CW01510840

The Exes

The Exes

LEODORA DARLINGTON

MICHAEL JOSEPH

PENGUIN MICHAEL JOSEPH

UK | USA | Canada | Ireland | Australia
India | New Zealand | South Africa

Penguin Michael Joseph is part of the Penguin Random House group of companies
whose addresses can be found at global.penguinrandomhouse.com

Penguin Random House UK,
One Embassy Gardens, 8 Viaduct Gardens, London S W I I 7 B W

penguin.co.uk

Penguin
Random House
UK

First published 2026

001

Set in 13.5/16 pt Garamond MT Std
Typeset by Six Red Marbles UK, Thetford, Norfolk
Printed and bound in Great Britain by Clays Ltd, Elcograf S.p.A.

The authorized representative in the EEA is Penguin Random House Ireland,
Morrison Chambers, 32 Nassau Street, Dublin D O 2 Y H 6 8

A CIP catalogue record for this book is available from the British Library

HARDBACK ISBN: 978–0–241–72560–3
TRADE PAPERBACK ISBN: 978–0–241–72561–0

Penguin Random House is committed to a sustainable future
for our business, our readers and our planet. This book is made from
Forest Stewardship Council® certified paper

MIX
Paper | Supporting
responsible forestry
FSC® C018179

To my mother. Thank you for helping me fall in love with literature. I remember how much we enjoyed my reading my books to you. I wish I could read you this one.

Well, the less scandalous parts, perhaps.

Chapter 1

Now

What they don't tell you about betrayal is that it eats you slowly. Long after the raised voices and slammed doors, after the tears – if there are any – it makes a home where your Good Feelings live and begins to gnaw at fond memories, trust, intimacy. And gnaws until you're full of holes, nothing left untouched but paranoia and the distinct sense of having loved a stranger.

Paranoia and loneliness are what I'm left clinging to as my husband cries in the room next door. I think about banging on the wall, telling him to quieten down. There is still music and laughter vibrating up through the floorboards from the party downstairs, but I'm worried that people will hear him. I've already been humiliated enough; I don't need our guests to hear our marriage going to shit, too.

A hollow wail pierces the room and my hands curl into tight fists. I close my eyes, breathe evenly. I'm not sure how or why he's the one in pieces when it's him who's destroyed our relationship, but here we are. Once I would have gone and furled myself around him. Made myself soft, pliable. A petal around a wasp. That might be how my mother raised me, but I've long since grown tired of watching women like her try to sweep dust from men's eyes while they have planks in their own. Planks the men usually put there.

Downstairs, someone changes the track to ABBA's 'Dancing Queen'. A dull pain begins to throb through my thumb, and I realize that the kitchen knife is still gripped in my hand.

The fleshy tip is pressing into the blunt edge of the steel above the handle. I will myself to let the knife go. For a moment, it feels like I can't. I won't. But then I remember the blood already on my hands, still unclean after all these years. The violent rages I can't clearly remember. And with the ghost of that darkness haunting me anew, I tuck the knife beneath the crisp, cold underside of the pillow on the guest bed.

I can't let that white-hot rage loose. Not again.

I sometimes wonder, if we'd met at a different time, in a different place, whether things might have ended differently, too. I don't think there was ever really the possibility of a happy ending. So much stood between us — so much history, so much blood — that the way things have worked out is sort of fitting.

Despite that, I really do think it's a shame that things have turned out this way. I did love you. I think. Perhaps.

I would have certainly given you almost anything you'd have asked of me. I guess, though, when the chips were down, what you wanted was something I just couldn't give.

I'm sorry for everything I've done.

I'm sorry for what I've put you through.

But now, after everything, I think we both have to agree that what we have between us needs to come to an end. As much as we've been at odds, I don't believe you'd fight me on that. As much as we've been at odds, I think you'd agree that only one of us can come out of this marriage alive.

Chapter 2

Then

Watching without being seen is an art I've mastered, but this afternoon, I'm sort of hoping I am. Seen, that is. It's a surprisingly sunny afternoon on Christmas Eve, and I'm sitting in an East London food hall, pretending to work on my beat-up laptop, half-paralysed by a desire to be noticed and an abject fear of it. He's several benches away from me, a devastatingly handsome smile on his face as the dark-haired man beside him speaks. My eyes latch on to the firm press of their shoulders against each other and I wonder what it would be like to have his shoulder against mine. Wonder what the over-tinselled tree behind him would look like in a home of our own. Although at this point in my life, not feeling lonely at this time of year would be a true Christmas miracle.

Occasionally, I lose sight of him as the abacus rows of heads shift between us, but it's enough for me, for now. Right on cue, as if to stop me from gorging myself on him, the table of twentysomethings sitting across from me slide along to let a new friend onto their bench, obscuring the view of the man I came here for. They snap pictures and squeal, mouths wide, eyes gleaming. I'd probably look that jolly, too, if I were a bottle and a half of prosecco deep.

For a moment, my stubby, bare brown fingers hover over my keyboard, the speed-typing test on my screen counting the clock down to zero. It takes an effort not to waste time staring at the young women, disappointed. I can't afford to drop so much money so often to look like they do. I can't even really afford to be sitting here, knocking back oat milk flat whites at almost four pounds a pop, but he's here, as I knew he'd be. Can't a girl allow herself a little treat?

I can imagine what life would be like were he mine. Or not quite 'imagine' – I've never seemed to have the creativity for that – but I slot myself into visions I've seen. The happy couple next door with the six-grand pram (I've googled it). The loved-up newly-weds on the latest season of my favourite reality show. I can take the scalpel of my limited imagination to cut around the young woman, lift her out of the picture and insert myself in. And in doing so, I can see how I would be happy with Him. Secure, for once.

'Anything else?' a voice asks behind me. I jump, startled. The incredibly friendly staff here have an incredibly quiet way of creeping up on you.

My eyes try to see through the throng of bodies. See if he's seen me. If he discovers I'm here, he'll want to know why, and I'm not sure my flimsy excuse will cut it.

'Um, sure. Another oat flat white, please.'

'Sure! Coming right up.'

Anxiety supercharged by caffeine hitches my heart rate up a notch. I can't tell if my man has looked this way. A break in the sea of heads seems to be forming but is quickly filled by a middle-aged couple taking a seat a couple of benches down. My eyes snag on the way the man catches the woman's elbow to ease her down, her pale hand going to cradle what I can now see is a rounded belly. I'm elated for her. I'm terrified by the force of the Want that rips through me. A hand goes to my flat stomach.

I come to the conclusion that if I can't see him, then surely he can't see me, albeit aware that I might be falling victim to toddler logic. Truth be told, I'm not sure James has ever really seen me. I first met him a year ago when he was showing me around the office. I say 'office'; really, it was a single tiny room in a co-working space. His business with his brother, Will, was still very much in its infancy, although things had been growing, fast, and they suddenly found themselves with more employees and admin than they could handle. The business, East London Chill, was an organic CBD-infused lager company. It was a rapidly successful venture. I was the thirteenth employee to join the company and liked to think of that as a lucky thing, despite the fact that I, entirely inexperienced, somehow represented the company's whole HR department in addition to my role as office manager. Now there are thirty of us, and I'm still the entirety of HR.

Fortunately, James is a good boss. Hard-working, fair and kind. He's pushed to get his brother, Will, into line (although, admittedly, Will might have just run out of employees to sleep with). His unwavering sense of Goodness is exactly what's drawn me to him and why I'll never have a chance. That, and the way his cheeks dimple when he's trying to hold in a laugh. The zeal he has for the small details, for how and why things work, making the most mundane process feel interesting. The easy way praise trips off his tongue – easy but earnest – I could bathe in it. His passion. His drive. His togetherness.

Liking James is Nice. If there's anything the therapy I can't afford has taught me, it's that I'm normally drawn to the wrong men like a moth to a flame. Therapy, and what happened to my sister.

I don't like to think about it. The mere thought makes me want to peel my own skin off and hide in it.

It would hurt.

And it would deserve to.

Still, even if my taste in men is improving, I have a lot of damage to heal. Too much to allow myself to get close to someone new. As long as I hold James at a distance, as long as I only allow myself to daydream about him, we can both remain safe.

The sea of bodies between us shifts again and a merciful parting in the waves brings him back to me. He's in a soft-looking jumper with sleeves pushed back and jeans, Will in his customary sharp suit beside him. They have always had this yin and yang pull, Will's loud, impulsive recklessness a foil for his younger brother's reassuring calm. Even visually, Will's dark hair and blue eyes seem a deliberate challenge to James's sandy colouring and brown irises. The brothers seem to be in opposition in every way possible, aside from the timbre of their voices. Sometimes I have to wonder how long it will be before that friction ignites into a fire that will burn the whole business to the ground.

'One oat flat white!'

I'm startled, hand flying up in surprise and knocking over the glass of water in front of me. Straight onto my laptop.

'Shit!'

I expect a dramatic snap, crackle and pop, or at least a gentle fizzing. Instead, the screen slowly flickers, a quiet death. Cursing my incurable clumsiness, I take the laptop, turn it to its side and give it a shake. The waitress behind me is flapping unhelpful concern.

'Oh my god. Sorry. Are you okay?'

Trying my best to rescue an unsalvageable situation, I flatten the laptop as best I can and flip it onto its front to drain. The backup laptops at work are even older and buggier than this one, and while Will might have declared them fit for purpose, it's not like he does enough real work to know.

'Some napkins would be great, please,' I say.

She claps her hands together in decisive agreement. 'Yes, of course.'

When I look back up from the mess before me, my body goes stiff. I have taken my eyes off the brothers for a moment and now looked back to where they were to find them both gone.

Panic digs its fingers into the crevices of my jaw and squeezes, clenching it tight. While my eyes dart across the room, I try to keep my head still. Try not to make my scanning too obvious, lest I give away my intentional watching of them, should they now be watching me. Keeping my wits about me, all I can do is –

'Natalie.'

My head swings around. James stands behind me, eyes crinkling gently in the corners, face lighting up like it's made his day laying eyes on me. In his hands are large fistfuls of white napkins from the bar.

'God, James!' I'm good at faking surprise. I'm good at faking a lot of things. But I know James always comes to this food hall with his laptop to work, and I knew he had set up a meeting with Will and the owners today.

'I heard the ruckus all the way across the room. Thought I'd save the waitress a trip.'

'Um, thanks.' I try to tell my body to relax.

'Here, let me.'

He starts dabbing at the table, allowing me to take a handful of tissues from him and mop at the ruined slab of tech.

'Sorry about your laptop.'

I shrug. 'It's a piece of shit anyway.'

'Your boss should really get you a new one,' he says with a knowing smile. 'Taken?' He points towards the slice of space opposite me. I shake my head, trying to smother my surging excitement. 'I wasn't expecting to see you here.' He leans

9

against the table as he slides onto the bench. I try not to stare at the momentary tensing of the muscles in his fore-arms. James gestures at the laptop that I've left face down, draining. 'Please tell me you weren't working on Christmas Eve. I know I have to, for my sins, but if Will's asked you to –'

'No.' My palms flash honesty at him as they fly up. 'No, I promise no work stuff.' There's not even a trace of suspi-cion in his eyes. He can't have seen me lurking here. 'Is Will around, too?'

He shakes his head and I'm embarrassed by how quickly the excitement leaps up again. 'No, he's off to meet some friends. I said I'd say hello to you and help rescue you from your laptop situation, then fire off a few more emails.' His head cocks to one side. 'I'm in here all the time. How come I've never seen you before?'

My stomach tightens. 'Well, I usually prefer sitting in a café nearer my flat, but it was closed. I remembered you'd recommended this place, but I didn't think you'd be here today of all days.' Lie.

James gives me a curious look. 'What's the c—'

'Anyway, forget me, I can't believe you're working on Christmas Eve.'

He laughs, a laugh that comes from deep within his chest and wraps the both of us in a gentle warmth. If he'd planned to grill me, it seems the plan has been quickly forgotten. 'True,' he says, 'but that's the price of being the boss.'

The waitress drifts back into view, sets another wodge of napkins down in front of me. I thank her, not taking my eyes off James as I try to assess whether he's seen through me. If he can smell the deception and desperation. 'Well, please, don't let me stop you if you need to be cracking on.'

I've already noticed the glances at the MacBook poking

out of his rucksack. The weariness that crosses his expression. Will gets to be Mr Charisma, never slow to volunteer for a sampling meeting with a potential new stocker, spending an afternoon laughing and schmoozing over beers. James is the one who keeps the books in order, the orders on time, the time-blind new hires on track. Without him, the business would surely fall apart or descend into chaos.

'But I think you've probably earned yourself a break?' I add.

That smile returns, broad shoulders relaxing as he looses a sigh. 'I think you're probably right.' He juts a chin towards my coffee. 'What about you? Maybe we can swap that for something stronger?'

I've already watched him sink a beer – otherwise, I'm sure this offer wouldn't have come. James has always been good at keeping boundaries in place with his employees, where Will has not. But now he wants a drink. With me.

I'd have been content even if my excursion only went as far as watching him from a distance. It's better than sitting at home alone, tempted to embrace the company of a mother who's mastered an art of cruelty so casual that you often don't know you've been wounded until you find yourself bleeding many hours later. But this . . . this is everything I've dreamed of.

'I think I'd like that,' I say with a level of chill I don't feel.

'Excellent.' A naughty grin stretches across his face, and I'm left a little breathless by how inviting it is. I flash a grin back at him, ignoring the rising alarm in the back of my mind. We have the distinct energy of two teenagers bunking off school.

'What d'you fancy?' he asks.

What would the alluring cool girl order? 'Assuming they don't stock any of our stuff, I'll have an Old-Fashioned, please.'

His eyebrows shoot up. 'Oh, so you mean business.'

I laugh. 'I do.'

'D'you know what, I'll have the same.' He gets up from his seat and begins to head for the bar, but something makes him spin back around. 'Hey, it's Christmas – shall I make it two apiece?'

'The bar *is* slow . . .'

He winks and sets off without another word. And as he walks away, as he leans over the bar to order our drinks from the bartender, I can feel something shifting in my brain, a question rising up that I'm doing my best to shove down. But I can't escape the thought that I'm playing with fire. Until I'm sure what happened with my exes can never happen again, I need to keep my distance from romantic interests. But James . . . James is not like anyone I've dated before. The worst thing you could accuse him of being is boring. And even then, Mr Double Old-Fashioneds is showing me that he might be more fun than I've given him credit for.

You've got to stop this, Natalie. You can't go there.

My infatuations always end in tears, I know that. It's why I've so diligently sworn off any romantic relationships for years. It's tough, starving myself of the one thing that's brought me . . . if not release, then distraction from my other problems for so long. But I've learned that until I heal, until I fix what's inherently broken within me, romance only compounds my problems in the long run. What happened with my last ex is a stark reminder of that, the pain from the fallout so bad that it still sometimes has me gasping awake at night, covered in a sheen of sweat. The cost of that relationship was too high. I'm still paying it. Perhaps I'll always be paying it.

Dear Marc,

I suppose, in some ways, you were where it all began. My first, in more ways than one.

I hate how much your opinion of me made up my opinion of myself. I hate that I ever let anyone have that much control over my self-esteem. If I hadn't been so weak, my life would look very different. Becky was right, you never really liked me for me. And I might have seen through the nice words if I hadn't been so insecure.

Perhaps I might even be normal.

What happened was a shock. But that shock was like dunking my whole body in ice water. It woke up something inside me. I now live in constant fear of that thing. I'm trying to starve it out, but I don't think it's working. It wants feeding.

If only you hadn't brought it to life.

Chapter 3

Ex Number One

Marc

You can still hear the cringe prom music from the school hall, even if it is a bit faint. The corridor is dark, as is the classroom we're in. It's kind of creepy. Like a scene from a horror movie before the two teens who've snuck off get murdered. Marc says it's better to keep the room dark, though. And Marc's smart. Or at least he says he's smart, and people seem to agree.

Apparently, no one should be coming this way, but I can't help but feel nervous every time I hear the slamming of a door echo from somewhere in the school. It's an old, pile-of-shit building. The roof blew off one winter. Nothing is soundproof. Which is part and parcel of why I feel about as comfortable as I would in a one-to-one with our pervy careers adviser in the library, but here I am.

'For god's sake, Natalie! Would you relax a bit?'

I want to bite back and ask Marc how I'm supposed to relax with Latin textbooks digging into my back. He has me on the teacher's desk, and he's standing between my legs. One hand is grabbing at my chest, feeling more padded bra than anything else, and the other is between my legs. I've never really stopped to reflect on how I'd feel if my younger sister was dating someone like Marc. But perhaps that's intentional. Perhaps I know I'd then like him less.

'I'm relaxed,' I lie. And he's obviously heard the lie. His

nostrils flare for a second and that faraway look glazes over his blue eyes. I hate it when he gets that look – it always means he's pulling away from me. And he does, physically. Suddenly, the skin on my body where his hands were feels ice-cold, almost as cold as the look he's giving me, dark curls falling into his eyes, dark brows stitched together.

God, he's so hot. He's so hot and he's mine.

Well, I'm his, and he's not with anyone else, and that's the same thing, really.

'I'm relaxed,' I insist.

'Is this about Becky? What she said?'

I feel my body stiffen at the mere mention of her, picturing her stupid face and her new burned-toast glow. She's still furious that she tanned that dark and that streaky. She swears up and down that someone switched her tan out for the wrong colour in her gym bag, but I don't know who'd be dumb enough to risk her going off on them.

'Because I thought it was really out of line,' he continues. 'I can't believe people still say stuff like that. I mean –'

'It's fine.'

'You know I'm not with you just 'cause you're Black, though, right? I mean, you don't even look it.'

I'm dumb enough at this age not to catch the insult.

'Really, Marc. I'm fine. Like, I'm not even thinking about that. Come here.' I tug on his shirt to bring him close to me again. The material feels good beneath my fingers. Thick, good quality, like the shirts Dad used to wear to work when he still had a job. They're in a box somewhere in the attic now. I found a load one day, and Mum caught me sniffing at them to see if there was any of him left in the fibres. She totally freaked out. They're probably still there, getting dusty and damp.

Marc's lips are on mine again, and I try to stop thinking

16

about Dad. It turns out it's not too hard. Marc tends to transform into Tentacle Boy when we kiss, his hands going everywhere. It's a lot. You know, the sort of jabby, windscreen-wiper tongue action. I used to think it was because I got him so excited, but now I sort of think that he just doesn't know what he's doing.

Speaking of not knowing what he's doing, and speaking of jabby, his hand is now in my underwear doing something I imagine is meant to feel good but feels incredibly uncomfortable. I want to tell him to stop, but I don't want him to pull away again. That feeling changes when I hear his zip come down.

'What are you doing?' I ask.

He pulls out a shiny packet from his pocket and grins. The cocktail of Pimm's, whisky, vodka and gin churns in my stomach. I'm beginning to think Emily's idea of taking a little off the top of each bottle in her parents' drinks cabinet wasn't such a smart one after all.

'Here?' I ask, not quite believing it. 'Now?'

The excitement in his eyes is snuffed out. 'Look, Natalie, you know I'm not gonna make you do anything you don't want to do.' It doesn't sound comforting. 'I think, maybe, though, I got this wrong, like . . . I dunno. I just thought you and me made more sense than maybe we really do. And it's not what Becky said. I guess, maybe, you're just a bit too . . . too uptight for me.'

It's a strange sort of feeling, but it's almost like halfway through the dumping I stepped out of myself, and now I'm watching this happen to someone else from a dark corner of the classroom. It's easier to do that sometimes; disappear while someone is trying to hurt you. You can't feel the blows land if you're not really in your body. Another choice life lesson.

I want to tell Marc he's wrong. I want to show him I'm not a silly kid. I want to prove to the other girls that not only can I take Marc Baxter, I can keep him, too. But before I can get a word out, he's already edging away from me.

'I'm sorry, Natalie. To do it like this, I mean. Here. I just – you know . . .'

I don't know. Prick.

'I guess I'll just –' And the coward doesn't even finish the sentence. He just slinks off.

Perhaps if that'd been it, if dumping me at prom was the worst of it, maybe things would have been okay. But that humiliation wasn't enough for Marc. No. He had to push me further. Had to make things worse.

In the end, I was sorry for what happened next. But Marc was sorrier.

Chapter 4

Now

James's snivelling has worn my patience thin. I get to my feet, the imprint of my body still on the covers. The clock tells me I haven't been lying there, staring at the ceiling, wondering about the disintegration of my marriage, my life, for long. But it has felt like an age. Not quite my life flashing before my eyes, but the life James and I might have shared suddenly bleaching out like film left lying in the sun.

Now I find myself creeping into the corridor. A gentle, rhythmic buzzing hums into the soles of my feet. The party downstairs is too loud. I should do something, turn the music down. The neighbours. We've just made nice with them and made this neighbourhood feel like our own. It's wild that we're even going ahead with this belated house-warming, but when James fled to hide in his parents' home, I warned him I wouldn't cancel. He could show up, face me and save face, or I could tell all our friends what he did. At least it sounds like the guests downstairs are having a good time, distracted. No one should disturb us.

When I open the door to our bedroom, I find James curled up in a ball at the foot of the bed, sobbing his little heart out. The tips of his ears have gone pink, and he looks like a little pig awaiting the butcher's knife. Like he knows just how much danger he's in. He catches my eye and, well, not quite straightens up, but rocks up into a seated foetal position.

'Please, I just —' He pauses to choke out a sob. 'I'm so sorry. I love you. You know that.'

My hands clench into fists and unclench. It feels like a rope is pressing itself against the soft flesh of my neck. When he proposed, he promised that, together, we'd forget the ways in which our families have disappointed us. Be each other's chosen family. But what kind of family would choose this?

'If you loved me,' I say, 'then how could you do this to me?'

He shakes his head, hugs his knees to his chest. 'I don't know. Really, I don't. It's the worst thing I could have done.'

'Yes,' I say, closing the door behind me. 'Yes, it is.'

Chapter 5

Then

My palms are always itchy when I'm nervous, and they're practically on fire as I make my way over to James's flat. It's only a short walk across London Fields from my own. A fortunate proximity, as I have already turned back on myself five times. This is stupid. Reckless, even. At first, it was just that one night. A friendly couple of drinks without so much as a goodbye kiss on the cheek. And yet, something shifted that evening. Suddenly, it felt like James saw me. I'd taken one of the equally old and useless backup laptops at work to replace my now dead one, but when the gift-wrapped MacBook landed on my desk, I'd looked up to see James watching me from his office, a gentle smile on his face, and knew what he'd done. Sometimes, I'd glance up from my desk and catch him doing that, one ear to his receiver, deep in doubtless important conversation, but still watching. He'd smile, shake his head and then go about what he was doing.

The first sign that we were slipping from something known into the unknowable was the Friday after Christmas when he caught me by the lifts on the way out of the office, the shadow of a fading bruise under one eye.

'Hold the doors!'

My guts clenched at the thought of our bodies penned into the same space, lungs breathing the same air. There was something intimate about sucking in the clouds of vapour he puffed out. Like I got to hold a little piece of him inside me. I held the doors.

'Wow – leaving before six. That's almost skiving by your standards,' I said.

He laughed, slipping into the lift a moment before the doors slid shut. 'Well, if you don't tell the boss, I won't.'

It had been a surprise to me when James hadn't made some excuse to peel off or hang back as we headed in the aligned direction of our respective homes; does the MD really want to be stuck talking to the office manager for his entire commute? But as we paced along the chilly East London streets, squeezing together and breaking apart in narrowing and widening pathways, he stuck with me, face bright and engaged. He had this new zest for life since Christmas that was infectious. And I was outwardly engaged, too – delightful even, I'm sure – but inside was sheer panic. I wanted him desperately. I wanted to hand in my resignation and never speak to him again.

My pocket started buzzing a notification. When I checked the screen, I saw the round photo in its centre. The white text that floated above it: Melissa Doe. It's perhaps a quirk of mine that I save her contact info under her full name, rather than just 'Mother' or 'Mum'. It's been this way for ever. All my contacts are saved like that. There's just something about having the whole name saved that soothes me. I suppose it's a reminder to look at the whole picture of who people are, rather than taking them in parts.

In any case, I did what I had done for the past few years and quietly declined the call. I knew I was damaged. Wrong. I didn't need her reminders of that fact. Didn't need to hear the unspoken insult beneath: *You're so like your father.* Didn't need to feel like any more of a freak. A monster.

My therapist once asked me why I'd not blocked the number. Sometimes I considered it, but I was at once terrified of and drawn to my mother. She was a bottle of vodka and I an alcoholic who couldn't live without it, even if I knew it was slowly killing me.

I shook all thoughts of her away, eyes latching on to the black-shuttered bar coming up beside James and me as we walked.

'I love this place,' I said, nodding towards it.

'Oh really? I've never been.'

'Never? They do this thing called a beer and a bump for only seven quid.' I suddenly felt silly and childish for extolling the virtues of cheap alcohol to this clearly wealthy man. 'It's, um . . . It's their house lager with a shot of your choice. I know it sounds silly, but –'

'It sounds like a hangover waiting to happen.' The laughter in his eyes told me that this wasn't necessarily a bad thing.

Something shifted in my periphery. A guy in a suit was hurtling towards us down the pavement, phone to ear, yelling obscenities. For a moment, I thought he might barrel into me, but James stepped between us, hand firmly pointing Phone Guy towards the clear stretch of pavement. 'Watch it, mate.'

I thought Phone Guy might turn his puce-coloured rage on James, but he simply sidestepped, throwing an angry look over his shoulder.

We were stopped now, James and I. It felt like fate.

Words fought each other in my mouth. I found myself blurting out, 'No worries if you have plans, but d'you want to stop in and try one?'

His eyebrows shot up. I wonder if he knew what I was doing, what I wanted, despite every reasonable bone in my body knowing I shouldn't. He made a show of looking at his watch and then looking back at me. I could almost see his mind sorting through where he felt the lines of propriety were. How close to those lines he was comfortable colouring.

'I guess one wouldn't hurt.'

Inside it was dark and close, tables and chairs pushed up against each other in low light. It was busy, and James and I found ourselves equally pushed up together. It could have just been in my head, but I was sure I could feel the warmth of his leg seeping through his jeans and into mine. It was loud, so we found ourselves having to speak into each other's ears. I liked the feeling of his warm breath condensing on my neck.

I felt myself slipping into Cool Girl mode. Easy laughs, bright, engaged eyes. But never too engaged. Always just charming enough and aloof enough to seem worth liking. To seem desirable but not easily attainable. It's not that I wanted him to like me. I needed him to. People only tend to give you what you want when they like you. And what I wanted from him was to be allowed to exist within his sphere of handsome normalcy, even if it was a fleeting bubble that I'd enjoy before it burst.

As we spoke about inconsequential things – office gossip, Netflix binges, weekend plans – I could feel lines blurring, boundaries demolished by the promise of 'just one more drink', pints disappearing as quickly as they came. I plucked up the courage to ask about the fading shiner, unsure which of the office rumours were true. *Nothing that exciting, I'm afraid; just an enthusiastic nephew with a new ball and terrible aim.* And then the conversation shifted, our words stumbling through the shallows and over an unseen precipice that plunged us somewhere deep.

'I just sometimes wish she'd see me,' James said, removing his tortoiseshell glasses to rub at his eyes. He'd never looked so boyish. 'She funnels so much into Will that sometimes it feels like there's nothing left for me.'

Emboldened by booze, I took hold of his knee. 'He's great, but I can't imagine it's always easy having an older sibling like him.'

'I feel like a traitor for agreeing with you, but it's true.'

'I mean, even at work, he's a bit of a loose cannon. More so, lately.'

My mind was flooded with recent memories of sour hangover breath fogging the air; alcoholic vapours steaming from mugs of coffee; overloud sentences with wild gesticulations drawing attention across the office; knocked-over files; knocked-over screens; an office sitting empty, unexplained, for two days that week. Will's fondness for a drink seemed to have mutated into something ugly that everyone in the office could see. I wanted to ask more about it, but my questions caught in my throat. It didn't feel like my place.

James gave out an exasperated sigh. 'Yeah, I don't know how much longer he'll stick around. Please don't repeat this to anyone. But Will's the kind of person who's interested in something until he's not. And I think the business is prime to join the growing pile of his discarded hobbies.' He paused to take a sip of his drink. 'I get why she worries about him. My mother. I get why she doesn't always take him seriously. But I don't know why she takes me even less seriously. If she'd just pay attention, then maybe . . . God, listen to me going on.'

'No. It's nice to hear you open up. And funny to hear everyone else's problems. As for me, I'd love my mother to see me less . . .'

'Oh really? How come?'

'You really want to get into it?'

'I do. If you're happy to, that is. You mentioned it's not your favourite subject.'

And so I went on to give him the sanitized version of my life story.

He blew his cheeks out, laughed. 'No way did an argument that big erupt over some dishes.'

'My inability to leave dirty plates by the sink is genuinely a trauma response – my therapist had a field day trying to unpick that. Me and my sister learned our lesson with the dishes, although Claire rebelled in other ways.'

He paused, looking down at me through thick lashes. 'Your sister sounds like quite the firecracker. You should bring her along to the summer party. I'd like to meet her.'

I realized my mistake too late. 'Oh, um . . .' I forced myself to look away from his stare. 'My sister . . . well, we had a big falling-out before she moved to LA. I kept dating arseholes, kept dragging her into my mess . . . I guess the main reason she moved was to escape our mother, though . . . It's complicated.'

There are a lot of questions on his face, but the next one out of his mouth surprises me. 'Is there much of a culture clash there? With your mother, I mean.'

I looked at him quizzically.

He continued. 'Just for people growing up in the diaspora, I hear there can be some intergenerational friction between what parents are used to and what's the new norm for their kids.'

'You sound like you've swallowed a stack of journal articles.'

He blushed and I realized that my joke may have accidentally hit the mark.

'Sorry. I just wanted to read up a bit. Educate myself, y'know?'

I took another moment to consider him. The earnestness made him bashful, dipping his head towards his beer. 'I didn't mean to be disparaging. It's cool you want to learn more. Although, I mean . . . have you dated Black girls before?'

'No. Not that I wouldn't. But why? D'you think I'd only be interested in your history because I was trying to get laid?' A vulpine smile now sat on his lips. I smiled back.

'Maybe. That's usually the reason.'

He simply shrugged. 'Sorry to disappoint. But if you ever want to chat decolonization, I'm down.'

It elicits a genuine cackle from me.

'Seriously, though,' he continued, 'we only have to talk about things you're comfortable with. I know you don't like talking about the past, your family, in particular. We don't have to go there again.'

'Is that a promise?' I nudged him with my shoulder, a grin on my face. His was deadly solemn.

'It can be.' His earnest gaze set my heart fluttering. He reached out a finger. 'Let's make a pact to leave the past where it belongs. Focus on the future.'

And my pinky slid around his, the promise made.

A soft heat pulsed at the edges of the evening as we talked. I could tell that the guy waiting tables – dangly earring, two phones in use behind the bar, clear fuckboy – was trying to flirt with me, not believing James and I could be on a date. On another approach to ask an inane question about my hair, James was curt: *We'll tell you if we need something, thank you.* I found myself reaching for his hand across the table and squeezing it. His palm was soft. Large. I felt small in his touch. Needing of his protection. From what, exactly, I'm not sure. Myself, perhaps, my therapist would say.

When the hours had worn on too long and we had to

make our way home, we were both unmistakably drunk. More so than on that Christmas Eve we'd spent together.

'I'm just going to quickly use the loo,' I said.

I found myself in the poky toilets, panic high in my chest, phone to my lips, recording a voice note for my sister.

'Claire, I know I promised no more relationships, but I think I want to hook up with my boss. And I think maybe he wants it, too. I don't know . . . Is this . . . I mean . . . Like, I know it's stupid and risky and it terrifies me . . . and I know what happened with the last guy. But this is okay, right? It's been years. What's the worst that could –'

Someone was banging on the door. I let the voice note send half-finished.

Outside, James took me in with a deep spark of curiosity behind a slightly glazed look. I wasn't going to let this spark of interest die. I pulled him to me.

'I want you to forget about this tomorrow, but I know I'll regret it if I don't do this tonight.'

And I kissed him. It was warm and wet, and I think he was startled at first. After a moment, he pulled away.

'Natalie, I really shouldn't. You're my – This is –'

'Do you want me to stop?' I asked.

'Not even a little bit.'

I kissed him again, his hands soon on me, steady and strong. The kiss was at once tender and firm. It felt like a kiss on a leash. There was a restraint in the meeting of our lips and the light pressure of his fingertips on my flesh. But the restraint soon came loose, James's hands reaching for my waist, pulling our bodies together.

A sharp pain suddenly bloomed on my lip, a metallic taste in my mouth. It didn't take me long to realize that he'd bitten me. Hard enough to break the skin. I pulled back, our eyes connecting. There was a challenge in his. My pulse raced quicker.

Perhaps this should have been a warning that James might hurt me more significantly down the line. That he might even enjoy it. But in this moment, I was so consumed by want, blood rushing through my ears and creeping across my tongue, that there wasn't any room for fear.

And I wish I could say that this was where things ended between us, but as I walk over to his flat, the promise of a home-cooked dinner and perhaps something more ahead of me, I'm ashamed to admit that this feels like the beginning of something new.

Chapter 6

Ex Number One

Marc

It's amazing just how easily a shitty boy can ruin your whole night. I'm sipping a Smirnoff Ice, already a bit dizzy, the usually sweet bubbles sour in my mouth. Across the teeming living room, Marc and his boys are having a laugh, elbowing one another and downing cups of foamy beer. They're red cups, just like the kind from American shows. Everyone says it's so cool he got them. Marc, that is. It's his house we're in for the prom after-party.

To be totally honest, Marc's got a weird hard-on for all things American. He says he's going to Harvard to study, but it's not clear to anyone whether he's actually got in. His parents, who are staying in a hotel for the night, could probably afford it, though. They're stupid rich. Which is kind of why we're at Marc's place in the first instance. It's huge – they've got four whole bedrooms and a pool. One time, Marc had me over and got me to give him a handy in it. When he came, his voice slipped into this weird American accent. It was strange as fuck.

Anyway, I'm at Marc's stupid big house looking at his stupid hot face and trying to make eye contact with him. I've been trying this for a good half hour now, and it's like he's deliberately not looking at me.

It's strange to say, but in this new state of crisis, I feel a little more alive than usual. Terrified, but everything drawn into a sharper focus. I hate it. I need it.

Emily's suddenly appeared, a bony arm around my shoulders. She's been hitting it harder than I have, shiny copper curls wild from all the dancing.

'Come on, Nat. You've gotta dance with me!'

'In a minute,' I say.

Emily tracks my line of sight.

'What's going on with you two anyway? You were all weird leaving the hall. You didn't even speak to each other. You fighting?'

'Yeah, you could say that.'

She hiccups and leans her head against my shoulder. 'Babe, he's kind of an arsehole. You're better off out of it.' She abruptly springs upright. 'Now come dance with me!'

'In a bit. Promise,' I say.

I watch her pout and leave, and I gather what courage I can. It never comes easily to me, bravery, but I've got good at faking it. I strut across the room, imagining I'm a sexy model or actress, hoping that this will mesmerize Marc, who is now, at the very least, looking at me. I catch the end of what his friend in the red hoodie is yelling, slapping Marc's back to punctuate his point.

'Bullshit. No way have you jumped from the roof into the pool!'

'Can we talk?' I ask, hand on hip. A chorus of 'oohs' erupts from the gaggle of twats around him.

He shrugs. 'I don't know that there's much to talk about.'

'Marc, look, I –'

'I've said what I have to say and that's it, okay?' More snickers break out around him.

I fold my arms across my chest. 'Oh, fuck off, losers.'

Marc gives me the world-weary look of a forty-year-old

divorcee. 'Actually, guys, if you could give us a sec,' he says, and they slink off, smirking. Once they're gone, he turns to me sharply. 'What exactly do you want from me, Natalie?'

The edge in his voice slaps more life into me. I want this. I want him.

'An explanation for what the hell happened today woul—'

'What more could you need? I don't want to be with you. I want you to leave me the fuck alone. Now, piss off.'

Despite the kind invitation, he's the one who actually walks away. I immediately scan the crowd around me. A few people are looking over, hateful smiles on their faces. Nosy bastards and bitches, the lot of them.

Even though only a few people will have heard what he said, everyone could read our body language, and the few people within earshot have already whispered their version of events to their neighbours. I can see the gossip spreading through the party like wildfire in real time.

For the third time that night, my face is hot with shame. Emily finds me – rescues me, really. She whisks me away to a bathroom, dabs away my tears.

'You're a bad bitch, Nat.'

'Yes,' I sniffle. 'Yes, I am.' Although I don't feel like one – and with Marc Baxter so publicly declaring me Unwanted, I'm not so sure other people will be convinced, either. Being an object of desire for a boy like Marc Baxter comes with social currency, social currency I wasn't born with, and social currency I've worked for. I can feel my balance depleting.

The party rages on. Emily and I unearth a bottle of top-shelf tequila that Marc has tried to hide away and we go to town on it. Before long, my dizziness graduates into blurriness. Everyone looks fuzzy. My casual clumsiness escalates into something more volatile, and several glasses are broken.

I'd love to say that my drama with Marc is quickly

forgotten, but it's obvious that people are talking about it through the night. About me. Some of his friends come over to say they're sorry to hear how things went down. They touch my shoulder, my waist, my arse, as they say this. I suppose I don't have a 'hands-off' rule on me any more. I no longer belong to Marc Baxter. I slip away from quick palms and into pulsating crowds of dancing bodies. The tequila bottle never leaves my side. Someone pinches my bum and I hate it, but I drink until I don't care any more.

And the rest is fragments.

Elbowing my way to the front of a toilet queue and chundering everywhere.

A text from my mother, asking if I'm going to bed at a sensible time at my 'sleepover', ignored.

More tequila.

More dancing.

Spilled drinks. A bottle of rum carelessly elbowed to pieces on the kitchen tiles.

More tequila.

Cannonballing into the pool with my prom dress on.

Shivering.

More tequila.

A search for dry, warm clothes.

I know where Marc's room is.

A door opened. A sudden scream. Two naked bodies interlocked.

Marc. Becky.

Pleading, tears.

More tequila.

In the bathroom again, face pressed against the cold plastic of a toilet seat.

Slurring, the world tilting on an angle.

My sister, someone's called my sister.

Softness, warmth. I'm lying down somewhere and it smells like –

Marc. Hands. Kisses I don't know how to return.

Pleading, tears.

I wasn't doing anything she didn't want.

Cold tiles.

Night air.

Fuck you.

Loud silence.

And then nothing.

The thing that draws me out of the darkness is the screaming. It's terrible, high-pitched. My whole body aches, muscles crying in a way I'm not used to, like I've actually hit the gym for a change. I'm in Marc's bedroom, which is immediately obvious from the posters on the walls: sixty per cent hot women, forty per cent cars. A gentle breeze is blowing in from the large window, left ajar. My legs swing out from under the sheets. The moment I'm upright, the dull ache in my head becomes a painful, looping throb.

There's a pile of soft blankets by my feet, and I get the notion that Claire might have stayed here. Claire. Where is she?

A quiet panic slowly rises through my body. The screaming outside has been joined by more voices, all alarmed. A new screaming voice has joined the first voice, a discordant wail echoing through the house. I'm rushing out of Marc's room and through the hall, down the stairs. The screaming is definitely coming from outside.

As soon as I step into the unusually hot summer sun, the location of the commotion becomes obvious. There's a crowd huddled by the pool. I can hear the sound of crying, blubbing. It doesn't make sense, but I'm suddenly terrified for my sister, that something awful has happened to her.

'Claire? Claire!' I shout.

She bursts out from the crowd and sprints to me, face wet with tears. I kiss her cheeks and look her over. 'Are you okay? Are you hurt?'

She shakes her head. 'No. I mean, I'm fine. It's – it's Marc.'

'Marc?'

My chest tightens. I rush forward, elbowing my way through the throng. On the stone slabs, two feet away from the pool, Marc lies with his head cracked open like an egg. He has a halo of blood around him and blood streaking down from his nose. One arm is sticking out at an unsightly angle. It's immediately obvious that he's dead.

Dread sinks in my chest. I look up to the place from which he's clearly fallen. This section of the roof is square and flat. At the back of it, facing the pool, is a large window that stands ajar. Something flashes before my eyes. I remember a voice shouting – Marc's voice.

What the fuck are you doing?

Cold grit beneath my feet, a soundless fall.

Pleading, tears.

I'm not sure what it means. But then Becky brushes past me, wailing. She manages to stop long enough to shoot me a dirty look that lingers, scrapes to my toes and back up again, so sharp it feels like it's raking my skin up like the peeler Mum leaves out for potatoes in the kitchen. I catch something just as sharp then. Sharper, perhaps. And white-hot. It's fleeting, but suddenly I think I know exactly what it means.

Under a mid-June sky, I hug my sister to my chest, and I pretend I'm not glad Marc is dead.

'Don't you know he was only with you 'cause he wanted to know what it was like to fuck a Black girl?'

And I pretend I don't wish Becky was dead, too.

Chapter 7

Now

The clock in this room is broken, but it still incessantly ticks.

Tick. Tick. Tick.

James said he'd get the battery replaced months ago and I'm mad at him for not doing it. But then again, I said weeks ago that I'd take care of it, too. And yet here it is, still stuck just before midnight, or midday, depending on how you look at it. Stuck, second hand flicking back and forth . . .

Tick. Tick. Tick.

Just like James and me.

From somewhere below, someone cranks up the volume on the speakers. I try not to let the panic about the noise preoccupy my thoughts. I try not to dwell on how absurd it is having this conversation with my husband while the 'Cha Cha Slide' takes place beneath us.

'So can you explain it to me? From the beginning?' I ask.

James nods, head hanging low, body still quivering.

'I'm going to need you to get it together if we're going to have this conversation, James.'

He nods again, sits a little taller. Exhales, slow and steady. The tears don't stop entirely, but the shaking stops. He looks like he's about to speak when a voice echoes through the door.

'Nat? You still up here?'

I'm unsurprised she's still here; she's always one of the last ones standing. Still, as much as I like my friend and old colleague, Ama, she has no need to see the sorry mess James and I are in, especially having worked for the business before. Ama had been the previous sales manager at East London Chill, and as she was the only other Black girl, we'd become fast friends. If she catches a whiff of something awry between James and me, the gossip will spread through the office like wildfire. It took one afternoon for the former office manager to become known as 'Mad Mary' to everyone. It's been years since she quit and people still call her that. Shit sticks. Even Ama, who'd slipped into a sort of filial relationship with the woman at work, started calling her that. She says Mary's dimpled smile reminded her of her aunties at first, but the increasingly crazy eyes morphed that smile into something sinister. Alien.

'Wait here,' I say to James in a hushed voice.

I'm up on my feet and out the door. One hand wants to hover on the handle behind me, guarding it, but I know how suspicious that will look, and so I let it go. Ama is just cresting the top of the staircase, neck craning to see me. When she does, she smiles, bright and wide. Despite the low light, her dark skin gleams, and I make a note to self to ask her for her skin-care routine again.

'There you are! Everything okay?' she asks.

The smile I return is almost as warm. 'Yeah, all good. James and I have just been having a moment. We'll be down soon.'

She gives me a knowing look, eyebrows raised. 'Getting some quality time in, eh?' She follows this with a mock frown. 'Kind of rude in the middle of your own party.'

I simply laugh. 'Did you need something?'

'Oh yeah – you got any ping-pong balls?'

'Surely not rage cage at this hour . . .'

She shrugs. 'You've got to give the people what they want.'

'There's a box under the kitchen sink.'

She claps her hands together, already turning to head back downstairs as she replies, 'If you two lovebirds can keep your hands off each other long enough, you should join us for a round!'

'We'll see!' I'm not sure she even catches my response in the din, swallowed by the party before the words escape my lips.

I turn back around, pausing at the threshold. I need to switch gears again and it's not easy. It doesn't feel good stepping back into that room with my broken husband and our broken marriage, but I have to. And so I open the door.

James is blowing his nose when I return. He seems more in control of himself. Perhaps Ama's interruption has been a useful reminder that he needs to keep it together; he can't risk coming apart entirely at this party. Half the people here either currently or used to work for his business. It's also perfectly possible that he's just been able to take a breath in the moments I've been gone. Either way, it feels like a conversation should be possible now.

Almost as if to prove this point, James gestures to the space next to him on the bed. I sit.

'I know how much having a baby means to you. Means to us,' he says.

I feel my own lip quiver at that, but it comes to a quick stop. I'm more adept at keeping my emotions under control than he is.

'And this was our only chance, James.'

He nods. 'And this was our only chance.'

He reaches for my hand and that dangerous anger flares up again. But the letters flutter before my eyes, tokens of blank nights heralding bloody mornings, and I quiet it. I can

39

do this. Be a good, normal wife. And if not good, at least not dangerous. Even if I'm soon to be an ex, let the separation be the end of it.

'So, can you explain to me why you cancelled our IVF treatment and stole twenty thousand pounds of my money?'

Chapter 8

Then

My plan not to spend too much time with James is failing miserably. Although perhaps 'plan' is too generous a framing – 'ambition' would be more apt. When you've not had sex in years, it's a bit like eating a slice of bacon after going veggie for a while, or having a few Kettle Chips after swearing off junk food. You just want more. And more. And more. I can't help but feel we're hurtling towards a dangerous inevitability, hard as I've tried to avoid it.

But new plan, new rule. Just don't fall in love with him. Don't get attached. Certainly don't become his girlfriend.

'Don't you think this is all a bit risky, though?'

Claire. Wonderful Claire. Her voice is like sunshine to me, as if she's sending the Los Angeles rays through the phone while I'm stretched out on my coffee-stained couch, wondering what to wear for my date with James. She's been out there for four years, chasing her dream. Mostly waiting tables, but her big break is coming, she can feel it. When I can finally afford it, I'll fly out to see her.

Claire's good with me. She understands the dark veil that sometimes descends upon my mind. She gets that it's harder for me to be good, to be likeable; I have to work at it. Not like her. She's magnetic, good at lighting up rooms.

It always seemed obvious that between myself and Claire, I would grow up the troubled one. Round face, wide eyes, and ringlets, Claire was the perfect portrait of a little girl. The cherub to my glowering demon who sat sullen in corners, wiping an always runny nose on the back of my sleeve.

There was a pointed feeling of failure in me, even when I was little. I managed to click well with Joy, Aunty Dev's daughter. Joy by name and joy by nature, she was all smiles and dimples, a head of thick curls to rival Claire's. But our mother being who she is, the friendship with Dev didn't last, and Dev and Joy disappeared from our lives.

Other children didn't like me. I was too withdrawn. Too watchful. I liked to observe people, even if I was too afraid to interact with them. It took me too long to understand that people don't like to be watched. They don't like you taking note of what they do.

I was the child in class who didn't always get a birthday party invitation. But then little Claire joined the school the following year and, oh! Didn't all the teachers love her? Weren't all the students clamouring to be her friend?

It was only a few days into the new school year that sweet little Claire noticed that her big sister wasn't loved by the other students as she knew I ought to be. And so she'd invited me to play with her new friends. She could tell that I didn't want to be playing with babies, but she could also tell that I didn't want to be alone any more. She was intuitive like that.

I fell in with Claire's friends. And I watched how she could smile or pause at just the right moment. Offer to share a toy with the right person.

As I grew older, I learned how to keep the right people around me, too. I never stopped watching, though. I just learned ways to hide it. Don't be too still; don't let your eyes linger on anything for too long; prattle about something mindless so that your brain can stay busy soaking things in.

For a while, I thought perhaps I really was growing

warmer, friendlier, kinder. I thought that my edges were softening. That I could be a normal girl. But on the eighteenth of June on a sunny day, I woke to find Marc Baxter dead, and I knew that I had simply been fooling myself.

'So, tell me more about him,' Claire says now, and I can almost hear her smile in her voice.

'Well, he's handsome, and smart, and kind. And he's obviously loaded. Not that that's so important, but it was always a bit annoying when Dad was between jobs, wasn't it?'

'Between jobs is one way of putting it,' Claire replies. There's a momentary discomfort lodged in the call. I know we both look back at our childhood through our own lenses, separate prescriptions pushing differing parts of our past lives into a soft blur and sharp focus. 'It's good he's got his shit together. But you're talking about him like . . . It just sounds like you're thinking quite long-term.'

'Don't start, Care.' Care, a remnant from when I couldn't pronounce her name properly as a toddler. The name just stuck. 'I promise I'm not getting attached,' I continue. 'It's just a bit of fun and great sex.'

'God, Natty . . . There are some details I don't need to know.'

'I don't think you can lecture me on that after all the times you –'

'Whatever.' A chuckle. 'As long as you're being caref—'

'Of course.' A scoff. 'He's sort of paranoid about people in the office finding out, I guess. Not that he needs to be – all anyone can talk about is what a mess his brother is at the moment. Turned up to a client meeting this week and was immediately sick in the recycling bin.

'Anyway, James and I haven't been out in public since we went to that bar. But I get it. And I sort of like that we have this little thing just for us. He's also so different than

I thought. He wants to live life to the fullest. It makes me feel more alive, too. None of my exes were like this, Care.' A drop in my stomach. 'I promise I'll be careful. This isn't . . . This is not going to end like the others.'

She's suspiciously silent for a moment. 'I really want to believe that.'

I shift in my seat. 'It'll be fine. Promise.'

'There's a chance it could mess up your career.'

I snort. 'What career? You care more about that stuff; I just want to be happy.'

'Okay.' She sighs. 'Speaking of, I'm going to have to go; my break's about to end, and these skinny half-caff lattes with double pumps of low-sugar vanilla syrup aren't going to make themselves.' She pauses to laugh. I laugh along with her. 'At least it pays the bills while I wait for a casting director to give me a half-decent job.'

'It'll happen,' I say. 'You're so hard-working. So talented.'

'All right, all right. I wasn't calling for you to blow smoke up my ass. Speak soon, and don't be a stranger.'

'I won't.'

'Okay. And be careful.'

'I will.'

'All right, Natty. Love you.'

'Love you, too.'

And then she's gone.

And then the words that feel too heavy to say. 'I miss you.'

Giving myself one final big stretch, I get up from the sofa and ready myself to leave the house. Before I know it, I'm out the door and walking to James's place, sure that I'm going to keep my word. I'm almost proud of the strength of my conviction. But I really ought to remember that pride always comes before a fall.

Dear Luca,

I'd love to say that the embarrassment of Marc leaving me to hook up with my racist bully cured my need to seek male validation, but you were proof that it didn't. If anything, it made it worse. I'd strut around on uni nights out with my tits pushed up to my chin and arse nearly falling out of my skirt on the hunt for someone just like you.

And then there you were, a varsity king who wanted to give me – ME – the time of day.

I can't begin to tell you how good the attention felt. How much it fed me. I was too busy gorging on your flattering words to hear how empty they were. I was too stupid to realize that just because you said you liked me, it didn't mean you respected me. Even a little.

In the end, my humiliation was so complete that I died a little before you did. And I wish I could say that when I heard you were dead, I was sorry. But the day you died, I made myself eggs royale for lunch with a mimosa on the side, and cashed in my birthday voucher for a hot stone massage.

It was bliss. Even if I had to start to acknowledge the monster living in me. Because I knew feeling this good about something so awful wasn't okay.

But I guess sometimes you just can't help how you feel.

Chapter 9

Ex Number Two

Luca

'Maybe see you after our social, yeah?' Luca says.

'Yeah, I'll probably be about. Drop me a text,' I reply.

'Will do, champ.' He gives me a wet kiss. His curls are still drenched from the shower, crowding his forehead. Fresh and strong cologne floats just above the smell of the varsity hoodie stretched across his broad shoulders. The hoodie is faintly damp, like the rooms in his student house, which is moist in all the wrong places. I left a pair of shoes in Luca's room for a few weeks and they grew actual mould.

It's late on a Thursday afternoon and I'm headed to meet up with some English Society members at the pub. They're a bit of an odd bunch – weirdly competitive and exclusive with an illusion of being cool – but it's nice to have some course mates. It feels like the kind of thing I should have. I think my not-whiteness automatically made me sought after to the Home Counties Hannahs and Hughs. Before I'd hardly said two words, they were fawning over me to tell me I was 'so cool'. But normalcy is something I have to work at and something they give me.

Luca's just sent me off after a night at his. I already ache for more of him, but escaping the dingy den that is his third-year house is a bit of a relief. He's living with four other boys from the football team. It's about what you'd imagine a house of five twenty-year-old boys looks and smells like, strewn with dirty socks. Grim.

But not Luca. He's wonderful. And although I fear my feelings for him risk tipping over into obsession, if I always listened to that pervasive fear that hums beneath my skin, I'd never do anything at all.

Luca's attention is like the sun: it warms you to your bones. A smile from him can make anyone's day, and people love him for it. He's a bit of a big name on campus – the wonder-kid with a hole in his heart who still manages to kick arse on the field – and I have to admit I like that. I like that cheeky grin, the warmth of his brown skin and the wicked glint in his eye. I even like the congenital heart defect. The promise of maybe being that thing to fill the tiny space in his chest.

I'm not sure if it was the attractiveness of Luca himself or the magnetic pull I could see he had on those around him that first piqued my interest. Perhaps it was a bit of both. I just remember being in the student union and Luca's gaze floating over the shoulder of a girl desperately trying to get his attention. His eyes wouldn't leave me, and it felt like a hook in my gut. I suppose I have a type. I want what other people want.

My phone. It's ringing.

'Oh, hey,' I say.

'Nat, where are you? I'm almost at the pub and I don't want to be alone with all your intense friends.'

I try not to snap back about how much more intense my sister's drama school friends are. After all, she has come all this way on a stuffy National Express coach to see me. I should be looking after her better than this.

'I'm not far off,' I say. 'Maybe twenty minutes? Emily will be there in five – chat to her.'

I'm certainly not winning any 'sister of the year' points

right now, I know that. And one might argue that a few clumsy shags on the still-damp patch in Luca's bed from the night before aren't worth keeping a sister waiting. It would probably be a fair argument, too. But like I say, Obsessed.

It's been eight months, my longest relationship to date. Claire thinks it's silly to be getting tied down in my third year of university, but when she meets Luca, which I hope she will tonight, she'll get it. In fact, it's this thought that allows me to smile so brazenly at her when I first appear, before the shame creeps in at the sight of her restlessness. Emily was not indeed 'there in five'. I ought to have remembered her fondness for being loose with the truth when it came to ETAs.

'Hi, Care.'

'And what time d'you call this?' she says, instantly melting into a smile. The curls she prefers to leave wild, the chunky Doc Martens boots, the oversized hoodie. She is home to me.

We hug outside the red brick of the student pub. It's built in the middle of campus, a heavy stream of student traffic flowing past it. I'm reminded of the way in which she attracts attention, her open smile an invitation for intrigue. While I've learned to cultivate a kind of friendliness, I've never had her natural warmth. I love this about her and am convinced this similarity she and Luca carry will make them firm friends.

'You should call Mum, you know. And don't bite my head off,' she says, immediately catching the look in my eye. 'Don't bite my head off; I know how she is with you. Just . . . It's been a while.'

'Sure.' My expression is as pinched as my voice. How very like our mother to use Claire to do her dirty work.

Eager to move past this, I take Claire's hand and lead her inside. We weave our way through tables sticky with snakebite residue and shuffle over scuffed floors. The briny smell of the dubious-looking hot dogs behind the bar permeates the air. When we find my friends, they're as fascinated by Claire as I imagined they would be.

'Gosh, I wish I'd chosen drama school instead; it must be so much fun! Not like slaving away in the library over these boring essays,' Rebecca says.

Claire catches the edge. I see a flash of anger in her eyes, her mouth opening to retort.

'It's a lot of hard work,' I hop in. 'And it's not easy to get in.'

Claire gives me a knowing smirk. 'Yes, I'm sure you could dazzle the admissions board with a sonnet or two.'

She returns to her pint. I'm relieved it's a relatively mild response. Claire feels things keenly – it's her superpower and her kryptonite. Rebecca seems to pick up on the returned sharpness nonetheless and her features take on that tight, alarmed smile middle-class people sometimes wear. Fortunately, she seems to land on the need to impress Claire rather than battle with her, and so the next few drinks are sunk without incident.

It's wonderful seeing Claire in her element, masterfully navigating this group of could-be-awkward pre-adults who are still trying to figure out who they are. And it's wonderful her seeing me in mine: confident, admired, powerful. Everything is going smoothly.

That changes when Emily arrives.

We were joined at the hip at school, so the first months we spent apart at uni felt like a punishment. She's always been a little territorial when it comes to me. I'm sorry to say that I even took her repeated assertions that I should dump Marc as jealousy at first. The all-consuming kind that only lives inside teenage female friendships. I was too slow to see Marc for what he was.

So when she arrives –

'God, look at your phone sometimes, Nat.' Beat. 'Hi, everyone. Emily.'

– she immediately takes against Rebecca. It might be Rebecca's sycophantic hanging on my every word, or it might be her ability to hide an insult in the doughy wrapping of a sweet tone. Or it's just Emily's temper. Much like Claire's, hers spikes at the smallest slight, and much like Claire, she doesn't like to back down.

'I know it's not your birthday until Sunday,' Rebecca begins – it's the reason Claire and Emily are both down simultaneously. 'But can I give you your present now?'

I shrug and voice a 'Sure', while Emily scowls in suspicion and Claire cocks her head in curiosity.

Rebecca shoves a small box across the table. I slide it open and find a charm bracelet inside. My mouth drops open slightly as Rebecca jangles her wrist at me. A near identical bracelet clinks on it.

'You said how much you liked mine, so I thought you might want one of your own.'

Emily, who's pushed herself up beside me on my side of the booth, peers into the box and snorts.

'It's a bit much, isn't it?' she says.

'Maybe to you,' Rebecca replies.

Emily narrows her eyes. 'What's that meant to mean?'

I do my best. 'Guys, cut it out. We're –'

But sharp words have begun firing, and I'm not sure where the ammo is coming from. Either way, the sound of the cartridges emptying is drowning out any attempts at peacemaking. Both Rebecca and Emily have begun making digs about their respective parents' jobs, in a strange sort of middle-class war.

I'm relieved when Harry returns from the bar with a fresh

pint and a packet of crisps, offering a moment of distraction that allows the conversation to move on, a tense residue left behind nonetheless. Harry is handsome in a country-boy way – tall, broad shoulders, a pretty face with rosy cheeks and unkempt hair. We hooked up on a social once, before Luca. We were incredibly drunk and never spoke of it again. I didn't know what to do with a boy that posh and I sense he didn't know how he'd introduce a Black girl to his 'old-fashioned' parents.

He glances at his phone uncomfortably as he sets his items down next to me. It's fleeting, but it's me; I notice things. The conversation spills out across the table, a debate raging over what the funniest sitcom is. Is it *Always Sunny*, *The Office* or *Parks and Rec*? I regurgitate my favourite Charlie Kelly one-liners as I watch Harry check his phone again, unmistakable anxiety on his forehead. He places it face down and glances at me, alarmed to see I'm already looking at him. He quickly averts his gaze and leans physically into the chat while remaining silent, an unconvincing smile on his lips.

I turn to him. 'Is everything okay?' The question is quiet, whispered into his ear. The anxiety on his face is now so loud, it's screaming. 'Harry?'

He quickly looks to the group, who seem content with the raging fire of their debate, attention fully diverted. 'Well, um . . . Would it be all right if you and I chat before you go home? Just, when the others have gone, I mean.'

It's not what I'd been expecting. 'Why? I mean, of course . . . Just, like . . . I hope you're okay?'

'Yeah, yeah, I'm fine. It's just . . . just better said in private. Actually, maybe if we –'

'Oh fuck.'

It's Rebecca's voice. My eyes dart across the table to where she sits staring at her phone.

'This is so fucked up. What the fuck?' she continues.

Our friends on either side of her are staring down at her phone. Chris, a sandy-haired dude who spends as much time with the surf club as he does with us, is grinning. Laura, on the other side of Rebecca, looks horrified. Rebecca smacks a hand over her mouth and looks up at me. She suddenly clocks Chris's gleeful expression and gives him a hard thump on the arm, slamming the phone face down. Perhaps it's my naivety that doesn't make the answer to what's happening immediately clear.

'What's going on?' I ask, just as Chris's phone buzzes. 'What is that?' I ask again. 'Show me.'

'Nat, babe, I'm so sorry,' Rebecca says. 'There's this video going round. It says it's you. It looks like you.'

Idiot that I am, I'm still confused. I'm not so stupid that I don't understand the implication; I know what it means when a video of a girl is said to be doing the rounds. But it's not possible. It's too early for the thought of a deepfake to even cross my mind, but the fact of the matter is I've not recorded myself in any kind of compromising position with anyone. I don't even send Luca nudes – I'm too worried about this exact kind of thing happening.

'Show me,' I say.

'Nat,' Harry begins, 'maybe here's not the right place to –'

'Show me,' I insist.

I'm half expecting that it's just going to be some other Black girl – it won't be the first time I've been confused for another girl on campus – but the video is worse than I could have imagined. First, it's unmistakably me. Second, although there's little to see bar his groin, it's obvious to me that the other person in the video with me, the person recording, is Luca. We're in his room, on his bed, and it's his hand travelling across my back, grabbing at my waist and my neck intermittently as he thrusts into me. Luckily, you can't really see my face, as I'm on my knees and forearms. But if you know me, know my head of fine braids, it's clear who it is. It's enough. I pause the video and switch the screen off, placing the phone down gently.

As I wrestle with the swell of looming dread, I count it a small mercy that the sound was off. And then, as if life wanted to have the last laugh, I suddenly hear my voice and Luca's voice, panting and cursing. The things he's saying to me felt sexy and daring and hot at the time, but now they feel degrading, shameful. For a moment, I go from being the girl who sees everything to seeing nothing, totally numb. I want to climb into myself and live there, in the dark. I think perhaps I already have. It's not until I feel the cold beer pooling in my lap, hear the deafening crash of the glasses, that I snap to and leap up.

Chris is sprawled across the pub table, nose streaming blood. His phone is smashed on the ground by my feet. Harry is being dragged out by security, and I'm under the impression that Emily must have been part of the skirmish, because she's getting marched out, too. Rebecca is running after them, pleading Harry's case. A couple of the girls are asking me questions in soothing tones. I can barely hear what they're saying. My sister is beside me. Her little hand is in mine. Well, it's not so little any more, but it still sort of feels it, you know? And her little hand is an angry claw. Her anger is filling the space where mine should be.

'Did you know?' she's asking, and her voice is the only one I can hear. 'Did you know he was filming you?'

I shake my head. 'No.'

'Then that's – that's against the law, right? We should do something. Something real. I can't smash every phone on campus.'

'I mean, it was impressively swift damage, but she's right,' Laura says. And of course she's here too. 'We have to do something. This is so awful, I'm so sorry.'

The pity emanating from the faces around me is so thick I'm suffocating. It's too stuffy in here, and I can't breathe. I need . . . I need . . .

'Thank you, sorry.' My words aren't making sense. 'I need some fresh air.'

I stagger outside, where the air is cooler. It helps and it doesn't. I can't organize my thoughts, and suddenly the swell of dread and shame is cresting. It breaks over me and I'm drowning. I'm drowning and I don't know which way to swim up. And so I let myself sink.

My sister is beside me and I don't know when she got there, and I'm on the ground, and my phone is in my hand, calling Luca's number.

'Natty,' Claire says, 'you've got to breathe.'

And she's right. I'm panicking, gasping and gulping, chest heaving.

She takes the phone from my hand – five consecutive calls to Luca with no answer – and places an arm around my shoulders. With great effort I close my eyes and try to see a way out of the hole I'm in. There's a small chink of light within me, of hope, but it's nestled in an ugly place. I snake my fingers towards that light and grip it tightly, ignoring the dark, oily sheen that covers it. And as my fingers take hold, I feel my despair and my shame and my dread sink into a leaden ball, and I feel that leaden ball sharpen into something white-hot. Something sharp enough to cut someone with.

Chapter 10

Then

Light pours through the crack left in the heavy curtains, dust motes dancing in the sunshine. This house seems to gather dust like treasure, memories of birthdays and Christmases past held in little specks that collect in corners. The ghosts of old photos remain in pale rectangles on the walls, frames removed when the seemingly permanent decor evidently changed. James is stirring beside me. He has this magic ability to sleep almost indefinitely, whereas my body wakes like clockwork at the crack of dawn no matter what time I go to bed. No matter where I am. It's as if I'm trained to be on high alert, to not allow myself to sleep while others are prowling awake.

James's lashes ruffle against each other as his face comes to life, eyelids slowly drawing apart. The youthful smile that breaks across his face when he sees I'm awake is instant.

'Morning, gorgeous,' he says, and kisses me. I've always sort of hated this, the vulnerability of being kissed first thing, teeth unbrushed, face unwashed. It's always made me feel exposed, like the naked flesh of a tortoise without its shell. But it's nice to imagine that James's kiss is my shell, my home.

'Hey,' I say.

'Sleep well?'

I nod, pushing my face into his neck. Our limbs are entangled like pretzels. He feels warm and smells good.

Yesterday's aftershave still sits on his skin. It smells so familiar, comforting. With my face entombed in his body, the forgotten-bedroom-smell surrounding us fades.

We're in the room he grew up in, tucked away in his parents' house in Surrey. It's clear that they have never used this room for anything else, never will use this room for anything else, despite James's no longer needing it. The room is all dark wood and faded carpet, in the same vein as the rest of the house. There's something about old-money folk and slightly shabby homes. I don't quite get it.

In case it isn't already immediately obvious, it's worth clarifying that my plan to not get attached to the man whose body is currently warming mine has failed spectacularly. And worse, it's failed publicly, too. There's been a zeal and excitement in James over the past few months that I've not previously seen. A zeal that's made him dogged about pursuing things between us, full steam behind the engine of his desire. I suppose I should be flattered that I've had such an effect on him, but suddenly, life was 'too short' for a lot of things. When it came to things like not making me his girlfriend, I was delighted. But with things like 'keeping us a secret', I found my anxiety spiking.

My track record with relationships meant keeping things quiet suited me incredibly well. Should things end poorly, better for there to be no audience to swivel accusing fingers my way. But if there was one thing the Thomas brothers shared, it was their ability to sweet-talk their way into anything, and so it was that I found myself ducking out of the office early on a Thursday afternoon while James prepped an all-staffer to the company explaining the new relationship to his staff. With it, he announced Will's new lead responsibility on internal promotions, to dissuade anyone from believing James was meting out preferential treatment influenced by our new relationship. I'm still not sure if James was naive about his brother's affairs or simply just believed the company to be. When it comes to Will, I remain stuck with the feeling that I shouldn't ask too many questions. I know how sensitive sibling relationships can be.

In any case, within a matter of weeks, Will admitted he wanted to wash his hands of the business, as James had predicted he would, and the responsibility moved back to James. No one seemed prepared to comment on this, although distinctly cooled temperatures towards me following the initial relationship announcement only seemed to cool further when Will went. I'm sure they thought I was attempting to sleep my way to the top, although there was nowhere to go in my role; I had no aspirations to trade James's affections for inflated titles. No doubt I'd have been sorely disappointed if I had tried to leverage sex for any kind of bonus. After all, James wore his nobility front and centre like a second tiepin.

What was bizarre, however, was the continued change in Will before his departure. James had sat the three of us down in his office after hours one day, the shutters drawn. James had just been returning to the seat behind his desk, Will looking churlish in his navy suit and smelling faintly of whisky beside me, when Will blurted out,

'So you're fucking her?'

James stopped halfway into his seat in a comical freeze. It only lasted a split second, James sitting down and leaning forwards on his forearms, but Will's arrow had evidently landed true, a smirk playing on the older brother's lips. Will cast an unreadable look at me with those blue eyes of his, then looked back at his brother, smirk widening into a smile. Sometimes, I worried that Will saw me more than I gave him credit for.

'I wouldn't put it like that,' James began, irritation hitching his broad shoulders up to his ears. He shook them out. 'Look, I set this meeting because yes, the nature of the relationship between myself and Natalie has changed, and I wanted the three of us to . . . discuss how to best navigate that within the business.'

Will licked his teeth, looked at me again. His lips were pressed together now, mouth shut, although there was something distinctly lupine about his lingering smile. We fell into an uncomfortable silence as he studied me, eyes sketching my face as if he could see behind the mask, see into the damage I hid.

'Will?' James.

Attention turned back to his brother, Will simply said, 'I don't care who you shag, James. Let's not make a whole song and dance out of this. Deal with it how you want.'

With that, he'd stood up and sauntered out of the office, not bothering to look behind him.

This was now several months ago. And this last piece, the parent piece, I've avoided for as long as I could manage. Almost a year since James and I shared our first kiss. The avoidance was bringing James to breaking point, and seeing as the rest of the world knows about us anyway, I've relented. With some logic behind it, of course. Meeting the family only increases my motivation to be good, and having been good for so long, if James wants to integrate me into his life, I should let him. I just have to hope to god that his family doesn't want to go digging into my past. Both they and James can never know what I've done.

James picks up his phone from the bedside table and sets it back down. 'We should try to get some breakfast in us before we hit the road.'

'Yeah, that's a good idea. Although what are the odds

your mother is going to start talking about how cute "cara-mel" babies are again over our toast?'

He chuckles. 'Sorry, I know she's a bit old-school.'

'It's fine. After what you've told me about her, I was sort of fearing the worst. But I can tell she's been making an effort with me. Maybe she'll even hit me with the "Gosh, don't you look young?" again. I like that one.'

James rolls onto his side, slips an arm across my belly. 'Yeah, she's a bit of a charmer. My friends at school didn't get it, either, when they met her. Kept telling me how nice she was. But I think she genuinely likes you.'

It seems true. At least, I haven't felt either parent is keen to chase me off their grounds with a shotgun. It's a surprisingly low bar, and the Thomases have cleared it easily, which is its own relief. And I know should his parents not like me, should they take against my lack of family, my unimpressive career trajectory, my preferred small talk – not to mention my Blackness – this would all soon come to an end. James is just that kind of guy: family is important, I can tell.

Being liked – useful.

James's fingers circle my navel, his eyes drifting across the sight of his knuckles ruffling the duvet.

'What are you thinking?' I ask.

A small smile. 'Nothing. Just feeling grateful. Thinking about the future, I guess,' he says, voice still foggy with sleep.

I curl my body further into his. I know I must look as giddy as I feel. 'Yeah?' It makes my heart hum with happi-ness when we talk about the future. Not that any promises have been made. But as his hand comes to rest on my stomach, I can't help but feel reassured that our dreams might be aligned.

'My mother was asking again about meeting yours, you know,' James announces, moving the conversation along before I can dig any deeper. 'And your sister.'

I try not to let my body tense in his arms. 'You know that's not possible, James. I haven't seen my mother in person in years. And Claire really doesn't want to be brought anywhere near my romantic relationships, not after that's gone so badly in the past.'

'I know, I know. To be honest, I think my mother would be secretly relieved to hear they won't meet. Last time she got close to an ex's family, the mum hung around like a bad smell even years after things ended. We practically had to get a restraining order.' He laughs, shifts his body weight. 'You never have to do anything you don't want to do. I'm sorry I mentioned it.' He plants a kiss on my forehead. 'I love you.'

I'm tempted to ask more about the ex's mum, but I remember the pact we made to keep the past where it belongs and force the feeling away.

I like the way James makes me feel: normal, loved and secure. There are no games with him, none of that playing it cool or waiting three days to text me back, like there was with Marc and Luca. I try to feel guilty as he continues to insist on covering our dinners, our trips, but I can't. I've never known 'cared for' before. Not like this. I want to gobble up as much of it as I can.

James and I have sex, trying not to make any noise on the alarmingly creaky bed, and then ready ourselves to go downstairs. His father is reading the paper in an armchair in the kitchen. His mother is busying herself pulling pastries out of the oven. I hardly have to think about it; I grab an apron and set to helping, shuffling things around the hot stove and soaping dirty dishes. In my mother's culture, it's just good manners, but Hettie is bowled over.

Hettie and I natter while we work: the garden, favourite recipes, best *Bake Off* hosts. Even this trite conversation is a Cool Girl act of its own. A demonstration of how easy I am to get along with. James tries to join in, asks Hettie a few questions she doesn't seem to hear. He turns to his father, and they have a discussion of their own. For a moment, it feels as if this family has opened up a space for me and said 'welcome'. It feels wholesome, normal. Or at least what I always imagined 'normal' might look like. It feels nice. I think about what it would be like to create my own normal. To provide a safe space in which my daughter eats fresh pastries on the weekends and we talk about her favourite things she's seen that week on TV. I smile.

Will doesn't appear. He's here, somewhere, tucked into a corner like the persistent dust, too hungover to haul himself out of bed yet, or having an inadvisably early whisky in the bathtub. This seems to be his favourite pastime. He's sleeping in the guest room; his old bedroom is now being remodelled. When I ask James why his own bedroom remains untouched, he simply says an update 'isn't necessary'.

Hettie seems to catch a corner of our conversation, James having joined the two of us by the sink to help me put away the clean dishes.

'You're not complaining about the renovation again, James?' Her smile and raised eyebrows suggest she's joking, but there's something hard in her eyes and tight in her voice that betrays the tension.

James's reply is just as tight. 'No. I was just telling her about it.'

'Because if it really matters that much to you, we can absolutely work something out for you, too. Even though you're never here. It's just that Will happens to visit mo—'

'I'm not sure bolting here to dry out for a day or two while Vanessa's mad at him quite counts as "visiting".'

If I were Will's wife, Vanessa, with two small kids to look after, I wouldn't be pleased with his drinking, either.

Hettie tilts her head, smiles. Hands me a wet plate. 'Are you sure we can't tempt the two of you into joining our holiday?' she asks.

I freeze, tea towel pressed against the plate in my palm. Something in the gesture, the tone of voice, tells me the question is a snare, but I can't get away with ignoring it. 'Holiday?' I ask, turning to James.

Hettie answers before James can. 'Yes, we're off to Corfu. We go every year. Although James never sees fit to come with us.'

'You know why I can't, Mum,' James says, words snapping back like plucked elastic.

I've never heard this tautness in his voice before. Not with his family. I don't want to ruin a wonderful morning, but he's never mentioned Corfu to me. Not once. 'Why is that?' I ask.

He turns his brown eyes to me. I don't think he means for me to see the minute scrunching of his brows. I've upset him. 'It's just work. They always pick our busiest season to go.'

'Will always seems to manage it,' Hettie says.

'Mother.'

She waves her sponge in the air, casting a net of soapy droplets. 'Oh, don't make a fuss, James. We know how committed you are to your little brewery. And at least the lively one of you will be there to keep us entertained.'

When I turn back to Hettie, she's already swivelled to face the sink, hands working their way merrily around a pan as she whistles a tune. The ease with which the poison slipped from her mouth leaves me wondering if it even happened. I try not to let my own mother creep into the kitchen. Slip her feet into Hettie's slippers. Fill Hettie's robe. Frown disapprovingly at me with her back as she scrubs, scrubs, scrubs, her closed-off posture rejecting me anew, reminding me of my Wrongness.

I want to reach out and hug James, but it feels like the wrong thing to do, like making a spectacle of what is only a small moment of friction between mother and son. Instead, I continue to dry the plate in my hands while the safe space I'd imagined sags a little under the weight of this interaction.

'James.' His dad, Peter. 'Be a good lad and help me with six across, will you?'

James's eyes snag on his mother's figure as he crosses the invisible threshold between kitchen and living room, moving towards Peter's chair to help with the cryptic crossword. 'Mum –'

And then the williwaw of Will falls upon us all. He cuts across James's path, dark hair gleaming wet from his bath, fresh aftershave radiating off him even more boldly than his glassy-eyed smile.

'Mummy, looking particularly resplendent this morning.' He sweeps her up in a bear hug, rocks her like a metronome. The years fall away as she giggles. She either doesn't notice that he's already been drinking, or chooses to ignore it. When it seems he's squeezed the brightest laughs out of her, he lets her go. 'Edie,' he says with a smug nod to James, whose expression goes blank. Hettie cackles like Will's told the world's greatest joke. He turns his attention to me. 'Natalie.' And he plants a kiss behind my ear. The cloud of cologne isn't strong enough to completely mask the sweet and sour smokiness of the single malt. His hand on my back is too low. I step away.

'Morning, Will.' Because it is morning, but I am less sure it is any good. He gives me a long look, mouth twisted in a way that suggests he's holding back laughter.

I turn away, ask Hettie where the plate in my hand belongs. Bored of me, Will heads for Peter, eyes alive with mischief. He comes to rest on the arm of Peter's chair, back to James, who can no longer see the paper spread across his father's lap. Will and Peter laugh conspiratorially. Peter's need of James seems to have been forgotten. James retreats to the dining table, drinks his cold coffee.

It only takes a moment to file away the plate and then I'm beside James, my hand on his thigh, my breath in his ear. 'You okay?'

He gives me a 'yes' devoid of conviction. Hettie seems to finally notice us, drying her hands on a tea towel and laughing.

'Jesus, James. What are you sulking about now?' she asks.

Knowing it's often easier to kill a blossoming argument with kindness, I whisper, 'Don't rise to it.'

James nods his acknowledgement. 'I love you, Mum. Let's not fight.'

She only laughs again in response. 'Oh Jesus. Edie as I live and breathe.' She turns her attention to me. 'Be careful when you have children, Natalie. They're so manipulative.'

Will cuts in. 'Bloody *ouch*, Mummy.' He leaps off the arm of Peter's chair. 'Are we not your pride and joy? Am I not the greatest gift you've been given?' He sweeps her into another bear hug.

Fresh giggles leap from Hettie as she and Will pick up a creepily flirtatious banter. She swats at him, bats her lashes, tells him how much he looks like James Dean. But he shouldn't forget how much of a smoke show she was in her day, either. I've seen one or two videos on socials about middle-class mothers who flirt with their sons and never really got it. But watching Hettie carry on with Will, I want to unfasten the gold brooch from Hettie's blouse and blind myself with the sharp end.

When breakfast is over, James and I prepare to leave. Will stands in the doorway of the country manor as James slams the car boot shut, a trace of last night's wine appearing in shadows beneath Will's eyes. James and I brush past Will on our way to say farewell to their parents, and after stilted hugs, we make our way back out the door. Will is still there, muttering a tired goodbye to his brother. He throws a wolfish look my way.

'Nice to have you. Hope you enjoyed your stay.' And he pulls me into a tight hug that I don't know how to escape. As he lets go, he leans into my ear and whispers, 'It's never going to work between you two.'

I hardly have time to process this before Will is retreating into the house, the front door closing.

As we begin our drive, I can't help but turn to James and ask, 'What's the Edie thing?'

Emotion flees James's face. 'It's a remnant from a long time ago that's brought up to make me feel small. I don't like it. Don't like talking about it. Can I please invoke our pact to leave the past where it belongs?'

Message received. I wonder if this Edie is a she, an ex. The one who got away?

Curious as I am, I can see James's walls coming up and so change topic. 'I don't think Will likes me much.'

James's brows stitch together for a moment and then release. 'What makes you say that?'

A pause for consideration and then a simple shrug. 'I don't know. Just a vibe, I guess.'

'He's not . . . He's not said anything inappropriate, has he?'

I turn my chin towards James, curious. 'What do you mean, "inappropriate"?'

Eyes flash mild panic at me before resettling on the safety of the road. 'Oh, nothing. Well, just, I remember he made some uncomfortable jokes with my first serious girl-friend. Nothing . . . nothing horrible, just a bit ignorant, you know.'

'She was Black?'

He shakes his head. 'No, but . . .' The thought is left unfinished.

'Will's not . . .' I flick through the pages of our inter-actions across the span of our history. His penchant for sleeping with staff is significantly problematic, but I can't think of any micro- or macroaggressions pertaining to race. He's certainly no Sandra, who consistently harps on about diversity but, despite hiring a range of brilliant overachiev-ers, only seems to promote the assistants with the most generational wealth. 'No, he's never said anything culturally insensitive.'

'Good. I'm not sure why I even mentioned it. That was so many years ago, it's silly of me to even bring it up. If he's a little off, he's probably just playing up to get at me. It's . . . it's our business. Him leaving might have been more fraught than I let on.'

I raise an eyebrow. 'Oh really?'

'It's nothing for you to worry about. Just . . . just, I guess I encouraged him to go in the end. Pushed the buyout. It's done some damage to our relationship.'

His jaw is tight, a telltale sign that he's repressing sadness. 'Sorry to hear that,' I say.

'Yeah, well, I guess it is what it is. And anyway, Will's never been responsible with money; it's part of why I thought it best we part ways. But he's blowing through what I gave him for his shares and is feeling hard up for cash. And seeing as our parents are smart enough not to lend him more money after he lost their last loan betting on horses, he's more pissed about being out of the business than usual.'

'Oh.' I don't know what to do with this significant piece of information that James has just casually dropped like a tissue that's been fluttering loose in his pocket. After watching Hettie fawn over Will, I'm surprised he's unable to weasel his way into more handouts. 'Have your parents fully cut him off?'

James shifts in the driver's seat, flicks his eyes to me and then back to the road. 'Looks like it. What with the drinking and the gambling . . . It's . . .' He raps his fingers against the steering wheel. 'D'you mind if we talk about something else? I know Will loves attention, but I don't much feel like giving it to him even when he's not here.'

For a moment, I'm tempted to push James, but as I part my lips to ask more, it dawns on me that ours is not a relationship in which we push; ours is a relationship in which we live and let live. I suspect James has never had that before, in the way that I never have, either. It's comforting, it's nice and I don't want to disturb the peace we've built between us.

'Okay, okay, forgotten.'

The rest of the drive is peaceful. I almost doze off curled up in the passenger seat, chair reclined. There's something soothing about being driven by James, about the gentle muscles on his forearms standing out when he grips the wheel, about the self-assured, confident way he manoeuvres the vehicle through traffic. There's something about a Competent Man or a man doing Competent Things that I can't resist. It's not lost on me that this is likely because I'm not

69

used to it, have never seen it before, spending a childhood trying to survive my parents' incompetencies. I suppose all our childhoods are spent trying to survive our parents' incompetencies.

Fading echoes of raised voices loop in my mind, the press of a small, warm hand in mine almost tangible in my palm. Our parents loved each other deeply, I know. But that passion was a volatile one that left Claire and me clinging to each other in corners, waiting for fevers to die down.

Claire.

I miss her so viscerally. It's like I'm walking down a staircase to find the last step removed again, and again, and again.

Wind beats against the windows as I pick my phone up from my lap and bring it to life. I hop into our chat, an unread message waiting for me there.

> Am I allowed to put paprika in my jollof or will the ancestors flog me?

I chuckle.
'What's tickled you?' James asks.
'Just a silly text from my sister.'
He smiles. 'Tell her I say hi!'

> James says hi. Also, you can do what you like with your rice – let me know how it tastes.

A beat, and then I add:

> But if it's not good, don't be sharing it with anyone. We're already losing the jollof wars.

Her reply comes quickly.

> You made any for your oyinbo boyfriend yet?

Of course not. My jollof is terrible. I'm a professional taster.

> Like he'd be able to tell anyway.

Behave.

It takes a moment for the next reply to come through.

> Have you left the parents' yard yet?

Yeah en route home

> And???

It went well in the end, I think. I think his rents are overcompensating a bit by telling me how beautiful my complexion is a ton of times, but think they mean well.

> Are you being careful?

I am.

> Are you sure?

I don't reply.

It's only when we're stopped in traffic that I really look at James again. I don't often look at the people I love, not in the incisive way I look at everyone else. And yes, I've used that word, 'love'. I love him, or at least who I am when I'm with him. But as I take in his form, hands on the wheel, eyes on the road, I notice that there's something dishonest in the set of his shoulders. Like his voice, the echoes of a private education sounding through the London twang that sharpens his vowels. When we first met, it immediately struck me as affected. A false easiness. Having met his family, I now know that it is. The tightness is gone from his jaw, but it still threads its way through his body, almost imperceptible. Almost.

The echo of a rusty tang coats my tongue. And for a moment, I'm back with James outside that bar, his teeth sinking into my lip. And then I'm curled up on a hardwood floor, my body rattling with shock. And with this second memory, I know what the echo means. What that taste is trying to tell me. James and I are more similar than I knew. He sometimes needs protecting from his family, too. But it's okay. Perhaps we can be each other's family now. Perhaps we could one day start a family of our own.

Even so, as I look at him, really Look, I can't help but let Will's words echo in my head. *It's never going to work between you two.*

Chapter 11

Ex Number Two

Luca

This is the worst place I could be, and the only place. Foreheads boast a sweaty sheen as bodies jostle and jump together, bass-heavy music vibrating through my chest. In the crowd I can see some people I like and many I don't. The party is being thrown by some of the football boys, Red Bull sponsoring the sprawling debauchery, free cans flowing between hands and little baggies passed around behind closed doors. I know Luca will be here somewhere, and I know I have to find him.

It's been hours since I first saw the video. Hours of calls and texts to ask what the fuck is going on, only to get some half-hearted apologies back.

So sorry. No idea how the fuck this got out.

And

I know babe. Someone hacked my phone I swear.

And

I swear I told you about the camera you were just drunk remember? Maybe you've forgot. We'll talk properly later yh? So sorry about all this.

I've seen Luca's casual way of fobbing people off in

action before. It looks like you're getting his care and attention when really, you're getting none of it. I can feel it in the three messages he's sent today. If he really cared, he'd have been by my side in an instant, not straight to the pub with his football boys after the game and straight to a house party after that.

And he knows he didn't tell me he was filming. For a split second, I almost believe that he did, but I don't get blackout drunk like that, not since Marc, and I know in my bones that I would never consent to what he's saying even if I did. Still, a seed of doubt writhes in my brain, and I hate him for planting it there. It's far too hard to kill a thought.

As I make my way through the crowd, hunting for Luca — and I am unmistakably hunting — I feel eyes sliding over me when in close enough range. Sometimes hands, too. The smirks would tell me all I need to know even without the crude words that follow. I've leaped into a lion's den.

It takes me some time, this hollowed-out student house vast and cavernous, the building converted from an old pub. But eventually I find him. He's slouched in a corner of a basement room, body making a solid imprint on the faded sofa as his friends pass a small plastic pouch filled with off-white crystals between them. Although Luca declines the contents of the bag, his smile is so easy, the slump of his body so relaxed, that I want to scream. He gets to his feet as I approach him, an unsteady rock as he straightens up. I eye the beer in his hand and wonder how many he's had.

'Babe, you made it!' he says, as if he's expecting to see me here. As if I've not obviously tracked him down from a passing comment made about these plans. He kisses me on the mouth, and it's too quick and I'm too shocked to prevent it. Before I know it, his arm is slung around my shoulders. 'Max, get us a beer.'

One of his friends slides off the sofa and lopes off upstairs, leering at me as he goes. I'm so knocked off course by Luca's easy-going demeanour that I let myself be pulled down to the sofa, squeezed in next to another of his friends.

'Babe, I'm so sorry about all that mad business with the video, yeah? It'll all blow over before you know it.'

I manage to find my voice. 'But that's not the point, Luca. Why the fuck does it exist in the first place?'

'Look, I —'

Before he can finish, the sound of pantomime shrieking and grunting erupts in front of us. Two of Luca's football buddies are on the floor in front of the sofa, one on his knees making high-pitched, farcical whimpering sounds, and the other making exaggerated thrusting gestures behind him.

'Leave it out,' Luca says, laughing as he kicks them both over. It's clearly a joke to him, to all of them.

For a moment, my weaponized calm is almost shaken loose by Luca's cavalierness. It would be so easy to scream at him, to beat at his chest, but it's clear that Luca doesn't care, and all I would do is embarrass myself. There's nothing more despicable to a man than a hysterical woman.

'Can we please go somewhere quiet?' I whisper in his ear.

Arrogant as he is, it's possible he thinks I want to fuck him, even after everything, and so he obliges. Together, we weave our way out of the packed basement, up through various rooms of dancing bodies, past the kitchen, and up more flights of stairs. I clock each room I can as we make our way through the house, finally arriving at a mercifully empty bedroom.

'This is Max's,' Luca explains, flicking on the light to illuminate a room dingy enough to belong in his own student house. 'No one will be coming in here.'

I almost laugh when he leans in to kiss me, but instead, I let him, gut churning. He gently pushes me towards the bed, and as he climbs on top of me, I push against his shoulders. His breath reeks of beer.

'The video,' I say. 'Why did you do it?'

He laughs again, like I've told a corny joke. 'Really, Nat, are we going to keep talking about it?' He kisses my neck. 'You said you thought it'd be kinda hot, and it was. Have you seen how fucking hot you look in it?'

Jesus Christ. He's looking at me again now, clearly trying to temperature-check my expression. Trying to see if I'll buy the lies he's trying to sell me. If he can confuse me just enough to get away with this. For a split second, I have to pull myself back from the brink of believing him, and that terrifies me.

'Can I see it?' I ask.

'You don't have it?'

'Not on my phone, no.'

He rolls onto his back and digs around in the pocket of his joggers. In a swift movement, his phone is in his hand. I watch as he unlocks it, my body tense. He navigates to the hateful video and hands the phone to me, expectant. With care to look relaxed, I reshuffle on the bed, ostensibly to get comfortable.

Halfway through my apparent settling, I'm off the bed and out the door. Luca's reaction is quick. He grabs at me, managing a painful pinch of my arm, which ultimately slips out of his grasp, tripping him as he loses balance. I'm across the landing and into the bathroom I'd spotted on the way up within seconds, the door locked behind me. If it wasn't for Luca's stumble, I might not have made it.

Inside, my fingers tap at the bright, glassy screen. Luca's fists are immediately on the door.

76

'Nat, what the fuck? Open up!'

I find his WhatsApp and open his chats. Immediately, I spot what I'm looking for. My intuition tells me it's where I need to be. The football group chat. The bathroom door starts to tremble under the weight of Luca's blows. In turn, a quiet fear sets my own limbs trembling, so quick, like a muscle memory of panic I didn't know I had. Unsteady thumbs tap my name into the search bar. A flood of messages appear – some from Luca, some from his teammates:

Be there for 9. Earlier if not balls deep in Nat

> Yeah, Nat's so sexy for a black girl. I bet she fucks like a champion. I bet Nat's nudes are hot . . . Sharing is caring, bro

No way Nat lets you hit it raw. Proof.

And then the pictures and videos start coming through.

Nat's hotter than your girls, sorry about it

> Fuck me, man. You got any more pictures of Nat?
> That's so hot.

Shit, the way Nat moves is crazyyyy

There's only a handful of images and videos, but it's enough to make it crystal clear exactly what's been going on. As the drumbeat on the door grows louder, I take my own phone out of my pocket and snap images of the conversation on the screen. Evidence, if I need it. What a shit. What a horrible little shit.

For a moment, I wish I hadn't left Claire and Emily behind, abandoning them for this godforsaken plan when they've come all this way to see me. I want Emily's warmth, Claire's confidence. But how could I let them know what I know, see what I've seen? I think of Emily and her comforting mass of copper hair that always smells of the apple shampoo she still uses. I have friends here – uni friends, real-world friends – but there's something about my friendship with Emily that feels more honest. At uni, everyone decides to reinvent themselves. I'm not the only one pretending. And if two people in a relationship are lying about who they are, is their relationship even real?

Emily would tell me to suck it up. *Why be a sad bitch when you can be a bad bitch?* She loves the idea of bad bitchery, even if she grew up in a quiet cul-de-sac with a dad who was a dentist and a mother who taught at a primary school.

'Nat, open the fucking door!'

With Emily's imagined words still ringing in my ears, he gets his wish, terror in the brown eyes that lock on mine. Good. He should be scared. I slam the phone to his chest and he sees what I've seen. The terror seems to deepen.

'Listen, Nat, I can explain –'

I don't wait to hear it. I'm pushing my way back into the throng of the party, looking for 'numb', whatever it might look like and wherever I can find it. One of the party girls I always seem to bump into at these things is heading into another bathroom as I try to brush past. She sees my poorly masked distress, sees Luca grabbing at me, trying to get me to talk. Without a second thought, she pulls me into the bathroom with her, this secret den of sisterhood. We sit there, not saying much, until Luca gives up and disappears.

It's a relief to have her here. She always looks pleased to see me, has kind words to say, open ears for my thoughts. But I only seem to meet her when she's high on MDMA, so it's not entirely clear how much of this openness is her own. She listens to what's happened and holds my hand throughout. Her hands are soft and a little clammy. I want to cry at her kindness, but I won't let myself. My fingers are too firmly curled around my sharp rage now, holding it so tightly that it might be slicing into me, doing internal damage I'll never be able to repair. But it's my lifeline. I won't let go.

'It'll be okay,' Party Girl says, glittery makeup twinkling in the unforgiving bathroom light.

She hands me a bottle of water, instructs me to drink. The water is bitter and chemical tasting. When I realize it's spiked, I glug it more greedily, stopping at the point when taking more might be bad manners. She gives me a hug, holds me close, and then we make our way into the party downstairs. I find myself with her friends, dancing, trying not to think about how naked, exposed and ashamed Luca has left me. As the drugs kick in, this becomes easier, and easier.

Minutes later, I'm flying on this makeshift dance floor in this stripped-out living room. Luca is somewhere, but nowhere near me. I think about all the beers he's sunk that he shouldn't be drinking and wish his heart would just give out. Maybe one of these pills my new friends have given me would do the job if the beers aren't enough. But I'm not meant to be thinking about him, and so I push him out of my mind.

After that, all that's left is the music and the dancing and the pills. All that's left is the love of these kind strangers who, for tonight, are my best friends, and whom I'll probably never see again. For a few sweet hours, I can pretend the humiliation doesn't belong to me, reject it like incorrect baggage handed to me across a cloakroom desk. *Sorry, this isn't mine.* It's incredibly freeing.

At some point, and I'm not sure how soon, Emily materializes. She's worried about me, she says. I haven't been returning her messages. But she doesn't need to worry, and I tell her so. I'm having too much of a good time to look at my phone, that's all. But I'm not sure how convinced by my words Emily is, because it could be two minutes or two hours later, but she's insisting we go home.

Thanks to Emily, I make it back to my room. The night is not a blank, but it's a blur. A blur with some large holes in it. I immediately shut my curtains against the hideous morning light already illuminating my bed and tumble underneath the covers, snaking an arm around Emily's waist and holding on to it like a buoy in the waters of my rising despair, the dam of euphoria breaking, ecstasy draining away and leaving only dark thoughts in its wake. I want my sister, who's sleeping in the bed my housemate offered up given they're away, but I don't want to face Claire's judgement for falling apart like this. She can see me when I'm sober.

In the afternoon, when I eventually stir, my phone is drowning in notifications, and Emily is gone. A nugget of disappointment and anxiety wedges itself behind my ribcage at the thought of her leaving without saying goodbye.

I don't want to look at the messages. Amid the birthday texts will be more comments and links to the video. And I've done so many drugs that I know the comedown is going to be a killer without fixating on what made me get so high in the first place.

But then my eyes latch on to a few key words in the messages. I see they have nothing to do with my birthday or the video. Instead, I'm seeing:

In his bed.
MDMA.
Heart attack.
Dead.

It's easy to piece together the news across the outpouring of messages. One of Luca's housemates has found him dead

80

in his bed, of a suspected heart attack. Many people at the party saw him high on MDMA towards the end of the night, a drug he's historically avoided taking because of the hole in his heart.

The messages are all sympathetic.

Oh my god, Nat.

R u ok?

Let me know if you need someone to be with you tonight.

But the moment the news sinks in, any trace of a come-down lifts. I open my curtains, look up at the sunshine and let the falling rays warm my face. And for a moment, I feel grateful that Luca was such a master manipulator. Because everyone's convinced that the leaked sex tape had nothing to do with him, and save for Party Girl, everyone thinks I consented to that tape being made. So no one on campus knows the thoughts I had last night, how grateful I am that Luca is dead.

A foreign feeling settles over me.

Satisfaction.

Chapter 12

Now

'So where do you want to start?' I ask James, whose breathing is even now. 'That's the only real money I've ever had, James. My dad's mother might have been an arsehole who wanted nothing to do with us, but at least she had an attack of conscience on her deathbed and left her family something in her will. We were meant to use it to finally have a family of our own.'

He sighs again. 'Please, just before I say anything, I want you to know this has all happened because I love you.'

A swell of nausea rises in me and I want to shake him. I take a moment, steady my breaths, and I'm calm enough.

'Do you understand why I might find that hard to believe?'

He nods, shoulders so slumped it's like Atlas's celestial sphere is on his back, sky made stone. 'I understand, but it's true. And when I explain, I hope you'll see that.' He reaches for my hand, and I snatch it away.

'Talk.'

Raucous cheers erupt from what I assume is the living room. They come to a crescendo with rhythmic thumping undercutting the yells, beating through the house. So someone's just lost a round of rage cage, then. Spectacularly, it sounds like.

'Should I tell them to pack it in?' James asks.

I eye the snot bubble primed to burst from his nostril and find myself physically repulsed by James for the first time since we've been together. 'Leave them to it. Just explain yourself.'

'Okay, okay. Look . . . The truth is, Will found something out. He found something out, and I had to pay him whatever it took to stop him from destroying everything we have.'

The blackmail bombshell sits between us like a heavy weight. It's a lot, and I'm not sure what to make of it. For a split second, I think about Will's warning that day at their parents' place. I speedily dispatch the thought as inherently irrational. But then, what else?

'Why would your own brother blackmail you?'

He shrugs. 'I know you and Claire grew up close. But it's never been like that between me and Will.'

The thought of Claire almost winds me. The force of feeling will keel me over if I linger on it for too long, so I push it aside.

What James is saying is true, and I feel momentarily guilty for the judgement, but there's still so much pain and anger. Still so many unanswered questions.

'So was it something to do with the business, then? With you pushing Will to let you buy him out?'

James flinches. 'No, it's not that.'

My disgust is thick on my face and thick in my throat. 'An affair. Is that it? Will finds out you're cheating on me, and you use the only real money I've ever had to keep him quiet.'

'Jesus, Natalie. I've not –'

A knock at the door. Neither of us has even heard this person coming. James flashes me an alarmed look. I quickly slip out of my cocktail dress.

'What –'

'Just scoot over so you're out of the door's sight line,' I tell him. He does as he's told. Nobody needs to see his puffy face and pink cheeks.

'James? Nat? You in there?'

My fingers root into my braids and jostle them. It's impossible to make them look truly dishevelled on such short notice, but a gentle tousling should do the job. I pull the door open a crack, shielding most of my body with it. Waiting outside is a guy in chinos whom I recognize from the sales department of East London Chill. The moment his eyes take me in, he goes his own shade of florid pink.

'Oh! Oh, uh . . . Nat. Sorry, so sorry.' He's already turning to leave, eyes awkwardly looking anywhere but at me. He can hardly see anything, but it's clear from where he's standing that I'm almost naked, if not totally.

'It's okay. What is it?'

He risks a glance, then looks away, casting his eyes up to the ceiling. 'I, uh . . . We were just wondering if you have kitchen roll stashed away somewhere?'

'Yeah, there should be some near where Ama found the ping-pong balls, under the sink. They're tucked around the side on the right.'

He nods, chin leaping up and down in rapid succession. He looks like one of those bobblehead toys you stick on a car dashboard. In ordinary times, I might have found his discomfort mildly amusing, but all the humour has bled out of me. 'Of course, of course,' the man says, already making his exit.

'Is everything okay?' I call out after him.

'Yeah!' He doesn't risk a glance over his shoulder as he makes his way to the stairs. 'Just a bit of a spillage.'

I nearly jump out of my skin when I feel James suddenly behind me. 'Not on the wooden floors?' he asks, voice hopeful but words lost below the thrumming music.

This is so absurd it almost does make me laugh. But then again, James has always liked his Nice Stuff. And not just liked it – needed it. Sometimes it's hard not to feel like that's why he needs me, why he chose me: the Cool Wife to make him look like the Cool Guy. Another item for his collection of Nice Things.

I close the door. We're close now. Closer than we've been so far tonight. His stare, beneath tear-clumped lashes, is intense. One smooth sidestep, and I'm away from him again, safe.

'Pass me my dress.'

He does. As I change, he shifts from foot to foot, casting anxious looks at the door. 'Really, should I go downstairs and make sure everything's okay? We've only just finished decorating –' And now he's a wilting flower under my incredulous look. 'It was just a suggestion.'

He sits on the bed, offers me two raised palms in surrender or supplication. I suppose it doesn't matter which it is. In either case, I don't accept.

'You're in the middle of telling me why you've done this to us. Why? Why do it?' My voice is a desperate plea and a dismissal, all at once. I'm the one shaking now. I'd finally found a way to live normally, be happy, and then this . . . I sit beside him, defeated.

He sighs, shuffles closer, and reaches out towards me. His movements are ginger, testing the waters, but when he can see I won't lash out at him, he takes my hand.

'We'll get to the money, I promise,' he says, rubbing his brow, jaw tightening momentarily. Then he looks me dead in the eyes. 'I know I should have come to you sooner, I know I should have discussed it with you, not Will. But, Natalie, I found your letters.'

Dear George,

I suppose you were the point of no return. With you, there were the beginnings of an escape plan, thoughts about how you might not be good for me. I'm not sure why it was only possible to emotionally divorce from Marc and Luca once they were gone from my life, but with you, I found a way to see the light first.

That's why how it eventually went down is so ironic. It was a much messier divorce than either of us expected. I was cut so deep by everything you did to me that I wanted to cut back. I snapped, lashed out. What happened was violent and shocking. Ultimately, you could have seen me behind bars. It was a wreck. But my time with you left me in pieces, so I suppose that was fitting.

There was a lot you took from me, George, and I regret being too slow to notice what you were doing. To understand that nice gestures can cover a void of meaningful affection. But the worst thing you took from me was my sister. Like I say, I was sloppy. And this time, she saw the monster in me, and this time, it placed an insurmountable distance between us.

Not having her around any more is a high price to pay for not having you around. Too high. If you gave me the chance to do it all over again, I'd do everything differently with you. And then maybe I wouldn't have to live with this unbearable regret.

Chapter 13

Ex Number Three

George

George is the type who loves an outdoor activity: hiking, climbing, skiing, diving. You name it, he's into it. I like that he's into wholesome things and is sure of himself. It makes it easier to feel sure of myself, too.

We're in a cottage by the New Forest on a short stay-cation, just him and me. That's how we tend to like it. The two of us. My relationship with my mother remains strained, and my sister's too busy chasing her dreams to see much of me. He's not close to his family, either. I don't love that the trip is over Emily's birthday weekend, the same Emily whose parents always had a loosely watched liquor cabinet and who would have gone to war with Marc for me had he not died first. Luca, too, even though she hadn't really known him. She was that kind of friend. But George had already paid for the holiday before he knew about the birthday. There wasn't much we could do about it at that point, and the invite to Emily's was half-hearted in the first place.

Admittedly, I've not seen much of her over the past year or two. We're at different ends of the city now, her parents bribing her close to home by buying her a place in South, although the distance began after her visit for my birthday at uni. I was annoyed that she'd leave town early, on the day itself. She was annoyed for reasons she did not seem keen to divulge, nor I to press her on. I had drawn my own conclusions about what had happened to Marc, to Luca, and I wondered if she had drawn them, too. Either way, I could feel our relationship dying, slowly starved of oxygen. I didn't expect it to eventually end so dramatically. Didn't expect a catastrophe so big that it would sever my relationships with Claire and my mother, too.

With George, I know I fell into the trap of falling into a relationship and falling out of touch with everyone else. I've tried over the eighteen months or so I've been with him to maintain contact, but it's difficult. George prefers hanging out with me more than anyone else, which is flattering, and he often makes special plans for the two of us that he's sensitive about us missing. I'm lucky to have him, really.

A walking holiday? So I guess he picked out the activity again.

My sister's text this morning. The messages started materializing while I was in the cottage hallway, lacing up the walking shoes George bought me.

Don't you feel like he decides too much of what you get up to?

Even mum's started side-eyeing him and she has terrible taste in men.

Call me soon. Call mum. It's been too long.

As soon as I'm done with rehearsals, I'll come see you.

I wanted to tell her she doesn't know what she's talking about; how can she when she's so wrapped up in the relentless rehearsals and rapid carousel of romantic relationships that make up her last year of drama school? Where I get easily attached, she never does, her interest in partners only fleeting. But if I'm being honest, she's not entirely wrong about George. After so much chaos and pain with Marc and Luca, I like having someone with a good head on his shoulders to look after me. And so I left the messages unanswered.

My feet are sore after a long day of walking, boots caked in mud. George sits beside me in a small nook in this idyllic, cosy pub. A friendly waitress sets down two steaming plates in front of us – bangers and mash for me, and a juicy steak for him. We've been walking for five hours and I'm ravenous, tearing into the plate. Halfway through, I catch the corner of something tucked away in George's eyes. He sees me catch it and glances at my plate, only fleetingly. I set my cutlery down.

Don't get me wrong – George has never said anything negative about my appearance. Ever. But he does like to encourage us both to be healthy, to work out and watch what we eat. He's always been clear that our health is important to him, and I know the mountain of food on my plate is fat with butter, grease and cream.

'I've had enough,' I say.

'Are you sure?' he replies.

I nod. 'Yeah, I can feel my arteries clogging.'

He smiles, and whatever it was in his expression fades. 'God, I love how disciplined you are. It's so sexy.' He reaches over and skewers a plump sausage from my plate, dropping it onto his own.

I spend the rest of the meal watching George finish his food and most of mine, allowing myself another slimline gin and tonic while I wait. The second drink has me eyeing the dessert menu, but George's praise about my discipline is ringing in my ears. I push the menu aside, wanting to keep making him happy.

By the time we return to our Airbnb cottage, I'm light-headed and bone-tired. It's been a long, active day, and I probably shouldn't have tried to show off by declining to eat half of my meal. We discard our mud-clad shoes and shrug off our waterproof coats. The sofa beckons and we collapse onto it, laughing as our simultaneous bounce on the material threatens to throw us both off.

'What a perfect day,' George says.

'It was, wasn't it?'

He snakes an arm around my waist, kisses my shoulder. 'I can think of one way to make it even more perfect.'

It feels uncharitable to deny him sex – I rarely do – but my head is spinning. What I need is to fall asleep watching a cheesy film and to wake up refreshed. I tell him as much.

'Baby,' he says, climbing on top of me, pushing my legs apart. 'Please.'

I whack him lightly on the arm and laugh. 'I'm not your fuck doll. Off.'

He climbs off but looks visibly chastened.

'I'm sorry,' I say.

'What for?' he asks, tight smile. He gets to his feet and claps his big hands together. 'Right, a bottle of wine and that film you were talking about?'

'Sounds perfect.'

We make our way through a bottle of red surprisingly swiftly, George joining in as I take swipes at the bad acting and clichés on the small screen. We're good at snarky telly watching, although George doesn't like it when I take swipes at the more boneheaded comments on the men's podcasts he listens to. I protest when he uncorks the second bottle – my empty belly has sent the booze rushing to my head – but we're having fun, which was the whole point of this holiday, and so the second quickly disappears as we roll about laughing on the sofa. Unsurprisingly, I don't make it to the end of the third, my eyelids growing heavy as we approach the film's ending. It's everything I wanted.

It would be difficult to pinpoint exactly when it is that I fall asleep, but the moment I wake up will be for ever seared into my memory. The first thing that's immediately clear is that George is inside me, panting in my ear. My head is filled with painful static and it takes me a little while to figure out everything else: where I am, what's happening. Slowly, my vision comes into focus, the vague shape of the bedroom nightstand solidifying before me. I remember that we're in an Airbnb. We were watching a film. I fell asleep, and at some point George must have carried me upstairs.

There's a clock on the nightstand, red numbering blaring out '1:09'. The side of my face is pressed firmly into the hotel-soft pillow and it's all I can really see. It's not immediately clear to me whether George intends for me to have woken up or not, and that not knowing shocks me into silence. Distress begins to build and dislodge my stuck voice. At 1:10 I say,

'George?'

It's more of a question than anything else. I feel him falter, then push on.

'Oh, baby,' he says. 'You feel amazing.'

I'm still incredibly drunk – that's obvious. It occurs to me that we might have started this together, when I was awake, so I don't say anything else, just lie there until he finishes with a big grunt at 1:14. It's only five minutes in total, and when it's over, he holds me to him and kisses the canvas of my back. In this specific moment, it feels normal, like normal couple sex. I just happened to fall asleep in the middle of it. I wouldn't be the first, nor the last.

It's only in the morning, when I ask him gentle probing questions about the night before, really looking at him this time, that I realize he knew I didn't want to have sex with him, knew that I was sleeping, knew that I'd wake up and know he knew I didn't want it. There's an ugly word that I'm scared to ascribe to it. But when I look it up hunched over my phone with a hollow feeling consuming all other emotion – the definition, the law – it fits perfectly. And when I turn my eyes back to the night before, to the past year or two, I understand how much I've missed. I understand that last night was a punishment, a reminder to know my place in the shape of us. I can almost hear the brainless bark of one of his podcasters reminding him, *Sometimes you've just got to show your girlfriend who's boss.* I feel a fool for not having seen it sooner, that hardness at his centre, that need to dominate masked as willingness to support.

But I don't let him see any of this, don't say any of this to him. Because I've realized that I'm not the only monster in my relationship.

Chapter 14

Now

Thoughts are clanging together in my head, loud chaos. I've always prided myself on being able to keep my emotions in check, but suddenly there are too many for me to keep hold of, each one slipping through my fingers. James must see the maelstrom of feelings on my face because he squeezes my hand, still tucked in his, and places a reassuring palm on my thigh.

'Please say something,' he says.

'W-what do you mean? When you say letters . . .'

'I mean the letters you wrote to those guys. Your exes. The ones you . . . you . . . I'm not sure exactly what, Nat, but it doesn't sound good.'

I wrench my hand from his and spring to my feet, pacing. This couldn't possibly be any worse.

'Look, I don't know what you think you saw,' I say, forcing my feet to be still. From somewhere downstairs there's a shriek and a crash, followed by raucous laughter. I'm sure something James and I picked out carefully for our new home is now broken. He flinches at the sound but dutifully ignores it, pushing on.

'Nat, I found the box under the floorboards in the guest room. I've read every letter.'

My breaths become shallow, my panic a live bird fluttering in my chest, hoarding the space through which air should flow. Oh god, this is not the conversation I thought we'd be having.

'And y-you've read all of them?' He nods. I try to get my hands around the conversation, take control of it again, steer it where it needs to go. They're trembling fingers holding keys over a drain. 'I'm not sure the letters are quite what you think . . .'

'What I think is that you sound scary in them, Nat. You keep talking about this "monster" living inside you. What the hell does that mean? What the hell have you done? In the second letter, the one about Luke –'

'Luca.'

'Right, Luca. It says he's dead. I know you wouldn't, but, Nat, I need to hear you say you didn't –'

I keep my face straight and fire back quickly. 'Of course I didn't. It was a heart attack. He had a heart problem. Are you really asking if I murdered someone? Jesus, James.'

My own heart feels painfully tight. His eyes are bone-dry now.

'Can you blame me? Why bury the letters like that? And I saw the look on your face when I told you I'd found them.'

I let myself emote for a moment; he needs to feel the veracity of these words. 'Because I'm embarrassed! And horrified. Those letters are about the worst trauma I've ever experienced. I was trapped in these horrible, toxic relationships with these horrible, toxic guys and it fucked me up, James.'

He takes my hand gently, rubbing my palm. 'Look, I . . . I get that some things in the past are too painful to talk about. But I need you to explain it to me. Each one.'

'James, I –'

'Please.' The gas is pumping back into him now, reinflating him into the man I married – quietly confident, self-assured; there's no moving him on this now.

Deep breath. I pull my arm away, stumble backwards. And

then I tell him about Marc, about Luca, about George. Most of it anyway. Parts of it, at least. Fine. Snippets, in all honesty. I tell him the ways in which my exes were rotten. I tell him the ways in which that rot spread, taking root in me and growing into something that felt dark, unsafe. I confess to wanting to hurt Marc, to wanting to hurt Luca, to managing to hurt George, badly.

'You've married a monster.'

He squints as if the dust motes in the room might draw together to give him a clearer picture, fingertips massaging his forehead. 'So let me get this straight – Marc is also dead? He fell off that roof.'

I nod. 'A horrible accident.'

'And Luca had a heart attack.'

Again, a nod.

He gives me a knowing look. 'I read the letter; I know you weren't exactly cut up about it.'

I turn away. He immediately takes my shoulders, pulls me back around to face him.

'Look, I can understand that these were accidents, and I know why you might not feel all that bad after what they did to you. But George – Lord knows I want to hurt him myself – I still don't understand exactly what it is that you did. You're not being straight with me about it.'

Something like the truth is flaking off, ready to be picked at and flicked in James's direction. I'm nervous to tell him this much, but it's clear he has to know if our marriage is to survive. Perhaps beneath the dread, the conviction that it's stupid to let anyone see this much of me, there's also a flicker of relief in unburdening myself of my secrets to my husband. I've been holding so much in for so long. I relent, open my mouth to tell him more.

'One day, after . . . Not long after what he did to me, he

97

came home drunk. He was being aggressive, taunting me about the time he . . . he hurt me. I just . . .' I can't quite meet James's intense stare and turn my eyes to the floor. 'We were at home, and it wasn't much more than a slap at first, but when I hit him, it made him angrier, so I grabbed a knife to protect myself.' I see James's eyes go wide and hurry the next words out of my mouth. 'But he's bigger than me, stronger than me. He knocked me down before I could really do anything. Even if I – I tried. I cut him, but I didn't kill him.'

When I finally look up at James, he isn't reacting at all like I expected. Relief is plain on his face. He pulls me to him, hugs me close. 'I was terrified that . . . I mean, I know you could never, but for a moment I thought . . . Listen, you've been through a lot, Nat. That's not your fault. It's not your fault.'

'I don't get it.' I shake my head, pull away. 'How can you be so calm? I nearly killed a man –'

He cracks a dry smile, although I notice his eyes are wet again. 'I don't know if I'd call this "calm" . . . But these past relationships, the pain: you're getting help for it, right? I mean, your therapy . . . I get why it was so important to you now. And it – well, you've been saying therapy helps you. So it must be helping with . . . all this. And what happened with George was self-defence. Jesus, Nat, look at me – it's been a whole week since you found out about the money, and . . . and look. You've not hurt me.'

Something clicks. I feel physically sick. 'Is that why you went to stay with your parents? You were scared I'd hurt you?' His face crumples and I know it's true. My already waning confidence dies and guilt grows on its corpse. 'Oh god, James. Oh god, I'm so sorry.'

'No, I fucked up by not coming to you. I meant what I said in my vows; I want it to be us against the world. You're my best friend, my chosen family. I should never have gone to someone else without speaking to you first.'

I think of our vows, our shotgun wedding. It was wonderful, mad and probably too soon. I thought it was romantic that James didn't want to wait, liked that it gave me less chance to chicken out and a reason not to worry about inviting people I knew. But I'm sure James is learning what it means to marry in haste and repent at leisure.

'I get why you didn't come to me. I know what I sound like in those letters. I know I . . . I know I'm not normal.'

'Don't say that.'

'Why not? It's true. Would you have been so afraid of me if I was?'

He gestures for me to sit down, and I do. We both take a moment to stare at the bedroom wall. I'm not entirely sure how to navigate things in the new shape of us, and I don't think James knows how to, either. He married the easy, charming Cool Girl, and now he has . . . this.

'So,' I say, first to speak again, 'the blackmail. You went to confide in Will about what you read and he decided to extort you?'

'Yeah. I mean, the letters sounded like maybe . . . I worried – we worried . . . But I wasn't sure. I know you. I know the woman I married. But Will . . . He said he'd go to the police, tell them everything he knew about you, see if they could find out what you did, if you were a . . . I was shocked, and confused, and, yes, a little scared . . . but I couldn't let that happen. Nat, I love you to your bones; I wasn't going to let them put you away.' He rests a hand on my thigh again and gently squeezes.

'But you know that could still happen, right?'

'What do you mean?'

'George. I say it in the letter. If I'm reported, I could go to prison. I attacked him – it's actual bodily harm at the very least . . .'

James simply shakes his head. 'Will won't talk, and we say nothing more to him. That's what the money was for.' He reaches for my hand again. 'I should have just come to you and talked this out. If I had, we wouldn't be in this mess. We're meant to be better than this. We talk to each other, don't we?'

I pause, thinking of our repeated pact to not bring up the past. 'We do.'

'Please, Nat. Do you think you could find a way to forgive me?'

It would be hard to dig my heels in, punish him, when I've been hiding a secret of this magnitude. When I'm still hiding secrets. It's my messy past that's got us into this messy present, and as much as I wish James had kept a cool head and hadn't gone behind my back . . . God, I wish he hadn't gone behind my back.

It feels stupid to brush it under the carpet, and 'stupid' is not something I usually allow into my life, but I simply give a weary nod and say, 'Okay.'

'Okay?' he confirms, pitiful hope singing out in his voice.

'Okay.' I nod again.

He takes me in his arms and squeezes me close. For a moment, my face is buried in his neck. His aquatic and citrusy cologne brushes against my nose, that smell of home coming back to me again. He gives me a gentle kiss, salt seeping into it from tear-streaked lips.

'And what about me?' I ask. 'After what you've read, after what I've told you . . . Can you still trust me?'

He takes a beat. 'I trust you.'

And in that moment, I'm reminded of how good an actor my husband is – whether it's pretending to be less posh than he is; or to hate his privilege more than he does; or to enjoy Audre Lorde as much as I do. Because not everyone will have caught the minuscule shift in his register, but I know that when James says he trusts me, at least part of it is a lie.

And as I detect a curl of that anger, that white-hot rage still lurking beneath my broad relief, I can't be sure that I trust myself, either.

Chapter 15

Now

Dimple

'It's been a while since I last saw you.'

I'm sitting in my new therapist's office. It's a little more distracting than the corporate simplicity of Dr Foster's was. The walls here are peach, the carpet green. The furniture is largely old mahogany with gold details. It's a strange room: certainly not modern, but not old-fashioned in a way that adheres to any archaic rules; not trendy or cool, but very intentional and cohesive in its decor choices, which seem to gel in a discordant way. I sometimes wonder if this is part of the psychiatric evaluation – when you finally call out the madness of Dimple's room, you've passed therapy, free to go.

That's what she prefers I call her, by the way: Dimple. Just her first name. I suppose it's meant to foster a kind of familiarity. Almost like a friend. But she's not. Dr Foster, on the other hand, felt familiar. I'd been seeing her for so long before her retirement that she'd almost felt like family. Dimple, her replacement, I've seen only thrice. All the same, I do feel bad for how long we've gone without a session.

'You're right,' I admit. 'It's been a while. How have you been doing?'

She gives me a wry smile. Lines deepen around her mouth and her eyes in a way that captures her warmth. She is a woman who smiles a lot.

'Come on, now, Natalie. I think we both know we're not here to talk about me. What brings you back in to see me?'

My eyes fix themselves on the garden view over her left shoulder, trees gently rustling in the wind.

'I'm not really sure where to start,' I admit, fingertips digging into the velvety peach armrests beneath my hands.

Her head dips to one side, thick, dark hair swinging down a shoulder. I know she's about to go for the jugular. 'So how about we start with why you stopped coming to see me?'

'Oh,' is all I say. A small shuffle in my seat.

'Oh,' she repeats, eyes crinkling in amusement.

I know how this game goes. She pokes somewhere I don't want prodded, and I waste time and money dodging away from the jabs until she finally gets what she wants. The truth. She will sit there for as long as it takes for her to get it; I might as well cut to the chase.

'To be honest, I felt better. My violent impulses have been down for so long, and I was happy with James.'

'I notice that we're speaking a lot in the past tense.'

She's good.

'Yes, well . . .'

And I explain the whole saga to her. Me finding the money gone. James finding my letters, telling Will about them, telling me about them. The blackmail, the panic, the fear.

'That's a lot for one person to go through,' Dimple says.

'Yes.' I nod, feeling affirmed. 'Yes, it is.'

'I'm interested to know more about how your conversation with James went. How exactly did you discuss the letters you'd written?'

'He wanted to know more about my exes, about what happened.'

'And you told him?'

I scrape a shoulder blade against the backrest of my chair. 'Sort of.'

Dimple smiles. 'Let me reframe the question: what did you tell him?'

'I told him that Marc's fall and Luca's heart attack were accidents.' Her smile has turned knowing, and it's as irritating as the fabric of the chair against my back.

'Did the two of you discuss George in any detail?' Dimple asks.

'A bit. He knows I hurt him. He doesn't know he's dead. And I know what you're going to say about honesty in relationships, but this is what works for me for now, okay? I mean, haven't you ever lied to a partner?'

Dimple's eyebrows bob up and back down. 'You know I don't discuss my private life in this room.'

It seems an unfair trade. I like to think she's glad I sometimes ask her questions about herself, too. She should know that I see her as a human being.

Dimple taps two fingers against the side of her glasses and changes tack. 'Tell me, broadly, how have these new conversations with James made you feel?'

'Unsettled. Off-kilter, I guess. I felt like I had everything in control and now it's all spiralling away from me.'

'This feeling of impotence, of not being in control, how is that presenting itself?'

I look at her and look away. I can't bring myself to hold eye contact. 'The impulses. I suppose I've been feeling them again. Nothing I haven't been able to control, exactly. But when I first found out about what James had done, about the money he stole, what that meant for my ability to have kids . . . I could have really hurt him, Dimple. I wanted to.' I pause for a moment. 'Just to be clear, I'm not going to, though. You don't have to . . .' My words lose themselves on the way out of my mouth.

'Please feel that you can speak freely, Natalie.'

I massage a thumb into the groove of a knuckle, recall what Dimple has said about client confidentiality. She assures me that what's said in this room stays between us, and that if I say something that means that has to change, I'll be the first to know. I did my research before I started therapy, the threat of talking my way into a prison cell very present in my mind. She doesn't have to report past crimes, but if I say something that makes her think I might cause serious harm in the future, I'm screwed.

Dimple reclines in her chair, looks at me through the thick black rectangular frames of her glasses. It's clear that no more words will come from me unless she draws them out, so she continues. 'I notice we've slipped into the past tense again. Tell me, how are you feeling about James now?'

My head gives a small shake. I don't know where to start. 'He's been great. I can't imagine any other guy finding out about my past and . . . He just seems to want to protect me.' I shrug the simple truth out. 'I'm grateful for him.'

Dimple's head dips to the other side. 'Is there a "but" coming?'

My nostrils flare, and for a moment I think about shoving her backwards in her silly chair. 'But,' I concede, 'that thing . . . that blinding white heat, it's still there . . . It came back the moment I found out about what James had done, and although I understand now, although I don't want to hurt him, it's still there. Just buried, with nowhere to go. It's like I can feel that violence pricking behind my eyes at all times. Like if I don't unleash it, it's going to blind me. Destroy me, even.'

Dimple leans forwards again, elbows on knees. 'How long has it been since you've acted on one of your violent impulses?'

'Four years. Still nothing since George.'

'And has anything bad happened to you?'

'No. And before you say it, yes, I remember what I've learned in my sessions about this. I know why I sometimes feel this way and I know, I know it's not real . . . But in the moment, when the feeling comes, when the thing bares its teeth, all I know is how real it feels.'

Dimple nods. 'I understand. Still, remember what we said ab—'

'I get all of that. I do, I promise. But the problem isn't my conscious mind. Even now, when everything feels like a house of cards waiting to blow over, I have control over that. It's the other thing that keeps me awake at night.'

'The thing you cancelled our sessions to avoid talking about.'

A frisson of irritation runs up my spine, pulling it taut. 'I've never had a problem talking about the blackouts.'

Dimple's head tilts over once more, her eyes narrowing. Only slightly, but enough that her unbelief is stripped bare. 'I seem to recall you leaving our session early the last time we tried to talk about them. What might I have misremembered about that?'

'It wasn't the blackouts; it was the other thing you wanted to talk about.'

'Because it's not quite possible to talk about one without the other, is it?'

Silence from me.

'Is it?' Dimple insists.

The air in the room is dry. Too dry. 'Yes. No.'

Dimple nods. 'So, let's talk about your mother.'

Chapter 16

Before

There was a slight tremor in her hands as she set down the teacups. She glanced over her shoulder. Once, then again. Her eyes were tracking up the staircase: rickety, wooden. It needed repairing. It had needed repairing for a long time, and by now its repairs needed repairs.

The cups and saucers clattered down to the table, chipped red for Claire and cracked blue for me. It was subtle, but even at five years old, I knew there was intention behind her choice. Claire was small, but already her vibrancy, her energy, matched that ladybird red. Me, on the other hand, I was still watery, still placid. With something very definitely wrong with me. At five years old, cracked.

It might seem insanity to suggest that a mother would try to send her five-year-old subliminal messages through crockery, but insanity was the boldest and most consistent thread in the tapestry of our mother's parenting. I sometimes wonder if that's where my intense observation of people comes from. Mother would bury vitally important messages under layers of obfuscation, and woe betide anyone who missed them. Insane behaviour. A truly insane way to communicate, and yet . . .

Looking back, it's clear my mother's mental health was as complex as her communication style. But a Ghanaian mother seeking professional help for that? Chance would be a fine thing.

On this day, there were clear warning shots. They were

fired in the soft kisses she planted on our temples after she set the cups down and in the tight squeeze she gave our shoulders after. Her short braids tickled our cheeks as she pulled us to her, the faint musk of years-old Elizabeth Arden covering us in a cloud of sweet and sad faded glory.

'You look so beautiful today, babies,' she said.

I was immediately suspicious, my little hands becoming little fists on either side of my cup of steaming hot chocolate. She must have seen it in my face, too, because she then said, 'Oh, stop making that face, baby. It doesn't look pretty on you.' She tapped my cheek as if to knock the doubt away. I knew to play ball, thinking of my classmate's puppy that met her at the school gates last week, and her promise to bring him back on Monday. The thought soon brightened my face.

I kept my gaze fixed down on my cup while Mother started to tend to Claire. She was littler than I was, still needed help drinking without getting sticky chocolate all over herself. I say 'sticky chocolate' – hers was more milk than anything else, but that didn't stop it from being a nightmare when soaked through her clothes.

'I was thinking we might have an adventure today,' Mother said. 'How would you like to go to the big park near Grandma's? We can go on the big slide as much as you want and finally explore those woods.'

Claire let out a squeal, screaming, 'BEE PAAA!'

Mother's eyes widened, managing not to look at the rickety stairs, but also not able to stop her body from involuntarily twitching towards them. 'Hush, darling.' She turned to me, smile manic. 'Now, Mummy was thinking, seeing as we're going all that way, we might as well stay at Grandma's house for the night. If you're good, she might even make her peanut soup. You'd like that, wouldn't you?'

Yawning slides, cavernous sandpits, salty-sweet soup with tender chicken floating in it. I'd like it a lot. I kicked my dangling feet, fixed my brown eyes on hers, and nodded.

'Good girl. Mummy's just going to go upstairs and get our explorers' packs together.' My heart lifted. 'Mummy also needs to tell Daddy we'll be gone, but it won't take long.' And there was the catch. I was young, but not too young to know that this wouldn't be as easy as Mother made it seem. Dad knew how to behave better when other people were around – it's part of what made me miss having Aunty Dev and her daughter, Joy, around even more. Without witnesses, he was unpredictable.

The thing that always lived with me in that house, buried in my chest, reared its head just then. Fear.

One bubble, two bubbles, three . . . I stared down into my hot chocolate, watching the little spheres on the surface pop one by one.

Mother watched me turn in on myself and withdrew her warm touch. If I was looking at her in that moment, her mouth would have been twisted up, I know it. One thing my mother hated was weakness, and that's what she saw in me. Weakness undercut by a wrongness that made her wary. Hard not to absorb that feeling. Hard not to fixate on what inside me was broken enough to make me so unlovable.

'It won't take long,' she said again, retreating towards the staircase.

The echo of house sandals on wood started and then came to an abrupt stop. This piece always stays in my mind – it felt eerie, like she'd suddenly vanished. I realized years later that she'd just taken her sandals off so that she wouldn't be heard. And she was successful, in that sense, for a time.

As I stared down at my safe circle of brown, blowing ripples into the surface, ignoring the dwindling babbling of my sister, that's what began to fill the house – an absence of sound. It's not quite the same as silence. It's like the moon slowly drawing its way over the sun and drowning out its rays; it's not just darkness but the absence of light where it was, where it should be.

The quiet made me think, and what I was thinking was of our big adventure, and what I was thinking was that it was too good to be true, and what I was thinking was I didn't like it when our mother and father were alone for too long because sometimes when Mother came back –

A thud.

I looked to Claire, who looked to me. She didn't worry like I did. She was still a little too young for fear, still too well shielded from it. It was clear that Mother tried to keep Claire in a bubble of peace and safety. She didn't want her to turn out like I did. I'm not sure if it was this protection or something else that made Claire's eventual fear grow differently than mine. Smaller. Quieter.

Our house was without sound again. Everything was peaceful. Too peaceful.

I slid out of my chair, feet dropping to the ground. I made my way towards the stairs, but before I came close, a terrible shriek, crash and thud filled our home. Instead of rushing over, I found myself frozen, tiny feet with big ambition planted firmly on the wooden floor. Claire was wriggling out of her seat now, slowly learning to be afraid.

Perhaps that's what motivated me to move, the sight of her usually joyful eyes big and scared, her little sticky fist pushed into her mouth, ringlets bouncing as she looked to the stairs, then to me, then to the stairs again.

'Mummy okay?' she asked.

Another crash echoed through the house. This place wasn't big enough for the four of us. I couldn't bring myself to lie to

Claire, so I only said 'Wait' as I found the will to move again. When I reached the mouth of the staircase, narrow walls astride uneven wood, it looked yawning, ready to swallow me whole. My father's voice could now be heard, bellowing from the bowels of our home. I took the first step, heaving my legs up what seemed like a mammoth climb. I was big. I was a big girl going to sort everything out and make sure that Claire wasn't scared and that Mother wasn't hurt and that we would still have time to go on the big slide before it got dark outside.

More shouting, and our mother's voice was joining the chorus of crashes and barks to build the sound into a spectacular din. My short legs marched forwards, eyes fixed on the blank wall ahead. That wall represented my next feat of bravery. It was at this point that the staircase made an abrupt turn to the left, continuing a few steps up into the upper house proper. Something about making that turn terrified me, as if once I was in the belly of the house, like Jonah in his whale, I wouldn't be able to get back out. They'd been talking a lot about Jonah in Sunday school. I didn't think I could manage three days and three nights trapped in the storm of my parents' anger.

My progress came to a halt. The landing where'd I'd have to make a turn was just a few steps away, and the feeling that I might never come back was stronger than ever. The din had grown into a cacophony of screams, and the screams were overwhelming. I could feel them building to a crescendo, cresting into a wave that would crash and leave my lifeless body in its wake, small bones strewn among the wreckage of my family.

And as if I'd somehow dreamed it into existence, suddenly the pandemonium was upon me. My mother, wailing, hurtled into view. She crashed onto the landing. There was a gash on her head, blood on her face, terror in her eyes.

'Natty, go!' she screamed. And even as she screamed, she scrabbled to her feet. The heavy thud of danger was on the stairs behind her, descending. She turned and yelled, 'Stay back!' I turned and ran back the way I came, eager to be away from the horror behind me, eager to be anywhere else at all.

I took the stairs down as fast as my legs could carry me.

'Natty!' Claire.

'Wait!'

A horrible crash. More yelling. I think maybe I smelled her before I felt her. The sweetness of that old, faded glory. But when I felt her, it was too late to do anything about it. Her large, hard body, pinballing down the stairway, collided with me. I was helpless, a soft pin beneath her leaden bowling ball. We both landed at the bottom of the stairs, pain exploding across my body, pain exploding out of her mouth as she screamed my name.

And that was when my fear monster cloned itself, slithered out of my chest, and made a home in my sister. There, it raged. There, she screamed.

Chapter 17

Now

'Are you sure you're up to this?' James asks, running his palms over his shirt and checking his reflection again in the hallway mirror. He's changed his shirt three times but has settled on this one, geometric patterns and relaxed cut screaming 'trendy East Londoner'. Only the thing is we haven't been East Londoners. Not for the year since we moved almost to the end of the Elizabeth line, expressly in the interests of starting a family. It was only after we'd begun unpacking in our new Taplow home that the doctor had delivered the news about my endometriosis and how badly it had fucked up my fallopian tubes.

I used to feel a level of responsibility for taking James away from East London that I know is unhealthy. It still calls to him. It's where the company's headquarters are and where tonight's launch event will be. Now, with the money gone and the question of children in smoke thanks to James, I feel that guilt a little less.

'Yeah, I'm looking forward to tonight, babe,' I say, not entirely sure. It's been a few days since our big conversation and it feels a little like the wheels are coming off my newly renovated wagon, everything at risk of coming to pieces in a crash that I won't be able to stop. I curl my fingers around his neck and give him a gentle kiss. 'You ready?'

He smiles, face lit up like a child's at Christmas. 'Yeah. All right, then, let's go.'

The taxi is already waiting outside. It's only a fifteen-minute walk to the nearest station, but James knew I'd want to wear heels, which are murder on my feet over loose pebbles, cobbles and potholed pavement. He didn't even ask, just knew what I'd want and booked ahead of time. Two weeks ago, to be exact. This is who the man I love is: thoughtful, kind, attentive. And that is what he's been during the emotional turmoil of the past week: thoughtful, kind, attentive.

James suggested going to his parents about the money at first, and this idea ignited cruel hope in me for a moment, before I realized that his parents would want to know why we'd handed the money to Will in the first place.

No. We can't go to his parents.

And where that leaves us is with no money, no new doctor's appointment. Which I tell myself is fine. I tell myself that not everyone needs to be a mother. My mother certainly did not need to be one. But there's a gnawing feeling inside me. A need to do better than her. To prove I can do better than her. To love something, someone, completely selflessly. To love not for what that person can do for me, but for what I can do for them. To leave an indelible mark on the world in the form of a good human. I just want to make a good person. I think perhaps that might make me a good person, too.

I try not to dwell on this as we make our way to the station and onto the train. There's a desperation living in those thoughts that repulses me in the same way I know it would my mother. Instead, I sit nestled into James in the quiet carriage. There's a new intimacy between us since we've bared our secrets to each other. But it's a precarious intimacy, walking the tightrope of all the things we're not saying. The trust we're pretending hasn't been broken. I know it won't last.

All the way to the pub, snippets of teacups and old dilapidated staircases and Elizabeth Arden keep pushing their way into my mind. James speaks, and I half listen as I try to get myself together for him. I've got to show up to his party in top form. I nod and smile at what feel like correct intervals. I offer him kisses when it seems he's said something meaningful. And before I know it, we're walking into the venue, hand in hand, the picture-perfect couple.

There's a momentary flash of concern on James's face as he surveys the reasonably thin crowd. Despite my own doubt, I'm about to remind him that it's only six thirty, people will still be at work, when the marketing manager, Molly, springs forwards from the bar. She's a fun wine partner for a thirsty Thursday but is just as likely to stick a knife in my back as have it, depending on what's at stake for her. I've noted the increased warmth she's radiated towards me since James and I have been together, no doubt banking on some future usefulness I might have for her. She clearly misunderstands the kind of man James is.

'James! You're here!' She has a tray of full pints in her hands, the new CBD IPA that's launching. It wobbles a little as she does an excited shimmy, her severe black bob shivering with her. She turns to acknowledge me. 'Nice to see you, too, Nat.' Her eyes track back to James, spot the question in them. 'Everyone's catching the sun upstairs.'

And when we follow her up an almost hidden staircase reminiscent of a swanky hotel corridor and emerge onto a roof terrace teeming with plants, we can see that the party has indeed started. Thank god for a sunny day in London. Everyone's ready to power down laptops at four p.m. From some of the wide and slightly uneven smiles, some people have done exactly that and are already a few pints in.

It's easy from there, at least for the next hour or two. James mingles with colleagues and contractors. Outside his overbearing brother's shadow, he's the star of the show. People seem easy, relaxed. James is good at holding court and I'm good at allowing him to.

A not small part of me wishes Ama was here for company, even though she left the business a while ago, her warm smile and wicked quips a comfort. The ghost of Emily intrudes at that thought. She doesn't need to belong somewhere to show up and have a good time. Have everyone around her have a good time, too. The perfect plus-one. I miss her. But I don't know how to reach out. We haven't spoken, in fact, for years. I wonder if my mother is haunted by the phantom limb of Aunty Dev in this way, too.

I shake the melancholy away. Dutifully listen to holiday stories from co-workers and exchange home-reno ideas with local shop owners. It's important to give James space to mingle, let him feel he doesn't have to babysit. He'd do it without complaint, but I know first-hand how annoying it is to have to try to entertain a spouse when it's their partner you really want to be talking to.

'God, he's good, isn't he?' It's Molly the marketer, hands free of a drinks tray this time and occupied with lighting a cigarette instead. 'Lucky you. He really looks out for you, you know?' I'm not sure what she means by that, but the look that lingers on James, a few feet away, is clear admiration. And more than that. She may as well have cartoon heart eyes bulging out of her head, despite the existence of her long-term boyfriend, Brian. She's not the only woman I know who wants to sleep with James, and I've never particularly minded when women do. Even the previous office manager, Mad Mary, was said to have held a candle for him before her infamous nervous breakdown and abrupt departure. He's an attractive man; it's only human. But there's something new this time as Molly lets invisible drool spill down her chin – something white-hot. Something sharp enough to gut a man with.

It takes me so by surprise that I take a physical step back from her. This sudden movement draws her eyes back to me, a subtle question in them as she tries to assess whether I've read her thoughts, whether she's been staring too long. But it's nothing to do with Molly and everything to do with me. Because suddenly I can imagine James's longing stare turned her way. Picture him leaning closer to her in the office after hours. Nonsense, I know. He's not Will, would never cross that line. But I can feel the trust James and I have built is on even shakier ground than I've admitted to myself. I don't like it.

'You okay, Natalie?' Molly asks.

'Yes,' I say with a small nod that speaks of weariness and mild embarrassment. 'Sorry for the thousand-yard stare; I just remembered an important email I forgot to send before logging off. It's not going to be a fun day for me tomorrow.'

Molly relaxes a little, smiles. 'It's okay, we've all been there. I'm sure whatever it is can wait until morning. Worst-case scenario, at least you're sleeping with the boss.'

A tight smile.

Molly continues. 'Although, god, it's a relief not having to do damage control for Will's chaotic emailing any more.' Her body language is conspiratorial, a cheeky glint in her eye. It's becoming increasingly clear that the pint in her hand isn't her first.

Not one to pass on a performative bonding opportunity, I lean in, too. 'Honestly, I don't know how it wasn't a total shit-show before James took the reins.'

'Wasn't it? I had to have a bottle of wine after work every day, just to wash away the trauma. I was one small crisis away from having a nervy b and going full Mad Mary. Just totally sodding off without telling anyone. When Will started drunk posting on our socials, I almost did!' There's unbridled delight in her laughter. Okay, so she's loving this. I'm happy to indulge her further.

'I don't know why James taking over didn't happen sooner. James is really grateful to those of you that stuck it out, by the way. Think he'd have lost his mind without everyone's support.'

She takes a puff of her cigarette and shrugs. 'Well, it wasn't so bad to start with. But I guess sometimes when the wheels come off, there's no putting them back on.'

I try not to think of my wheels, of my wagon. Instead, I think about Will, piercing blues staring into your soul as he talked you into doing something that really should have been his job and made you feel glad to do it. At one point, he was a force to be reckoned with. If any of that Will has survived, he's a dangerous person to be holding my secrets.

It's as I'm thinking of this that a loud laugh pulls my gaze over Molly's shoulder. At first, I thought it was James. It would be psychotic of me to think I've suddenly acquired some kind of psychic ability, but it's as if I've manifested Will by sheer power of thought, as he's suddenly there, staring directly at me with those icy eyes. He's dressed up for the occasion in yet another navy suit, an espresso martini glass in his hand. The martini in the midst of James's beer event feels like a very distinct 'fuck you', and I'm sure he knows it.

My pulse spikes with terror and rage as I take in his appearance, but I do my best to quickly smother the fear and fury. This might be the first time I'm seeing Will since the blackmail, but I need to keep it together. Otherwise, he wins. How or what is not clear, but reacting unmistakably feels like a loss. Another one.

Will and I are still staring at each other. The elegant blonde chignon of his wife, Vanessa, drifts behind him as she chats with someone in what looks like stilted conversation. I'm all for spousal independence at parties, but rather than voyaging out on her own, Vanessa always has a sense of drifting unmoored at these things. Her husband is not a good life raft.

Will's eyes narrow and I wonder if he has been reading my thoughts, given the hostile look on his face. Although I suppose, if he suspects I'm a murderer, to look at me fondly would indicate a level of insanity. His mouth is opening as if he's standing right in front of me and is about to speak, when a hand takes hold of my waist. I know immediately that it's James's hand, just a breath before the hot words are whispered into my ear.

'What the hell is he doing here?'

I don't have an answer. At least, not one I like.

'Do you want to go somewhere and talk?' I ask, voice low.

James looks to Will and back to me. 'I don't like the idea of leaving him unsupervised with everyone. Who knows what he might say or do? Even if he does seem weirdly together.'

But when I look at Will, I catch the scent of something else, something nudging his spine straighter and holding his shoulders broader. What does he want, and what will he do with what he knows? That ever-present fear sitting beneath my skin begins to crawl out of my pores.

'Do you think he's going to say something?' I ask. 'Is this about me, or is this about you?'

'I don't know.'

I weigh our options up. 'Let's just talk to him.'

James's eyes flash panic. 'Here?'

I shake my head. 'Downstairs, where it's quieter.'

James nods, takes my hand, leads the way. The crowd parts for him like the Red Sea, only the path to Will is no road to salvation. Smiles follow us as we pace the terrace, but people back away when James and Will finally draw near. There's an implicit understanding that this is not a conversation for other ears.

'Lovely to see you could make it,' James says. Will's expression is almost defiant in the sarcastic arching of his eyebrows – they both know he's not welcome here – although his eyes flash an unreadable question as they flick to me. Before Will can say anything, James pushes on. 'Actually, I'm glad you stopped by. I'd really love your opinion on some of the flavours we're experimenting with for the IPA. We've got some samples downstairs. Come with me.'

It's too firm and reasonable a request for Will to justifiably protest. 'Sure,' he says, clearly anything but.

'Nice to see you, Will,' I say as we turn for the staircase, suppressing a smile at the frown that draws his brows together and sends a glance my way. It's the little things, sometimes. It's work understanding people and how to get them to feel comfortable around you, but it's fun to make them uncomfortable, too, now and then.

We're silent as we make our way down the stairs and into a booth, tucked away at the back of the pub. It's less quiet down here than it was before, but this area is empty. Will sits on one side of the table, James and me on the other.

'Well, this is cosy,' I say, trying my best to suffocate the fear and draw on the simmering anger as I sit across from the man who's stolen my IVF money. It was only a couple of months ago I got it transferred from my estranged grandmother's estate. Only a couple of months to live the dream of having a family before it was snatched away. I'm putting on a good show, but I feel sick to my stomach.

Now we're no longer in full view of everyone, Will's energy is nervous, jittery. He's leaning as far back as the bench will allow him, as if I might reach over the table at any moment, a knife unsheathed, going for the carotid. But that's not me. I can't let that be me. In fact, I'm relieved to find the thought not particularly tempting. Perhaps James is right; I'm healing.

It's too silent for a conversation, Will's lips stitched together in a new but apparent wariness, and James's lips forming a thin line of something alien on his face: anger. I don't like having to be the one to show my hand first – it's the worst possible way to start a negotiation, if that is what this is – but someone needs to get the ball rolling.

'So, who wants to sta—'

'I didn't know you'd be here,' Will says coldly, running a hand over his chin. The gesture makes it look like he's trying to hold in more words from blurting out. 'Vanessa's just upstairs. If anything happens . . .' He leaves the sentence unfinished. Takes a sip from his drink. A little droplet of brown splashes onto the pale blue of his shirt collar.

'I'm not going to hurt you, Will,' I say.

He simply looks away from me, pointedly staring at James as if I'm not there. James takes my hand, squeezes it. He eyes the almost-empty glass in front of his brother and looks up at Will. 'You seem out of sorts. Need another?'

'No, thank you,' Will says, grinding his teeth. 'Have you forgotten I have a problem with drink?'

'No, but I was wondering if you have,' James says, cool as anything.

The friction between them is beginning to grow so rapidly that I can almost smell smoke rising from it. If unchecked, it will soon fan into flame. While a not insignificant part of me would love to watch Will burn, now is not the time, nor the place. Too many other things would catch fire.

'Look, Will, we're a little surprised to see you here,' I say. 'We're just curious, that's all.'

'Yes,' James cuts in, consonants clipped. 'Why did you come?'

Will's back straightens a little. 'I don't know why you're surprised when the idea for the new range of beers was mine. And now you're taking all the credit and the profit from it, too. And swanning around with your crackpot wife as if nothing has happened!'

James bristles, his first words a violent hiss. 'Watch your fucking volume. Or did we not pay you for your bloody discretion? And you were piss-arse drunk and high for the last couple of months you were "at work".' He makes a point of making air quotes with his fingers around those last words. 'What could you possibly remember? I was working on this idea long before we even had a conversation on it, and I bought you out of the business fair and square.'

'No, you pushed me out. And the idea for the flavoured IPAs only exists because I was talking to you in the pub about how much of a brilliant invention I thought flavoured cider was.'

'Is this what this is?' That tight anger is pulling the muscles in James's jaw taut. 'Are you here to shake me down?'

Will thumps a fist on the table. 'I'm not shaking you down; I just want what's mine. I've cut back the drinking. I've stopped the gambling. I want back in. You know what I know.' He glances over at me, daring me to speak.

I'm uneasy. I'm uneasy and James is apoplectic. Will can't quite see it, that he's pushing James to his limit, but I can. Only I don't know what that means. I've never seen him there before.

'You promised,' James says again.

Will softens, both physically and in tone. He slouches against the backrest of the booth bench and his hands fall to his lap. He takes a moment to gaze at his thumbs, then looks back at his brother. 'Please, James. I need this. I'm trying at home with Vanessa, with the kids, but . . . My life is . . . This is all I have left.'

James looks to me, and his eyes seem to be begging me to

help somehow. But I need to watch Will more, understand him more, first. James seems to see that I have no Hail Mary and slumps back against his own bench, shoulders drooping, defeated.

'I need you to stay clean for a year. No more drinking. A year, and then we'll talk.'

'Four months,' Will fires back, eyes eager. 'I can't sit around like I am for a whole year, James. I need purpose. I need this.'

James looks at me, a clear question in his eyes. I give him an *I trust you* shrug and he turns back to Will.

'Six months. Six months, but you can't put a toe out of line. And absolutely no showing up at work or company events before then.'

Will's jaw jostles in thought before he eventually says, 'Six months. And everything you said.'

'Six months.'

'Okay, it's a deal.'

The grin on Will's face is so earnest that, for a moment, he almost looks sweet. Almost. There's a greedy glimmer in his eye, and I can't shake the feeling that he's the kind of person to always want and never be satisfied. Takes one to know one. And I know that want is an addiction; the more it's fed, the hungrier it gets. I don't have room in my life for another junkie.

'So?' James asks.

'So what?' Will replies.

'So, no showing up at work, no company events . . .'

Will looks taken aback for a moment, but then nods, smiles. 'Yes, of course. Right. Right you are.' He slides out of the booth and smooths his suit. 'I really appreciate you hearing me out. I can't tell you how much this means to me.'

'Sure,' James says. 'Just don't let me down again.'

Will nods, says an awkward goodbye, and leaves. I watch quietly as he retreats, and when he's safely out of earshot, I turn to James.

'Are you sure letting a man like that back into your business is a good idea?'

'No, but I'm sure I've just bought us six months of time while we figure out what to do about it.'

I can only hope that the house of cards we're stacking stands that long.

Chapter 18

Now

Dimple

Dimple's jumper is pink today. A fuchsia, really. It's distracting. I want to tell her it's distracting, but I know that normal people don't do that. That level of honesty is for people who live on the periphery and I very much want to be an in-the-thick-of-it everyday Jane. The kind of wife and, one day, mother who hosts the social events of the season and who everyone says 'God, isn't she great?' about.

I try not to let the desire for this to overwhelm me. For the unlikelihood of this to overwhelm me. I try not to think of my useless fallopian tubes, my inevitably dwindling egg count. I try not to think of how easy it seemed to be for my mother. So easy, in fact, that neither Claire nor I had been planned in the first place. And here I go, thinking about her again. My mother. I try not to do that too often and have become quite accomplished at it over recent years. But the worse I feel about myself, the more I feel her hostile ghost. And now Dimple is reopening the doorway to the cardboard box of memories I have of her tucked away in the recesses of my mind.

It's painful, Dimple forcing me to pull back the heavy curtain of my trauma like this. I don't like it. I want it to stop. And yet –

'You once told me you had a generally positive impression of your childhood.'

'Mmm.'

'I notice that you struggled in our last session.'

I shrug. 'I suppose I did.'

She tilts her head, sighs. Today she wears her hair in loose curls and the longest strands only just about tickle the tops of her shoulders. 'Are you just verbalizing your agreement with me for ease, or do you actually agree?'

I shift. 'No, I agree. I mean . . . even though I'm estranged from my mother, I never really thought things were that bad back then. I know they weren't great, but I always supposed they were fine. I guess I suppressed a lot.' I pause. 'You asked me to talk about where the real difficulty started with her – my mother – and I started, but I – I clammed up. I froze, I know I did.'

'Why do you think that was?'

My sister's screams echo in my ears and I feel my little bones clattering against hard wood.

'It's just difficult to talk about,' I say.

Dimple's mouth twists to one side in thought. It's a strangely comforting gesture. I like it when I can tell that people are being careful, being considerate of me. It's nice to be considered.

'What exactly is it that you want out of our sessions?'

This isn't what I was expecting her to ask. I blink in surprise and rummage for words. 'I – I thought we've been over this. I don't want to hurt anyone again.'

'I'm going to ask you a challenging question, and you'll have to forgive me in advance for the bluntness of it.' She pauses. 'Are you sure that's true?'

It's like she's taken the smooth palm of her hand and struck me with it. It stings. 'Of course it's true. Why do you think I've been coming here, pouring money down the drain, if it's not true?'

She narrows her eyes and leans back in her chair. When she speaks again, there's a gentle provocation in the high pitch of her register. 'If someone had hurt your sister, badly, what would you want the outcome to be?'

'I don't know what you mean.'

'Just entertain me here for a moment. I know your relationship with your sister is important to you, and that you feel deeply bonded with her. There's a fierce protectiveness and love there.'

'That's true.'

She spreads her hands. 'So, if, in theory, someone hurt her – badly – what would you hope would happen to that person?'

I'm beginning to understand the trap she's laying for me, and I resent her for it.

'What would you hope would happen to that person?' she asks again.

I lick my teeth and pause.

'I would want them to hurt, too,' I say.

'Even if it means hurting them?'

The tree over her shoulder takes my attention for a moment. I need a second of Zen to compose myself.

'Even if it means hurting them,' I agree.

'So,' she says, seemingly satisfied, her elbows coming forwards to rest on her knees, 'I think it's safe to say that you're not here because you never want to hurt anyone again.'

'That's an extreme example. That's not fair.'

'I know,' she says, offering me a small smile. 'I'm just trying to get us to address the root of things. To help you as you need to be helped. Everyone is capable of desiring violence. What exactly is it about your situation that needs to change?'

She's right. She's always right. 'I need to be confident that I can control myself.'

'And how do you think we do that?'

'By unpacking where my lack of impulse control comes from.'

'And how do we do that?'

'By talking about my past.'

'And?'

'By talking about my mother.'

'And?'

'By talking about what my mother did to my dad.'

Chapter 19

Before

The hours after the fall were like a surreal pantomime. The humanity switch seemed to flick back on in our father at the sound of our collective screams and the sight of my little body in a heap. He ran to me, scooped me up in his ham fists, poking and prodding through tears, asking if I was okay. I was not. But beyond a cut lip, it seemed the worst damage that was done to me was psychological. At least, he hoped it was.

My father was no doctor, and my mother, a part-time nurse whose split brow was gushing blood into her eye, was determined to get me in to see one. That humanity wavered in Dad then, and he raged, screaming blue murder about Mother trying to get him 'done in'. But when the conversation was dropped, when it was agreed my mother knew enough to know I was okay, that we wouldn't be going anywhere, he was all apologies, tears and kisses again.

It wouldn't happen again.

He was so sorry.

He wished she wouldn't drive him to the edge like this, it killed him.

She'd heard it all before. Although to my young ears, it sounded like maybe he meant it this time, that he was capable of change. After all, the way Dad would cuddle me, toss me in the air, play dinosaurs with me . . . he couldn't be a bad guy, could he?

My little brain and bruised body didn't know how to

compute these thoughts, and I just screamed, as did Claire. Screamed as he tried to hug us; screamed as he set down ice-cream bowls adorned with our favourite sprinkles; screamed as he waved our most-played-with toys before us and tried to get us to engage. With Mother little more receptive to his attempts, even the gentle dressing of her injuries, he eventually gave up, wailed that we didn't love him and left with a slamming of the front door.

I took my little sugar-sick belly over to Mother, who was still cowering on the floor. She'd hardly moved from where she'd fallen at the foot of the stairs. She put her arms around me and pressed her nose into my hair.

'Ouch, sweetie. Not so tight there,' she said, pulling my tiny arms loose from her waist.

'Are you okay, Mummy?' I asked. In retrospect, I know how stupid a question that was, but I didn't know which other questions there were to ask.

'Of course, baby. Mummy just might need you to watch Claire for a few hours, and maybe get the two of you something from the fridge to eat at dinner time.'

I blinked. Watch Claire, dinner. I'd watched Claire plenty and helped Mother with dinner before, but this was the first time I was being charged with both on my own. I simply stuffed a small fist into my mouth and nodded.

Looking back, I'm not quite sure how we managed it, but Claire and I spent the next couple of hours, and then days, looking after ourselves and looking after Mother, too. I couldn't cook anything for us, but I managed to find some bread buns, crisps packets and chocolate, which tided us over for the first day. And when that ran out, I messily cobbled together some bowls of cereal.

Mother had crawled to her room on the first night and stayed there since. Claire and I would run in to check on her, but she didn't want to speak. This was and wasn't new. I was used to Mother sometimes hiding in herself when Dad's screams were in her ears and his hands were on her body. That vacant look in her eyes always told me she'd gone away. I slowly learned that this disappearance was pain relief; she let someone else take the blows while she went elsewhere. Eventually, I would learn to do that, too. It helps, I think.

On the third day, life began to leach back into her. She came downstairs, still slow, still wincing, but she came down all the same. Her bruised eyes took in the chaos, the stream of crumbs and souring milk on the floor, the scattered pages and broken crayons. Neither Claire nor I had bathed, and we both looked as dirty as the room smelled. We had been doing our best, but we were still so small.

Mother straightened a little at the sight of us. Early-morning sun was flooding the living room, illuminating our sorry states.

'Right, girls. Let's get you a proper breakfast and then bath time.'

I do remember crying at this point. Crying because the woman who had been living in my mother's skin and didn't want to talk to me was gone, and our real mother was back. Flaws and all.

Again, hindsight is a useful thing, and looking back, I should have known that this was too abrupt a recovery. Emotionally, I mean. I should have known at that point that she was planning something. In any case, I simply rejoiced as she set down steaming plates of eggs in front of us. They came with cold glasses of orange juice, condensation beading on the glasses, and sides of hot, freshly buttered toast.

I sort of recognize that eerie calm now, the peace after the storm. She'd grabbed onto a lifeline, the only one she could find, and it had a dangerous edge.

The house over the next few days was the most peace-ful I remember it being. The three of us stayed at home, Mother's wounds slowly healing. She read to us, we built forts in the kitchen and the garden, we ate okra and banku and all the other things Dad said he couldn't stomach when he was around. But he wasn't, not for a whole week.

I'm not sure if Mother called around to ask where he was. I'm not sure exactly where it is that he stayed. All I know is that a week later, he came stumbling into the house, a faint whiff of whisky wafting over the perfume of the obscenely large bouquet of flowers in his hands.

There were no harsh words from either parent, simply a wary sizing up as they locked eyes until Dad eventually grunted, 'I'm sorry.'

More silence. The flowers were placed on the dining table and then: 'I'm going to bed.'

The festivities ended then. We didn't quite cower in his presence, but we all tiptoed around the landmine-infested soil of his feelings. He was still somewhat contrite, it seemed, so it was easy enough not to set him off. How long that would last, however, was uncertain.

One evening, a couple of days later, Claire and I sat cross-legged in front of some cartoons while Mother and Dad lay on the sofa behind us. Mother was feeding him whisky, one glass at a time. With each glass, his mood turned more and more sour, and his words became meaner and meaner.

'Off to bed now, darlings – it's past your bedtime,' she said.

It was rare for us to give up TV time in any hurry – it was a real treat – but with the storm clouds gathering, we were only too happy to comply. Mother followed us upstairs, tucked us into bed and kissed us on our cheeks.

'Everything's going to be okay, promise,' she said.

We both let our eyelids close and our minds drift to sleep with that promise echoing in our ears.

It was the loud crash that eventually woke us. Our room was still dark, so I knew it was still night-time, my body eager to get back to sleep. But little Claire was scared.

'It's okay. Wait here, Care. I'll be back.'

It's a big sister's job to look after her little sister, no? Even when you're just as scared as she is. Even if you just want to get back under the covers and chase the thought of night-mare monsters away.

But I was going to be brave.

I inched out of the bedroom and slowly made my way to the landing. Mother was standing at the top of the stairs, back pumping up and down with heavy breaths, fists clenched tight by her sides. She looked at once ready to spring into action and frozen. Totally frozen.

'Mummy?' I asked.

I walked my little legs over to her, small hands reaching up into the folds of her nightdress and yanking. 'Mummy?' I asked again.

When no response came, I followed the track of her eyes, staring down the narrow hallway into the near distance. As I followed her line of sight, I realized that we weren't alone. Dad was sprawled at the bottom of the stairs, one arm and his neck at an unnatural angle. His eyes were staring, unsee-ing, back at Mummy. I wonder if she was the last thing he saw, or if he was already dead when his gaze fell that way. In any case, he never saw anything else again.

Chapter 20

Now

I wish I could say that my sessions with Dimple are sewing me back up, stitching my torn pieces together into a beautiful, sturdy quilt. Instead, it feels like old scraps of trauma are being dredged up and assembled into an ugly, unwieldy thing.

It's just weird how much stuff comes up when I think too hard about it. It sounds fucked-up when I say it out loud, but we were okay, right?

I hardly remember that time. I was too young. But I think we've always had very different definitions of 'okay'.

Claire. I consider sending her more messages about it, about what it's like reliving all this. But when she can't really remember it in the way I can, when I've seen before how upset it makes her talking about it, I don't know what good it will do.

Instead, I send her inane memes and TikToks I think she'll like in our chat. It takes all my willpower to actively avoid Self-HelpTok as I hop between skits. Ex-boyfriends aside, I don't tend to hyper-fixate, but there's something addictive about the promise of better mental health packaged into neat thirty-second clips, presented by pretty people who don't acknowledge they have a beauty filter on their videos, but you know they have a filter on and aren't admitting it, which makes you feel a bit superior as you scroll with Kettle chip crumbs down your front, and you realize that maybe everyone is a little bit messed up and maybe you're not that special.

Okay, so I've watched some videos.

James is throwing himself into work more. It's a distraction, I guess. And when he's present, he tiptoes around me, cautious. He pretends he isn't, but that false easiness has crept into his smiles and kisses. His eyes track me when he thinks I'm not looking. I've noticed he doesn't touch our joint account statements any more, leaves me to open them when they're pushed through the letterbox. I've noticed the dribs and drabs he's started depositing. It's nowhere near enough, and won't be for a long time. When I ask him about it, he simply flushes, promises he'll do what he can to get us back where we need to be, and changes the subject.

His guilt is palpable in the supercharged softness he's treating me with, and I wouldn't mind it, save for the litany of traps now peppering our conversations. His performed softness is a veil draped over my eyes, not allowing me to see his difficult feelings. To see which step might be deadly, which word might drop me into a trap that could sink the both of us.

We're curled up on the fluffy white rug in front of the sofa. It's date night. We've finished watching a nondescript film I'm already forgetting, and the TV now displays a faux fireplace, embers turning to ash on a gentle loop. There are glasses of red wine on the coffee tables either side of the sofa. Soft, low, sensual music hums out of the speakers around the room.

'Talk to me.' James. His fingers trailing my leg. A cocking of his head to one side, lines framing his eyes as they smile at me. He's always had reassuring eyes. I hate that there's a glimmer of wariness in them. 'You've not said much about how you're feeling.'

I want to tell him that he hasn't said much, either, but am scared of spoiling the mood. I'm not sure we're good at talking beyond what's comfortable, what's easy. I've tried to get him to open up, too, but he's always *fine*; he's always *glad to know more of you, to know you better, despite everything*. And I don't want to say too much. Don't want him to bolt to his parents' place again out of fear.

Instead, I want things to feel like they used to. Want to feel him, close.

'Can we not talk?'

It's meant to come out sexy, but it comes out shy, small. James seems to understand me all the same, takes a hand from my lap, places the palm to his mouth, and kisses it. His kisses still send shocks sparking down my veins, setting me alight with crackling electricity. That hasn't changed, at least. But this shallow pit that's appeared in my stomach of late. This wanting . . . I want to understand why James still wants me; I want to know what to do about Will; I want to understand why my childhood fucked me up so much more than everyone else's fucked them; I want to know where the blackouts come from; I want to know if James will be my next victim; I want to feel confident that he's definitely not; I want my mother to leave me alone; I want my sister to come back home; I want James to fuck me like an animal; I want to have a baby

I want

I want

I want

And I'm afraid that all my wanting, my bottomless pit of need, will pull James into its orbit and swallow him whole. He will be crushed under the weight of it.

'I miss you,' he says, lips planting an offering on my neck.

I let him kiss me, and the hunger and the want almost yell

139

their excitement, needy black fingers reaching out from the waking pit within. I kiss him back and he can feel my hunger in my eager mouth, in the hands that reach into his hair and twist and pull. And I can feel his hunger, too. It's in the heat and the urgency of his hands on me, the pressure of his body against mine.

Perhaps it's because it's been a while since we've last done this, but something about this time feels more primal, more urgent, than it usually does. When we're done, we're both left sweating and panting on the carpet. James pulls me into him, my head resting on his slick chest, our legs loosely tangled.

'I can't keep lying like this,' I say, smiling. 'I'm too hot.'

James sighs, laugh barely disguised.

I slip my knee out from between his and peel my head off him. My eyes stare up at the ceiling. I try not to think.

'Uh-oh . . . where are you going?' James asks.

'What?'

'In your head. Where are you going?'

He shouldn't be able to read me like this. If I start letting him see behind the mask, see the real me, I'll lose him for ever. Him, and the family we've planned.

'Nowhere. I mean, it's fine. I'm fine.'

He sighs again, and it is heavier than before. 'Are you thinking about Will?'

I shake my head. At least it's honest. 'No. Well, not in particular. I suppose I'm thinking about everything. Kind of.'

He laughs. 'That doesn't help make things any clearer, Nat.' He runs his fingers through the fibres of the shaggy rug. 'I'm worried about it, too. But he seems to mean what he says . . . about not saying anything, I mean. He's been quiet since anyway. As long as you and I talk to each other, communicate, I think we'll be okay.'

I think about pushing him in this moment, pointing out the irony when it's clear we're both holding back from being entirely honest, but I'm pretty sure this would spring one of those hidden traps that would leave both James and me wounded. Besides, he only wants me to tell him I'll be an open book, but then keep my darkest thoughts to myself. I've been one of his favourite Nice Things, and if I can convincingly continue to pretend to be that for him, he'll be happy. I look at the video of fire flickering before us, watch the flames slowly consuming the wood.

'Yeah, I agree. We'll keep talking and we'll be okay,' I say, trying not to linger on how well James lies. Trying not to dwell on what else he may be lying about. A flash of Molly enters my mind, and then the yoga teacher who always wants to chat a little too long when James picks me up from class. Nice, normal women.

I do my best to suppress the thought. It's not easy. James is not George, not by a long shot, but I've allowed him to own so much of my life: my job, my home, my heart. And, with my determination for a fresh start, shedding friends from my life before James and I were even romantically involved, he's now the centre of my world. The power is his to abuse if he wants to.

'I know we haven't been able to make it work yet,' James says, 'but maybe we could have your sister come visit. Might do you good.'

I shake my head. 'She's busy with auditions and she can't afford to take time off. And it's not like we can afford for me to go over right now.' A thought. 'But it has been a while since I've hung out with my friends,' I say.

'Friends' is a loose term. It's still the case that very few of my friendships, if any, feel real in the way that my friendship with Emily was, but I haven't seen her since the Big Fallout.

She wasn't even at my wedding. Not that many people I knew were.

He studies me a moment longer, cool eyes scraping my skin. His mouth opens, closes, then opens again. I think, a little unkindly, that he resembles a goldfish.

'Maybe you do need to go out, blow off some steam,' he eventually says.

I do. I need to get out of the house, broaden my world beyond James. He's kind, generous, and loves me. My rational mind knows he's safe, safer than anyone else. Even my family. Especially my family. But I can't shake the irrational feeling of needing a safety net. Like knowing there's almost no chance of dying on a flight, but spending the whole journey with visions of plummeting planes and smoking wreckage anyway. I might have lost touch with my uni friends, with almost everyone who might remind me of the horrors of my past, but I need to nurture the friendships I have left.

A wine-soaked night with a couple of friends will be just what I need. Maybe a girl just needs to let her hair down to stop herself from falling apart. It feels like a good idea. But then again, so many of my worst ones do.

Chapter 21

Now

Dimple

Dimple's enviously thick hair is straight again today. An attempt to tuck it behind her ears has been made, but as usual, it pushes forward of its own accord. Her probing style is similar; an attempt at reining in an irrepressible curiosity.

'How are you feeling today?'

I shrug. It's knowingly petulant, but I resent how much she's making me dredge up and I want her to know it.

'I'm uncomfortable. Apprehensive, I guess. These sessions haven't been easy for me; I've told you too much, and I've no idea which scab you're going to want to pick at today. But I know it's important I'm here if I'm going to straighten myself out.' After all, I love James. My love for him and his longevity are proof of my ability to get it right, my potential to be a good human being. The kind who'll make a great mother.

'That's an interesting expression.'

'What is?'

'Your framing of our sessions as picking at scabs. Why do you think of them that way?'

I sigh, knead the flesh of my thighs with the heels of my hands, then bring the movement to an end.

'I don't like it when you do that, by the way.'

'What?' she asks.

'Ask questions you already know the answers to.'

She smiles, taps the back of her pen against her notepad. 'It's not my job to put words in your mouth or assume how you're feeling. I wouldn't be a very good therapist if I just made these sessions about what I think,' she says. 'So, why do you describe our sessions as like picking at scabs?'

Inside, I'm twisting my mouth, stretching my fingers across her intent. I still think she's on my side, that she wants to help me. But how do I know? At the very least, I know I can't let the knot of paranoia that's beginning to churn in my gut grow. I don't need more problems.

'I describe it that way,' I say, 'because it hurts to pick at it. I don't think those old wounds ever properly healed.'

Dimple simply nods once – whether intentional encouragement or a betrayal of inner thoughts, I don't know.

In the gap, I finally build up the courage to ask my next, most important question. 'I need to know I can trust you if I continue. That being open with you isn't going to land me in trouble.'

'Given what I already know, and what you've already disclosed, it would be difficult at this stage for you to shock me. But please feel free to try.' She gives me a look that I imagine is meant to be encouraging. 'We ran out of time last week, but you were telling me about the day you found your father dead.'

I try to shift my brain into gear, to focus back on where we are in the room. The thought of my dad is still a complicated one. It's difficult to disentangle the emotions knotted together around it. All I know is that it hurts.

'Yes, it's – it's a difficult memory.'

'I noticed your retelling was suggestive, but unspecific about how your father died.'

My eyes snap onto hers. 'What do you mean?'

The quirk of her mouth tells me she's holding back her own rebuttal about asking questions one knows the answer to.

'How do you believe your father died?' she asks.

My eyes look away and scan the fuzzy peach, forest green and gold of the room. It's tempting to try to force her to revisit the present instead, to ask that we talk about James. He's why I'm here, after all. Because if these resurfaced feelings go unchecked, who knows what I'll be capable of? But Dimple doesn't seem particularly interested in James today.

'Can I have some water, please?'

She pours me a glass from the jug on her table and then looks at me expectantly.

'Are you okay, Natalie?' Dimple asks.

I nod.

'Are you able to answer the question?' she presses on. 'How do you believe your father died?'

The truth is unavoidable.

'My mother killed him.'

'And how do you feel about this?'

It's easy to talk about how I feel about it. Feelings, I have a lot of. Talking about it clearly, however, is another matter. And so, in disordered fragments, I tell her about my Feelings. I tell her how I felt relieved at the thought of not waiting for his tightly coiled anger to spring loose again. I tell her how disgusted I was, how my stomach churned at the strange angle of his neck, limbs all wrong like a collapsed mario-nette. I tell her how I felt scared of my immediate numbness, that I felt my feelings ought to be bigger somehow. I tell her how frightened I was of finding out what my place in the world meant without my father in it, of finding out whether my mother might grow into a bigger monster than he was with her whims unchecked. I tell Dimple many things, and through it all, she nods like she understands. I don't see how she can, but I don't blame her for pretending.

'Those are a lot of feelings,' she says.

'It was a complicated time.'

She shuffles, shoulders shimmying as she sinks into the soft back of her seat. 'If you were to pick the emotion you felt was strongest in the weeks after your father's death, what would it be?'

I take a moment to Look at her, tongue running across the back of my teeth. Her hunt carries a scent of its own and it is strong. If there's a point she wants to get to, then she should get to it directly.

'Listen, I know what you want me to say.'

Dimple's eyebrows rise in question. It's almost provocative, and perhaps she realizes this, as they soon drop. She squints and opens her mouth to speak. 'A reminder that it's not my job to put words in your mouth or explain your feelings.'

I want to huff and slouch and scowl. Instead, I give her a small smile. 'You're right. Sorry . . .' A pause. 'Relief was definitely the most powerful feeling . . . Yeah. I can't remember being more terrified than when he'd hurt our mother and disappeared, leaving Claire and me to fend for ourselves. Things were unmistakably better after he was gone. We were all happier. We were all safer. We had a little bit more money, too, as it turned out Dad was drinking away more than he was contributing. And before you try gently nudging there, I know what you're getting at . . . My mother hurt my dad, and it felt good. I saw and felt how good a decision that was for our family, and so now, when my partners fuck up, badly, my brain is wired to think my life would be better if I hurt them, too. Don't you think I already know this? That it's obvious where it comes from? But I'm not the only woman in the world with a dead deadbeat dad, so . . .'

146

Now I do allow myself to huff and slouch and scowl. It's petulant behaviour, I know. But I want her to see my frustration. Perhaps revisiting these old childhood memories is encouraging a regression into childish behaviour. Perhaps.

'Do you have any dead relatives?' I ask.

She looks somewhere between bemused and amused. Her face looks pretty when it's contorted like that. It's infuriating. 'Dead relatives? Yes.'

She can't be much older than me, if older at all. The power dynamic makes me think of her as more grown up, but when I look beyond the glasses and the sensible clothes, she could be even younger than me. 'Glad any of them aren't around any more?'

The smile on her lips flattens into a thin line.

'I'm going to take that as a yes. Any murderous tendencies of your own? No? Well, you see my point.'

As usual, Dimple is unflustered. She simply takes a moment to adjust the glasses on her face. 'I'm interested. How much remorse would you say you feel for the people you've hurt?'

In my own way, I do feel bad about it. It would be nice to say that hurting them keeps me up at night, but it's not so much what I've done as what my actions say about me that plagues me. After all, if they hadn't hurt me first, I wouldn't have had to hurt them worse. I'm sure I've saved countless other people from being hurt by them over the years. But I don't want to become the kind of person for whom the ends justify the means. That kind of person will inevitably hurt the people they love. My mother was that kind of person. I'm sitting in this chair because I won't be that kind of mother.

Dimple scrutinizes the expression I'm determined to keep placid as she waits for my response. Eventually, I have to accept that if I want to get better, I'm going to have to be honest.

I smooth a thumb across the slightly oily slick of an eyebrow. 'If I'm being honest, Dimple, I'd say I feel worse for what I've done to me than what I've done to them.'

Chapter 22

Now

Over the next few days, my phone is more alive than ever with unanswered calls from my mother, as if she's sensed me looking through the windows of my memory into her past life, transfixed. Horrified. On the twelfth missed call I answer.

'Are you dying?' I ask.

'No.'

Silence. Irritation creeps up my spine.

'Then what is it? Are you sick?'

'No.'

Her breathing is heavy on the other end of the phone. It's unlike her to leave gaps in conversations for other people's words to fill. A wariness creeps in.

My voice quietens. 'Is this about Claire?'

'I suppose it is about your sister in a sense. It would be easier if you came to see me.'

Aha. 'Mother, this is a new one for you.' She was always 'Mother' to me. Never 'Mummy', 'Mum' or 'Ma'. All those diminutives were too warm for her. Too familiar. She hadn't earned them. 'I'm not coming home. If that's all —'

'Natalie, I need to talk to you. I need to tell you some things.'

'I'm sure you do, and given the things you've said before, I'm sure they won't be true and will be designed to hurt me.'

A sigh, and then a classic. 'Sometimes, you're so much like your father. Natalie —'

'Goodbye, Mother.'

The call only leaves me more on edge than before. For years after he died, I couldn't mention Dad without Mother becoming apoplectic, but now she unsheathes his memory to slice me with when I'm unprepared, defenceless. I can't deny the truth of it, though. Despite my best efforts to hide it, sometimes I am so much like the monster he was. No wonder she hates me.

I'm relieved to be away from it all for an evening, finally sitting in this bar, on James's earlier advice, sandwiched between Ama and Marketer Molly. Although Ama's no longer at the same company, our offices are nearby, and on this Thursday night, we're crowded into a generic bar in Central. The walls are almost sweating, it's that hot, but the lights are dim and so everyone looks more attractive than they should.

This includes the group of suited City boys eyeing us up from the table nearby. They've been watching us for a while now, casting glances our way that are less subtle than they think they are. There are four of them. The easiness between them suggests that they are close, although one is clearly on the periphery of the group, and one is the leader. Not that friendship groups should have leaders, but this is the kind of friendship group that does. Work friends, which the location of the bar and the attire speak to.

Ama and Molly are in good spirits. Ama has finally just been promoted and Molly has got a raise. More good news than usually runs in junior employee circles, but our respective businesses are booming – even when times are hard, people love a beer.

The two of them are enjoying the looks being sent our way by the nearby suited gentlemen. Or not gentlemen. Almost gentlemen. Whatever. The point is, they're enjoying the looks. Ama is single and Molly has a boyfriend she doesn't much like but whom she will likely marry. Perhaps it's the certainty of this, of being stuck with him for ever, that makes her so desperate for the attention of other men. For an evening, she can pretend that she would be bold enough to leave him, to start a life with someone else.

I straighten my spine, try to shake out the mean thoughts with a shimmy of my shoulders.

'What's the matter?' Ama asks, hand on my back.

'Nothing,' I reply, slouching down again on the chair.

'Are you sure?' she asks. 'I know sometimes things just kind of get . . .' She gesticulates vague shapes in the air. 'Just kind of a lot, you know?'

It's a strangely incisive and left-field question. I don't like it at all.

A distraction. We need a distraction, something fun.

'Let's call them over,' I say, noting that the gazes are now a two-way street from table to table. Aren't I the fun, Cool Girl after all? The one guaranteed to make a party more interesting, a family barbecue less dull?

When the men arrive at our table, the leader is right into names. None are worth remembering, so we'll call them Suit 1, Suit 3, Suit 2 and Mr Periphery. I'm not sure why it makes sense to name them in that order, but it does to me. Suit 1 immediately turns his chair around as he sits so that he can rest his forearms on the low back. I've already decided to make Mr Periphery my co-conspirator for the evening, using the fleeting moment in which our eyes lock to roll mine. He clears his throat and looks away.

Hmm. Not what I expected from the clear outsider.

Mr Periphery is quiet, and Suits 3 and 2 don't have much of interest to say. Neither does Suit 1, but he's happy to carry the conversation nonetheless. Ama and Molly titter along to vaguely funny and mildly offensive jokes. It's clear that they also know how to ingratiate themselves with guys like these, make them adore them. It's simple, really – shut up and laugh. But tonight I can't stomach playing that role. Instead, I go into Cool Girl overdrive, raised eyebrows and unimpressed smirks that carry enough humour to suggest that, beneath it all, maybe I do want to fuck them.

The suits, entertained and alive in the presence of women to perform for, keep the drinks coming. Martinis and palomas and mojitos and prosecco. It's obscene. I hope they're paying. Implicit as it is, you never know when an ego might get bruised, or an attack of conscience might appear after a glance at the white line that marks where their ring usually sits. Men can up sticks and leave at any moment if you're not careful, and neither Ama nor Molly nor I can afford to be stiffed with the bill.

Before long, we're all a little sloppy – we girls more than the four men, and even then, me far less so than Ama and Molly. In fact, it's a stretch to call me sloppy at all. I've made a point of not letting myself get too loose for several years. There have been too many dark nights followed by fatalities in the mornings. Too many blank spots in my memory clouded over by nice tequila and narcotics. What I can do is keep my faculties about me. I'm terrified of what I'll do if I don't.

Suit 1 and Molly are jostling each other with their shoulders. There's a palpable tension in their locked eyes and loose smiles. I wonder if I should put a stop to this, seeing where this is going. I want to. And not just because Suit 1 is obnoxious, bigoted, too handsy – but because I know what it will mean for Molly if she takes this too far.

'Molly?' I ask. I try to make the question sound carefree, a cheeky raising of the eyebrows, a laugh. But it's clear she knows what it means.

'Oh, give over, Nat,' she says, garnishing the comment with an eye roll of her own. I don't love it.

'What?' Suit 1 asks. He jostles her, bleary eyes scanning between the two of us. He finally settles his gaze on me, laughs and says, 'I think our girl here needs another shot.'

Great. The last thing I need is to stand out as the sober friend. I accept the shot handed to me by Suit 2, laughing along with jokes and mentally planning my route home. The night has been disrobed of its facade of fun and is shrugging on something unseemly in its place.

Before long, Ama announces her intention to head off. It is late, after all. Suit 2 surprises me by saying much the same. Suits 3 and 1 and Molly are keen to head to another bar. I look at the time and my heart sinks.

'Molly, babe, I don't think I can. I'm sorry.'

She scoffs, grabs her bag. I try to tell her not to go and she looks at me like I have three heads. An alarm is whirring in my brain. I stand, physically take her arm in mine, stare her down.

'Molly, go home. Brian will be wondering where you are. Get an Uber, and text me when you get in.'

A pout forms on her lips as a question settles on her brow. The sound of his name has been at least a little sobering. She glances at the suits, perhaps begins to see what I see. She nods, straightens.

'Yeah, I'll order an Uber now.'

'You sure we can't convince you to come for another?' Suit 1 asks me.

'I think I'd best head home soon.'

He shrugs. 'Your loss.'

The tension leaches out of me and I realize how badly I need to pee. The girls and I hug, promise to meet each other outside. I run to the loo, cool plastic beneath my thighs as I sigh and relieve myself. It's clear to me that I've drunk more than intended, forgoing my usually extensive wipe-down of the seat. My phone pings. A message from Molly.

Uber's here. Hopping in but so fun catching up,
speak more soon x

By the time I re-emerge, there's a girl waiting outside my cubicle door, slightly smudged mascara under wide eyes. It's clear that she's desperate. I sidestep out of her way.

'Sorry, it's all y—' The sight of the empty stall next to mine stops me. All the other stalls are empty, in fact.

'You're with that guy in the bar, right?' she asks.

I make my way to the sink, soaping my hands. 'Which guy?'

She shifts from foot to foot, fingers twisting together. 'The guy in the grey suit, brown hair. Looks a bit like James McAvoy. You were with your friends, but they just left, I think.'

Mr Periphery. 'Oh, him. Yeah, we're not really friends. We just met.'

'Yeah, well – Sorry, I don't know how to say this . . . but I'm pretty sure I just saw him put something in your drink.'

I freeze for a moment. 'Wait, what?' The tap goes off and I don't bother with a paper towel, patting my hands on the sides of my jeans. 'What do you mean?'

'It's just, I was watching everyone leave, and it looked like he did a weird thing with a glass after they went. I wasn't paying proper attention, but I noticed him pushing a glass across the table, and it wasn't his own drink, and I'm pretty sure he was putting it back where it was, and I'm pretty sure where it was is where you were sitting.'

'Fuck.'

'Yeah, it's so fucked-up. But also, maybe it's nothing. And I didn't want to report it and be wrong, so I thought I'd just come tell you and you can decide what to do. If you want to come join our table or if you want me to wait with you while you call a taxi, I'll –'

'Actually, no. It's okay.'

I'm thinking.

'You know what,' I continue, 'I asked him if he wanted to try my drink before I got up. I think that's all it is.'

Her relief is so palpable and complete that I don't even feel bad for lying to her. Isn't she happier now that I have?

'Oh my god. Oh my god.' She laughs, slaps a hand to her chest. 'Oh, thank fuck for that. I'm so sorry to panic you.'

I give her a smile dripping with warmth and reassurance. 'No, babe; you did the right thing. We've got to look out for each other. Thank you for looking out; I appreciate it.'

She nods, already inching towards the door. She wishes me a good night and disappears. I stare into the mirror and think about what to do next. Mr Periphery has surprised me. Perhaps this night hasn't been wasted after all.

When I return to the table, true to the stranger's words, everyone else has already left. Mr Periphery is still finishing his drink. I approach him.

'A girl goes to the toilet for five minutes and everyone vanishes,' I say, voice friendly and bright.

'Yeah, I think your friend Ama was worried about missing her train.'

'Which is wise. I should probably shoot off before I miss mine.'

He gestures at his glass. 'Are you going to make me see this off on my own?'

'I dunno . . . It's late –'

155

'You've hardly touched your cocktail! Seems wasteful to leave our drinks here. Join me, so I look like less of a loser?'

It's easier than it should be to say 'Sure.' I sit, smiling. 'Oh, but d'you mind grabbing me a napkin from the bar, please? The bottom of my glass is dripping wet.' So is his. Beads of condensation have clustered on the tall glasses, collecting in pools at their bases. And Mr Periphery is happy to oblige, leaping up from his seat.

The switch takes only a few moments. I trade our drinks, using the water jug to make sure his new one looks full enough. When he returns, napkins in hand, all looks as it did before.

'Bit cluttered on this table – you want to nip into one of those booths?'

I shrug. 'Sure.'

And so we find ourselves tucked away into an almost-hidden corner of the bar, sitting opposite each other on sticky faux-leather seats. He's more talkative now that the others are gone, and I let him talk. At the very least, talking seems to be thirsty business for him. As he tells me about Suit 1's performance improvement plan at work and how it's hard to find trustworthy females who bring enough to the table for high-value men in modern relationships, his drink disappears.

Within ten minutes, I notice the beads of sweat forming on his forehead, the occasional quizzical look that shades his face as his gut churns. His words are slurred, and his body is hanging over the table. It's like there's a very thin string between the wall and his back, keeping him upright. It looks like it might snap at any moment.

Knowing that it's only downhill for him from here and that I'm safe, I get up from my seat and squeeze into the seat beside him.

'You don't look too good, angel.'

He looks at me, and in his eyes is a hazy challenge and understanding.

'Whurrrrr—'

'Hush, pet. Not much point trying to speak now.'

He slouches towards the wall, the effort of holding his body weight up no longer worth it.

'So this is what you wanted me to wind up like, huh?'

He groans. I feel sick. It's all too easy to think of what he'd be doing to me right now had I drunk my own drink, as he planned. My little monster is roaring – furious, white-hot anger. And it's not so little now. It wants to clamp its jaws around this sick creep and feed.

I'm terrified of how angry I feel and can't help the feeling that the anger has to go somewhere. That Mr Periphery needs to be punished. That the world would be better off without him in it.

The thought feels alarmingly right and wrong at the same time. I don't want to do this. I promised myself I wouldn't do this. But if it releases the anger, keeps James safe, our marriage intact, my future family a possible, if slim, prospect, then perhaps it's worth sacrificing another corner of my soul.

I think about it. I think about taking a blade and pushing it into his carotid. The feeling it brings surprises me. I feel a little sick. It strikes me that perhaps my vision is too bloody, and a pillow stretched over his face would do instead. Still, I feel queasy.

It should be easy from here, no? Check his licence for his address, or use his thumb to unlock his phone, where it's sure to be nestled in his Uber or Maps history. And what then? Splay him out on his kitchen table and set at him with his knife set? Or simply leave him lying face up in bed, in the hope he chokes on his own vomit at some point in the night? But he might have a security camera at home. What then? There's many a steep stairwell in the narrow and twisting streets of London that he could take a tumble down.

The churning in my gut intensifies. I've not yet considered that the girl in the toilets saw me with him, as have most of the people in the bar, and his colleagues will definitely throw my name out if he's discovered suddenly dead . . .

Shit.

I suddenly feel utterly powerless. What am I doing here? What am I doing? I don't want to kill a man in cold blood – this is not who I am.

Mr Periphery groans. Between the stretched, slipped and skipped-over syllables, I can just about understand that he feels sick. He wants to go home.

And I have to let him.

It makes me angrier than I was before. Angrier than I was walking into this bar. But there's no scenario here where I don't end up fucked, albeit not in the way Mr Periphery was planning.

The cocktail stick lying beside a saucer of olive pits taunts me. I'm so furious I can't help myself. I grab it and press it against his crotch. He grunts. I pinch the tip tightly and drive it as hard as I can against the fabric. I feel it burst through the membrane.

He screams. Well, I say 'screams'. He tries to. It is a low, animal wail that thunders. I've not driven the splinter as deeply as I would have liked, but he is sure to feel this tomorrow. For a while. I yank the stick out and toss it to the floor. Just in time, too, as one of the bar staff rounds the corner, peering in.

'Everything okay?' he asks.

My expression is apologetic, earnest. 'Yeah, I think he's just had a bit too much to drink.'

'Right.' He gives me a sympathetic look.

'To be honest, I'm in a bit over my head, here. I only just met him tonight and I need to be getting home. Any chance you'd be able to help him sort a taxi? Sorry, I know it's a lot to ask but –'

He's sceptical. Who wants to be landed with a loaded suit to look after? 'We close in half an hour.'

'And my last train home leaves in fifteen. Please.'

His shoulders relent before his mouth does, deflating in a long exhale. 'Okay, love, get off home. We'll sort it.'

'Thanks so much,' I say with my biggest, most grateful smile.

That smile remains fixed to my face, painted on with the uncanny quality of a porcelain doll's. The moment the fresh night air hits me, it wipes it off. I want to cry. I want to hide and scream and rage. The whole point of tonight was to make me feel better, not worse, and yet now . . .

Somewhere in the distance a siren wails, a lamplight flickers overhead, and I try to pretend that I'm not a ticking bomb waiting to explode.

Chapter 23

Now

Dimple

It's a sunny view I'm treated to in Dimple's office today. The trees beyond the window look particularly verdant and lush. I'm decidedly more on edge.

'I'm in a funny sort of mood,' I announce, fingers stroking across peach fuzz.

'How so?' she asks.

'I think I get it. My impulses, I mean.' My mouth twists at the euphemism. Say what you mean and mean what you say, after all. 'I have a better understanding of why I hurt people. It's always been obvious with the others that they've pissed me off in some way. But it's not just that. It's not just annoying me, or even betraying me. It's about power. It's about injustice. It's about them taking something from me and me needing to take something back.'

Dimple makes a movement of her head that could be agreement or a simple checking of her notes. 'What makes you say that?'

I consider her for a moment, whether I'm still prepared to embrace this unbridled honesty I've decided will help her help me. Well, I do want to be helped . . .

'I tried to kill someone last weekend.'

She blinks once, twice. Her mouth flops open and then clamps shut. An involuntary shake runs through her head as she readjusts her glasses, readjusts her whole body in her seat. 'Could you please talk me through what you mean when you say that?'

My eyebrows scrunch together. 'I mean I tried to kill someone last weekend.' Her eyebrows rise, asking for more. I worry that she might now think I'm dangerous enough to report. 'Well, I couldn't do it. I wanted to, but I couldn't.'

'Let's dial back a little. How did this decision come about?'

My mouth twists. 'I've been feeling . . . unsettled since this whole business with James and the letters. And our sessions, I know they're helping me on some level, but they're also making me feel worse. I came away from the last one feeling . . . feeling like a monster. I thought that if I didn't channel my anger and my hunger somewhere, I'd hurt James.'

'And you don't want to hurt James?'

'No.' Have we been wasting the time we've spent together? 'No. I love him.'

'I've upset you.'

I look over her shoulder, focus on the tree. She doesn't fill the silence – she rarely does. My eyes flit back to hers and I speak. 'What is it you're trying to get from me? Just ask.'

She smiles, a kind warmth flushing her cheeks, and this irks me further. Her kindness is polyester against my skin right now, chafing. 'I'm asking,' she says. 'Let's try this; talk me through the day you tried to kill someone. Was it someone you knew?'

'No, a stranger.'

'And how did you meet the stranger?'

And I tell her the story of my evening out. Of cocktails and cocky corporate bros. The words spill out of me. It's like I've snagged the hull of my guts on the sharp edges of her patient inquisition, and the black oil of my confession is purging itself from my belly. It leaves the room, our conversation, feeling slick with the shame of it. I am ashamed. But I can't stop.

'Obviously, I wasn't thinking clearly. I hadn't thought any of it through. That's not like me, you know? But if I had, and if I'd known what that guy was going to try to do to me . . . If I'd had the means, I think maybe I'd have hurt him worse. And I'd have felt better for it.'

Somewhere outside, a driver thumps down on their horn. Once, then twice more.

'What makes you so sure you would have hurt him worse?'

It doesn't make sense that I flinch, but I do. 'It's what I do. Someone takes something from me – something I don't want to give, something that hurts – and I have to take something back.'

'By "take something back", do you mean their life?'

The walls seem to darken. I'm silent.

'Natalie, I'm not sure it helps us to keep talking in code.'

I can't speak. Can only see the cage drawing around me.

'Natalie?'

'You already know I feel responsible for my exes' deaths. We acknowledged it in our first session. It's all in Dr Foster's notes.'

Dimple sighs. I'm not being as explicit as she wants, but this is as good as she's getting for now.

'This transactional revenge you're describing . . . I'm just not entirely clear on why you wouldn't have hurt this stranger worse, if it were that simple.'

'Well, I don't fancy spending a life sentence behind bars. Chances are, I would have been caught if I did.'

'Let's take a moment to consider Marc and Luca. Where were you when they died?'

My nose twitches. 'What do you mean?'

'On the nights they died, where were you?'

'Well –' I take a moment, seeing where she's nudging me. 'We were at parties.'

163

'So, chances are, you could have been caught?'

'Caught doing what?'

Dimple takes a moment to consider her notebook. Her thick but elegant fingers flick through pages. For a fleeting moment, I want to be annoyed that she needs to check her notes, but then I remember that she has many other clients. It's not fair for me to expect her to have everything committed to memory.

'You've never quite finished telling me what happened with George.'

Another unexpected blow. 'I don't like talking about it.'

She gives me a look that says, *What do you think we're here to do?* and I feel like burying her pen in her eye.

'Okay.' I sigh, steel myself. 'What do you want to know?'

'Take me back to the moment you realized he was dangerous. I'd like us to follow the weeks leading up to the "Big Fallout" you've alluded to. Can you do that for me?'

'Every time you ask me to revisit something I don't want to, I end up feeling worse.'

She shrugs. 'I don't know how to help you if you hold things back from me.'

'And this? We have to go back to this?' A beat. 'And how can I really trust you?'

She doesn't answer, simply prods me for more. 'Feel free to have a drink of water. Start in your own time.'

I do as instructed, shaking inside. As the water slides down my throat, I steady my nerves and prepare to talk about the worst day of my life.

Chapter 24

Ex Number Three

George

It's been barely a week since we got back home from our cottage trip, but I've been walking on eggshells the whole time. Easy way to make a week feel like a year. Not that George seems to notice any difference. I wonder what that says about me, about how small I've made myself around him.

He's been in and out of the house for work, same as usual. When he comes home from the office there's always a big smile and a kiss for me. It would be easy to convince myself that nothing really happened, that it was all in my imagination, but I know in my bones what he did to me.

It was a relief when he announced his weekend away with the boys, fishing. I should have been annoyed at the short notice, at the cavalier disregard for the film I'd mentioned I wanted us to see together – anything to get out of the house, to be perceived by public eyes, safe – but the relief was so complete that I simply said, *Have a nice time.* I didn't even press him on who these 'boys' were, despite his having nowhere near enough friends to amalgamate into an ensemble. Instead, my fingers were soon on the lightly cracked black screen of my phone, hesitant, dancing towards and just stopping before numbers on the dial pad. I was ashamed of how long it had been, of what the voices on the other end of the phone might say.

But, of course, a brief dial tone and a little conversation later, it was all okay. How could it not be? And now Claire sits in front of me, tea steaming from the full belly of the round mug warming her hands as she looks at me, contemplating.

'Emily should be here soon,' I say for lack of other words. 'She's on her way.'

Claire's nose wrinkles in distaste. Upset as I was at Emily for abandoning me on my birthday all those years ago, it seems Claire has held the grudge in a tighter grip on my behalf, as a sister is wont to do. We sit in silence for a moment.

'So are you going to tell me?' she asks.

'Tell you what?' It's only in contrast with hers that I hear how thin my voice has become, how it seems to rattle inside of me.

'It's been months, Natty.'

'I know.'

My thumbs preoccupy my attention for a moment. It's as if by the time I look back up, I will have escaped Claire's scrutiny. As if.

I think of the distant memory of Aunty Dev for a moment. Wonder if Mother let their friendship wither and die because she knew the reunion could be this painful.

'You look thin,' Claire says.

'I know.'

The next moments take me by surprise. She bursts into tears. Of the two of us, she has never been the crier, her bravery more real than my performances of it. A hand clasped over her mouth does little to stifle her sobs. Under normal circumstances, my arms would be around her shoulders, holding her close. But these circumstances are anything but normal, and the months that have stood between us feel like a yawning chasm with her feet planted on one side, and my feet treading crumbling rock on the other. I don't know if she wants me to touch her, and that little uncertainty is a knife in my chest.

'Are you okay?' I manage to say, her sobs quietening.

'Are you?' she asks. In her eyes is an accusation. *How dare you do this to yourself? How dare you let him do this to you?* 'You look like Mum,' she adds as another knife in the gut.

'Stop it.'

'You do. You look like Mum. Whatever's going on here, you need help. You should talk to someone.'

'Like who?'

'Like a therapist.'

I don't want to be our mother, but I can't escape the fact that I seem to keep dating variations of our father. Callous, selfish men who know how to turn on the charm when it suits them. I look away, out of George's kitchen window. Staring at nature soothes me, even if being in the thick of it gives me the heebie-jeebies. I've never been able to do spiders, creepy-crawlies, or big trees at night. Not up close. I look back to my sister.

'I'm not sure what to say.'

And then she does what she always does. The perfect thing. She gets up from the other side of the kitchen island, walks over and hugs me. The weight of her love is crushing, so firm that it squeezes the pent-up emotions out of me, and I finally cry, too. I haven't once, yet. Not after what he did. Not when I realized that, just as Claire said, I was becoming our mother. Tiptoeing around a home that didn't feel like mine, with a man who felt like he was poised to hurt me.

When we finally let go of each other, it's like all the awkwardness has been wrung out of us. We laugh, feeling the weight of it lifted, cheeks still wet. Claire drags her stool over beside mine, shuffles up, clasps my hands on the counter.

'Go on, then,' she says. 'Tell me everything.'

And I do, Claire's hands intermittently becoming claws on

mine. She keeps her face passive for the most part, flinches flashing across her expression at some of the worst of it. It's only when I get to the very worst that it gets too much, her nails suddenly in my skin.

'Claire, ouch! Fuck.'

'Sorry.' She's obviously contrite. 'I just – I just can't believe he . . . Oh my god, Natty, this monster raped you and you're still living in his home?'

My voice is smaller than ever. 'I don't know what to do.'

'What do you mean?' Her voice is bigger than ever. More desperate, too. 'Shit, Natty, have you learned nothing from our parents? You take your shit and you get out!'

She's wrong; I learned plenty from our parents. I learned that sometimes playing dead keeps you safe, that confronting violence can simply raise the stakes, turning what would have been bruises into open wounds. But I'm beginning to realize that playing dead can just as easily make you a predator's plaything, just as easily leave you dead, a baby seal thrashed in an orca's jaws.

'Nat, after Marc, after Luca . . .' She pauses for a breath. 'You've got to be smart enough by now to see you've got to leave him. I can't keep watching you make horrible decisions.'

For the first time since she's arrived, I feel calm, icy certainty in my words. 'Move out and what? Just let him get away with it?'

For the first time since she's arrived, Claire seems unsure. 'What do you mean?'

'I mean he did something pretty fucking awful to me, and he deserves to be punished for it.'

And there it is, that hunger. That knowledge of what I'm capable of, which I've tried to ignore and deny for years. It's obscured by the frustrating veil of black that descends upon my memories, blank nights followed by bloody mornings.

But through the darkness, a flash of roof, the sound of a fall. A pill between two fingers, a water bottle, and an idea.

Tempting as it is to manufacture another staircase accident, George doesn't have the alcoholism that ultimately gave our mother an easier time in getting the police to believe Dad fell. Still, I've learned there's a saw, hammer, and shovel in the shed in the communal garden. Learned it's smart to dig your holes before you have your body. Learned where the good places to dig might be. If George looks in the wrong place, he'll find plastic tarp in the attic. If I hadn't secretly borrowed a spare work phone, he'd see Reddit pages on hermetic containers, pigs, slit arteries in bathtubs, flooding my browser history. But my fear of him leaves me frozen with indecision. I don't know how to convert my anger into action without the rush of alcohol or Class As, and yet I can't afford to lose my faculties around a man like George.

'I don't get it, Natty,' Claire says, although from her hushed tone, I think that she does.

'I get such heinous dick fog, but now that it's lifted, I can see things more clearly. Sure, he has a good job and looks like a nice guy, but he's abusive. Why doesn't he have any friends? Why have I never met his family? He hurt me, and I'll bet he's hurt other women. Bet unless I stop him, he'll hurt someone else.'

Claire's question is barely a whisper. '"Stop him"?'

'I'm talking about Marc, Luca . . .'

'They're dead.'

'I know.'

Fear and concern wrinkle her forehead. 'You're not mak— They were accidents.'

'Were they?' The look I level her with is even and cool. There's more calm composure in those two words than she's seen from me in the past two years.

'I don't get it. Wh—'

'I'm telling you I killed them, Care.'

Liquid catches at the back of her throat, and I think it's the tea until I realize she's choking on her own saliva. I get up, pat her back. She leaps up and away at my touch, and the air beneath my fingers turns icy at the absence of her.

'What the *fuck*, Natty? What are you talking about?'

No matter how much I want to retract it, I can't take it back. 'I don't know how else to say it. I killed Marc and Luca.' And speaking these words out loud for the first time is a huge weight off my chest. Despite the horror on Claire's face, eyes wide, mouth agape, I feel relief.

She steadies her hands on the counter. 'Jesus Christ! You wouldn't. I mean, how?'

My palms itch. 'I'm not sure the details matter.'

Her mouth hangs open. I encourage her to sit back down, tell her as much as I can. By the time I'm finished speaking, Claire's head is in her hands.

'What the hell, Natty? This is . . . I mean, talk about dropping a nuclear bomb.' She rubs her eyes, sits up, looks to the ceiling, looks to me, casts her eyes back down. 'Wine. I need fucking wine,' she says. 'Do you have some?'

I stand, pause. The smooth counter is cool under my palms. 'We do, just . . . I can't quite stomach red any more. Is white okay?'

Understanding flickers across her eyes and she nods. 'Yeah, of course.'

I uncork a bottle and as the wine pours, so does everything I've wanted to say to her over the past few months. We spend a lot of time chewing over my relationship with Marc and Luca at first, Claire asking questions, frozen panic on her face.

'You're not going to report me, are you?' I ask.

She scoffs. 'But, Natty . . .' She squeezes my hand and gives me a nervous look. '. . . I don't know what to say.'

'Then don't say anything.' My grip on her hand tightens, desperate for reassurance. 'We're ride or die, right? I mean, you always said you'd help me bury a body, no questions asked.'

Wine slips into the wrong stream on the way down. She splutters again. 'That's just something people say, Natty.'

'I know.'

'I guess there's no actual body you're asking me to bury, so thanks for sparing me that much.'

'You're very welcome.'

'And Emily . . .' She taps her phone screen to bring it to life, the time glaring up at her. 'Does she . . . I mean, I assume you haven't told her.'

'Of course not.'

'And are you going to?'

I pause, bite my lip, shake my head. 'No. No, I don't think that's a good idea.'

'Agreed.'

There's a hesitant smile in her eyes, but it's genuine, and it melts some of the tension. She can see me faltering, my energy dropping; she knows we can't talk about this any more tonight.

I double-tap my own phone screen to assess the time for myself. 'Where is Emily anyway?'

A new message is waiting for me.

So sorry, babe, but I'm not sure I'll get out of these drinks in time to make it. It was really nice to hear from you, though. Let's get a catch-up bev in, just you and me, yeah? xx

The disappointment shouldn't be so crushing.

'I don't think she's coming,' I say.

'Great. So that means I get you all to myself.'

And to steer me away from the impending sadness, she talks about literally anything else. Starts to tell me about life after her graduation. The new, if unimpressive, agent she's signed with. The manic pixie dream girl she's grown bored of and plans to break up with. And it feels like we're Care and Natty again, gabbing about the good and bad stuff. When the front door clicks open and shut, I'm fleetingly confused more than anything else. An optimistic part of me wonders if Emily's text was a misdirect so she could surprise me. Has somehow let herself in. But then I recognize the familiar heavy footsteps in the hallway. I hate that my body immediately goes rigid with fear. Again, I'm reduced to being a quiet, fragile mess. I hate this. I hate that he's made me this.

He says nothing at first, just storms into the kitchen, eyes clearly scanning. They stop when they land on Claire and me, frozen. For a moment, he looks disappointed, but he soon finds his voice.

'What's she doing here?'

'No "hello", then,' Claire says. I'm alarmed to see that her hackles are already up. I can almost hear her hissing.

'I thought you were going away for the weekend. I thought it might be nice to have some company.'

'Hi,' Claire says.

George quickly scans the room once more and then stares at me. 'Trip's cancelled.'

It's late and he stinks of beer, so he's certainly been somewhere. But the timing, the expectant look he wore when he entered the room . . . I'm beginning to suspect that there was no trip, only a trap. Claire is not quite what he expected to catch in it.

'Who did you say you were going away with again?'

He ignores the question. 'What are you up to?'

'She just told you, genius.' My sister jumps in.

'Anyway, I could ask you the same question,' I say, throwing myself into George's crosshairs. I didn't like the way he was glowering at Claire. But now I don't like the way he's glowering at me.

'What do you mean?'

'It's just . . .' I can't keep letting these men make a fool of me. 'It's just a bit sus that you've announced this trip out of the blue and come home in the middle of the night on the first day, stinking of booze. Something isn't adding up.'

He smiles, and I'm reminded that a smile can be ugly. 'If anyone here is up to something, it's you. Why would you sneak your sister into my house without telling me about it? What were you two talking about?'

Claire's stool groans as she scrapes it back a few inches. She doesn't actually stand, but every part of her body looks ready to spring up.

'What are you scared of her telling me?' she asks.

George glances between the two of us. 'Seriously, Nat. What have you been saying?'

This isn't how I want this to go. Sure, I can be brave, but not stupid. George is bigger than the both of us, drunk, and has already proven he's capable of violence. 'Why don't you sleep this off, and —'

To my shock, he's actually turning to leave the room, when —

'You're lucky you're not in prison right now,' Claire calls out.

'You what?' He swivels around again, fresh anger in his eyes.

'I said you're lucky. She told me what you did to her.' She finally stands, and her eyes are burning, too. 'You deserve to fucking rot.'

173

His smile returns, although there's no light behind it. 'And what exactly is it that I'm meant to have done to Natalie?' He looks at me. 'Well? What have you said?'

'It's nothing. Go to bed, and we can —'

'It's not "nothing".' A crack echoes through the room as Claire slams her wine glass on the counter. A segment from the foot goes skidding across the marble top. 'You raped her.'

He actually laughs this time. My stomach gurgles like it's alive. I feel physically sick, but in the churning of my guts, I can feel my monster waking.

'Is that funny to you?' Claire asks.

'Actually, it's not. Not if you're serious. Do you know what accusations like that can do to a guy's life? Where are you getting this idea from?'

Again, he looks to me. I try to warn her. I say, 'Care —'

But she doesn't listen. 'That trip. Just last weekend. She told you no and you forced yourself on her while she was sleeping.'

'Did she tell me to stop at any point?'

Claire glances at me. 'No, but —'

'So what's your point here?' He turns to me. 'And what the fuck have you been telling people?'

I'm angry now. Angrier than I planned to be. 'You hurt me, George. You know what you did.'

He laughs again and I find myself flexing my fingers as if to keep control of them. If I don't think very consciously about keeping my hands still, I don't know what they might do.

'Just because you like it a little rough sometimes —'

Hands move quicker than my brain does, a palm striking him across the cheek. Stupid, I know. He immediately lunges forward.

'How dare you —'

Claire steps between us, hands pushing his chest back. Well, as much as her small hands can. 'Oi, back off.'

Hands move quicker than my brain does, George taking Claire by the shoulders and throwing her to the floor. She yelps and I want to cry again. The shove is rough, her body slamming into cabinets and rolling across the tiles. The tears are starting. I've done this to her; it's my fault.

No.

It's his.

My hand finds the segment of glass on the counter and I lash out with it. I make contact. I wasn't expecting to make contact. There's an angry red line across George's cheek and shock on his face. He's stepped back once as a reflex to the pain, but when he sees my paltry weapon, he simply smacks it out of my hand.

'Care?' I ask.

She's groaning, but angry. Body rocking like she's aboard a ship, but rising nonetheless to throw herself once more at George. George, in turn, is ready to lunge. I try to thrust myself between them, but George simply gives us both a rough shove with each hand. My back cracks against the counter. I'm so focused on stopping George in his tracks that I don't see Claire's head make contact with the corner of the kitchen island, hard.

Her crumpled body is still.

I can feel that George is ready to leap. My hand roves behind me over the kitchen counter looking for new help. The knife block. I've found the knife block, and I've found a handle, and George is suddenly lunging at me. I draw the knife out. George draws his fist back. I feel the blow before I see it.

In fact, I'm not sure I see it at all.

The next thing I know, I'm coming to, my temple

throbbing. I can feel the cool tiles of the kitchen against my face, cold seeping through my clothes and into my bones. It takes me a few seconds, but I manage to sit up, and when I do, I can see that George is right in front of me, slumped against a cabinet, the knife buried to the hilt in his chest.

Chapter 25

Now

'And how is everything?' the waitress asks.

I try to blink away images of George's lifeless body as I root around for an answer about the overpriced and under-seasoned eggs in front of me. The bright, brassy decor of the restaurant fails to push away the dark memories.

It's the reason Claire finally upped sticks to LA and left me here, I'd found myself explaining to Dimple. *She was tired of sacrificing for me. And who could blame her? I was dating another douche, and this time he hadn't just hurt me, but hurt her, too.*

My mother was livid, of course. Called me every name under the sun. It's why I stopped seeing her. Why we don't talk. And then Emily . . . She heard what happened. Reached out to me. It was a hard phone call when we finally spoke. She told me I needed help. Guess there were too many dead boyfriends around me to ignore.

So that was it. The Big Fallout.

It's why I wrote the letters, why I started to see Dr Foster. I wanted to make sense of things, break the pattern, make healthier choices. Had to at least prove to Claire that I was willing to do the work so she'd let me back in again. It took time. But we got there.

Even after all these years, I still hate him. George. Hate him for what he did and hate him for filling me with so much hatred. So much that it's pushed out many of my happier thoughts and feelings to make room for itself. At the very least, he made the story I spun of him attacking me easier to swallow. Turns out he had quite the rap sheet: aggravated assault, harassment, stalking. I'm not stupid; I'd looked him

177

up online, but he'd given me a fake surname that hid his history, and given his socials didn't use his surname I'd no idea he was living a double life. His list of charges included cracking his mother's jaw when she refused to give him a larger share of his dad's will after the cancer killed him. Some nonsense about George, being head of the family, deserving to manage the funds. His family's testimony also helped me out in the end. Someone ought to arrest the podcasters George was poisoned by, too.

I make a mental note to call Claire in the evening. Hearing her voice would do me good. A wave of pain hits me at the thought of how unreachable she is, leaving me winded. An unsent message sits drafted in our chat.

> I miss you. I know you won't come home, but
> I need you here. I'm falling apart without you.

'The food's delicious, thank you,' James says for both of us with his most charming smile. I've clearly been lost in my head for an uncomfortable amount of time. The waitress blushes and I try to tamp down the stab of jealousy that flares up as she walks away. It's too easy to wonder if James's betrayal of me with the money is just a precursor to more betrayal. Is that how it will start? A seemingly innocent smile and a coy look, right in front of my face? After George, I promised myself I'd never be too trusting of a man again, but I can't let myself become paranoid, either.

It's not hard to see why our waitress is besotted with James. His chunky knit jumper, tortoiseshell glasses and softly styled hair make him look like the romantic lead in a festive film, somehow lifted straight out of the movie and plonked in the middle of this mid-range brasserie opposite the witch who stole Christmas.

'How are your eggs?' he asks.

'Yeah, good.' The answer he wants to hear. I even manage a smile.

It's date day, which James has been good at making sure we keep steady at, even while everything else around us rocks. He's still cautious around me, even as his words tell me that there's nothing to worry about. But at least he's trying. We both are.

Today, date day is brunch, followed by a couple's massage and a trip to the cinema. As usual, I'll take a few turns around the spa pool post-massage, while James simply sweats it out in the sauna. It's sweet that he's organized this, that he wants to organize these things for us. It's what made falling for him so effortless – from acts of service to quality time or gifts, he's fluent in all the love languages. It's so easy to melt into loving a man who holds you that securely.

My eyes linger on the olive pits that sit in a small cup between us, chewed up and spat out. I feel like one of those pits. Life has sunk its teeth into my flesh and scraped the meat away from my bones. My eyes linger on the cocktail sticks sleepily crisscrossed within the cup. I think of that night in the bar with Mr Periphery. It's the first time I've thought of him in a while. Perhaps I should be more nervous about potential repercussions, but after a quick news scan the next morning didn't turn up results, I let it go. The only thing that keeps me up at night is the fear that he hasn't learned his lesson.

James and I enjoy inconsequential chat as we eat. I'm telling him about Ama being headhunted for a new role when he sheepishly mentions an executive assistant opening he's seen. For me. At another company. I've not begrudged him bringing work home with increased out-of-hours calls, texts and emails recently – I know that world is his safe space – but now removing home from work? It's hard not to catastrophize, to think of how maybe seeing me all day in the office and then at home is now too much for him. Now that he's seen behind the facade of the Cool Girl and has the Crazy Wife. It's hard not to think of the unspoken concession I'd be making in terms of my right to maternity leave if I leave the business, and what James's acceptance of that means for our future.

'Are you okay?' he asks, trying to clear the cobwebs of my guardedness away.

'Yeah. No, I get it. Probably healthy for our marriage for us to have a little space.'

'That's not why I –'

'I know,' I interject.

'But it's probably also true. I'm not so sure I always get being your husband and being your boss right.' He smiles. It occurs to me that he smiles a lot, like Dimple. 'Well, at least I'm a better boss than Will would be.' A dry laugh. 'Christ, I know we've still got a few months to go until he becomes a problem again, but it doesn't feel like enough time.'

Suddenly, the knife feels very present in my hand: the weight of it, the bite of the spine against my fingertip, the coolness of it against my skin. It's a feeble thing, too blunt to do any real damage, but in that moment, I can't help but imagine that with enough force applied, perhaps it might. After all, James and I might have broken each other's trust, but it's Will who's really destroyed everything for me. If he had left things alone, hadn't been so greedy, hadn't been so reckless in the first instance, I'd be well on my way to being pregnant right now.

The feeling is so ugly it frightens me. I do my best to wrap it tightly in impenetrable denial and pack it away somewhere in the recesses of my mind.

'You know that's not just your problem to handle. It's my mess, too. I'll help clean it up.'

'How?' James's look is weary. The question could be rude, but it's not. I understand what his face is saying: *What exactly can you do without Will ratting you out to the police and turning you in? The police aren't going to believe you over him.*

As if the very mention of him has summoned him into our sacred circle, like a whisky-soaked Beetlejuice, James's phone pings. Time was once that his work notifications would have been on silent when we were together, but I guess people change. He flips the phone over and unlocks it. I watch as his face falls.

I don't want to ask but am too anxious a person not to. 'What is it?'

'Nothing. Nothing for you to worry about anyway,' he says, a smile repainted onto his face. The words are delivered as sweet and smooth as honey, but they also feel like a lie.

'James.'

His eyebrows pinch together in concern for a split second and then settle back into their rightful place.

'James, for god's sake, just show me.'

He slides his phone across the table, screen lit up. His emails are open, one particular email filling the screen. From Will. The words are what I've long feared were inevitable:

Look. You know this is the last thing I wanted to do, but I'm in trouble again. I don't want to hear 'I told you so', but I need another £15K. I know it's a lot to ask, but I know you can afford it, and it's the least you could do after I've been so good in keeping Nat's secret. I promise this is the last time. I swear.

'Fuck. So much for having a few months until we need to worry about him,' I say. James reaches for my hand again,

181

and this time, I clutch it like a lifeline. 'I mean, we definitely don't have the money. Where are we supposed to find fifteen grand?'

'If I hadn't sunk all my liquid assets into the company, it'd be easy, but after buying Will out . . . I imagine he wants me to steal it from the business. Or take out a loan.'

'You can't afford to do that.'

If James steals that money, he'll be putting himself at huge risk for the mistakes I've made. And if he gets a loan, then we'll be even further away from affording the help we need to have a family. But if we don't pay, don't give Will what he wants, one day soon we'll arrive home to find police on our doorstep with questions I can't answer.

Those ugly thoughts spring free from their constraints. A plan seems to be forming in my mind. I need to be better. I want to be better. But if I play things right, I have a chance to remove a huge problem, and allow James and me space to work on our marriage, our future family. After all, I want a family more than anything. A family with James. Despite everything, he's still here, fighting my corner. I don't think I'll ever find a love like this again.

There's only one problem – it's going to be painfully obvious what's happened if Will suddenly dies.

Although I do seem to be criminally good at making murder look like an accident.

Chapter 26

Now

Dimple

I remember what it was like when I first fell for James. It was a heady thing unlike anything I'd ever experienced before. I have a distinct memory of walking to work through London Fields on an otherwise ordinary weekday morning. It was raining, and I had a project overdue at work, and I'd forgotten to spray deodorant under my arms, so I was already a little damp in the pits and conscious that it would only worsen as the day wore on.

And it was the best morning of my life.

It's a real mindfuck very literally seeing the world through different eyes, an intoxicating cocktail of hormones flooding your brain and altering its chemistry. Going to work felt like going on holiday. Everything was through rose-tinted glasses. It was impossible to have a bad day. It was true magic.

This is how I feel now that I've given in to the idea of doing something about Will. It's a strangely euphoric trepidation. At once relieved that there's a solution to our problems and terrified about what I'm letting loose in myself.

Whether it will be an unfortunate tumble down some stairs or a horrible crash, his proclivity for drink and drugs makes him a relatively easy target. And it will be different this time; I will be meticulous. I won't make intricate plans only to throw them out the window in a fit of temper. Won't have to keep looking over my shoulder, like with George.

James will inevitably grieve for a while, but once he's over it, we can get back to the way we were. But better.

A small voice in my head whispers that I'm being over-confident. That I've never killed a man with a clear and sober mind at the steering wheel. But I do my best to smother those doubts. Giving them too much oxygen feels unwise when Will's elimination feels like my only lifeline.

'You seem in good spirits today,' Dimple says.

Said good spirits seem to be reflected back to me in the friendly squint of her eyes. Or perhaps it's just my positivity-drunk brain imagining this.

'I am,' I reply, smiling.

I'm not imagining the smile that Dimple returns; that's for sure. 'I'm so glad to hear it. Can I ask what's put you in such a good mood?'

Honesty, transparency. That's what I've promised myself and Dimple. But this is different. This is premeditated murder, and if I tell her I'm going to do it, she'll have to tell someone else. I can't risk that.

An unexpected sadness suddenly surges over me, a grey cloud over my perfect-blue-sky day. It occurs to me that aside from Claire, Dimple is the person I'm most myself with. Sure, there are moments I try to avoid talking about things, or want to hold things back, but that's normal, isn't it? No one person bares the entirety of their soul without restriction to any one person. That would be psychotic.

'James and I have been doing well lately,' I say. 'He's making an effort to fight for our marriage.'

Seconds tick by. There are only maybe three or four of them, but they stretch between us, bloated and pregnant. Whatever it is Dimple is thinking in those moments, what it is she almost says, I see her pack away for safekeeping. Instead, she draws out the following.

'So, your blackouts . . .' The change of topic is so swift that it almost gives me whiplash.

'I'm sorry, what?'

'Your blackouts,' she repeats plainly.

'I thought we were talking about James.'

The blank look she gives me tells me that maybe she's seen through my bullshit. Perhaps an unfortunate side effect of letting her see me so completely; she may now be impervious to my lies.

'Entertain me for a moment, please. We can always return to James later on in the session, if we have time.'

I'm wary, but I give her a nonchalant shrug. 'Okay.'

'You seem to have found new clarity and understanding around your violent impulses.'

'Yes, that's fair to say.'

'If your desire to hurt is rooted in the desire to take back power, to exact revenge, then what do you think the reason is for not being able to remember the details of historic violent incidents?'

Each death is interwoven with fog and haze. It's one of the things I was most keen to address when I started coming to Dr Foster; making healthier life choices and keeping my impulses under control while conscious is one thing, but I'm afraid of what I might do if I'm asleep at the wheel. Dimple knows this. Knows I struggle with why these memory holes exist.

I frown. 'We're dancing around what you want to say again, I can tell. Just say it.'

Dimple offers her hands up in a peaceful gesture. 'I'm only curious as to whether you might have your own theories on the matter.'

My nose twitches and my mouth twists. 'I assume it's some kind of dissociative memory loss, triggered by trauma.'

She nods, lithe fingers flicking through her notepad. 'You've said before that you believe you've inherited your proclivity for violence from your mother. Specifically, your father's death.' I note her avoidance of the word 'murder'.

'Sure.'

'What was your mother's response to the event? We've spoken a little about yours, but in the aftermath, how did she respond?'

'I'm not sure I follow your meaning.' I do; I'm just being difficult. Suddenly, she feels less like Claire and more like my mother, laying traps with her words to catch me in.

Dimple seems unfazed, although we both know what I'm doing. 'Did she seem to experience any forgetfulness? Any blackouts?'

My lips press tightly together. The skin pulls taut, a fissure left in a dry patch splitting open. It hurts. 'No, she didn't as far as I know. But I'm not sure what difference that makes. I didn't expect something like this would be hereditary. It's psychological.'

She just stares at me with a lukewarm smile. There's something off about it, like milk sitting all day on the counter of a hot kitchen.

'So, returning to my question, what do you think might be the psychological factors behind your mind dissociating to such an extreme degree?'

My hackles are up, but I want to answer. I won't understand what she's playing at until I do.

'Well, take George, for example. What I did was quite an extreme act. I imagine that on some level, I found the act deeply traumatic, even if I felt compelled to do it.'

She sets her notepad aside on the little round table next to her. 'If your mind could insist on rejecting such violence, what makes you think you're capable of enacting it in the first instance?'

Static crackles through my head, making it hard to think. 'What do you mean?'

'The other day, in the bar, you described a feeling of nausea overcoming you at the prospect of more seriously harming the man you met.'

'That's true.'

'And you say you were afraid of getting caught.'

'That's right.'

'But you weren't afraid of getting caught when you stabbed George in his own home?'

'I thought you weren't supposed to put words in my mouth.'

She taps her pen against her thigh, smiles. 'Well, were you afraid?'

'Before it actually happened, and after, sure.' The room is too warm. 'But I can't remember how I felt in the moment, can I? That's the whole point.'

'Does that not strike you as particularly odd? You were drinking heavily on the night that Marc died and were under the influence of other substances at the time of Luca's death. Gaps in your memory are easy to explain on these occasions. It's this one that stands out.'

I run my tongue across my teeth. 'Yes, that's why I'm here.'

Dimple leans back in her chair and removes her glasses. She takes a moment to rub the bridge of her nose before fixing them back into place. She looks me dead in the eyes, the grey of her irises now steel, now flint. I want to look away, but I'm caught in her net.

'Have you ever considered that perhaps you don't remember killing these men – I think we're beyond the point of euphemisms – because you did not, in fact, kill them?'

The room feels like it's sliding away beneath my feet. Someone has tipped my world over, setting it at an angle. My nails are digging into the flaking crust as I attempt not to fall away from it completely.

'What do you mean?'

'Think about it . . .'

I don't want to. The static is louder in my ears now, abuzz in my brain.

'Is it possible that you've made a mistake in assuming your anger means you are directly responsible for these deaths?'

I shake my head. 'For Marc or Luca, maybe I'd get it. But George –' That rage I'd felt, that I can still feel now, that was clear. I'd had some wine, but I wasn't blackout drunk. I'd known what I was doing when I'd reached for the knife. 'It's just not possible. Who else would care to bump off all of my exes? Because they didn't just drop dead by magic. I mean, who else was even there?'

The last sentence is a desperate throwaway, but I wish I could swallow it back down as soon as it flies out of my mouth. I see the words forming on Dimple's lips even before she says, 'Your sister.'

Chapter 27

Then

Claire

It alarms me, how easily Natalie lets insult or injury roll off her. At home, with Mum, the knives might come out, but outside of the house, it's like she's disarmed. I get that it's her defence mechanism, balling up like an armadillo and letting her passivity be her armour. Truth be told, I'm jealous of this ability to not let barbed words find their hooks in her skin. Despite how hard she works to make people at school like her, how elegantly she weaponizes that Like, I know she doesn't care in the way most people do. She doesn't get any warm fuzzies from people thinking or saying nice things about her. But she knows that being held in people's good opinion can get her things, and that . . . that she wants. Needs, maybe.

My popularity is more personal to me. Perhaps that's why I've never been able to bite my tongue the way she can; any kind of slight feels like being told that I'm not important. I have to remind the person that I matter, even if I do it with a smile. Perhaps my easy step to anger is simply my own defence mechanism, resisting the urge to become the pliant rag doll our mother became. That Natalie's becoming. I'm never going to be anyone's punchbag.

Natalie's right about how useful it is having people think well of you, though. Becky didn't even think to accuse me of being behind the switching of her tan a couple of days ago. Even though it's my sister she's being a total cunt to.

The thought of her stormy, charred orange face when she marched into school still makes me smile. She deserved worse than that.

At school, it's hard dealing with slights, but it's always worse watching it happen to my sister. Maybe because I know she'll never do anything about it, and I know some people see her as an easy target. Our mum is poor, our dad is dead, and we're among only a handful of Black kids in school. Then to top it all off, Natty just swallows any insults. And so, to balance the scales, I've developed a fondness for hatching little revenges. Feels like the acts should have a chic French name: *petites vengeances*. Still, once you get a taste for something like that, for making people get what they deserve, it's difficult to ever stop.

It's with all this in mind that I sneak out and rush over to Marc's party when I receive Emily's call about my sister. Sober Natty is vulnerable enough, but I don't like the thought of her drunk in a den of vultures. And when I arrive, finding her curled around a toilet bowl like a cat, I know I made the right choice. Fortunately, this isn't the only bathroom in Marc's house, but people are still drunk enough and desperate enough for use of it that a lot of people are banging on the door, pissed. There's sick down Nat's prom dress, which is soaked through and smells of chlorine. Her skin is cold, and I worry she's going to make herself even sicker than she already is. I'm not someone who feels fear often, but I do feel afraid for my sister; she doesn't seem to know how to look out for herself.

'Come on, Natty. We've got to move.'

She's unresponsive.

'I've been trying for ages,' Emily says, hands flapping. 'I just don't know what to do. You've got this, though, yeah?' She's already getting up to leave.

A bolt of irritation runs through me. 'Hold on a minute – you're probably the reason she's so wasted in the first place. Can you at least go get three of the least creepy and least weedy boys here to give me a hand? Heavy on the "least creepy" part.'

'I did not force your sister to down half a bottle of tequila,' she slurs. 'But sure – I'll be right back.'

A few minutes later, three boys are releasing my sister's limbs on top of Marc's bed. It takes me more time and effort than seems reasonable, but I eventually manage to strip Natalie down and dress her in a dry T-shirt and joggers found in a wardrobe.

Duty done, I decide to go find my sister's boyfriend and give him an earful for not looking after her properly. There were rumours of him being out on the rooftop, attempting to make a heroic dive into the pool, but I've just been in his room, overlooking the square patch of roof closest to the pool, and there's been no sign of him.

Emily finds me before I can find him, shoving a shot glass in my hand and yanking on my arm to come dance. I can't stand how desperate she seems for me to like her, but look, I'm not a bloody saint; I'm a teenage girl at a house party with a cool older crowd and no parents. I want to have fun. I also know the brownie points this is going to score me with the other kids in my year. So of course, I take the shot, and then a Smirnoff Ice.

I don't go crazy – I've no intention of getting as wasted as my sister – but I enjoy myself, flirting with whoever seems open to it and dancing with whoever has rhythm (not a huge number of people in that crowd). As the party quietens down, I start to catch snippets of the hushed conversations and throwaway comments traded in clusters. By the time the last of the party guests are heading to bed or hopping in taxis, I've realized that Marc and Natalie are no longer together, that there has been some kind of scene with Becky. There's still no sign of Marc, but I think of my sister lying sprawled out on his bed and I realize it was a mistake to leave her there. From the sound of it, it's the last place she'll want to be.

Moving quickly, I make my way back up to Marc's room. When I get there, the door seems jammed, but with a firm shove, it comes tumbling open. A chair topples over, clearly propped against the handle mere moments ago. Marc is in the bed, hunched over Natalie, his mouth on hers. She isn't moving.

'What are you doing?' My blood is suddenly cold in my veins, feet planted on the floor.

He throws a hooded look my way, clearly also drunk. As he turns to face me properly, I notice his hand sliding out from Nat's trousers. I'm glad, at the very least, that they're still on. But that doesn't stop the bile from rising in my throat.

'What the fuck are you doing?' I ask again.

Still not moving, Natalie gives out a low groan. Marc swings his legs out from under the duvet and gets out of the bed. He's naked.

'Claire!' It's a slack-jawed greeting and a reminder that I'm not supposed to be where I am. He ambles over to me, arm outstretched. 'Come on, you gotta go.'

He's strong, but he's drunk and unprepared for my righteous anger. 'I'm not fucking leaving you alone with her. She's passed out. What the hell are you doing?' I smack his arm off my shoulder.

'C'mon, you've got to get out,' he says. 'She doesn't want you here.'

'Nat?' I run to her side of the bed and shake her. More gentle groans, but nothing coherent.

Suddenly there's a hand on my arm. I stagger back with the force behind it.

'You gotta go,' he says.

'If you make me leave, I will scream up and down this house about what you were trying to do to her.'

He glowers at me, storms over to the door and slams it shut. 'And what was that?'

'Christ, you could at least put on some clothes.'

He still looks sullen as he staggers over to the bed, unsteady on his feet. Once he's unceremoniously plonked himself down on the edge, he starts scooping up discarded clothes and putting them back onto his body. 'You're a real pain in the arse, you know that?'

Natty stirs again, this time forming a semi-coherent sentence. It's slurred, each word bleeding into the next, but the question is clear: *What's going on?*

'Is there anywhere we can talk?' I ask him. I don't want her to overhear. Whatever he was doing was bad enough; she doesn't have to hear about it in this state.

'Could you not just *fuck off*?'

His growl is dark, menacing. But unfortunately for him, my amygdala only knows 'fight', not 'flight' or 'fright'. It's a seed of savagery I wish my father hadn't sown in me. A seed I've watered to grow over my fear. And so I find myself marching up to Marc and flicking him in the ear. Hard.

'Ow! What the —'

'Cut the attitude. Two minutes, and then I'll leave you alone,' I say.

A glowering Marc indicates that I should follow him, ambling over to a large window. I don't love heights, don't love the prospect of being out there alone with him, something menacing in the glazed-over look in his eyes — the eyes of a spoiled teenage boy with no one currently at the helm. A boy like that is capable of anything.

He prises the window open and steps out into the warm air. It takes more effort to climb through with my short legs, but I make it out after him, pushing the window almost closed so that the sound won't travel to Natalie.

'So, Marc, what the fuck?' I say. 'I mean, I saw where your hand was. And you were naked.'

He looks at me with those dead eyes of his. They've always been so cold, devoid of something. I'm never sure if Natalie likes him because of or in spite of this. But in any case, something in his energy has shifted. He isn't pretending to be pally any more.

'Look, your sister's a little fucking slut. I wasn't doing anything she didn't want.'

My temperature starts to rise again. 'How could she want anything if she's out cold?'

'She's always desperate for it. I can smell it on her.'

'Care?'

Natty. She's swaying unsteadily behind me, bare feet on the roof tiles.

'Natty, go to bed.'

'Yeah, babe, go to bed. I'll be there in a sec.'

She looks confused for a moment, memories from the night clanging together. They aren't together any more, are they? Or maybe they are again . . . She turns to go back inside, almost slipping. I'm relieved when one foot makes it safely back into the room and then the other follows. She almost falls over getting back to the bed, but, thankfully, it's a mere step or two away from the window.

Still furious, I turn back to Marc, who is gazing lazily out at the pool below. 'You can sleep somewhere else tonight.'

He laughs, and his laugh is pitying me. Who was I to stop him from doing exactly what he wanted? Was I really going to stop the athletic, rich white boy from doing anything at all?

'I'm going to sleep in my bed,' he says with a shrug. 'You can sleep where you want.'

I don't mean to do it. Or, at least, I haven't planned to. I can't say exactly what would have happened next if he'd remained silent, if this had been enough for him. But it wasn't. For boys like him, it's never enough, and he says, 'God, you lot are so entitled.'

And I lose it, storming up to him.

'Fuck you,' I say, shoving him firmly in the chest.

He's actually still smirking when he takes the first step back. It's only when the second step finds air and not roof that his face comes alive with fear. Perhaps it's the shock of it that means he doesn't cry out, but the only sound is the sound of his body hitting the concrete.

Part of me wants to run down there, to see if I can help him. I didn't think I'd pushed him that hard, didn't mean for him to go over the edge. There's a chance he just has a broken arm or leg. But the silence scares me. Marc is not the kind to bear pain in dignified silence. I creep to the edge of the roof and look down, see the blood spreading out from his skull. He already looks very dead. And I think of going to check for a pulse to be extra sure, but I know what it would look like; the brown girl found kneeling in a pool of the golden boy's blood doesn't get off with a slap on the wrist. There's nothing I can do for him now.

At first, I'm surprised I'm not freaking out. But his is not the first dead body I've seen. My dad's had looked much like this when I'd emerged from my bedroom on the night he'd died. Granted, this time there's more blood, though.

But I've already learned another lesson from my dad's death: some men are better off dead. And Natalie will certainly be better off without Marc in her life.

When Mum comes to pick us up in the morning, she gives Ghanaian professional mourners a run for their money. She weeps like Marc was her own son, even though Natty had pointedly kept them apart, clutching hands to her chest and stomping at the ground as she gets out of the car. The police have cleared us to leave, and parents are rushing in, grabbing their precious, alive children away and staring, hard, at our mother. Even they can see she needs the therapy she refuses to seek out.

Ultimately, these aren't really my friends watching our mother melt down, but I can see how embarrassed Nat is. How this is more difficulty heaped onto an already difficult morning.

The first words Mum says to Natty are, 'You look terrible.' She stops to pull Natty into a brief hug and then releases her, fresh scrutiny in her eyes. 'Really, baby, you look horrible. Have you not even washed your face?'

I watched my sister withdraw even further into herself. If she withdraws far enough, our mother's sharp words can't reach her. But I can't reach her, either.

'Can we go?' she asks, not waiting for an answer. Her hand is on the passenger door handle and her rear in the seat before Mum can give any kind of reply.

Mum is soon also in her seat, with me in the back moments after. As soon as the car door clicks shut, the theatrics stop. It was like that when the police came after Dad died, too. She was quiet as anything before they turned up, but the second they stepped foot in the house, she grieved like the most devoted of wives in ancient Greece, preparing to throw herself on her husband's funeral pyre to burn with him. The second they left, the house sank into quiet again. In the end, I think the quiet, how it persisted, was too much for her. In the absence of Dad, there was no chaos to control, nor an outlet for her tirades on her little lot in life. But it was better to just let Dad be gone than try to keep him alive. Our mother's paroxysmal fits at the mere mention of him weren't worth the upset for her or us.

Seat belt secured, Mum takes a moment to turn to me and pat my cheek. 'You're a good girl coming to look after your sister.' I'm embarrassed to have nothing to say to her. A defence of my sister has already risen and died in my throat. I'm not sure why it's like this, why our mother is the only person I can never speak back to, and the only person Natalie can. The irony is that Natalie follows our mum's rules far more than I do, but our family has somehow assigned Natalie the role of problem child, and me, the good daughter.

It was only a few months ago that a boy sent me flowers and chocolate to the house for Valentine's. He'd played the lead in the school play, had a talent I found compelling. He told me all about his auditions for drama school, mesmerized me with his monologues. We started hooking up in the drama centre on Thursday lunchtimes when it was empty. Our sessions were fumbled and juvenile, but they kept me entertained for a little while.

When Mum found the flowers and summoned us both to the kitchen, yelling about teen pregnancies and 'boryor matters', I stood frozen. In the end, Nat said they were hers. It was Nat who raged about Mum needing to let us have our own lives, a notion I've keenly felt and never been able to express. With Dad gone, Mum's depressive episodes are less frequent, but her attention, suffocating.

'If I hear anything about being up to no good with boys –' Mum barks.

'She was good.' Natalie. She has no idea if this is true, but she says it anyway.

Mum checks her mirrors, begins to pull out. She doesn't reply to Natalie, just throws her voice back to me. 'Good. Because you can't go blindly following your wayward sister.'

'Mum.' Natalie. 'Can you not?'

'What? I told you to stay away from that boy, to focus on your studies.' She pauses to huff for emphasis. 'You told me your party was girls only, at Emily's. And now I'm picking you up from that boy's place after doing god knows what, and the boy's had the fancy to go and split his head open like a coconut –'

I wonder if Mum thinks of Dad's dead body in that way. A piece of food gone wrong. A gingerbread man with his limbs snapped. He hadn't looked much like a gingerbread man to me when I'd crept out behind my sister that night. He'd looked very much like a dead body.

'Mum.' Natalie's eyes are screwed shut, fists flexing closed and open.

I lean forward. 'Mum, this is a hard morning for her. She's grieving –'

'Hard for her? Do you know how mortifying it was calling Emily's mother and having her realize my baby had lied to me about where sh—'

'Please, Mum,' I say.

But Natty simply waves a hand. 'Leave it, Care. It's fine.'

And so she sits there, absorbing it all so that I won't have to, as she always does. I'm indebted to her for this, I know. Not that she expects anything of me in return. But still, the guilt gnaws at me as I sit, listening. And I promise myself that I will always work to repay this favour. After all, Natty needs protecting sometimes, too.

Chapter 28

Now

If I floated into Dimple's office on a summer breeze, I leave with the howling of a storm cloud. Words have been said. I can't recall what exactly, but the words were fast and loud and vicious. I think I toppled the coffee table over on the way out. Doors were slammed, expletives hollered, sound ricocheting into the lobby as waiting patients averted their gazes. I've left before my time is up, already drafting scathing emails to Dimple in my mind, in which I demand my money back for time wasted.

My sister!

My sister . . .

There's a gnawing sensation in the back of my brain that I can't ignore. It's not even quite an idea, just a feeling. The gnarled bud of something waiting to blossom into something hideous. Its fingers are pressing on the inside of my skull, slippery against it. I can feel the pressure of them pushing, pushing, pushing.

I need an ibuprofen. I need some wine. I need an umbrella, because Jesus fuck is this weather awful. The heavens have cracked open, and I have to think this is some kind of sick joke. If the universe can transform itself into something wonderful for you, it can conspire to become your own personal hell, too.

Before long, I'm in the car, rain-drenched shoulders trying not to shiver.

My sister.

It's ludicrous to even consider it. And yet . . . And yet that Feeling is still lurking.

I tap out a quick message:

You around later for a chat? x

> Of course, Natty! I go on break in 2 hrs – that not too late for you?

Does it really have to wait two hours?

> Do you really want your sister to get fired?

No, 8 is good. Will call.

When I eventually get home, James is not yet back from work, always in the office, whereas I opt for an increasing number of days working from home. And today he's texted to say he'll be back late. I'm not sure how to sit with this, alone, for the next half hour. And I'm not yet sure if talking to Claire is going to make this better or worse.

Ibuprofen. Wine. An easy first step, and swiftly arranged. When I check the time, I see I still have twenty-two minutes left to wait. Great.

By the time eight o'clock rolls around, my nerves are shot, and I'm mildly tipsy. I'm sitting on the sofa, thumb hovering over the dial button, Claire's number up on my screen. There's something very final about making the call, about having the conversation. Whatever the outcome, I know something between us will be irreversibly changed. She's the only family I have left. I don't know that I can afford to lose her.

'Hi, Care.'

'Natty! What's up? God, you won't believe who I served in the café today.'

'Oh.' My voice is flat. Somehow, I'm already getting this wrong. 'Is now a good time to talk?'

The spark in her voice fizzes out. 'Yeah, I can – What is it, Natty?'

'Are you alone? Can you find somewhere quiet?'

'One sec, I'm just heading to the break room and then I'm all yours.'

As Claire describes it, the 'break room' is really a glorified storage cupboard, just about big enough for a table and chair to be pushed up against a towering stack of boxes. Claire says she's never minded it, though. Says it's one of the few places in LA where she feels truly at peace. There's something nice about being shut off from the rest of the world.

'I'm in,' she says. 'Just getting comfortable. What is it? Is it James? Has something happened?'

The words stick in my throat. And when, for a moment, it feels as if I've found them, they're fuzzy, strange and mis-shapen. I don't know how to say this.

'It's not James,' I say. 'Not really.'

'Oh. Then what is it?'

I force the headlines out of my mouth. The latest therapy sessions; the man in the bar; Dimple's theory. 'I couldn't sit there and keep listening to her, Care. But it – it sounded like she thought maybe what happened to Marc and Luca and George had something to do with you.'

'She did?'

I wish I could see her face.

'She did. And I was so mad – you have to believe me, I was so mad – I couldn't listen any more and I stormed out. I mean, it's crazy, right?'

The other end of the line is quiet. It shocks me how quickly my blood is up. Because why isn't there the immediate outrage, the shock? Why am I not hearing my baby sister curse down the phone at me? Keeping her temper has never been her strong suit.

'Claire?' I ask, and there are teeth in the question this time. I wonder if she can feel them biting into her.

'Claire!'

I pull the phone away from my mouth and watch the screen as it goes dark. She's gone. I try to focus on one thought at a time, but there are too many, and they're all so loud.

The house suddenly feels too big and too empty. There's too much room for my thoughts to roam free, colliding with one another, colliding with me. I glug down some more wine in the hopes that it will quieten the noise, and it does, in a fashion. Or perhaps it's the simple passing of time. Either way, the thoughts begin to come through to me in an organized line.

I have never clearly recalled the moment of any of my exes' deaths. Claire has always been there, in some capacity. I didn't invite her to Luca's party, but she was in town to see me, and she knew where I was. And what he'd done. She's always been more reactive than me, always had a stronger sense of justice.

The truth of these things does not sit comfortably in my body. It's a donated organ that I don't want, that doesn't match the story of the relationship I have with my sister. Every part of me wants to reject it. Because there's no way Claire would have allowed me to struggle like this, to believe I had this blood on my hands, to be driven mad by it. That's a kind of cruelty we'd never deliver to each other. Or, at least, I thought it was.

When the sound of the front door opening and closing finally echoes through the house, I still haven't moved from my spot on the sofa. I feel strangely without feeling.

'Hi, babe.' James's voice.

He wanders into the living room, eyes taking in my deflated

form on the sofa, a balloon animal with the air let out. His body goes immediately stiff with caution as he approaches me, eyeing the wine.

'Everything okay?'

Hey, babe, so it turns out I'm probably not a violent psychopath at all. In fact, it looks like maybe it's my sister who's been doing all the maiming. Surprise!

He sits next to me on the sofa, arm around my back, my head in the crook of his neck. Tears are soaking into his shirt.

'It's not just about George,' I say quietly.

'What do you mean?'

'My therapist, she got me to unpack Marc and Luca's deaths, too, and . . . I don't think they were accidents, James. I think she killed them. Claire.'

The blood seems to drain from his face and he goes so still that, for a moment, I'm worried he's stopped breathing.

'James?'

'Are you sure?'

I don't answer. Something in my gut feels certain. Of course it made me sick to think of murdering that guy in the bar. I'm simply not a murderer. 'I think it's true, though, James. It . . . it would explain a lot.'

'Well, I guess the good news is you're not a monster,' he ventures.

To his credit, I do actually laugh. Properly laugh. 'Fat lot of good it's done us, though . . . We've already lost all our savings.'

'Doing that to your own sibling . . .' He looses a heavy sigh, voice darkening. 'I don't wish to speak ill of her, but I don't think I could ever forgive what she did if I were you.' He pins me with a tense look. 'Do you think we could speak to her together? She owes us answers. Answers and apologies.'

The corner of a cushion is pushing painfully against my spine. I shift. 'I don't think that's . . . I mean, you've only been in touch over text . . .' I leave the sentence unfinished.

His eyes track away from me, towards the French windows. At first, I think something's caught his eye, but nothing's there.

'James?'

He comes to, looks back in my direction. Doesn't quite meet my eye. A hand rakes through his hair, balling into a fist and tugging at the roots. It hurts him to do this a little, I know, but he also considers it stress relief. I take his fist in my hand, gently pull it away from his hair, which is now sticking up at wild angles.

'I know it's a lot to take in.'

'No, I . . . I just don't get it. You said you reached for a knife with George. That was you. I don't understand how that could have been anyone but you.'

There's a little space created between us as he leans back to take me in. I don't see any option other than to admit, 'I did. I did grab a knife. But he punched me as soon as I grabbed it. Knocked me out. When I woke . . .' Deep breath. 'When I woke, he'd been stabbed. I thought it was me, that the knock to the head made me forget or I just blacked it out.'

The room is too silent, and my husband is too still. Even though I feel it coming, I'm still wounded when James removes his hand from mine.

'And you . . .' His jaw is clenching and unclenching. He takes a small shuffle away from me. It feels like a mile. 'And you thought you killed him, didn't you? You lied to me.'

I've made my bed and now I have to lie in its soiled sheets. My chin eventually offers James an acquiescent nod. Our marriage has been burdened with more secrets than I know if it can bear.

'But remember, I didn't do it,' I say.

He won't look at me. 'You think. And you lied. It's not a small lie, Nat.'

'I know, and I'm sorry. But this – my innocence – that's all that really matters. My therapist knows I didn't do it, and I know that, too, now. I'm not a killer. It means Will has nothing to hold over our heads any more. We're free.' Which is a blessing. My plan to remove Will from the equation was born of false confidence. If I'd tried, who knows how catastrophically I might have failed?

James's eyes meet mine and although the skin around them folds, smile lines engaged, the distinct emotion that reads from them is *wary*. 'Yeah, you're right. It's great news.'

The reassurance in his voice rings false. He's a good actor, always has been, which is why he's such a good boss; we never see him sweat. But not everyone is as observant as I am, and I can see the gentle sheen covering his brow.

Chapter 29

Then

Claire

When I find myself cradling my sister outside a shitty university pub, her eyes at once as manic and as vacant as a shell-shocked soldier's, what I immediately want more than anything is for Luca to pay for what he's done to her. I know he's a dead man walking.

It was sickening watching it unfold, understanding before Nat did. Or before she wanted to, at least. A couple of her friends were decent, concerned, but she was too wrapped up in her despair to notice the whiff of smugness that floated beneath some of the looks traded across the pub table. There's a certain delight to be had in Nat being put in her place. The failed Oxbridge hopefuls of the world don't like to be made to feel inferior, and Nat, who by now has learned how to be more well-liked than most of them, can afford to be taken down a peg or two. It makes me want to smack the smugness off their faces. They're lucky Chris's phone is the only thing I went for.

After freeing Emily from campus security, we retreat to Nat's student digs. Popcorn, chocolate, wine, ice cream, pizza. Emily orders it all to the house, insists we don't pay. I think of the coins in my bank account and am grudgingly grateful. We cuddle up together in Nat's bed, an afternoon sleepover. We play the 'fuck him, he's trash' game: endless volleys of insults about Luca traded across our small circle, but Emily and I seem to be the only ones with paddles to play. So we play the distraction game instead: movies, TV shows, thumbs scrolling social media. Did you see this? And this? And this?

It all passes over Nat. Words wash over her as she stares off and the sky outside darkens to an inky black. Emily and I trade worried looks. *Is she going to be okay?*

The three of us eventually fall asleep, tightly squeezed in beneath the covers, that question resounding in my head before consciousness fades. I do feel her get out of bed. Nat, that is. I assume she's gone to the toilet. Am too sleep-drunk to think straight, using the moment of lucidity to stagger out of the sweaty trap of her too-full bed and into the adjoining room that her housemate's offered up as extra sleep space while on holiday.

As a result of my new spacious, peaceful bed, I don't notice Emily leave at all. It's only at three when my phone buzzes beneath my pillow that I wake. Clearing the alarm I set, I see Emily's texts.

[02:03] Woke up and Nat wasn't here. Didn't want to disturb you, so headed out to look for her. Think she's at that party to find him. If she's not there, might need to call you in as backup.

[02:47] Found her. She's pretty high, but otherwise fine.

Fuck. I was hoping – wishfully, I know – to slink off to the party alone. I've heard Nat wax lyrical plenty about Wonder Boy's holey heart and the party felt like a good opportunity to test how much it can handle. Break my sister's heart and I break yours – fair trade.

It also irks me that Emily wouldn't think to wake me so we could go together. Or, more likely, intentionally left me lying there. Sometimes, it's like she's competing with me. Like she wants to prove that she's the better sister.

Anger creeping in at the thought of Nat anywhere near Luca, I dress as inconspicuously as I can and walk my way over to the party house through the lamplit streets, still littered with drunk students making their way home. By the time I spot Nat at the house party, watching from a distance as Emily tries to keep up with her wild dancing, she's clearly off her face. It tells me all I need to know. Things haven't gone well.

Part of me wants to stay with her, make sure she's okay, even though I can see that Emily is trying to do the same thing. I'm transported back to Marc's bathroom all those years ago. It's so easy for these boys to push her over the edge.

There's something grotesque that squeezes at my chest at this thought. The truth is, I love her so much and I hate her for what she lets them do to her, for the lesson she refused to learn after Marc. It's both that love and that quiet hatred that pushes me out of that basement room and up into the kitchen, where I've seen a group of varsity boys lingering. As I've hoped, Luca is still there among them. He spots me, a gentle crackle floating beneath the bass, under the pressure of the can now more tightly constricted in his hand.

'Hey,' he says. 'Claire, isn't it? Nat's sister?' His grin is a little too big and his eyes are a little too wide, darting side to side at the friends around him. I can spot another actor a mile off, can see that Luca's smile is painting over something a little desperate. I realize that, like my sister, he needs to be liked. But Nat's lacking the thing that makes Luca dangerous, the thing that makes him a little too loud, a little too gregarious, a little too reliant on 'good banter': crippling insecurity.

A couple of Luca's friends shuffle uneasily, sniffing and rubbing at their noses. It's clear that something that Natalie has done has rattled them. A little pride swells in me at that thought. She hasn't just let him get away completely scot-free. Still, I've been hoping he hasn't seen me in enough of Natalie's Instagrams to recognize me as her sister, let alone name me.

'Yeah.' My smile is equally fake. 'You must be Luca.'

He crosses and uncrosses his arms. 'Listen, you must have heard about the uh . . . the um . . .'

'The video?' I ask. However I approach this, I can't be too aggressive. 'I know Nat was keen to talk to you about that. How did it go?'

There's a flash of understanding in his eyes then. He stops fidgeting. 'It wasn't good,' he says, a demonstration of regret creasing his features. 'I've been trying to get to the bottom of what happened, but it's not easy. I leave my phone lying around parties like these all the time. Anyone could have got into it. Sucks for someone to betray my trust like that.'

Were I more like my sister, perhaps I would believe him, but instead, I'm having to hide my clenched fist behind my back.

'Damn, you really can't trust anyone these days,' I say. 'Obviously, poor Nat's a mess, but has anyone stopped to ask you how you're doing?'

He blinks, eyes widening. 'Wow, you're – Wow. No. People don't tend to care about the guy's feelings. But thank you. I'm a bit shaken up, but I'm okay.'

And like that, he melts. The guarded hiking up of his shoulders softens into a more relaxed stance, and following his lead, his friends adopt his new casualness. This is good. This is necessary. I've no intention of spending more time with Luca one-on-one beyond this, but I need to be able to remain in his periphery for my plan to work.

'All right, boys, shots!' Luca announces. I hide the unspoken question that threatens to sing through on my face. Do any of them really need them? Not one of them is anything close to sober, and if I'm right about Luca's heart condition, I'm surprised he's willing to drink so much, but his recklessness is of use to me. I don't complain when he hands me one of their oversize plastic shot glasses.

The boys quickly re-cluster in smaller groups, shots done. Some of them leave the kitchen. There's a guy with a mullet I have my eye on. I've noticed him dipping his finger into a baggie a couple of times already, sucking the crystals off. His slightly leery, slack-jawed grin and dilated pupils suggest a malleability and hunger that I can work with. I decide to make him my friend for the night and corner him to talk. He is studying biomedical engineering. He is also on the football team. There is a whole heap of uninteresting information I glean that I swiftly forget.

In any case, he is accommodating, and I float in and out of groups by his side; allow him to speak at me in corners of rooms; fall in and out of rounds of shots; strategically move whenever I feel there is a kiss incoming. There's a hairy moment in which we're heading to the kitchen for more shots. I hear the unmistakable timbre of Natalie's voice on the way, undercut by Emily's heady laugh. I make my excuses in this moment and flee to the bathroom. Nat will inevitably know I was here, but she doesn't need to see me right now. At least while I wait, I'm able to solidify my plan.

We're back in the kitchen a few minutes later, ostensibly chatting, materially waiting. I notice Luca re-enter. I almost want to tell him what I'm planning for him, just to see him scared, but I say nothing.

'More shots?' I ask Mullet. He's absolutely fucked on the cocktail of whatever he's taken but is obliging. I gesture to the bottle as he begins to pour. 'Anyone else want one?' A couple of people nearby give enthusiastic yeses, and the first part of my trap is laid. 'Might as well do a few.' More pouring. 'Could you do a couple of those MD ones you guys were doing? One for me, one for you.'

He looks at me quizzically for a moment. I've refused any drugs up until this point.

'Just a light one for me, thanks. If I do too much, I want to kiss everything in sight.'

'Yeah, of course.'

I watch as he tips the remaining crumbs of crystals from one baggie into one shot glass, and then opens a new baggie and tips almost the entirety of it into another.

'Isn't that quite a lot?'

'Oh, this stuff is a bit shit. You need quite a lot to feel anything.'

I shrug as hands reach onto the counter for shot glasses, disappearing, reappearing, repouring. 'Okay. A normal one for courage, first.' A plain tequila goes down my throat. I wince and then look over my shoulder. 'Oi, shot king! Luca. Want one?'

He gives me a hazy smile, eyes half-closed. 'Always.'

Mullet is already deep in fits of laughter with some nearby friends. I pick up my shot glass and another and head over to Luca. I ham up a burp as I approach.

'You know what, that tequila's sent me west. Have both of these – I've got to go.'

It's so easy. He just smiles, puffs up his chest and says, 'Sure.'

I give him my spiked one first, quickly pushing the second into his hand with a slightly furry-looking lime wedge to chase away any potential aftertaste.

'Fucking hell,' he says, grimacing.

The words have hardly left his mouth before I'm out the kitchen door. I've barely taken two steps when I find myself barrelling into a chest. I look up to find glossy copper hair and an accusatory frown.

'What are you doing here?'

Emily. Shit.

'The same thing as you. I need to make sure she's okay.'

She casts a look over my shoulder into the bright light of the cheaply furnished kitchen and sniffs. 'Your sister's in bed. I took her back in an Uber – she's good. I just . . . I wanted to come back to have a word with that bastard. I've been looking for him everywhere. I didn't expect to find him doing shots in the kitchen with you of all people.'

I send a glance behind me, cursing the time I'm lingering. 'I was palming off my unwanteds on him. And what good would you talking to him do?' I ask. Emily looks hard at me then. It's easy to underestimate her, but when it comes to defending her friends, to defending my sister, she's a force to be reckoned with.

'Since when are you the bloody voice of reason? If your fuse was any shorter . . .' She shakes her head and sends a glare over my shoulder into the kitchen again.

'You're right,' I say, using more push than is polite to steer her around the corner and out of the kitchen's sight line. 'You're right. Which is how I know my sister doesn't thank people for popping off on her behalf. She'll be more embarrassed than she already is, and she'll resent you for it.'

Emily crosses her arms, a slight stagger backwards accentuating the gesture. For a moment, I hope that she's drunk, that she won't remember this, but a disappointing assessment tells me she's just bungling, not battered. 'I guess you're right.' And before I can protest, her arm has swung itself through mine, and she's dragging us both out of the party.

We stagger, arms linked, back to Natty's student house. As we walk the quieter streets, I wonder what will happen to Luca. It's different than with Marc; I know I want to hurt him, badly, but what I've done isn't an exact science. If I'm lucky, he'll really suffer.

When Emily and I arrive back at the house, we say good night and head our separate ways. As I turn from her, make my way to the spare bedroom, I feel the press of her eyes in my back. Her suspicion follows me all the way inside until I close the door. Still, I know that, whatever happens, she can't make trouble for me. Because if I was at the scene of the crime, then she was, too. And I've no qualms about letting her know that if things become complicated for me, they'll become complicated for both of us.

Chapter 30

Now

James's grip is tight on the steering wheel. Mine is tight on my phone.

I still haven't heard any more from Claire, despite all the messages I've sent her.

Tell me you wouldn't do this to me

I'll never forgive this

This feels worse than what any of them have ever done

Please tell me I'm wrong. Maybe there's an explanation?

It's a warm evening, the car air-con on full blast. I'm not sure if I'm ready to face Will, the wet rag of Claire's betrayal wrapped tightly around my face, stymieing my breath, obscuring all my senses. But I am ready to end one of my nightmares if I can. The blackmail can finally stop. There's a literal bittersweetness beneath my tongue at that thought. It reminds me of the gentle sweetness that floods my mouth before I'm violently sick.

And I do feel sick. I should feel boundless relief, freedom and joy. But my sister's duplicity sits heavy on my shoulders. This silence, her inability to offer me the smallest relief or explanation, is slowly killing me. There's a sheen of sweat on my forehead; my fingertips tingle; my chest is tight. I thought it was the hot air, but despite the arctic blast pumping out of the air vents, I still can't breathe.

'Air' is all I say, jamming a finger down on a button that sends my window sliding open.

James glances at me, looks back at the road, then glances again. Things are a little strained between us. I've apologized a hundred times for the lies. But somehow, now, he seems even more on edge around me than before.

'You okay?' he asks.

Yes. No. Maybe. 'I'm just . . . It's a lot.'

He nods, eyes on the road and hands tighter on the wheel. I'm still a little drunk from all the Picpoul, which hasn't helped. And now, even the gaping window, fresh air beating my face, isn't helping. I wonder if I really might throw up.

'Are you okay?' I ask.

A bewildered look flashes across his face. 'Of course. Why wouldn't I be?' He shuffles in his seat. The car picks up speed. The set of James's shoulders is casual, and his face is ostensibly . . . well, if determined, still relatively relaxed. And yet there's an energy radiating off him that makes me uncomfortable. There's been something unfailingly artificial in every smile, reassuring hug and enthusiastic comment he's made to me since hearing the news this evening. I'm too tipsy to untangle it, and even sober, I'm not sure how much easier it would be. James is good at keeping a lid on his emotions.

We take a few sharp turns, and I can't help but feel we're hurtling towards an inevitability. As if the very thought has conjured her like a malignant spirit, my phone starts buzzing. A blank circle, photo long since deleted, but name clear: Melissa Doe. For the first time in years, I'm less conflicted about picking up the phone and speaking to her. After all, it's the poison she's tried to feed me about Claire that's driven us apart. More than the psychological warfare, more than never being enough for her.

I notice James notice my screen, but he knows me well enough not to bother to ask about it.

Deep, even breaths.

My finger hovers over the green answer button. James is doing his best to focus on the road, but I can feel him watching what's happening out of the corner of his eye. I hit the answer button. His jaw drops open.

'Mother.'

There's a faint, rasping breath, and then sobbing. Wild, unburdened sobbing.

The car speeds along the road, wind whipping my face. For the first time, I wonder what's prompting this call. The thundering wind doesn't leave much space for my mother's reply, but even beneath the roar I can tell that there is only silence on the other end of the line.

'Did you know?' I ask. 'I was talking to my therapist today, and she asked me some questions that . . . that got me thinking. About my exes. About what happened to them. Claire.' A wail on the other end of the line. 'Did you know?'

'Oh, my baby, my baby . . .' More crying. It is painful to hear. My mother is a woman who's suffered a lot. She's spent her life meting that suffering back out little by little as if she can give it away. As if it doesn't just multiply.

'Mum,' I try again. 'Mum, did you know the truth? About what Claire did? And I don't just mean George. I'm talking about Marc and Luca, too.'

'Oh, my baby . . .' She is choking. The words sound stuck in her throat. 'My baby, I should have told you it's not your fault. None of it.'

So she knew. She knew. And her confession makes this all real, thoughts sliding from strong suspicion to concrete fact. 'How could you not tell me? How could you let me live thinking —'

217

'Baby, you don't understand –'

My own throat is swelling with everything I want to say, that I can't say. 'Mum . . .' I'm dismayed to find tears gathering in my eyes. I take the sleeve of my shirt and drag it across my face. 'You could have . . . have –'

'How? I only –'

'I'm sorry. I thought I could do this, but I can't.' A furtive glance at James. 'This has really messed with my head, you know that? This whole time you've let me – no – *made* me feel like a stain. Like an evil –'

'Baby –'

'Goodbye, Mother.'

The line goes dead. I'm all too aware of the proximity of James's body to mine as he changes gears. He says nothing for a moment as I try to figure out if I can somehow recover my dignity, having just stripped bare in front of him. I close my eyes. Deep, even breaths. I count to ten. Feel a hand on my thigh, squeezing. It makes me want to cry more.

'I'm okay,' I say. James's thin-lipped smile tells me he knows it's not true. So we're both lying to each other now. Wonderful. I want to open my mouth to have it out with him. This idea of starting with a clean slate, this chance he says we've been given, it doesn't work if we're still lying to each other. But I want him to talk first.

Before I can raise the challenge, I see we're curving onto a residential street. The GPS is telling us we've reached our destination. It's time.

'Are you sure this is a good idea? Confronting him tonight?' I ask.

'Yeah. I want this over with.'

The car comes to a stop. There is only one light on upstairs in the detached house. It's very late. The kids will be asleep.

I wonder if Vanessa is letting Will sleep in their marital bed or if he's bunked up in the spare room.

A click echoes through the now deathly quiet car as James unbuckles his seat belt.

'Maybe you wait here, Nat. This is . . . I mean I . . .' He looks out the car window, breathes heavily, looks back at me. 'I've let you down a lot recently. The money, talking to Will in the first place . . . And right now you're going through a lot. I mean, even just now with your mum . . . I know you won't want to talk about it, but – I just . . . I think I should handle this.'

I reach out to take his hand. He squeezes our palms together.

'We're in this together,' I say, my stomach still secretly turning somersaults. Why did I drink so much wine?

'I promise I'll be okay. It's just . . . This is my brother. I think this is something I need to handle myself.'

I nod and squeeze my eyes shut, trying to push out the hundred other thoughts fighting for attention. I am not my best self right now. My sense of self, in fact, is on incredibly shaky ground. A strong gust of wind could blow it away.

'Okay,' I say.

'Okay.'

He leans over, takes me by the face and kisses me hard.

'Okay,' he says again, more to himself this time. With one final deep breath, he pushes open the car door and steps into the night. I watch him as he goes, chest puffed up, taking big steps. It makes me want to cry. He looks so much like a child like this. Like a little boy going to confront his bullies. Or maybe I'm just projecting. I was always so scared as a child. Of my dad, of my mother, of myself . . . Of everything, really. I know sham bravery when I see it. But it's time James finally learned how to stand up to his big brother. He's right.

Lights flicker on behind the windows downstairs and the door swings open. To my surprise, it's not Will's figure I see in the door, but the figure of a diminutive woman in her late forties instead, blonde hair swept up into a bun and a robe clinging to her body. Vanessa. I can just about see her look past James into the soundless street. James casts a look over his shoulder in turn, settling on me in the car.

After another moment, Vanessa steps aside, and James is absorbed by the house. I close my eyes once more, try to will myself into feeling less nauseous; try to push aside the feelings of deep betrayal; try to focus on one nightmare coming to an end, James snatching Will's leverage away from him, maybe even getting some of our money back.

Despite how it feels, despite the chasm of despair opening beneath me, threatening to suck me in, today has been a good day.

It has been a good day.

It's a good day.

Somewhere, a bird chirps in a tree. I wonder if it's an owl, this time of night. I've never really known much about nature in detail. I wonder if any future children of mine might take an interest. Would they want to go camping? James would make a great camping dad. I wonder if I'm even fit for having them at all. I wonder if it's stupid even thinking about them.

So much for distracting myself with a light bit of fantasizing.

My phone buzzes and it's my mother again. I want to pick up, embrace her, forgive her, but our relationship feels rotten beyond repair. If there's any chance of our building bridges, I can't yet see it, and I need time to figure out if I want to. I decline the call and block her number. I think about calling Claire again and then don't. This is all too much.

With nothing to pass the time, my mind races. I play over the conversations I've had with my sister over the years, try to spot warning signs, things I've missed. I'm meant to be observant, aren't I? But as hard as I try, I can't figure out how I could have seen this coming. My sister, the actress. She had me well and truly fooled.

When I begin to tire of this, I finally notice how much time has passed. Twenty minutes. Really? How long does it take to tell your brother, *By the way, my wife's not perpetrated violent crimes, so you've not got a leg to stand on; the letters won't hold up. She's innocent and you've got to leave us alone.*

My nerves begin to clamber on top of each other, at first a scattered pile, now building into a mountain. Another ten minutes tick by, and then another ten. My eyes scan the windows, looking for figures, signs of life. This might all still be okay. Perhaps it's gone better than we thought. James said Will had the decency to look guilty when he first asked for the money, although I find it hard to imagine that. Perhaps he's thrown himself at James's feet, is begging for forgiveness. Perhaps.

My fingers are itching towards the door handle when the front door flies open. Will is pelting towards the car at full speed, face flushed by a wild madness. James is hot on his heels. James lunges, yanks Will backwards with a handful of Will's faded T-shirt. Vanessa runs after them, screaming.

'For god's sake, stop! Both of you, stop!'

Will frees himself, spins to shove at James. Punches him once in the chest. James staggers, recovers. He gets his hands around Will's neck, and it's like he's trying to choke his brother to the ground.

I'm out of the car. One hand rests on the roof while I hover behind the door, unmoving. The metal is cold beneath my palm, reminding me that this is real, but the night air is still warm, stuffy. Stifling, even.

'James!' I shout. To stop him? Perhaps. To check to see if this is really my calm, smiling husband? More likely.

It's impossible for him not to have heard me in the deathly quiet of this suburban street, but he doesn't even offer me a fleeting look, his eyes fixed on the brother in front of him. Eyes full of a fury I've never known him to be capable of.

Will's eyes are burning just as brightly. They rage with the desperation of a man willing to do anything to come out on top. To confirm my fears, he spits in James's face, which contorts with disgust. James recoils, rubs at the wet flecks with his jumper. Will lurches back, freed from his grip. Before James can recover, Will shoves him hard, sending him tumbling to the ground. And Will is on him, taking James's shoulders and slamming him against the grass. His head bounces in a way that does not look good. This is enough to spur me into action, finally. I begin to run.

But now the pair are tumbling again, and James has mounted his brother; he has the upper hand. My feet freeze as James makes a fist and swings. Hard. I'm not sure if I'm imagining it, flashbacks forcing their way to the forefront of my mind, the loud den of violence my childhood home too often became flickering in and out of view, but a loud crack splits the night in two.

'James!' I shout, and I hear Vanessa's voice join mine.

He swings again. Will's head snaps viciously to one side. Another swing. A crack. A swing. Will's arms reach up, feeble, fingers slipping over James's face. Swing.

The wine in my stomach curdles. I clap a hand to my mouth, remove it to shout once more. 'James!'

'No! Go back to bed. Daddy's okay. Don't look.'

I look. Two small figures are hunched in the doorway, Vanessa curving over their small bodies protectively. No. No more.

I find the ability to move again. And not just move —
sprint. I'm upon James as he draws his fist back again. His
knuckles are slippery with blood. My arms are not as strong
as his, but I wrap both of them around his swinging arm and
dig my heels in, thighs screaming as my whole body fights
to stop his.

'Enough,' I say. 'Please. Please, enough.'

His eyes. He looks like a man who's dreamed himself
naked on a stage, only to open his eyes and discover it's
not just a dream. He looks at me, hair fallen out of its wax-
streaked structure and into his eyes. He looks at his fist,
bloody and balled up with anger. He looks to the house, sees
his nephew and niece crying, shivering beneath a mother
who looks just as scared.

He looks back at me. My voice is surer than I feel this
time. 'Please. Enough.'

He nods, a shell-shocked expression on his face. It wears
him, not the other way around. Wears him as I feel his violence has, eating away at him and leaving an impression of
my husband behind, his ghost, only. He lets me take his
hand, Will gurgling beneath him.

We near the car and his eyes still hold a vacant look.
Empty, like they're clutching on to the emptiness.

'I . . . I'll drive,' I say. I'm not a good driver. Never have
been. Or, at least, I've never enjoyed it. But I'm competent
enough, and in his state it's clear that James isn't.

He fishes in his pocket for his keys. Still zombie-like, he
slips them into my palm. Red transfers onto my fingers and
I gag. I try to stop it, but my stomach has had enough, this is
all too much, and the wine finally splatters onto the ground,
glossing the tarmac.

This seems to stir James and he wakes. He takes me in,
legs shaking, hands unsteady. He tenderly slips the keys back

out of my palm as if my hand is a broken bird cradling them for warmth.

'It's okay,' he says. It's not. 'I'm okay.'

Life seems to be returning to him. Letting him take control seems the safest option.

We clamber back into the car. As we pull away, I try not to see Vanessa over Will's still body, not to see her frantic on the phone, calling for help, her daughter running out against instructions.

There's nothing easy I can say, and so for a while, as I rack my brains to figure out what could possibly have happened, I am quiet. James is somehow quieter, his eyes on the road, his mind clearly elsewhere. Eventually, I muster up the courage to ask.

'What happened?'

A flash of . . . What is it? Anxiety?

'I told him everything and it didn't matter.' The car meanders along. The night is empty. We are alone here.

'What do you mean?'

'I mean he said he has copies of the letters and that nothing has changed. That whatever you thought you did is obviously serious. The letters sound like confessions, and he could still make the police believe that you attacked George. Still put you away. And that now he knows you're all bark and no bite, he knows he can destroy us.'

My nausea returns tenfold. This is all too much.

'You didn't tell him anything, did you? About Claire? About George being dead?'

He shakes his head. 'No, I'm not a total idiot. I made the mistake of running my mouth to him once; I won't do it again.'

I run my tongue between the grooves of my teeth and then over the points of my incisors. 'He wouldn't try to get me arrested. Not knowing I'm innocent.'

'He made it perfectly clear that he could and he would.'

The air is slapping me now. It stings. I roll the window up and shut it out – this is not what I need right now. What I need is an escape route out of this burning building.

I try to ignore the talon gently scratching at the pane of my churning thoughts. It tells me that despite what I know, despite my innocence, perhaps things would be better if Will never gets up from that grassy lawn. That maybe, just maybe, things would still be better if Will was dead.

Chapter 31

Then

Claire

A little guilt creeps in as I watch the distance blossom between Emily and my sister after Luca. I think even Emily's nerves of steel waver at the thought of her best friend's sister being a murderer, of Emily herself being an accomplice in some small way. I guess that's why she slunk off the morning Luca died, the morning of her best friend's birthday, without so much as a goodbye. But whenever that guilt flares up, I simply think of Natalie showing me Luca's group chats the next day as we sipped our mimosas, of her guiltily confessing her relief that he's gone between mouthfuls of eggs, and it all feels worth it.

So I know from the moment I see my sister that George has to die. She hasn't told me much about their relationship, but it's been clear as our torrent of regular phone calls dry into a drought that things aren't right. It's obvious that he's been slowly cutting her off, sealing her away from her friends and family brick by brick.

Change, after such a stretch of time, was inevitable in some way, but I'm still not prepared for how frail she looks. How much like our mum. The sight of her, shoulders curved downward, half hiding behind the door . . . It takes the wind out of me. I can barely speak, and I can tell that this makes her feel awkward as she ushers me in.

Awkward. Natty. It doesn't make sense. Even when she

was really small, when she hadn't quite understood how to make people like her, she was never uncomfortable. If anything, she was painfully comfortable in her own skin, in her solitude. Or, at least, that's how I remember it. And when she got it, when she understood that to make people like you, you have to lie, she was fine.

She seems to have a thinner memory of when we were really small, of nursery and home, than I do, despite being older. It struck me hard across the cheek when I once heard her refer to our childhood as 'generally happy'. The worst incident, the one that warned us that all we had was each other, she recalls. If a sanitized version. In her memory, our father's immediately contrite. In mine, after he'd beaten our mother and sent her flying down the stairs, I remember a strange performance of familial devotion. He was the great clown Pagliacci, invited to a funeral no one wanted him at, but that he felt a duty to bring healing to. Healing through warmth and laughter. He shook soft toys at a still-screaming me, pushed dolls into the hands of a still-screaming Nat, showered all three of us in frantic kisses too hard for our bruised bodies and feelings. Nat and I were hoisted back into our seats at the table, bowls of ice cream foisted upon us. Mother had a glass of wine pushed into her hands. She sipped it, eyes big and afraid as Dad dabbed at her cuts. Through it all, she looked like a cornered animal with a broken leg, folded in on herself, teeth bared. Her gaze tracked his every movement across the room, almost like she was waiting for the next attack.

I have a particular memory of a weekend afternoon with our dad. At least, I assume it was a weekend. I just know that it was sunny, and we went out to the florist's together, so it couldn't have been a workday. I remember Dad making a show of buying a nice bouquet for Mum, waxing on to the florist about how she just deserved a little treat. It wasn't their anniversary or her birthday or anything.

I remember it wasn't the first time he'd done this. It was a little pilgrimage we made every other weekend, until he could only afford to shell out for particularly bad fuckups. He'd do his little dance, and the florist would be all smiles. As part of the dance, he'd always pick the prettiest flower out of the bouquet and pop it behind the florist's ear. She'd almost lose her head giggling at that, every time. He'd disappear into the back of the shop for a while and leave me on a stool, teddy bear clutched in my hands and on my lap a book I couldn't read.

The florist would usually keep me company. Read a bit. Make silly faces. One time, she told me she'd 'just be a minute', needed the loo. While she was gone, a little old lady came in.

'Are you okay, love? Where are the grown-ups?'

I wasn't supposed to talk to strangers – the florist didn't count, as we had seen each other so many times – so I just stared at the lady with big eyes. There was some noise coming from the back room – quiet scuffling and gentle knocking. The old lady took matters into her own hands and crept over to see what was what. I remember the sound of a woman shrieking, how quickly the lady came shuffling out, my dad's face red, voice bellowing, spittle flying.

It's obvious to me now that my dad was having an affair. Not with the florist, who never went into that back room when Dad was there, but with someone the florist liked well enough, or who paid her well enough, to help keep the affair a secret. But I didn't understand any of this at the time. All I knew is that my dad would go to buy these flowers, be showered with praise by the florist, by our neighbours when they saw him bringing them home. People loved him. *She's so lucky to have you!* they'd say. I guess they didn't know how to spot bruises on dark skin. Not that Dad often hit her where people could see anyway.

When Dad got home, he'd slap the flowers down on the dining table and promptly forget about them. He didn't even hand them to Mum.

And there you have it. My first lesson that pretending to be what you're not could work wonders for you. I wondered how much of this Dad had learned from his own parents, but his choice of family was too different for their taste, and so I never met them to find out. Their loss.

The baffling thing about pretending is how easy it is. That's the scary thing about it, too. I'm so comfortable playing pretend that when I pushed Marc off that rooftop, when I could see that Natalie couldn't remember what had happened, that it was eating her up inside, I just kept on pretending. Pretending I had no idea, either.

I know I must confess the truth to Natalie. And not only because Emily is also on the way over and I haven't seen her since Luca. I've no idea what she might say. But it's clear as Nat's words tumble out of her mouth that she's taking on guilt that doesn't belong to her. That I've taken my secrets too far.

Still, I want to enjoy this – us – for as long as possible before it might be lost to me for ever.

This is the thought still at the forefront of my mind when the keys start jangling in the front door. I see how big and scared my sister's eyes immediately go, see her shrink in on herself, and my fury spikes, so that when George enters the kitchen and starts provoking Natalie with mean-spirited questions, I've no interest in playing nice. I hate him for how he's chipped away at her confidence, her support network, without her even noticing. How it's been a slow erosion on the coastal line of her life, over time leaving a barren island behind.

Part of me knows that I've made her this way. That silently standing guard, dealing with her problems, has smoothed away her edges. That acting as her armour has allowed her to shed her exoskeleton, leaving her fleshy softness alarmingly vulnerable when I'm not around. A fury simmers in me at that thought, fury at myself for weakening her, and fury at her for being so weak. But as the conversation with George continues, I see something shift in her, shoulder blades drawing together, spine straightening, breastbone rising, proud.

Angry words are exchanged.

Natalie slaps George hard across the cheek.

George lunges.

I block.

I'm on the floor, pain exploding through my head.

Natalie is up, reaching for the knife.

George is fast. His fist connects with the side of her face. The knife falls. She falls.

But I'm ready. My head is aching, a piercing pain splitting my skull, but my fury makes me fast. And the last thing George will see is my face as I sink the knife into his soft chest.

Chapter 32

Now

Dimple

So, this is awkward. Unmistakably, undeniably, teeth-clenchingly painful. The receptionist is looking at me like I'm a piece of gum she's had to scrape off her shoe. After the scene I caused last time, I'm not surprised. The other therapist in this office has clearly also come to the desk with a query but has stopped to watch the wreckage of whatever this is. Both were an unwilling audience to my performance the other day, vile words ricocheting around what is meant to be a calm and safe space.

'I'm sorry,' I say for the fourteenth time. 'It's just, if – if there's any kind of gap in her schedule today, I'd really like to apologize in person.'

I've taken the day off work. Used my married-to-the-boss privileges to pull a no-questions-asked sickie; I might as well use them for as long as he can still stand to have me working with him. James and I didn't say much to each other last night when we got home. Haven't said much to each other this morning, either. It feels like the next words I say to him will be very important, and I don't know how to choose them. What happened last night was beyond my comprehension. Yesterday felt like a collapsing domino line of bad news, and now I'm crushed under the weight of it all.

But I don't need to be a victim of my circumstances. I can take some power back. First, by righting the wrong of my misplaced anger. Dimple didn't deserve my vitriol. And it's not like me to care what people think unless I can use it in some way. But Dimple's different. I care a lot.

The secretary taps her fingernails against the desk, fires some characters into her computer, then looks back at me. 'I'm sorry. If you'd like to call to schedule an additional appointment, we can arrange a time for you at a later date.'

My automatic response sits sourly on my tongue, waiting. My mouth twists around its lemon sharpness and swallows it. Now isn't the time for acerbic retorts.

'Really, I know I was a mess yesterday evening, and once more, you have my deepest apologies for the scene I caused. If Dimple's diary is fully blocked out, I totally understand, but if she has a spare slot and is willing to see me, I'd gladly pay to take it just so that I can deliver my apology in person.'

The other therapist, pinned-up greying hair and loose shawl, is pursing her lips at me. I fear I'm making yet another scene.

'Actually, never mind,' I say, cursing this car crash of an idea. 'It's fine. Again, I'm so sorry for yesterday, and sorry to have disturbed you this morning. I'll just—'

The phone on the receptionist's desk rings once, twice. She picks up the receiver. As I turn away, I notice a curious look settling on her features. She flashes her eyes up at me.

'Are you sure?' she asks. A pause. 'Okay. Fine, I'll send her in.'

My heart lifts.

'You're in luck. Dr Das has had a cancellation this morning. She'll see you now.'

I don't need to perform my gratitude; it's an immediate huge weight off my shoulders. 'Thank you so much.'

I'm walking to Dimple's door when she opens it. She looks elegant in her at once soft, loose and structured clothing.

Her hand beckons me in, but the set of her jaw is tight, face pinched. It's anything but welcoming. I can't blame her.

'Come in,' she says.

'Thank you.'

The door clicks shut as I make my way to my usual seat. It all feels oddly formal. I watch Dimple take hers, a deep breath directed at her lap. She looks up at me and adjusts her glasses.

'How can I help you today?'

I'm sure I'm not imagining the absence of warmth in her words. It had felt like we were on the same team before, but now it's like I've broken something between us.

'I won't take up too much of your time. I just wanted to apologize . . . For yesterday, I mean.'

Her face is remarkably still. I can tell she is working hard to remain a blank canvas. I wonder how much strain it's causing her.

'Really,' I continue. 'I'm so sorry. I can't even remember everything I said, but I should never have raised my voice at you, never have caused a scene. Not only was it entirely inappropriate, but it was unfair. You were just trying to help. You've always just been trying to help.'

Dimple's face remains a smooth mask. 'Why do you think you reacted so strongly in our last session?'

Formal, emotionless. I suppose that's fair. She's here to do a job. 'I suppose . . . I suppose my relationship with my sister is precious to me. I've lost a lot in my life, been hurt a lot. She's the only person who's consistently been good to me, and . . . and I guess it felt a little like you were trying to take her away.' Dimple remains unmoved. 'But that's not to excuse my actions. Really. I know you say my feelings are valid, but I also know I don't get to act any which way because of them. I should have known better. I'm sorry.'

She nods once, a half smile on her face. Well, I call it a 'half smile' – it's more a British tightening of one corner of her mouth. But it's better than nothing. 'Thank you. I accept your apology.'

Relief floods me for the second time that morning. 'Thank you. I'm glad.' I scan the room, rub my legs. 'That was it, I guess. I don't want to take up any more of your time. But like I said to Sarah outside, you can bill me for the full hour.'

I'm already out of the seat when Dimple speaks. 'If you're paying for the full hour, you might as well stay.'

This catches me by surprise. It's not remotely in my plan. Get in, apologize, get out. Stew in inner turmoil. That's the deal I've made with myself.

'Well?' Dimple asks, gesturing to the seat.

I sit. I always do what Dimple tells me to do. Or, at least, I feel that way. 'Well, what do you want to talk about?' I ask.

'I'm curious as to how you're processing what I raised at the end of our last session. You had an initial reaction, which you've apologized for, but how are you feeling now?'

My tongue prods around my gums. I'm not sure where to start.

'I'm not sure where to start.'

Dimple narrows her eyes, offers her familiar head tilt and then says, 'Do you still feel directly responsible for what happened to your exes?'

Pride blocks my airway. It stings to admit the answer, but I cough it out nonetheless. 'No. I don't. I . . . My mother . . . I . . . We spoke. Briefly. It's obvious that she knew all along. I suppose I can't blame her for not knowing that I blamed myself for all of it. But if she'd just told me the truth . . .' I lean forward, elbows on knees, palms against closed eyes, pushing down until it starts to hurt and patterns spark across the darkness.

'So you saw your mother?'

I shake my head. 'No, we spoke on the phone.' The pain in the darkness begins to intensify.

'Natalie.'

I take my hands away and sit up straight. Dimple remains unreadable. 'So, to be clear, you do believe it was your sister who was responsible for what happened to Marc, Luca and George?'

I nod. 'I'm not sure how, but yes.'

'And how does this news about Claire make you feel?'

I suck air into my lungs and blow it out, chest heavy. 'Beyond the crushing betrayal, I feel relief, I suppose, but . . .'

Dimple waits for me to fill the opened space with words. She's good at waiting, but today, it seems she'd prefer not to. 'But what?' she pushes me on.

'But I thought I'd feel more different, knowing I'm not a killer. And yet . . . I don't know. Should my impulses, these dark thoughts, should they have gone? Because I'm not sure that they completely have. And if they haven't, then what exactly is it that's wrong with me?'

Chapter 33

Now

At home, I try to keep my mind occupied as I wait for James to come back. I watch TikToks of people pretending to be happy, but they make me sad. I watch some of people who are genuinely happy, and I feel worse. I take myself for a restorative walk, as that's something people do, isn't it? But this town is a leafy kind of dead. I realize I hate it. With no chance of starting a family on the horizon, giving up London for its green barrenness feels like a sin. A cookie from a corner shop does little to lift my mood. I struggle to understand why I thought it would. And then I see her. The blur of a woman in a greedily large hoodie, wild dark curls pushing out of the hood. I catch a flash of brown skin and a blink of bright yellow from the back of her Doc Martens as she disappears down a side street. And it's not just the outfit lifted from her uni days; the too-speedy smudge of her features looked just like her. Claire. It's too much. Too much a reminder of how much I miss her and how much I now hate that I do. I return home. Pick my phone up time and time again, start trying to call Claire and stop. I want to scream at her until I'm hoarse. Want to tell her about James. Want to hear her beg for forgiveness. That I can't see a way to work through the betrayal leaves me feeling wrung out like a wet rag.

I wish I could say that I'm not dreading my husband walking through the door, but this morning was tense and uncomfortable. I'd almost convinced myself to have it out with him while brushing my teeth, but by the time I'd left the bathroom, he'd gone. No goodbye kiss.

Not long after my fourth attempt at reading something and my second glass of wine, I hear the sound of the keys in the door and straighten. For a moment, I think about discarding the wine glass. It's becoming a habit, and I don't want James to think I have a problem. But also, if I am developing a problem, probably good to have someone to hold me to account. When I start hiding the bottles, I'm already a lost cause. He materializes in the kitchen doorway, handsome as ever, but face taut. I'm not sure if it's his day at work or the prospect of this conversation stretching his nerves thin.

'Hi,' I say.

'Hi,' he replies. 'People were asking after you in the office.' A beat. 'I told them you're okay.'

It's awkward. I know it's awkward. He knows it, too. But so much has happened between us that I don't know how it couldn't be. He tells me that Will's recovering fine. They've not spoken, but Vanessa accepted a call from James to check in. Black eye, broken nose. Looked worse than it was. He reassures me that his violence was a one-off. I reassure him that I believe him. I apologize again for lying about George. He reassures me that he understands. Neither of us seems convinced by the words tumbling out of the other's mouth.

When we go to bed that night, I curl up on the far side of the bed. I'm not sure what else to do with myself. And when I feel him move up beside me, pulling my back into his warm body, for a moment I consider telling him to move away. But I feel his regret, feel my own and hold his hand in mine. I think he's preparing to let himself fall asleep when breath fogs warm on my ear.

'I can get the money. I've got some stuff from my father

that I think I can . . . I mean, I know it has value. We'll be okay.' A beat. 'And I'm sorry things have been so shit, Nat.'

'It's okay.' I want it so badly to be true.

In the morning, I'm almost convinced that things might not turn out totally horribly, that James and I will find a way. After all, it seems that perhaps we're just as damaged as each other. It's this thought that allows me to head into the office, fire off emails through the workday, contribute to meetings, act like a fully functioning member of my team, the threat of Will still present, but a bearable heat on my skin.

But when I get home, stepping into the lightly jasmine-scented air, my foot finds itself treading on a crisp white envelope. It stops me in my tracks. Turning the cold paper over in my hands, I can see it's been sent by priority mail. I also see my name hand-printed in clear letters above the address. It's not a bill or junk mail. This is something important.

Taking care not to slice my finger open on the paper, I rip the envelope open and pull the contents out. Staring boldly at me are words I recognize all too well.

I hate how much your opinion of me made up my opinion of myself. I hate that I ever let anyone ever have that much control over my self-esteem.

My letter to Marc. Or a photocopy of it, at least. And on the next page, my letter to Luca. And on the next, my letter to George. It only takes me a second to connect the dots. Motherfucker.

The feeling is stronger when it comes again this time, and unlike the last, it doesn't take me by surprise. Will is fucking with me. He's taunting us. Wasn't it enough to steal the money? Wasn't it enough to worm his way back into the business? Did he think he could really send me to prison for something I didn't do, too?

He might feel safe in the knowledge that, in the past, my sister has fought my battles for me. Might make the mistake of thinking of me as powerless, someone he can walk all over. But I'm not the girl I was back then. Not powerless, just patient. Patient enough to get rid of him properly.

Chapter 34

Now

There was a profound powerlessness I felt with Marc, with Luca, even with George. I don't want to let myself feel powerless again. And so this is how I find myself pulling my second sickie of the week, trailing Will on a Friday morning.

He always goes to the gym on weekdays. A quick scroll on his socials gave me a good idea of which one, provided he hasn't changed subscriptions in the last six months. I try not to tally how much of our money he could have paid back if he simply adjusted his lifestyle; I need a level head if I'm going to avoid being caught.

I'm currently staked out in the car, tucked away on a side street opposite the gym, waiting for him to appear. I'm not entirely sure exactly what it is I hope to see today, but I need to understand Will better before I make any moves. And nobody is more themselves than when they don't know they're being watched.

Eventually, Will strolls out through the gates, sweat drenched. I must admit that he doesn't look as bad as I was expecting. I'm not sure if it's my callousness that makes me think that, or the memory of his unmoving face and James's bloodstained shirt. His eye has a few purple marks around it and looks the slightest bit swollen. His nose is much the same on the bridge. Otherwise, he looks okay, expression suspiciously sunshiny on a newly ruggedly handsome face. I suppose extortion puts one in a good mood.

I watch as Will disappears into the nearby car park, turning my engine on. When I notice his car pull out, I slip out into the road, too, relieved that there aren't too many cars between us when I join the main street. After about ten minutes, he stops. I panic a little but manage to find another side street to turn into with a space near the junction. I want to be able to see what he's doing.

It soon becomes clear that he's stopped for a pick-me-up, hopping into a café. I can't see what's happening in great detail, but it looks like there's a woman at the front of the queue flapping. She's rifling in her bag, looking up at the barista, and then rifling again. Her hand gestures grow increasingly large as she dips in and out of the bag. I can see her head sink and her body begin to turn towards the entrance when Will darts forward. I see him slip a hand into a jacket pocket. Some passers-by obscure my line of sight, but the next thing I know, the woman is walking away, a to-go cup in her hand and a smile on her face. She keeps touching a hand to her chest and waving at Will as she goes.

This act of charity grates against my perception of James's older brother. The gesture seems nice. Selfless, even. Although perhaps he feels he can afford it when he's stealing our money.

I'm preparing to pull back into the road when Will exits, but he surprises me by walking past his car and continuing up the street. I think about it for a split second and then throw caution to the wind, hopping out of my own car and pelting down the pavement to join the high street. I can only hope that Will doesn't choose to turn around. After only a minute or so, he makes an abrupt left turn into a shop. I look up. The chemist. A visit for something mundane or something more interesting? Pushing my luck, I creep towards the windows of the shop and watch him approach the pharmacy counter. It's not a huge revelation, but for now, it's enough. I file this stop-off away in my memory and return to the car.

The next few minutes are more confusing than ever. I assume he'll be heading home to shower, but I know where his home with Vanessa is, and it's not where he's driving. When he pulls into a quiet residential street, I make a point of finding a space as close to the turning as possible, hoping he hasn't stopped close enough to spot me. It's a relief when I can see him several houses down: small, but discernible. What is he doing here? Is it a secret family? An affair?

He rummages in his gym bag, pats his pockets.

He takes a moment to lift the corner of a hanging plant and unearths something. He opens the front door.

Aha.

So Vanessa has finally kicked him out, has she? I wouldn't blame her if this week's display of violence was the final straw. It's what a good mother would do. It's what I'd do. Protect my children first and foremost.

The adventure is already growing dull, but I haven't seen quite enough yet. And so I wait. And after a painstaking hour, he leaves. This time, there's a car waiting in the middle of the road for him. A Prius. A Bolt or an Uber, then.

It's harder to follow him this time. The streets are quieter here, and so I need to leave a bigger gap between us. But eventually, I manage to follow him to a pub. It's relatively unremarkable, nestled on the high street. It's a little early in the day for drinking, but it's a sunny Friday and it already looks relatively busy. Perfect. Risky, but perfect.

There's a small charity shop a few doors down. I buy myself a satin scarf and a new jacket, ignoring the musty smell shrouding both. With the scarf tied around my head and the dark green trench coat wrapped around my body, I look a little silly, but I hope a passing glance would spare me recognition with distance and dim enough lighting.

When I enter, I'm delighted to see that it's even busier than I expected. God bless the British and our sunny Friday afternoons. I order myself a lager and look for where Will has settled. When I spot him, hunched over a beer in a corner, for a split second I fear he's seen me. But his eyes are glazed over, staring into nothing.

I find myself a seat not too far from his table, sufficiently tucked into its own nook. It's easy to watch him from here. And I watch him sink two, three, four pints. Alone. All while I sip my one. Over the course of my stalking, I have to admit my voyeurism loses its shine. What I'm watching is an unmistakably sad man. An unmistakably sad, lonely and depressed man. It's easy to see how James felt sorry for him in this moment. As he laps at his fifth pint, a little spilling onto his T-shirt, he looks so pathetic, so woefully without hope, that I almost want to cry.

There's no pleasure to be had in what I'm doing any more. Watching Will feels like watching those videos circulating on social media of vulnerable people having cameras shoved in their faces for laughs. I recently saw one of a drone repeatedly knocking into a homeless woman's head. It's incomprehensible cruelty. I take my phone out and take a subtle snap of him. Considering he's promised to stop drinking to get back into the business, it could come in handy.

I push my hardly touched pint away from me and rise to leave, the hops still bitter at the back of my mouth. For now, I've seen enough.

Chapter 35

Now

Sifting through my feelings about Will is a challenge. The sharp anger is undeniably still there, but he doesn't feel like someone who deserves to have his life cut short. The man I saw today was capable of kindness, more pathetic than anything else, and yet he'd still conspired to make my life a living nightmare.

My mind shifts back to my exes. With my hands washed half-clean of Luca's blood I find myself able to acknowledge that he could be capable of kindness, too. He was cruel, sure. But his cruelty was born of carelessness. Just a cocky boy who thought he could rule the world. And who did, I think, know how to love with that defective heart of his, until it stopped beating. A needle of grief pricks my own at that thought, catching me off guard. I can't take on any more complicated feelings without collapsing, so I swat it away.

I'm still trying to arrange my feelings into a picture that makes sense when I arrive home. James is already here, appearing in the living room doorway.

'Where have you been?' he asks. There's an unfamiliar note of accusation in his voice.

'Just out,' I reply.

'Natalie . . .' A clear warning.

'Okay, just hear me out,' I say, setting my bag down in the hallway. How do I start? 'Come on, let's sit down.'

He's clearly on edge as he follows me to the sofa, nostrils

flared, mouth tight. It's so unfamiliar, so off-putting, that I can't ignore it.

'What's got into you?' I ask.

'I thought you were going to start explaining yourself.'

'Jesus, James. I'm back an hour later than usual. It's not like I've disappeared for days on end.'

'Well, were you in the office today? We both know I was out with clients, but where were you?'

Admitting I wasn't there feels like losing the argument we're suddenly having.

James keeps going. 'You might not care about your career enough to take it seriously' – *ouch* – 'but you can't just pull vanishing acts. Do I need to embarrass you by reminding you that I own the business, and people tell me what's going on? Particularly if they're concerned that the office manager, who is also my PA, who is also *my* wife, has gone AWOL. They worry. You're making them worry about you. Besides, you wouldn't have driven to the office, and you clearly took the car. So where were you?'

'Okay, babe, can we please calm down a little, and I'll explain.' I can almost hear his teeth grinding. 'I was with Will.'

His eyes darken. 'You were what?'

'Okay, not *with* Will. I was following him.'

Confusion flares up on his forehead and camps there. The frustration is still present, but it seems lighter than it was a moment before. 'What do you mean?'

'I mean I was following him.' It's silly of me to be this glib, but I'm not sure how else to deliver the news. 'Look, I just . . . I just wanted to see if I could get a better sense of why he's doing this to us.'

'So you stalked him? Nat, I surely don't have to tell you how irresponsible that is.'

'He didn't see me.'

The innocent act doesn't seem to be working, because James is now on his feet, pacing the living room. 'Jesus Christ, Nat. I thought we were done with the crazy. You're officially not a violent psychopath. Great! Fan-fucking-tastic news. But now you're stalking people?'

I'm more than a little put out. 'Person.'

He stops in his tracks. 'What?'

'Person. I'm only stalking the one person. And it was only a one-time thing.'

He looks at me, incredulous. 'My god, Natalie. What is wrong with you?'

This one cuts deep. He watches me recoil as if he's physically struck me. It almost hurts just as much. I don't know what to say to him, so instead I bring my knees up to my chest and hug them. He's soon beside me, arm around my shoulders.

'Sorry.'

'No, I'm –'

'No, I wasn't thinking. I didn't mean it. I'm sorry.'

'No, you're right. I'm not normal.' I wish I was, but I don't think I know how to be.

James plants a kiss on my head, holds me tighter. We search for what to say next. He gets there first.

'So what did you see, exactly?' he asks.

I pull away so that I can look at him properly. 'What do you mean?'

'Well, you spent the day following my brother. What did you see?'

I pick at a bit of loose skin on my thumb. I like that it hurts. 'Not much. Gym, coffee shop, chemist. But, James, before he went to the pub –'

'Wait – he's still drinking?'

'Yeah, I took a photo. In case you need to fob him off a while longer about starting to work again.'

He half smiles, covering his mouth with a hand. 'Don't take me smiling as encouragement.' I do anyway, and he knows it. 'This is useful. He's broken our terms. I'll figure out a way to deal with it without incriminating you, but that's it. He's not coming back.'

'There's more. He went to the pharmacy section of the chemist. Does he take medication for anything?'

James stops, thinks. 'Well, he struggles with anxiety some-times, I guess. He's got a prescription. Valium, I think.'

'Oh.'

I try to keep my face passive, try not to show how I'm storing this piece of information away.

'And is that it?'

'No. I think Vanessa's kicked him out. He's not staying in the family house any more.'

'Probably serves him right.'

'Probably.' I take James's free hand, squeeze it. 'I have to admit, he didn't look like such a threat to me, just watch-ing him on his own. He's a sad and desperate man. Is there nothing the two of you can do to fix your relationship? This can't just be about the money.'

'After everything with Claire . . . do you reckon you can fix that?'

'Claire's not here. It's not the same. Isn't there anyth—'

James lets go of my hand and looks away. 'No. It's too late.'

In the distance of his gaze is a solid resoluteness that tells me, family or no, once James is done, he's done for good. It scares me a little. How close am I to crossing a line I can't come back from?

'What do we do?' I ask.

'I've checked – I'll have enough, from selling some cuff-links and a few other things my dad gave me, to make the fifteen thousand. It means . . . It means clearing out the savings we've been trying to rebuild, but I should be able to settle with Will within the week.'

Another setback.

'What if he asks for more?'

'I don't know.'

We become two playhouse dolls, silent and still on the sofa. James stirs first.

'It would give me peace of mind if we could start sharing our location with each other,' he says. 'It's easy enough to do on Maps. And before you start' – he's right; I was about to start – 'I know I say couples who do that are insecure, but Will's making these threats and . . . and . . .' And there's a lot he's not saying. 'Please?'

Protests wither in my mouth before they have a chance to sprout. I know what he's thinking. That I'm reckless and need minding. That I'm not the tough fighter we thought I was and I need protection. He's not entirely wrong.

'Okay,' I acquiesce. 'But how do we stop him from holding this over our heads for the rest of our lives?'

He pinches the bridge of his nose. I realize, with horror, that tears are building. 'Nat, I don't know. Short of him drinking himself into an early grave, I don't see how this ever ends.'

Chapter 36

Now

Dimple

It's a murky sky outside this evening, already darkening into a depressed grey. I have been working up courage for today's session. I'm not afraid, exactly, but I know that what I have to say is a Big Deal, and I've no idea how Dimple will receive it.

I'm trailing my fingers up and down the velvety armrests of the chair where I'm sitting, waiting for her to speak.

'It's nice to see you today,' she says. 'How have things been since last week?'

'Much the same,' I reply.

She hitches up an eyebrow in question. *Anything else?* This time, I don't indulge her.

'Last we spoke, you were concerned about your ongoing anger. How have you been finding the meditation exercises we went through?'

Perhaps they'd be plenty useful if I was using them, but alas, I am not.

'They're great. Thank you.' I clear my throat; I need to lie better. Lying is something I'm usually good at, but lying to Dimple is not something I usually do. This muscle is weak, untested. I must do better. 'I mean, it's not a fix, but it helps when I can feel my temper flaring.'

Dimple adjusts slightly in her seat, jaw jostling from side to side in contemplation. If I was trying to avoid triggering her bullshit radar, I've failed.

'Tell me, has your temper been flaring often over the past couple of days?'

Sort of. Not really. When I think of Will hunched over his pints in the pub, there's no anger there. But when I think of Claire, the void of answers from her, the way her secrets have ruined my life . . . When I think of Will's blackmail, the greed, the desperate hole he's left James and me in, I'm so furious I can barely see. James is right. The only way out Will's left for us is if he ends up six feet under, and it's only when I'm at my most angry that this even feels possible.

'I'm fine.'

Dimple closes her notebook and sets it aside. 'Your answers seem guarded today. Why might that be?'

It's annoying how transparent I am in this room. Yes, my answers are guarded, because she can't know what I plan to do. I'm not about to sit in front of her and detail my plans for murder. I take a moment to make sure I'm composed, making a show of picking at some fluff on my shirtsleeve.

'To be honest, Dimple, I think our sessions might just be coming to a natural end.'

Her surprise is fired across the room in a rapid series of blinks. 'You're saying you'd like to end our sessions?'

'Yes. Don't get me wrong – you've definitely helped me. More than you could ever know. Talking through my urges, my relationships . . . Helping me understand myself better. And, of course, now we know I'm not a psycho killer, there's a less pressing need for me to keep coming.'

Dimple shifts in her seat, more dramatically this time. Her fingers flex out and in on her knees. She shifts position again. 'I'm not entirely sure we've really unpacked what this revelation means. You have indeed done a lot of excellent work in this room, but in my professional opinion, there is still more work for you to do.'

She's probably right, but whatever help I need, I can no longer get from her. This has to end soon, before I say something stupid and get myself caught planning to hurt Will. That, she'll have to report immediately.

'I appreciate that, Dimple. Really, I do. But a huge reason I started coming here was thinking I was hurting people. I thought I'd hurt my exes, worried I'd one day hurt someone else. But I don't have to worry about that any more. And with everything with Will . . . We need to be careful with money right now.' I shrug, displaying an Oscar-worthy composition of contrition.

'It's true, therapy isn't inexpensive, but I do believe there is still important work for us to do here.'

'Dimple, I —'

'What about George?'

I'm stopped in my tracks. 'What do you mean?'

'Whether you landed the fatal blow or not, you still reached for the knife.'

I can hear muffled voices outside Dimple's door. My skirt is itchy beneath my thighs. There's a loose thread hanging off Dimple's sleeve. My skin begins to prickle with heat, that familiar nausea setting my mouth swimming with saliva again.

'I guess that's true. But wouldn't anyone in that scenario? It was self-defence.'

'And your mother. You've spoken for the first time in years, and we've hardly discussed it. How do you feel about that?'

'I don't know. I'm conflicted, I gue—'

'And what will you do the next time she calls?'

'I'm not sure. But I have her number blocked.'

'And what about Claire?'

'What about her?'

'Well, how do you plan to process this betrayal?'

'Okay, Jesus!' My hand flings out emphatically, making

contact with the water glass on the table beside me. It topples over to the floor, spilling its guts out into a darkening wet patch on the carpet. 'Shit. I'm sorry.' I drop to my knees, retrieving the glass. I grab the box of tissues that had stood next to it, frantic, and use the sheets to mop up the liquid. 'Shit.'

Silent as a cat, Dimple is suddenly beside me, hands gently taking the glass and tissues away. It's rare that we're this close, her perfume stronger than I've smelled it before. It's a little sweet and musky, vanilla and sandalwood, I think. She gently rests one hand on mine.

'Relax, Natalie. It's just water.'

I'm not sure she's ever touched me before. It's so unexpected and electrifying that it feels like perhaps it's not allowed. She removes her hand and rises, placing the tissues and empty glass at a safe distance on her desk. The skin on the back of my hand now feels cold.

'It's just a little water,' she reiterates as we both take our seats again.

'Sorry. Yes, you're right.' About everything. I hate that she's always right about everything. 'Look, maybe you have a point. Perhaps I could come for a few more sessions and we can check in on where I'm at in a few weeks' time.'

Dimple gives an acquiescent nod. 'That seems like a plan to me. And how about next time you're here we talk a little more about what happened with your sister all those years ago? The Big Fallout. I think it would be useful for us to revisit that together.'

'Okay.'

A look that's meant to be reassuring. 'Okay. So for now, let's talk a bit more about your anger.'

I grit my teeth and prepare to try my hardest not to fall into any more traps. But I have to wonder if I've already been caught.

Chapter 37

Now

Although things between James and me have thawed, they remain a little awkward. Now, more than ever, he seems to not want me around. At the same time, I find myself yearning for him a little more now that my connection with my sister has been severed, a void of affection to fill. She's never been the one to initiate a call, but now I can't call her, either. I've been blocked.

Over the past couple of days, James has insisted that, while things are stressful, I elect to work from home. But working in the office is a nice distraction from everything else happening in my life. Here, there is order, and if and when there's chaos, the stakes are so low that it's easy to keep a cool head about it. People seem to think I've attained some guru level of inner peace, but the truth is that I simply don't care enough about work problems to go into a panic about them. And so, for the past few weeks, the office has been a strange haven.

I'm returning from my lunch break today, earbuds pushed in as deep as they'll go, Euro rock blasting on loud. It's not my usual music of choice, but of late, I've found angry screaming soothing. It's nice to hear from people who seem more enraged with the world than I am. It's nice to take these lunchtime walks, inhale some not-quite-fresh but at least outside air. It's easy in the gaps between task seven and task eight on the to-do list to clear my mind, take in the people pounding the pavement, the old buildings, the secret alleyways, the tiny hidden parks.

The lifts are half-broken again today, and so those of us who have braved them, packed in shoulder to shoulder, must wait at each floor for the doors to close before jabbing the next floor choice repeatedly until the button sticks. By the time I get to the fifth floor, a little of my lunchtime Zen has been eroded, but not enough to stop me from looking forward to blasting through the next five or so hours of tasks. It feels good to get this done.

Most of the team is still at lunch, but Molly is back, eyes focused on her screen. She glances up as I shrug off my bag and jacket. There's a scrutiny in her expression I'm not used to, eyes tracking me as I sit.

'Good lunch?' I ask with a brightness I don't feel.

She nods, the false sunshine in my voice not banishing the shadow that undercuts hers as she says, 'Will called for you.'

My mouth goes dry, tongue sticking to my teeth even as I say, 'Oh yeah?', with an easiness even faker than my smile.

I realize too late that her scrutiny is naked suspicion. I wonder if this is how Mad Mary felt when the tide began to turn against her in the office: afraid. Wonder if people have already started to align my increasingly erratic behaviour with hers.

'Yeah, you were out, so I answered the office phone for you,' Molly says.

I want to point out that she's not answering the phone for me – anyone can answer; it's just that most people in the office are too lazy to, and I always seem to be first to cave. But now doesn't feel like the best time to debate the issue.

'He said your time's up.' She continues. 'What does that mean?'

Play it cavalier, cool as a cucumber. 'Oh god. I have no idea.' A look of fear I don't have to fake.

Molly is fast to pounce on it. 'What?'

I shake my head. 'I shouldn't say anything. It's just that . . .' A dramatic look into the distance and a flicker of reluctance back her way.

She's all in now, swivelling to face me in her chair and leaning forwards. 'What?'

'Well, James said he'd been drinking again . . .' A pause for added drama. 'I didn't realize how bad it must be, but this . . .'

Molly nods, sombre. It seems like she's genuinely onside now. 'Christ. He did sound off, now you mention it.'

The tempo of my pounding pulse slows even as my thoughts race. It must be about the money. Although James said he was handling that. Perhaps he gave Will more than just the cash. Told him he knew about the drinking. Told him he can't come back to the business. Did James give away that I'm the one who caught Will in the act?

I punch my log-in details into the computer and try to look normal. But then Molly pipes up again.

'I noticed that in the pigeonhole for you, by the way.'

Confusion clouds my mind for a moment, but then I spot it. There's a gleaming white envelope, almost blending in with the polished white desk. My name is clearly written on the front of the envelope, our company address beneath it. I take my seat and pick up the post. The all-too-familiar scrawl glares at me. I'm already holding my breath, but when I slip my finger under the folded corner, when I slip out the first sheet of paper, my heart stops.

In the end, my humiliation was so complete that I died a little before you did. And I wish I could say that when I heard you were dead, I was sorry.

'Anything interesting?' Molly asks.

Panic and fury flare in my chest. I fold up the contents.

'No, just . . .' I rack my brain for something she won't want to see. She's unendingly curious. 'Just an overdue invoice from one of the freelancers.'

'Oh! Printed? Old-school. Which one?'

For god's sake.

'Jess Williams.'

She wrinkles her nose. 'Oh god.'

And that's the end of that, at least, her attention firmly on her screen again. I turn to my own, forcing myself to wait a couple of minutes before slipping the letter into my bag in a way that I hope is surreptitious. The rest of the afternoon is ruined, my thoughts preoccupied with Will. From my desk, I can see into James's office, see him hunched over his computer. I want him to look up, try to catch my eye like he used to when we'd just started connecting. I want him to notice something's wrong, pull me into a conference room, pull me into a hug, tell me everything's going to be okay. But he's more distant from me than he's ever been.

As for Will, proving he had copies by sending them to my home was one thing, but calling up the office? Sending copies here? That's unconscionable. Even for him. It's clear he's trying to scare me, but all he's succeeded in doing is firing me up. This simply can't continue.

The rational part of my brain advises caution, wants me to think things through. But I'm tired of thinking and waiting. Tired of hoping James will somehow fix things.

I quietly slip away from my desk, phone in hand. Outside, I dial James's number once. No answer. I try again. More of the same. On the third attempt, he picks up.

'Is everything okay? I'm about to go into a meeting, so if it can –'

'I'm outside. Can you spare five minutes to just come talk to me?'

'Nat . . .'

'Please.'

'This meeting's important. If anyone else in the office asked, I'd give them the same answer. I promised no special treatment.'

'James, I'm your wife.'

'Nat, please. Can you just tell me what it is?'

I'm frustrated, but James's unwavering sense of fairness is not going to let him budge on this.

'He's sent copies of the letters to the office.'

A beat. 'What?'

'Will. And he called. I came back from lunch and . . . Jesus, James, he bloody called the office phone and Molly picked up. He told her my time's up, whatever that means. Has something happened? Why is he doing this?'

'Shit.'

That's a 'shit' pregnant with meaning.

'What is it, James?'

He's silent.

'James!'

'God, I didn't think he would – Bloody hell.'

'James.' A 'James' pregnant with warning.

'I sent him the money, but I was a little short. Just a few hundred pounds.'

'James . . .'

His voice is pained. 'I know.'

'And you didn't think to tell me?'

'I'm sorry. I just didn't think it was enough for him to be unhappy about it. I'd obviously tried.'

'So this is him retaliating, then? This is a nightmare. At least for now, no one's seen the contents of the envelope.

And I think I managed to fob Molly off with a story about Will drinking. I'm okay.'

'Thank god.'

'Look, we can talk about this later. I've got to get back to my desk and you've got your meeting.'

'Oka—'

I'm quick with my next line. 'Actually, I'll be back a little late. I think I need to take myself off for a massage, maybe even a film or something on the way home. My mind's racing. It will make me feel better.'

I almost feel guilty for lying to him. Almost.

'Sure, whatever you need to do.' A beat. 'I love you.'

'I love you, too.'

The hours ticking down to home time stretch longer than ever. I'm usually one of the last to leave, but today I'm the first, bolting out of my seat as soon as the clock strikes five. I notice Molly's eyebrows shoot up as I shoot out. A question that approximates concern for my well-being chases me through the dusty office air as I race toward the exit.

Outside, my fingers jab at my phone screen as I pace along the pavement. I need to know how to get to Will's new place without my car. An ugly idea is forming, half-baked but there. It relies on a lot of luck – more than I should be comfortable with – but I'm determined to make this work for me.

Before I know it, I'm out of the city and into the suburbs, knee almost tired from all the jostling it's been doing while I've been sitting on the train. It's only as I near Will's street that anxiety begins to peek over the ledge of my anger. I'm very exposed here. If he's out anywhere, I'm easy to spot outside the confines of my car. This is blatantly stupid. I wonder if Claire was as reckless as this, or whether she enacted her plans with more meticulousness and attention to detail. I wonder if I'll ever know.

The anxiety is a very real knot in my stomach as I turn onto Will's new street. It feels like everything in my life hinges on what I'm about to do. But at least this particular nightmare will have found a conclusion. At least I'll be able to wake from it.

As I creep closer to the terraced house, I can see that the lights are off, ostensibly no one home. This offers some relief, but I wouldn't put it past Will to be passed out inside somewhere, having started his day with a pint of Guinness. All the same, I can't afford to dawdle; I don't know what kind of curtain twitchers live on this street, but a Black person lingering outside a house too long means police getting called. On this occasion, they'd be right about my being up to no good. All the more reason to avoid them making an appearance.

Step one, slip fingers into plant pot. I'm relieved to find the spare keys still there.

Step two, unlock the door and go inside.

Inside, it smells a little like Luca's old uni house. Stale. There's a faint whiff of cigarettes, unwashed laundry and festering bins. The living room is immediately on my right and I poke my nose inside. There are clothes, plates and other crockery strewn around, take-out containers still on the coffee table. Propped up on the windowsill is a photo, frameless. Will's little boy and girl. Through an archway is the small kitchen, dirty crockery crowding the surfaces, rubbish spilling out of the overflowing bin. It's a depressed man's kitchen if ever I saw one. A flicker of sympathy threatens to flare into life, but I snuff it out.

I back out of the living area and into the micro hallway. It's a small, square patch of carpet that immediately leads to a narrow staircase. Upstairs is also empty, which is good news. A quick look shows me there's a good-sized bedroom and one bathroom. That's the lot. I imagine what I need will be in the latter and so brave re-entering.

And, yes, I mean 'brave'. The room is almost entirely beige, but I can tell that the tiles, the toilet, the bathtub, should be white. I shudder at the thought of the thin layer of grime covering everything. My eyes lock onto the bathroom cabinet. A couple of steps forward and I'm there. I prise the door open and peek inside. I can immediately see what I'm looking for in two small cardboard boxes. The Valium.

I flip the flaps of the boxes up and slip the contents into my palm for a check. A smile cracks across my face. It's like he wants to make this easy for me. As with everything else in his life, his blister sheets are a mess. The pills seem to have been taken sporadically across the packs, a couple of sheets still full, but most with at least one pill missing. It will be easy to slip out a few more without raising too much suspicion.

Eenie, meenie, minie, moe. I choose fourteen pills at random, popping them into my hand. I hope it's enough to knock him out, and not so much he'll notice their absence. Done, I replace the packs in the cabinet and close the door. I may need to wash them first, but there should be some spoons in the kitchen that I can use to crush up the pills. And then all I need to do is find the whisky. If there's a lot in the bottle, I'll pour some out first, swill the powder around in it, and then let nature take its course. I just have to hope that, without his wife to clean the tub, he'll still love his bathtime whisky enough to enjoy this indulgence here, despite the grime.

It's the perfect plan. Well, perhaps 'perfect' is stretching it, but it's something, and that's enough to make the weight on my shoulders feel a little lighter. I'm doing it. I'm succeeding where James has failed. Where I've failed before, leaving Claire to swoop in for me. I'm taking control of my own destiny for once – who needs my traitorous sister to rescue me? All I need to do is sort out the whisky, leave and wait.

There's practically a spring in my step as I descend the staircase. This couldn't be going more perfectly. Will really thought he did something with that nasty little phone call, but he's only sealed his demise. I'm sure James will mourn him for a while, but even he knows that we're better off with Will dead. And it will be hard for Will's kids at first, but they're better off without the poison influence of a dad like that, too. Life is really going to be so much better for ev—

The front door swings open. I'm still sandwiched by the narrow staircase walls, feet almost at the base of the stairs. In fact, I'm so near the entrance that when, Will blunders into the house, it feels like we're nose to nose. There's no hiding, nowhere to turn. His eyes immediately land on my frozen figure.

'What the hell are you doing here?'

Chapter 38

Now

My mouth is dry, the pills suddenly growing claggy in sweat-slick hands. I am thoroughly screwed.

'I –'

Will's eyes go wide; his mouth gapes. 'Oh god. Oh god, oh god.'

'Hi,' I say. I can't seem to think of anything else. Fuck's sake. My brain is meant to operate better than this.

Will starts to back away slowly, then all of a sudden breaks into a run back into the evening. I don't understand it but I take off after him, hot on his heels. I catch the back of his jacket at the gate. He spins, takes hold of my shoulders and throws me to the paved ground.

While I'm still righting myself, Will turns again and dashes into the house. I hear the lock click. He obviously hasn't thought this through. How does he think I managed to get into the house in the first place? With a roll of my eyes, I stroll up to the door, scrape the pills into my pocket and fish the keys out. A twist in the lock and I'm back inside, careful to close the door behind me. I just hope we haven't yet caught the attention of the neighbours. Will is standing in the living room, panicked to see me here, eyes darting from side to side as if they might find a new, magical escape.

'Stay away from me!' he shouts.

'Will –'

I take two steps forward into the room. He's dashing into the kitchen. Next thing I know, he's hovering in the archway, a big knife in his hands. His weight is on his toes, ready to spring into action. I don't come any closer.

'Stay away from me!' he says again.

'Stay away from you?' I hiss, acid fizzing in my voice. 'Stay away from you? I'm only here because you won't stay away from me. From me and James. All we want is to be left alone.'

Will's voice is indignant, knife waving as he speaks. 'What the hell are you talking about? I haven't once shown up at your home. Not once! So I don't know what you think gives you the right to break into mine. Because that's what this is, by the way – breaking and entering.'

My anger emboldens me, and I take a step forwards.

'I said stay back! How did you get keys to this place anyway?'

'The plant pot isn't the most original hiding place, Will.' His brow folds in on itself, face sour with grudging admission. 'But that's beside the point. I wouldn't be here if it wasn't for your threats. You're making our lives a misery.'

'Are you mad? You're the one threatening me. And that's why you're here, isn't it? You're here to kill me.'

This stops me.

'Hang on a second. What do you mean I'm threatening you? You're the one who's been sending copies of the letters to my home, calling up the office with vague threats.'

The knife lowers a fraction in his hand. 'I've never called you at the office.' Molly's words echo in my ears. *He did sound off, now you mention it.* 'And the letters? You mean the ones you wrote to the exes you did god knows what to, you total psychopath? Why the hell would I do that?'

I've always thought of Will as a good liar, but I never thought of him as this good. 'Because James was a few miserly pounds short on the payment.'

The knife drops to his side. 'What payment?'

Everything seems to freeze in the room while we try to slot things into place in our minds. We are looking at each other, reflections of anger and confusion on our faces. Our understanding of what's going on is worlds apart.

'You . . . you emailed James a couple of weeks ago, asking for more money.'

'No, I didn't.'

'I saw it.'

'But that's impossible. And stupid. Why would I provoke you when I know what I know? I'm not trying to get myself put in hospital, or worse.'

'But James told you the other night . . .' I can hear the conviction leaving my voice as I speak. 'He told you what we found out. I – I didn't hurt anyone. Not like I thought I did anyway. I'm innocent.'

'Wait. What? Then how –'

'It's complicated. I used to . . . I used to find a lot of comfort in alcohol and pills, like you. My memory wasn't . . . Short answer is I put two and two together and got five.'

Will shakes his head. 'You're lying.'

I spread my palms. 'I'm not. It's the truth.'

The knife thuds to the coarse carpet. Will staggers over to the shiny black leather of the sofa and collapses, his head in his hands. 'I don't understand.'

I walk, zombie-like, to the armchair a couple of feet away on the other side of the archway, kicking the knife back into the kitchen as I sit down. 'To be honest with you, Will, I don't, either. A couple of weeks ago, when we came to your house . . . James told you I was innocent, that you didn't have any leverage any more. That's why you fought, right? You said you could stitch me up for what happened to my exes anyway, using the letters.'

He looks up, brows furrowed. 'James came over that night

to tell me he'd changed his mind about the deal we made for me to come back to work. Said I should forget about it. Not contact either of you again. He promised that if I pushed him, if I went to the police, you'd shut me up for good.'

'So you *were* threatening me?'

'Not you. James.'

It's like someone's toppled the chair and I'm falling backwards, a violent drop in my belly.

'What?'

'I wasn't thinking about turning you in. Well, that's a lie – I'd considered it – but this was mostly about James. It's always been about James.'

'What about James?'

Horror and pity inch across his face until they're the only things I can see. 'You don't know?'

'Know what?'

'He told me you knew, told me you'd do anything to protect him. That's why he told me about your past. He wanted me to know you're dangerous, too. That you'd hurt me if I spoke.'

'Spoke about what?'

'The girl he killed.'

Chapter 39

Then

James

She's pretty. It was the first thing I noticed about her when Will and I held her interview, and the thing that's clearest to me now as I watch her flap at the oil spill of water on her table. It's not very progressive to say this about her, but it's true. I'm gearing up to do some light admin on a bench across from her. I don't mind it. Someone needs to be online today, and I'm not going to ask any of our hires to work. In theory, Will could also do it, but as he's explained on his way out, he's got kids to panic-buy stocking fillers for and a rare catch-up with friends after. I still remember how Will and I used to sneak downstairs on Christmas Eve after our parents were asleep. Will would tear the corners off our presents to get glimpses of what was beneath, get me to guess what was coming before it came. It was the world's greatest guessing game, even if it did our parents' heads in.

In truth, I've been working my way up to saying hello to Nat for some time now. I caught a glimpse of her as Will and I emerged from our meeting with the bar owner, although she didn't seem to see me.

Part of my reluctance to say hello is I can't trust that Will, despite all his promises, won't try it on with her. He's already a couple of pints deep. But now that this water fiasco is happening, now that Will is excusing himself, it feels like the right time to say hi.

So I do. And before long, we're sitting together, drinks flowing. When she says she didn't expect to see me here, I want to challenge it – I know she's able to access my work calendar – but I don't want to spoil the mood by becoming the interrogating boss. This light banter is better than going back to the blue glare of my laptop screen.

The conversation is easy, easier than I'm used to. She's fun, no showboating, no expectations of me picking up the bill, although I'm the managing director and, obviously, I do. And when I ask about her family, when she skirts around the pain I can see she's buried in her past, I feel a kinship in our secret keeping and a thrill in having sniffed out another loner. I'm so totally charmed by her that I regret having to leave.

We exchange personal numbers, and buoyed on by the festive spirit or the literal spirits, I almost kiss her. And as I observe the gentle disappointment in her eyes as she leaves, I realize she wanted me to. This solidifies my suspicion that she was lying when she said she wasn't expecting to find me here. And while this engineered run-in would alarm most, I have to admit that it makes me feel seen. Chosen. And I find myself still thinking about our not-kiss, what her lips would have felt like, when I get to my car.

I felt a little bad lying about Will being the designated driver, but I'm good at holding my drink and driving when I need to. It's Will who's always been the lightweight. He stayed in town to join me for this meeting, Vanessa and the kids heading down to our parents' first. Fair play to him; I'm the one that accepted a Christmas Eve meeting, so I don't mind doing the drive.

It doesn't take me too long to source a double espresso to shake off a little of the drowsiness of the alcohol. As expected, Will is half-cut when I collect him, but his loud obnoxiousness is of use for once, keeping me on edge, alert, as we wind through the already midnight-dark streets. I manage to snake the car out of the city and over the motorways without incident. I relax a little as we enter quieter country roads. And then the deer leaps across my path.

'Christ! Look out!' Will roars.

I slam on the brakes. The car skids to a stop. The deer glibly prances out of sight. Will and I pant out heavy breaths, the panic slowly leaving our bodies. The car crawls for the rest of the journey, but at least we arrive without incident.

Our mother must have heard the crunch of tyres on gravel, as the front door flings open before we come close to knocking.

'Will!' she says, bright smile.

He knocks my shoulder as he barrels past me, sweeping her up into a hug in the yellow glow of the doorway. She's so busy drowning him in kisses that I have to announce myself more than once.

'Hi, Mum,' I say again.

Will casts a smug look over his shoulder, our mother still trapped in his arms. 'Looks like little Edie wants some attention.'

She registers me this time, unpeels her face from Will's chest, and looks up at me as if waking from a dream.

'Oh, James.' Her tone is warm, but the energy has dropped. She steps back to allow Will into the house and then pats my cheek once he's out of the way. 'Welcome home, darling.'

It's as good as I can expect to get.

Once Will and I have dumped our bags in our rooms, we're ushered to the dining room, where our mother serves up plates of pasta to everyone. Dad is in a good mood, occupied by his grandkids flitting about the table. Another point in Will's column tallying up to his title of 'favourite son'. But as the wine flows, I find myself in a good mood of my own. Find myself thinking about Natalie.

When everyone else has gone to bed and it's just Will and me, Will fishes out a bottle of Dad's good whisky and we sit by the fire in the living room. Steadily sipping in quiet contemplation all night, I'm already more drunk than I have been in a while. Will is prattling on about some inconsequential drama with his friends. Tommy sleeping with his nanny. Or maybe it's Guy and his secretary. Something equally cliché with someone equally unremarkable. I can't help myself. I find myself wanting to talk about the dark eyes that won't leave my mind.

'What do you think of Natalie?'

Will stops in his tracks, eyebrows scrunching in question. 'Natalie as in Natalie from the office?'

'Yeah.'

He takes a sip of his drink. His right ankle is resting on his left knee. The foot begins to shake.

'Nice arse, nice face. Bit flat-chested for my taste.'

I laugh. Good. She's not for him. Not this time. 'That's not what I meant. It's . . . She was in the bar earlier. Where we had our meeting.'

His foot stops shaking. 'Oh yeah. What was she doing there?'

Curiosity and caution creep over his expression. I'm reluctant to say more, and bursting to tell someone at the same time. It's stupid. It wasn't even a real date. But something is telling me that I've just connected with someone special. 'I'm not a hundred per cent sure. She was sketchy on the details. But I . . . I think she knew I'd be there. Wanted to see me.'

Will's nose wrinkles in distaste and I fear I've made a mistake. 'What? Like a stalker?'

I try to shrug away the tension I feel crawling up my neck. 'Yeah. I guess. But isn't that kind of . . . I dunno. Nice? To care that much, I mean.'

A gentle click sings through the room as Will places his glass down on the coffee table. The crackle of the fireplace fills our moment of silence.

'I know I keep telling you to get back out there, but I think you can do a bit better than a bunny boiler who's essentially your assistant. It's been years since you've seen anyone seriously. Why her?'

Because she's choosing me. Because in a world where even my own family chooses me last, Natalie's choosing me. And I tell Will as much. Drain my glass, refill it as he stares at me, bewildered.

'James, what the hell are you talking about? We don't choose you last. You're not chosen last. You're Mr Perfect. I mea—'

'Sure, I'm Mr Perfect, but everyone loves you more. Our mother certainly does. Everyone at work, too, despite you doing absolutely nothing –'

'Now, hang on a minute.'

'Even my girlfriends always eyefucked you.'

Somewhere over the course of the conversation, my mood has turned sour. I hate that my jealousy exists, rears its head like this. Its very existence in the face of Will's calm seems to be confirmation that somehow, my fuck-up brother *is* better than me.

Right now, he's staring at me, incredulous. He's stopped drinking, which is saying something, but I continue to swallow big mouthfuls, hoping they'll erase the memory of my embarrassing myself like this.

'James, you've lost your head. None of your girlfriends hav—'

'*All* of them have.'

'*All* of them? Really? What about the girl you dated at sch—'

'She was the worst of them.'

His voice drops a scale. 'That's not nice, James. She was sweet. I liked her.'

'Yeah, I know you did.'

'And a bit low to speak ill of the dead.'

'If she wasn't such a bitch, then maybe she'd still be alive.'

Even in my drunken stupor, I know I've said too much. I freeze. We both do.

'You what?' he asks.

'Nothing,' I mutter.

'What did you mean by that?'

'Nothing. I was just talking.'

'Because when we were out in Corfu . . . that was an accident.'

'I know.'

'You said it was an accident.'

I've had enough. 'You don't believe that. None of you do. You've always blamed me for what happened, even though I was only eighteen. You think I don't know? You think I can't feel it in the way Mum and Dad treat me? In the way you look at me sometimes? In the end, what does it matter if she was pushed or if she fell?'

When it comes, his voice is barely a whisper. 'James . . . James, I don't . . . If you're saying what I think you're saying . . .' He gulps a big mouthful of air and seems to find it's not enough. Gulps again. 'Christ, why the fuck would you . . . Tell me you're joking.'

I simply pick up my drink and glower into the flames. It's all the admission he needs.

And then my world is spinning. My brain catches up

to what's happening as the pain begins to blossom on my cheek. I'm staring at the wooden beams of our living room ceiling. The heat from the fireplace is close to my face. Will towers above me, shaking with rage, fists clenching and unclenching.

'Tell me you didn't do it.'

Even if I could, it's too late. I just stare at him, feeling the shame lurching over me just as large and looming as my brother. His fist crashes into my mouth. It floods with blood.

I'm glad. Glad for this small moment of punishment, of his disgust, his violence. It's not even a fraction of what I deserve. And that feeling of release, of guilt, of relief at telling someone, anyone, overwhelms me. The tears are upon me before I can stop them, and suddenly, I'm a grown man crying open-mouthed on the floor.

'I didn't mean to do it. I promise. We were just – We started arguing, and she slapped me. Then she shoved at me, so I shoved at her. She lost her footing. I did'n—' My voice gets caught on the sob building at the back of my throat. 'I didn't mean for her to fall like that. I didn't want her to die. God, I loved her so much, I . . .' I can't say any more.

Will's hand is drawn back, hovering over my face. Muscles twitch with the agony of holding themselves where they are instead of leaping down to beat me again.

'Why would you tell me something like this? I can't . . . What the hell am I meant to do with this?'

I spit blood onto the tiles by the fireplace. 'You learn to live with it. Like I have.'

Blood flees his face, giving him the pallor of a dead man. Fitting. Because I'd sooner he die than let people know what I've done.

Chapter 40

Now

'Are you okay?' Will asks.

What a stupid fucking question. What a stupid fucking idiot. Me, that is. Not Will. I want to stand up, crack a window for fresh air, but standing feels like risking a fall, and my pride is already dented enough – my body doesn't need to take a ding, too. Somehow, despite telling myself I was choosing better, despite the seemingly infinite time spent in therapy to make me choose better, have I chosen another man just like my dad? Worse?

'Is all of this true?' I ask.

'I don't think I'm capable of this elaborate a lie.'

'Me neither.'

'I'll pretend it didn't hurt my feelings that you agreed so quickly.' He holds up a hand. 'Wait here a moment.'

Will disappears into the kitchen and reappears moments later with two glasses of water clutched in his hands. Even now, the life I know swirling down a drain I can't plug, I'm circumspect enough to eye the glasses with caution.

He sighs. 'They're clean.'

'Thank you.' And I mean it, too, a steady gratitude creeping over my body as I accept one. This may not have been the outcome I wanted or was expecting, but I'm glad that Will has been honest with me.

A beat.

'So on Christmas Eve, James confessed to you that he

killed his girlfriend. And you want to come clean to the police, but he doesn't.'

'That's right. I mean, I feel horrible about it. Her parents were trying to get the case reopened for years. Kept shelling out money they din't have on private investigators, the lot. And Chioma was always so nice to me, I –'

'Chioma?'

He pauses, puzzled. 'Yeah.'

At once, I can feel my head getting hot and my blood running cold. 'But that's a Nigerian name.'

Will only looks more confused. 'Yeah. She was.'

So I am not the first Black girl my husband has dated, despite everything he's said. 'Will, I'm going to need to know exactly what happened with Chioma, and why James refuses to talk about her.'

Chapter 41

Then

James

Some people have hazy memories of their childhood, brains wiping away and fogging up the past until it remains only a vague impression, brief flashes of clarity. It's not like that for me, my early years as sharp and clear in my mind as my adult life. In some ways, those early memories are clearer, purer.

It's because of this that I can't forget how potent my parents' indifference towards me has always been. Sure, I was the youngest son, and stories of spoiled youngest children would constantly be spilling out of people's mouths: friends, family, teachers. But it just wasn't my reality. I actually used to embarrass myself arguing about it in school.

Well, Mummy wanted one child and to be named partner at her firm, but instead she has two children and nothing interesting to say at dinner parties. We all do things we don't want to sometimes, darling. Eat your greens.

I was four when she said this to me. Shockingly, that knowledge of being unwanted has stuck.

Boys are cruel at the best of times, and the boys at my boarding school might have been even worse, so when I accidentally called one of our teachers – the hottest one – 'Mum' in the lunch hall when I was twelve, the already existing mummy issues I'd put on display made my life a living nightmare. One of the older boys overheard and nick-named me Little Edie after Oedipus. Few of the boys my

281

age knew the full origin story, but everyone knew that it meant I was a 'mummy-fucker', as it was so eloquently put.

It fucks up a boy's brain having the concept of fucking his mother become a constant throughout his day, Little Edie picking up steam as a name. And if that didn't suck enough, I'd then return home in the holidays paralysed by the need to spend time with my mother and the opposing need to not seem like a needy, mother-loving freak. To prove them all wrong. Because I wasn't Little Edie. Just James.

Whatever I wanted or was trying to do was irrelevant in the long run. My mother's indifference towards me was so violent that the more I pulled away, the more content with me she seemed.

It was with all this in mind that when I met Chioma in the leisure centre in the next town over, I was immediately drawn in. It was the summer I was fifteen. I'd been with Will at the time, his friends larking about doing laps while Chioma and her friends were practising handstands in the shallows. I was in the middle of a race, eyes blind to the gleaming legs stuck into the air with pointed feet.

The collision was slow but embarrassing all the same. I was ready for the angry words and mean looks. I'm some-one who was always in the way, it seemed, and here I was in the way again. But as I gabbled out an apology, she gave me a smile with kind eyes.

'It's okay,' she said.

We got chatting. She laughed at jokes I didn't know I was making. Laughed at my 'posh voice' but seemed to like it. When I told her things, she didn't immediately try to argue with me. Prove me wrong. It was easy as we bobbed around in the water. And although I noticed Will's friends elbow-ing one another and pointing our way, the creeping rash of embarrassment that started to rise over me was eventually transformed into something else.

'He's not bothering you, is he?' one of them said, splashing over.

'No.' Her voice was bright, beautiful.

'Because I can always get him to fall in line, you know,' he continued.

I then noticed how he was puffing his chest up. How he wanted to look important in front of her. And I looked at her again and took in how pretty she was. Fine braids, bright eyes, white smile. The boys didn't put up posters of girls who looked like her in the dorm rooms, but I could tell that they thought she was desirable.

'I can do a wicked handstand, you know,' he went on.

'Actually, we were kinda chatting if you don't mind,' she said. He looked confused. 'As in this is an "a" plus "b" conversation, so please "c" your way out of it.'

She crossed her arms and raised her brows at him expectantly. He muttered, slipped beneath the water, and slid away.

'God, I hate boys like that,' she said with an eye roll.

'Tell me about it,' I said, matching the roll and determined for her not to ever think of me as a 'boy like that', either.

Things with Chioma snowballed quickly after that. The texting was fun, even if a lot of phrases went over my head. And there was fresh attention in the school corridors. A lot of the questions were derisive, but a lot more were pure fascination. I'd hit it off with a pretty Black girl from the local comprehensive, and suddenly I was the most interesting boy in my year. Suddenly, I was no longer Little Edie or Eeds. I was James again.

The nature of my schooling meant I could only see Chioma in the holidays, but that was fine by me. People's interest in me tended to wane as soon as it waxed. Other boys at school, teachers, family friends, were used to my loud and gregarious older brother. Expected the same of me, only to find themselves rapidly disappointed.

A large and vocal part of me worried Chioma would eventually come to the same conclusion as everyone else. That I was a little boring. But with term time enforcing so much time apart, she never had the opportunity to get bored. A few days stolen together here or there felt special. So much so that our relationship lasted until we'd both graduated from our respective schools. She found me interesting, my Latin recitals impressive, my family home astonishing. I hadn't known how good it could feel to be admired. Hadn't known how a few superficial things could make me worthy in the eyes of someone as smart, as funny, as genuinely cool as she was. I wanted it to stay this way for ever. It triggered something unsavoury in me when other boys were too friendly with her, but she was always clear she only had eyes for me. Reassuring. I was fully out of my brother's shadow and in a spotlight of my own for once.

To celebrate our last summers at home before uni – me going to Exeter to study economics, and Chioma off to UCL to do medicine – my parents invited Chioma to join our family holiday to Corfu. They knew how cut up I was about our plans to land at the same university failing. I didn't get the grades for UCL, and Exeter had rejected Chioma for reasons she couldn't make sense of.

I could already feel the distance between us. And I mean that in a tangible way. We had months to go until we'd be so many miles apart, but I could feel her already withdrawing from me, our conversations shorter and farther apart. *Long-distance relationships at uni never work*, she started saying. I wanted us to be the exception.

It took three meetings with our parents for Chioma's mother and father to eventually agree to let her go on the holiday. It was one of those moments that reminded me of how culturally different we were. But once they gave their permission, we were so excited we could barely contain ourselves. I suppose we didn't know how badly things would work out.

The day that it happened, we were in our villa, enjoying a lazy morning. Will and Chioma were getting on like a house on fire. I didn't like it. I'd come downstairs in the morning to find them huddled together at the kitchen island, laughing around mouthfuls of muesli.

Maybe on balance, I'd been a bit naive about the whole holiday. Even with the trepidation of our impending distance cooling the relationship a little, being with Chioma still made me feel like a rock star. After almost two years of dating, my family, while friendly, hadn't made the effort to spend masses of time with her. I thought spending more quality time with someone so great who clearly thought I was worthy of adoration might get my family to start seeing me through Chioma's eyes. But all that happened is they found a new appreciation for how clever and smart she was. Fell more in love with her. Over humid lunches where we kids were allowed a little wine, Dad would crack jokes about what she was doing with me. Mom would sit beside her in the evening shade of the pergola, books splayed open on their laps, and later over dinner, they'd trade passionate whispers about what they'd read. And Will . . . They'd never spent a huge amount of time together before. I always thought he fell into the category of 'boys like that' in her eyes. But there could be an edge to their respective senses of humour that they'd found slotted well together.

On this morning, Will and Chioma were turned towards each other on their sun loungers, nattering away as I lay silently beside Chioma in the shade. It was too much sharing her with Will, of all people. Seeing her distracted by his dazzle. So I hatched a plan for us to have some time to ourselves. A couple of hours on the beach, just the two of us.

'Wait – you're not gonna take me with you?' Will asked.

Chioma threw me a *Well, shouldn't we?* look with her eyes. I threw a *Please let me have some alone time with my girlfriend* back at Will. He let it fall, uncaught, and waggled his brows at me.

'C'mon, you two lovebirds aren't gonna leave me alone with the old folk?' he asked with a wink. 'Besides, only I know how to get to that secret beach with the good diving rock. You got lost for an hour trying to look for it last year, James.'

'Oh, James, the pictures looked incredible!' Chioma says. 'Let's go there.'

And so the three of us went off.

When we came back, red-eyed and without Chioma, it was immediately obvious that something had gone horribly wrong. It's one of the only times I remember my mother's arms wrapped so tightly around me. And when I was able to find my voice, I told them all what had happened. How Chioma had drowned. How we couldn't save her.

The coastguard was called. The police, too. But after two weeks looking for her body, they gave up the search. It would have taken thousands that her parents didn't have to hire a commercial diving team to keep looking. Thousands my parents wouldn't give them, no matter how many times Chioma's mum showed up on our doorstep asking. That was when the restraining order was placed; they said it was about protecting me, but, really, they just wanted the problem to go away. If Chioma's mum stopped showing up, then people would eventually stop asking questions, and the shame of Chioma's untimely death on their watch would die along with her memory.

I don't think Chioma's parents have ever forgiven us – me – for what happened to their future doctor. They've certainly never forgotten.

Chapter 42

Now

The cogs are turning in my head as I sit in Will's living room trying to digest everything I've learned. I've been so relieved that James has never pushed to talk about the past that I've never questioned how that might be benefiting him, too. Will looks sheepish as he cradles his glass of water.

'So it wasn't, like, a murder? James isn't a murderer?' I ask. There are so many questions, but it feels like a good place to start.

Will shakes his head. 'No, it was genuinely an accident. And, I mean, she did hit him before he pushed her away. She wasn't meant to fall off the rock. I guess it'd be manslaughter, to put a definition on it.'

I bite my lip, try to keep my thoughts straight. Is this how James felt reading my letters? I feel like I've married a fraud. A stranger.

'And everything going on recently. The blackmail? Because you say you didn't go to James asking for more money recently, but I know our IVF money disappeared from our account and had to go *somewhere*.'

Will clears his throat, rolls his neck. 'I did take that money . . . but I didn't exactly ask for it. I'd been cracking for a while, saying we should go to the police. Help Chioma's parents find peace. The years of them trying to explain how their daughter who loved swimming would just drown destroyed them. Drove them mad. In the end, I heard from an old school friend that her dad turned to drink. Liver cancer. Not sure how long he's got left. The guilt of knowing the answer, of not letting Chioma's parents know, too . . . It was a lot.

'Then one day, James came to me bragging about what you were capable of, telling me I'd better keep in line or else. I made the point that it seemed like you both had a lot of secrets worth hiding, that you'd be smarter leaving me alone. He didn't like that. But then he started talking about the drinking, the gambling. He wanted to know how much of a hole I was in – just looking for a new angle, I guess – and when I told him, he offered the money to me to keep quiet.'

A lightning bolt of anger strikes me, so bright, it's blinding. 'He *offered* you the money?' Offered. Knowing it would stop us from moving forwards with starting a family. A careless move, or a calculated one?

Will's eyes are avoiding mine now, but I can see the shame in them nonetheless. 'I'm sorry. I was desperate.'

'But you asked for more money. James got an email . . .'

He looks back to me. 'I didn't ask for the money the first time, and I certainly haven't asked for any more. Did you see this email?'

I did, but I didn't interrogate the address of the sender. Has James employed one of the most basic scammer moves to deceive me? My silence says it all. The fight is fleeing my body. 'You had to know what that money meant to me.'

The carpet keeps an iron grip on his focus. 'I did. I do. I'm sorry. It's just . . . The only way I can numb the guilt of living with this secret is by making my way to the bottom of a bottle. Ironic given what's happened to Chioma's dad. It's fucked up my life. I've lost everything. The business, my family, my home . . . At the very least, the money would sort out some of my debts, keep a roof over Vanessa and the kids' heads.' He pauses, braves eye contact again. 'Did you really not know any of this?'

I shake my head.

'He made out like you knew and you were right behind him the whole time. He showed me the letters you wrote. I was terrified.'

It's hard to piece James's story together with only the fragments he's handed to each of us. I think about that fight on the lawn and take my fingers to my temples and rub, hard.

'But you never threatened to turn me in?'

'Never. Although, like I say, it crossed my mind. Many times. But my conversations with James have always been about what happened in Corfu, about my guilt.'

'I'm just trying to get this straight. James has been convincing me you want to turn me in, to what end?'

We're quiet as we shift the puzzle pieces around, trying to get a clear picture. It begins to crystallize. I'm not sure if Will is actively choosing not to see it or if he's just blissfully ignorant.

'Oh, Will . . .'

'What?'

My eyes scan the crumbs and stains on the carpeted floor before looking back to the man sitting across from me. 'James thought I had a violent streak. What if . . . What if he's been trying to trigger me?'

'You mean . . .' Will stops to suck dry air down his throat. 'You think he wants you to hurt me?'

'And I think he wants me to believe it's my idea.'

'You think he's been sending you the letters.'

It's a statement, not a question. And despite the profound betrayal that would require, despite what I've wanted to believe about James all this time, I nod. The beliefs I've held of him in my mind are milk teeth coming loose. Almost in real time, I can feel them dislodging: bloody, painful, dropping one by one. This New James, the new truths of what he is, are wisdom teeth pushing through my gums: slow, persistent agony as they show themselves. And between this Old James and this New James, there is still a score of gaps, a mouth of gaping wounds. He has somehow left me toothless. Defanged and disarmed. I see some of him, but not all.

'Nat?'

Will. I blink too hard and fast for a normal person, but I'm back in the room.

'Sorry. I'm just thinking. Molly said you called the office today with a message for me. Said my time's up.'

He's shaking his head before I've even finished my sentence. 'That wasn't me.' He gulps, looks around the room as if for the answer. 'I suppose if he adjusted his voice a bit, it could have been –'

'James.' I nod. 'But if he knows I didn't hurt my exes, then why the latest mail?'

Will shrugs. 'I don't have an answer to that. But I don't know who else it could be. In any case, he's got to be scrambling. Everything's coming apart.'

And with these words, my sense of certainty shifts again. How can I be sure that Will is telling me the whole truth? That he didn't instigate the blackmail, send the letters? It makes more sense than James voluntarily giving away the cash, provoking me when he knows I'm innocent. The stakes are so high that I feel dizzy looking down from the peak of them, feet wobbly, unsure. A migraine is threatening my head, and I've no idea what my next steps should be.

James will be home soon, if he isn't already. I've bought myself some time with my self-care lie, but that time will eventually run out.

Perhaps my silence speaks of my paralysis, because Will suddenly asks, 'What are you going to do now? What do we both do?'

Wary of Will's and my too quickly becoming a 'we', I give him a guarded shrug.

'You can't go back there. If he's willing to . . . If my own brother could want to hurt me, then I don't think it's safe for you, either.' His eyes rake across the detritus of the living room. 'You could . . . You could stay here if you need to.'

The concern on his face, the offer, it seems sincere. And it's not the yellowing bathroom, overflowing bins and solitary bedroom that prevent me from accepting. It's James.

My brain is ticking so loudly, I wouldn't be surprised if Will can hear it.

'Will, you never saw me here,' I say.

He pushes himself back into the sofa so hard, it's like he's trying to disappear. 'Wait, what?'

'I came here to find dirt on you, some kind of leverage that would get you off our necks for the blackmail.'

'You did?'

Sure.

'But I didn't find anything, and you didn't find me. I came and went; we never spoke. I don't know he's been lying about you blackmailing us, and you don't know he's been lying about me threatening you. Have you got it?'

His thumb rubs his index finger in circular motions. 'But what's the plan?'

'I don't have a perfect plan formulated, which is all the more reason to bide our time. All I know – all we both know – is that James is reactive when backed into a corner. I don't want to see what he'll do if we force him into one.'

'Okay,' he says, wiping a running nose on his shirtsleeve. 'But . . .' He takes a moment to scan the room again. 'But I need concrete answers. If he's been doing what we think he has, he has to pay.'

Chapter 43

Now

Dimple

Two hours. That's how long I have to pull myself together on the way back from Will's to my home. Home. What an absurd joke of a word. What I'm going home to is a long-running lie. A large part of me can understand why James would want to hide Chioma from me; I don't really have a leg to stand on in that respect. But there are too many pieces of the puzzle missing from Chioma's story. Pieces that I'm convinced will help me make sense of everything else. After all, Will was there the day she died, and I can't help but feel he's deliberately obscuring something important from view. Somehow, I have to find answers.

If Will is telling the truth, James believed I hurt my exes, that I was capable of hurting Will to shut him up if pushed . . . But finding out my sister was responsible? That would have rocked James's plans.

I'm not sure how, but he must have still sniffed out the danger in me. Known that I could still hurt Will, despite the adhesive in his hot-glue-gunned plan dissolving. That he was right, that he played me so well, is terrifying. I could have killed a likely innocent Will. Although a small part of me, the part nestled in that dark place, says, *See? He knows you so well. You might actually be perfect for each other.*

I think I need that right now. To have someone. Not be so alone. I know I'm desperate for some sort of connection, belonging, because I think about unblocking my mother. I even pull my phone out, pull up her contact, then decide I'm not quite that desperate. Yet.

Despite the churning thoughts that threaten to overwhelm me, I pull myself together string by string. This is what I've spent a lifetime doing: pretending. I can be just as good an actress as Claire and James – all I have to do is return to form. I have two hours to swallow my heartbreak. Because this is what it is – I have loved James, do still love him in a sense, but I have to accept that the version of him that I love doesn't exist. That I've somehow chosen wrong again, having thought I'd learned my lesson. I'm too fond of falling in love with ideas and ideals, not anything real. And if I've learned anything from the heartbreak that's gone before, it's that sometimes it's best to throw the whole pear out when you first notice the rot. There's no point trying to cut around it, not if you want to be sure of not poisoning yourself. Still, like I said to Will, I don't want to make any sudden moves. Because if I'm right about James and he knows I'm onto him, he'll have no problem eviscerating me to protect himself. I need time to be sure of the truth and then make my move.

Despite the cool calm I drape around myself when I get home, I worry that James will smell the distrust on me, the deep betrayal. But he doesn't. Ironically, he seems to have finally relaxed his close monitoring of me, while I'm watching him more closely than ever. Questions about everything – about Chioma – rise and die on my tongue. Even to ask about his ex would give away that I've been speaking to Will, leaving me exposed.

I find my way back to Old Natalie, stepping out of myself to protect myself from the bad feelings. There are too many, and it's easier to live as a passenger in myself. Numb, not feeling at all. This pulls me through the late dinner I have with James when I get home, pulls me into our marital bed, allows him to kiss me and for me to kiss him in return. And the next day, I find myself able to continue to perform normality while I try to see a way out of my hole. I tell him I want to work from home and spend my lunch break googling him, finding nothing new at first. But when I stitch in the name 'Chioma', a couple more pieces pop up. Nothing as far back as the day she died, but there's a local press piece about her parents' attempt to reopen the case again. It features a small picture of them standing together looking lifeless, leaning against each other as if they'd collapse without the counterweight. Marionettes with their strings cut. A couple of blogs picked up the story and reran it, but there's no new information in it. Just that she drowned. That her parents think there's more to the story. At least it confirms what Will's told me. At least it gives me her full government name. Her parents' government names.

I discover an old but public Facebook post from Chioma's mum with an email address for people to send information to if they might know more about what happened to Chioma. She asks for people to share it. It's all very aunty-on-Facebook-coded, lots of her friends adding their prayers in the comments. It's the kind of thing that would have gone nowhere, but I sit and stare at it. Wonder how fair it is to open an old wound. And then I send a message I expect will sit in an unseen void. Send a friend request to her account from my own, untouched for several years.

When I think about James, I'm not struck with the impression of a man who's methodical in his violence in the same way that someone like Marc or George was. I'm sure he may even think of himself as an actively good person. But he's a coward. This is his ultimate flaw – ruled by fear beyond the point of reason – and that still makes him dangerous. Dangerous enough for me to not risk slipping.

When I find myself in Dimple's office the day after, I am still successfully holding myself together, although all my pieces are being kept in place by a single taut string.

'How are you doing today?' she asks with a kind smile.

'All things considered, okay.' I need to work my way up to talking about this. There are limits to what I can share, but I need to talk about James.

'I appreciate you coming back here despite your reservations about continuing our sessions.' Head tilt, hair swish. 'But, Natalie, I have to remind you that for this to work, I need you to be honest with me.'

I nod. 'You're right. I'm sorry for that. I'll try to do better today.'

'Thank you.' She looks genuinely grateful. I wonder if this is an honest reflection of her feelings, or if she's just as good a liar as James. 'So, how have you been managing your temper over the past week? There are still several stressors in your life and –'

'Actually, if it's okay, I'd like to start with something else.'

Dimple blinks. It's one thing for me to agree to play ball, and another entirely to start volunteering information.

'Sure.'

'It's James.'

'What about James?'

And so I tell her what I've found out. In an approximate way, at least. She needs to know about Chioma; about faking the threats from Will; about . . . well, I can't say I'm sure he was trying to get me to attack Will – it hardly reflects well on me – but I tell her I suspect he wanted me to hurt him, that he was promising Will I would.

Dimple removes her glasses and pinches the bridge of

her nose, eyes sliding shut. I'm alarmed; Dimple doesn't emote. A second ticks by, and then another.

'Dimple?'

Eyes ping open. 'So you're telling me that your husband killed his school girlfriend.'

'Yes.'

'And that he has been threatening his brother with harm if he went to the police.'

'Yes. I mean, it sort of makes sense why he looked so unsettled by the news of my innocence. It totally messed up his plan.'

She replaces her glasses, mutters something under her breath and then looks back at me.

'This is all quite a lot, you know,' she says. I wonder if she has her own therapist. I wonder how many of our sessions have sent her to them. I wonder if this new update will finally send her to the police. Right now, it's hard to care that it might. 'And how are you feeling about all of this?' she asks.

'It's strange. It's like someone's stabbed me with a nine-inch blade, and it's healed badly. Like if I'm still, I can almost forget the wound is there, aside from a dull throb, but if I move the wrong way, there's this breathtaking pain that threatens to topple me over. I'm pretty good at moving carefully with it, though.' I see Dimple opening her mouth to ask another question, but I need to get this out of me, my next words verbal vomit. 'The thing that really gets me, though, is that I thought I'd learned my lesson after George. I thought I knew how to spot the wrong type of guy, so how the hell am I still here?' I feel the string pull tighter. I'm not sure how much more it can take. I'm not sure how much more I can take. I close my eyes, swallow hard – tears, panic, pain, in that one gulp. I fear how naked I've made myself in front of

Dimple, but when I open my own eyes, I see that hers, too, have been closed.

Dimple's fingers are on the bridge of her nose again. I'm beginning to wonder if this is too much for her. If I'm too much for her.

When Dimple opens her eyes again, they're alive with incredulity.

'So you're positive that James killed this "Chioma"?'

My mouth twists. 'I can't be one hundred per cent sure, but I've done some research. Chioma really did drown on holiday with his family in Corfu. Of course, Will might not be telling the whole truth.'

She sits back, removes her glasses entirely and tosses them onto her side table, mouth hanging open. 'Fucking hell.' She touches her fingertips to her mouth, tries to wipe the words away. 'Sorry, I shouldn't have said that.'

A burst of laughter leaps out of me. 'No, I . . .' The laughter is a little wild, unhinged, but it's nice to feel something nice for a change. 'No, I'm sorry and glad that you're having to unpuzzle this shit with me. But how did I get here?'

We dance around the answer to this question – the 'how the hell have I ended up with a killer' one – spending time revisiting my relationships with Marc, Luca and George. Something's different about this session, though. Dimple's like a hound that's lost the scent. Her heart isn't in it.

I've been white-knuckling it through the past couple of days in anticipation of this session, hoping Dimple would help me see a way forwards. But Claire's the only person in this world who's ever truly looked out for me. Besides, I've made the mistake of expecting too much of one person with her. It's now up to me, and only me, to save myself.

Chapter 44

Now

Mint-green flecks of paint dust my fingertips as they press into cool metal. I only just repainted the hallway radiator in the renovations. The paint job shouldn't be disintegrating this quickly, but, then again, neither should my marriage.

There's something grounding about standing here in the stillness of the house, James not back from work yet. Not due back for likely at least another hour. Maybe more. I rub my fingertips together. Drive away the debris. Handbag is shaken off and shoes kicked away. The moment of pause is welcome. Needed, even. But I can't be still for long. I make my way to the sofa, check my personal emails. Obviously nothing from Chioma's mother yet. Friend request not accepted on Facebook, either. I remember an article describing her as a healthcare assistant. Look up the nursing homes in the towns closest to where James grew up. I do the math; she might not be retired yet. I scour websites, seeing no sign of her. Then I start jotting down addresses. There aren't too many. If she's still working, I can drive to them. I can find her.

Everything okay? You've been a bit quiet.

Will.

> Yeah, all good. It's going to take time, but I'll let you know if I find anything useful.

Maybe. Because am I really going to throw all my trust in the alcoholic and very married Lothario who fucked his way around the junior women in the office? He's no saint. I'm caught between the secrets and lies of two extremely dysfunctional brothers. It would help if I knew for sure that James had sent those letters. That he's been the one threatening me. Evidence. There must be some evidence.

Instinctively, I head for the bedroom with no idea where to start. Wardrobe. Unassuming rows of shirts, jackets, trousers. Nothing pushed into the dark corners but dust. Rows of neat, folded jumpers, no secret missives filed between them. Chest of drawers. Just socks, pants, casual T-shirts. I traipse over creaky floorboards throughout the house, hands passing over one unassuming object, then another, left empty.

My hands are rifling through the drawer of letters in our living room cabinet when I hear him come in. I step away, his cold-flushed face appearing in the living room. His handsomeness has a haggard edge to it today. Eyes track to the open drawer and back to me with a question in them.

'I was just looking for recent proof of address. Found a new savings account with a great rate.'

Now they narrow at me, crowded with confusion.

'For our IVF pot,' I explain.

The confusion is expunged by surprise. 'Oh.' He rubs a hand across his forehead as he pulls away his scarf with the other. 'Also, hi.'

We both jolt forwards as if we're onstage having just remembered lines momentarily forgotten. We kiss, give each other a quick squeeze.

'Hi, my love,' I say.

His gaze around the room is furtive, eyes trying too hard to avoid the open drawer. He leads me to the sofa, cups my hands in his big ones.

'Listen, baby, with everything that's going on . . .'

And although the mention of the new savings account was a ruse, I already hate him for what he's about to say.

'. . . I just don't think now is the best time for us to be planning a family.'

I withdraw my hands from his. They feel cold outside the warmth of his palms.

'Right.'

'I just . . . Everything's still so volatile with Will.'

'Yeah, I know.'

'And the past couple of weeks have been rough for us, Nat.'

'Sure.'

'And the money –'

My temper spikes then. I can't help but provoke him.

'I know we decided it wasn't safe, but maybe now we know I'm innocent, we could think about asking your parents again.'

I watch the words curdle in his ears and then on his face, lumps of fear creeping across his cheeks. Avoiding his parents has never been about protecting me. It's always been about him. His dirty little secret about why Chioma really died. And it's in this moment that I finally understand that there is never going to be a baby. This dream of creating the family I never had, being the mother I never had, raising a daughter who is happy and healthy and good. It's dead. I can hardly hear James's words over the bright and brittle sound of it shattering.

'Baby, I just don't think it's safe. Will's clearly serious about using your letters if he has to.'

And I could almost believe that the fear on his face is really for me – if I didn't already know everything else.

He continues. 'And I just think we need to be on more

even ground as a couple before throwing IVF into the mix. I mean, the process –'

His phone begins to buzz in his trouser pocket. He pulls it out, frowns, and declines the call, discarding the phone on the coffee table.

'Like I was saying, the process is rough on couples and –'

His phone again. When he picks it up and looks at the screen, a weary look descends upon him.

'Sorry, baby. Horrible timing, but I need to get this.'

I shake my head with easy understanding. Cool Girl mode reactivated. By all means, take another call in the middle of telling your wife you no longer plan to have babies with her.

'Don't worry about it,' I say.

'We'll continue this conversation later.'

I suspect we won't.

I hear him answer a 'hello' as he hurries up the stairs, guest-room door snapping shut behind him.

I wish I couldn't feel this, was able to be a ghost in the room watching this happen to someone else, but the disappointment, the pain, can't be numbed. Grateful that James is out of the room, I let a few tears fall, breathe deep, and then use all my strength to push this grief into a corner of my body where it can sit until I'm ready to deal with it. Right now, I need every reserve of strength and focus to figure my husband out.

The amorphous sound of James's conversation whispers through the doorway. It's nothing I'd ever have questioned before, countless supplier calls stretching into evenings and weekends. But now I can't help but wonder who's on the other end of the line. Who's been on the other end of the constant emails and text messages.

It's never going to work between you two.

When Will said that to me, was that meant to be a warning, rather than a dig?

Feeling brave, careless, or desperate, I punch Will's number into my phone. I'm not certain I can trust him, but if I keep applying pressure to both brothers, eventually one of them will break. After only a couple of rings, he picks up. The words are garbled out with a sobriety and concern I find in equal parts surprising.

'Hello? Is everything okay? James isn't onto you, is he? You're safe?'

'Yes, I'm safe. I just . . .' I pause to listen for the muffled sound of James's ongoing call upstairs. 'I'm just trying to figure some stuff out . . . I know it was ages ago, but when I first met your parents. When James and I were leaving. You said, "It's never going to work between you two." What did you mean by that?'

Will's silent for a while. 'Oh.' Another beat. 'Really? That's what you're worried about right now?'

Thanks for the patronizing tone, Will. 'I have my reasons for asking.'

He sighs. 'I guess it was a lot of things. He hadn't held down a serious relationship in years. Could never really seem to get into a girl. And he'd told me he thought you'd stalked him to the bar when you had that drink at Christmas, which he seemed to be into, but I thought was off . . .'

My stomach flips at that. He'd figured out what I was doing and *liked* it? I guess he's got his own issues, too. Is attracted to damage. It would explain why he didn't immediately run when he found the letters. My heart swells a little with hope at that thought. That James really sees me and loves me for who I am. But if everything Will's told me is true, his love is either a lie or too twisted to be any good. If. Big if.

'. . . And a part of me thought maybe you *would* work,' Will continues, 'but I was pissed at him for the stuff about

Chioma, about trying to push me out of the business, his life, so I wouldn't be a problem.'

'So you were just trying to fuck with him?' I ask, disappointed and relieved.

He pauses, and the longer he doesn't speak, the more dread I feel.

'Listen, I . . . I guess I was also trying to scare you off a bit. I was plastered at the time, not thinking straight. But knowing what he did to Chioma and then what happened to his most recent ex . . . It was stupid.'

His most recent ex?

It's a little too quiet upstairs. I get up, stand in the doorway of the living room, straining to hear more. The shuffle of James's feet upstairs tells me he's pacing, which means he's in an active part of the conversation, just listening. Will and I should still have at least a minute or two before he's done. I walk back into the living room, try to keep my voice even on the call.

'Will, what happened to his ex?'

A beat. 'She killed herself.'

I drop back to the sofa.

'And I know it's sick to say it,' Will goes on, 'but I couldn't help but feel that maybe being with James didn't help. He's got this darkness in him, you know?'

Do I know this for sure? If I ignore Will's words and focus on James's actions, he's been nothing but kind to me. But if Will's telling the truth . . . 'Does any part of you think James might have killed her?'

'No. That's not what I'm saying. It all seemed pretty clear-cut at the time. I just wouldn't have been surprised to find he pushed her over the edge.'

Quite the thing to say about your own brother. 'Text

me everything you know about her. Her name, socials, job. Everything.'

'God, it was a while ago . . .'

'Do your best to remember and I'll do some more digging. But I've got to go – I don't want to push my luck and have James catch me speaking to you.'

'Oka—'

I end the call.

Stupid. Had I not been so relieved at our pact to leave the past where it belonged, I'd have pushed more about the women who came before me.

One dead ex is a tragedy. Two is too much of a coincidence. I should know.

Chapter 45

Now

I've been sitting silently for a few minutes when James comes traipsing down the stairs. He's jittery in a way I'm not used to. Hair a nest of tousled tufts that suggests he's been pulling at it.

'Rough call?' I ask.

He nods. 'You could say that.'

'How come?'

His eyes scan the living room. Land on me. 'One of our biggest customers is thinking about pulling our range off their taps. They're starting up their own brewery. Thought I could talk them around, but . . .' He paces. 'Drink? I could do with one. D'you want one?'

It's getting a little easier to read James now that I know to look for his dishonesty, and this whole performance is a little much. Still, his suggestion makes my plan a little easier.

'Sure,' I say. 'You sit down and try to cool off. Just let me know what you fancy, and I'll pour us two glasses.'

He takes his specs off and crashes down onto the sofa. 'Thanks, baby. I don't know what I'd do without you. I'll just have a beer.'

'Of course.'

A quick kiss and then I'm off. It doesn't take me long to fish out two of the lint-furred Valiums buried in my coat pocket in the hallway. It's the perfect dose to gently send him to sleep. I crush the pills into a fine powder in the kitchen, swill them around in his beer, and return.

'Sorry I took a minute – couldn't find the bottle opener anywhere.'

We throw something on the telly. Our new modus operandi. The perfect way to avoid someone while so physically close you're exchanging breath. Easier to ignore the lack of anything to say to each other when fictionalized characters' words are filling the silence.

Eventually, he nods off, breathing deep and even. The cold, flickering light of the television dances across his face as he sleeps. I test him with a gentle nudge. Nothing. A firmer nudge. Not even a gentle moan. No change in his breathing pattern. With care, I take his hand in mine, wave it a little. Still sound asleep. Perfect.

From here it's easy to press the soft pad of his thumb to his phone screen. Bring the device to life. Irony is, if he'd trusted me when I told him Face ID is definitely secure these days, I wouldn't have been able to get into his phone.

I start with the call log. The number he received the call from tonight isn't saved. No messages in their text history, either. But there's an extensive series of calls back and forth between them over the past few weeks. A prickly sensation creeps up my spine and I google the number from my phone. Nothing. Which is no comfort, as surely if it were a business number, some sort of information would have surfaced. I decide to try my luck, prefixing the number with 141 to hide caller ID and dialling it. No answer. No luck.

Even though I've learned more about my husband in the last forty-eight hours than I cared to, it's clear that James still has more secrets to hide. But it's only when I get to his Instagram account that I learn just how many.

Because at first there's just the pared-back Instagram account that I already follow. The most recent photos on the grid are mostly of the two of us looking happy, smiling, blissfully unaware of the shitstorm due to hit us in the coming weeks.

But then I see the little arrow by his profile name. Click on it. See the second profile nestled there.

The account hasn't posted in the past couple of years, but across it are several images of James and a pretty Black girl I've never seen before, the latest image of them together from seven years ago. She's also younger than him. Much younger. Thick black liner rims her eyes in most photos, a silver ring gleaming proud in her nose.

I can't help but stare at the screen, at James, back at the screen again. My brain is short-circuiting.

A tap against an image pulls up the girl's handle: jadedacosta_x.

Her profile is quiet, few followers. A snap of her then new custom phone case makes me realize her name is Jade. Jade Dacosta. I kick myself for reading her handle as 'Jaded'. And then I notice another chilling detail.

She hasn't posted in years.

The phone feels hot in my hand.

I tap back into James's secret account. Want to see how he spoke to her when no one else was looking. Get a flavour of their relationship. What I see in his private messages confuses me. Dozens of flirtatious messages sent to a range of girls flood his inbox. All very different-looking, but none white. The timeline suggests the messages were sent after Jade had died and before we got serious, which is something, I guess. He gets a few responses. A few threads show me he even has the occasional success of meeting up with a girl in real life. By the looks of the acerbic messages in those same threads, he sleeps with them, ghosts and then blocks. When I look, I find almost nothing in his DMs with Jade.

I want to throw the phone across the room. Slam it down. Crack it against the floorboards.

Instead, I reach for my own phone, open Instagram, create a finsta of my own. With the new profile, I find the accounts of the women he's met. One by one, I send them the same message.

> Hi. I know this is a random message, but I am currently seeing James – the guy you dated a couple of years back. I've linked his profile at the bottom of this message. Have found out some things about him and am not sure if he's safe. Can you tell me anything about what he was like when you were together? I'm writing from a new account for my safety. Please take this seriously if you see it.

It goes to Jade's account, too. A long shot, but there's a chance someone who knew James back then is monitoring her account. Better than nothing. I slide the incriminating phone away from me and stand up for a breath.

I can't ignore what this looks like. Can't help but wonder anew why James made such a big song and dance about me being his first Black girlfriend. Wonder if Will knows about these women, too. Something about the set-up makes me think these women are James's darkest little secret to date.

Chapter 46

Now

Dimple

'I must apologize again for yesterday's little outburst. It wasn't very professional. I promise to do what I can to avoid it happening again.'

I offer her a small smile. 'It's okay. I know it was a lot.' A beat. 'I hope I'm not dumping too much trauma on you?'

She flicks her gaze away to something so solid in her mind's eye it's like the thought has taken form in the room and she's studying it. From my peripheral vision I try to stare at it, too. I see nothing.

A silence unwoven by her stretches out across the room. 'Dimple?'

And she's back from wherever she drifted to. That she zoned out last time, the news fresh, made sense. But this is so unlike her.

'Sorry. Yes.' Her words beat out a staccato rhythm of false fineness. 'I'm okay. Thanks. Sorry.'

'I appreciate you seeing me again so soon. I know it's late in the day for a session.'

She waves a hand. Pushes her glasses up her nose. 'It's the least I could do. So. Last we spoke, you were telling me about this big secret James had been hiding. The dead girl-friend, Chioma.'

'Yes.'

'It was quite the revelation. It must be a lot for you to process.'

'It is.'

'And have you discussed Chioma with James?'

I shake my head. 'Like I said, it doesn't feel safe. If he could want me to hurt his brother for what he might do with the information, then what might he do to me? No. I need to figure out the full extent of what he's up to before I can decide anything. Because there are obviously many lies. I've got this sinking feeling that I've started pulling on a thread that's going to unravel everything around me. That there's worse to come.'

Dimple quirks an eyebrow. 'Worse than killing someone?'

When I went to sleep last night, I could see them. A slideshow of women's faces that James had wanted to hide from me.

'I know it sounds stupid in the grand scheme of things, but I found out I'm not the first Black girl he's dated. Not by a long shot.'

'And that makes you unhappy?'

'Yeah. It's a bloody weird thing to lie about. Feels . . . sinister. But it gets more sinister. I found out that another one of his exes is dead.'

Dimple blinks rapidly, flashing her surprise in the bright whites of her eyes. 'I'm sorry?'

'It was suicide. Apparently. I can't seem to find anything about it online, although the last post on her Insta is flooded with "RIPs".'

'So how did you find out about her?'

'His brother told me. The other day. And I know I have nothing to base it on except gut instinct, but I can't help wondering . . . What if . . . What if the reason James didn't immediately leave me when he found my letters to my exes is because he related to them? What if . . . What if he hurt these women?'

Dimple's jaw jostles a little as she studies me, as if she's weighing up the next words on her tongue.

'You think I'm delusional,' I say. She says nothing. 'Don't worry, you're not the only person in this room who thinks I might be.'

'I'm not calling you delusional.' A relief. 'But I do have to wonder if you're being dishonest.'

This stings. 'Right.'

'Well, given your sometimes long-distance relationship with the truth, you can see why there's room for doubt.'

Fucking ouch. 'Well, what do you think I've been lying about?'

'Among many things –'

'Many things?'

'– your sister. I feel like there's something vital you're not telling me.'

Of course. There's a lot I'm not telling her. But the thing that's burning a hole in the fabric of my mind where it sits tucked away does not bear bringing to light.

She takes a moment, pursing her lips. 'I'd like to revisit what happened in the aftermath of George's death. The "Big Fallout", as you call it. In the session before the last, you said you might be willing to explore this with me a little more.'

'I did say that, didn't I?'

She offers me a small smile as consolation for giving up the big, secret prize. 'Well, why don't you try telling me about it again?'

Throat clears. Mind reaches for words I've repeated countless times.

'Would it . . .' She takes a deep breath, starts picking at a loose bit of skin on her thumb. Why so nervous? 'Would it help you to know that your mother has been in touch?'

Fear climbs up my neck and traps my words in my mouth. Dimple's eyes almost disappear behind her lenses as she squints to take me in. The anxiety is so loud on her face, I can almost hear her wondering if she's made a massive mistake.

'You've spoken to my mother?'

'Yes. I'm not at liberty to share with her anything you've discussed with me, nor even confirm you as my patient. But she had plenty to say to me, nonetheless.'

'About the Big Fallout? About Claire?'

'Yes.'

'So you know what happened.'

'I know your mother's version of events. And now I'd like to know yours.'

Chapter 47

Ex Number Three

George

The skirmish with George is messy, animal. Care and I both seem intent on throwing our bodies as shields into the other's path. But we don't know what we're doing, and George is winning.

Until he isn't.

The punch he landed is still hot and angry on the side of my face, the other cheek cold against the tiles. When I peel my torso off the floor, sit up, glance around, I'm almost shocked to see George's still figure slumped across from me. I remember the feeling of the knife handle in my hands. A few feet over, Claire sits propped up against some cabinets, glaring at his corpse.

'Oh fuck' is all I manage to say.

I expect a similar expletive in return. Nothing.

'Care?'

And then I look at her properly. See the unnatural tilt of her head. See the blood pooling beneath her.

I scrabble over to her. See the split skin and bleeding red on her temple. Hear again the crack of her skull against the countertop as she went down. See the sharp corner with a small slash of red so delicate it couldn't be part of something so ugly.

'Care?'

Her eyes are open, searching.

'I'm here, Care.'

A low, gravelly groan comes back to me. 'Natty.'

Desperate, I crawl closer. I try not to touch the blood. Try not to look into the eyes that have a hard time locking onto me, although I'm right in front of her. My hands cup her soft face, so warm. My desperation is clawing its way up my throat. I want to scream. And the pain and panic are only intensified by the knowledge that this is my fault; I keep being drawn to monsters like a moth to a flame, and this time it's left my sister bleeding on a kitchen floor. I know I'll have to come clean when she recovers. I know she'll never forgive me.

Fix this. I have to focus, fix this.

I'm up on my feet lightning fast. Phone. Where's my phone?

Aha. The counter.

And then, 99 . . .

I freeze before the final digit. There's a dead man in my kitchen, after all. I take a brief second to think. Time is not on my side. I have to get help. I have to save Claire.

And so I dial. I don't know how I do, but I dial, and after a few rings, she picks up.

'So you've remembered your mother exists, then?'

'Mum.' It's more a guttural choke than a word.

'Baby? Baby, what's wrong?'

'It – it's Claire.'

Perhaps it's her mother's intuition. Perhaps it's my obvious distress. She goes quiet for a beat and then says, 'Where is she? What's happened to her?'

'She's hurt. I need you to tell me what to do.'

Immediate denial. 'What are you talking about?'

'She came over to see me. I hadn't seen her in so long. And I was in trouble, Mum. George was meant to be out, but he came home and . . . I don't know how, but things got so out of hand, and he shoved her. I didn't think it was bad, but she hit her head on the way down . . . Mum, I don't know what to do, I –'

'She's not going to die from a silly fall. Is she conscious?'

I can feel the muscle memory of my mother's time on the wards snapping into place. Thank god. This is what I need. I rush back to Claire's side, try saying her name, louder this time. She gives a soft groan.

'Yeah, bu—'

'And she's breathing normally?'

The back of my hand goes to her pillowy lips. Soft breath fogs on my skin in a regular rhythm. 'I guess so, Mum. But you don't get it. Her head's bleeding. Like, a lot.'

'It's *what*?'

'It's bleeding.'

'Natalie, you need to get your sister into an ambulance immediately. Why are you wasting your time calling me? I'm hanging up. Keep me –'

'George is dead, Mum. Here.'

'How –'

'I killed him. Mummy, he was out of control and . . . and . . .' And I don't know what else there is to say.

'One thing at a time, Natalie. Let me see her,' she insists.

'Mum, I don't think –'

'Let me see her!'

'O-okay, I'll call back on video. But I think we need to be quick. One . . . one sec.'

And I do what I say I will, trying to ignore the wailing alarms in my head. Trying to ignore the hollow gurgle in my stomach. Claire groans.

'Nat?' It's soft, sort of falling out of her mouth.

The call connects and my mother's face comes to life on

the screen. The years have drawn the anguish on her face in harsh, unmissable lines. It's pain that can't be ignored. Suffering that cannot be subtle.

I tap the video, switching the image to the back camera. Claire's figure comes to life on my screen. Was there always this much blood? Her eyes. God, I can't look at her eyes, now seemingly staring into nothing.

A sob erupts from me so loud and so alive, its own beast, that it takes me a while to register my mother's scream. It is primal, so deep it must begin in her toes and end at her gaping mouth. It's all too much. I take the camera off my sister.

'My baby. Oh my god, my baby.'

She repeats this. It feels like it's endless. It feels like it's punishment, each cry a lashing against my skin. Because I know I have done this to her. I have done this to us. Both of us.

'I'm sorry,' I say. 'This is stupid. I'm wasting time. I'll call an ambulance.'

'Wait. Turn your flash on. Show me her eyes.'

'Mom, we have to get to hosp—'

'Show me.'

I do as I'm told. The call goes deathly quiet.

'Mum?' Nothing. 'What is it? Say something.'

She sniffs. 'This is your fault. I hope you can live with that.' And the call goes dead.

What the fuck?

I try redialling. Nothing. Look at Care. Still.

What did my mother see? Or not see?

'Care?' I ask.

Silence.

I pull up my phone torch again, flash it in her eyes. And then I see it. Her pupils are blown out wide like she's flying high, jaw slack. And no matter how near or far I hold the light, her pupils don't change size.

I collapse to the floor, reach for Claire's wrist. Two fingers press firm and urgent into her skin, heat already leaching out of it. Nothing. I try her neck, nothing.

I want to scream, but it's like I'm trapped in a nightmare, my mouth yawning wide but no sound coming out. And this is a nightmare. The worst nightmare. I collapse back, and I look at her unmoving face, and I do scream this time, not caring who might hear me. Because my world has ended. There is no surviving this. My whole heart has been carved from my chest and left on the floor.

And I know I need to move, but I don't know how to move, don't know where to go. The only person who might have helped is our mother.

Our mother.

My god.

And in an attempt to look at something other than my sister, my eyes find their way to George. My mind flashes to the plastic tarp stashed in the attic, the saw in the shed, the burial spots I've marked out.

I'm not thinking clearly but think maybe I should deal with him. That everything will be easier after that.

With legs so shaky I don't know if they'll support me, I struggle to my feet. I take two steps, collapse, heave, shake, scream.

There's nothing smart about trying to hide what's happened here. After all, if by some miracle I rid myself of George's corpse, what am I going to do with Claire?

Nausea overwhelms me. Vomit, acid and sour, races up my throat. Slips through fingers, a hand clamped to my mouth. Splatters against cream tiles.

Chapter 48

Now

It's started to rain outside, the pitter-patter of droplets on the window preoccupying my thoughts so I don't have to think of anything else. Anything else is too painful.

'Is that a relief?' Dimple asks. 'Facing what happened?'

I give her a sidelong look while I try to swallow the torrent of pain and regret threatening to turn to tears. 'Was it ethical? Speaking with my mother?'

'I hope I can assure you that I didn't seek her out. In fact, I have been doing my best to evade her. She's persistent.'

I can give her that much. 'She is.'

'Would I be correct in assuming that your distance with your mother since the "Big Fallout" is born of her refusal to entertain the fantasy that your sister is still alive?'

'There are many reasons for the distance between me and my mother,' I say with a mouth full of acid. 'But, yes. You'll have to forgive me if I want to avoid recurrent calls to berate me for my sister's death.'

'It must have taken quite a toll to lose them both at once.'

I try to shrug around the dart of truth in what she says. It will hurt too much if it finds its target. 'I needed a clean start after Claire died. It meant leaving a lot of people behind, but it meant she got to keep living in a sense. Got to finish drama school. Got to go chase her dreams. Got to see me go to therapy, work on myself. Got to see me fall in love, get married. Got to live her life uninterrupted.'

'And the conversations you've been having with your sister . . . Do you want to tell me a bit about those?'

I feel embarrassed. Protective over them, somehow. 'I, um . . . I downloaded one of those apps. Fed all of our text history into it. Voice notes, too. And I . . . I spent a few weeks writing up Claire's life story. Just the headlines, you know. I fed it all in and . . .' My voice breaks. More embarrassment. 'And then Claire's voice came back out. It's . . .' I stop, grab some strategically placed tissues, and continue. 'I know it's not her. But it feels like her, and it sounds like her, and that was good enough for me.'

Dimple says nothing, but her eyes implore me to continue.

'It was just to say sorry at first. To apologize and hear her say she forgives me. But then the reply came through, and . . . I just . . . Suddenly, I didn't have to let her go.'

She nods like she understands. How can she possibly understand?

'Dimple, I . . . I don't think I can do this.'

I'm embarrassed and heartbroken. This feels like a version of Claire dying all over again.

'We're making great progress. I'd really encourage you to stay.'

But all I can see is my sister's dead face. The life taken out of it. A waxy doll. I haven't allowed myself to see it since that day, and now I don't know if I'll ever unsee it.

'I'm sorry,' I say. And then I'm out of my seat before she can stop me. Dimple moves more rapidly than I've ever seen her, voice imploring me to stay as she pursues me through reception, eventually giving up the chase.

My mother's words ricochet around my head as I make my way home.

This is your fault.

And Claire's face crowds my vision.

You look like Mum.

And the letters swim in my mind, lines disjointed. Everything feels as if it's coming to a head.

I suppose, in some ways, you were where it all began. My first, in more ways than one.

I can't begin to tell you how good the attention felt. How much it fed me.

I suppose you were the point of no return.

I now live in constant fear of that thing. I'm trying to starve it out, but I don't think it's working.

In the end, my humiliation was so complete that I died a little before you did.

If you gave me the chance to do it all over again, I'd do everything differently with you. And then maybe I wouldn't have to live with this unbearable regret.

My thoughts concertina against themselves until I can't make sense of any of them. I can feel the string holding me together growing more taut by the minute. My cup is primed to overflow; I simply cannot hold anything more. And yet, it feels like there is more.

More.

Somehow, more.

More than my father's fists.

More than my mother's words.

More than the death of my sister.

More than Marc.

More than Luca.

More than George.

More than James.

I stop in my tracks. The string is fraying, I'm sure it's fraying. I stagger to a bus shelter and collapse on the red plastic of a free seat. My neighbours glance at me, shuffle

323

away. My breath has fled my chest and is in my mouth. It does no good in my mouth. I cannot breathe, and I know it is pure panic, only panic, but it feels like perhaps I'm dying.

For a moment, I wonder what I'll leave behind if I go. I once thought I'd leave an indelible mark on James, that I'd leave an indelible mark on our children. And I suppose that at least on James, I have, in a fashion. But it's not a beautiful tattoo, handpicked and carefully drawn. No, it's a scar acquired in a horrific accident. A scar he'll pull his sleeve down to hide. To hide with the other scars I suppose he's been concealing all this time.

James.

I'm twisting around that deep wound now. I've been doing my best not to wriggle, but my god, I can't keep still any more. It's clear that I never really knew him, and he never really knew me, and it hurts. My god, does it hurt.

Breathe, Natalie.

My own breath fights me, the shallow rise and fall of my chest seeming to shout, *No.*

A bus pulls up.

The car. I was making my way to the car. I should go.

And I do. I get to the car and climb in, hands almost shaking. I want to tell myself to get a grip, but I'm not entirely sure what I should be holding on to.

My phone.

It's in my hands, and I'm staring at it, and then I'm in the app looking at the call button for Claire. I'm not coping. And I wish she was here to answer for what she's done and to help me breathe. I want her here to please, please make everything okay in the way only she ever could. Please.

But Claire cannot fix this for me. She will never be able to fix anything for me again.

And my head is on the steering wheel. And my heart is somewhere out of my body, unprotected, already attacked, already failing. And I'm desperate. And my mother's number is still in my phone. And she was so contrite when we last spoke. So contrite. And my finger is hovering over the unblock button. And I want to. And I almost do.

I almost do.

My thread is badly frayed and I'm moments away from it snapping. But I can't let it snap. If it snaps, if I come undone, James gets away with everything, and I'm left vulnerable. And I've been working hard to change. So hard. But the only thing I can see to hold myself together, to seal up the fraying thread, is that ugly anger nestled inside me. I can't even say it's been sleeping. It's been wide-awake for so long. But I've kept it in a cage, or at least behind a fence. But I need it. I need it if I'm going to survive this.

And so I think about James. I think about everything he's taken from me. I think about everything he's allowed me to believe. I think about the time he's wasted, and the daughter I'll never have. The daughter I would have raised right, and loved, and shaped into a Good Person. And I think about how she'd have finally made me a Good Person. I think about how much I've failed. My biggest failing after Claire.

And I feel how angry it makes me. I feel how much it makes me hate him. And I reach out to that feeling like the last lifeline. I twine my fingers around it, sure of finding myself steady again, solid in my anger.

But the lifeline is slippery this time. I can't quite get a firm grasp on it. Just as I feel I'm heaving myself upright on even feet, it slips through my fingers and I'm drowning again.

Once more for luck. I think about Marc, about Luca, about George. I think about Claire. I think about what my weakness allowed them to take from me, and I find a semblance of steadiness.

A text flashes up on my phone screen. Will.

I tap the message open.

Spoken to some lawyers like we said. It's going to be hard,
but I think we can nail him for this.

The words float in front of my eyes. Don't sink in. What am I meant to do with this information right now? How am I meant to feel?

You should speak to some lawyers, too.

Jesus. I toss the phone onto the passenger seat, try deep breathing.

In, two, three, four.

Out, two, three, four.

Letting the push and pull of breath become my entire world feels good. But I know I can't sit here in my car for ever. Even so, how can I go home to James right now? How much more of the truth can I swallow? How many more lies dipped in honey can I speak? If my suspicions about him are right, then he might be more dangerous than anyone I've known. Falling apart in front of him could be a deadly mistake.

Will? My eyes flicker to the discarded phone and away again. I'm still not sure I trust him. And if I go there, if James finds out, he will immediately know that I'm onto him.

My fingers shake as I turn my key in the ignition. I wonder if my racing, chaotic thinking is the same thinking that Mad Mary submitted to in her easy slip into insanity. This woman I've never known suddenly looms large in my mind. I don't want to be like her. Can't be.

A pause. A deep breath. All I need to do is focus on the next five minutes at a time, on just getting through those five single minutes. And then the next, and then the next. That's doable. I can keep an even head if only thinking about that, and I need an even head in order to move this car.

And so it's the next five minutes I'm thinking about as my car slowly pulls into the road. I'm not entirely sure where I'm going yet, but that doesn't matter. I just need to drive. And this five-minute focus is working, although it's a little like having goggles, blinkers and earplugs on in a neon rave. I can focus on what's immediately in front of me, but I can feel the weight of everything else pulsing against me, fighting for attention.

After the first five minutes pass, I know that the next must be spent formulating a plan, or at least a destination. Not to Will's. Not home. Not yet. Friends. Good friends. I had those once. Not any more. Not in the same way. But I do still have friends.

Friends I can call on?

Five minutes.

That's all I need to do. That's all I need to plan. And it works. I have a destination in mind. It's a very long drive away, and I don't even know if she'll be there, but it's something.

I think about texting a heads-up, and then don't. And then I do my best to think of nothing at all except getting to where I need to be. If I try to think of anything else, I might fall apart.

And so when Emily finds me on her doorstep, approaching ten o'clock in the evening, she's surprised to say the least.

'Natalie?'

There's no delighted surprise, only confusion, and this already feels like a horrible mistake. I thought I was so smart with my little five-minute trick, but it's prevented me from thinking through what would happen when I landed here. If

I'd thought about it at all, I would have known it was a bad idea.

'Hi!' I say, and my hello is too cheery, too forced. It alarms Emily, who physically recoils. Even before the Big Fallout, it had been months since we'd seen each other in person. By now, it's been several years. It was a gamble coming back to this house, but I knew owning it greatly increased the chances of her staying put.

'Nat, it's been . . . What are you doing here? Is everything okay?'

'Yes. Yeah.' *Be normal, Natalie.* 'I just . . . I had a bit of a day and was in the area. Started thinking about you, I guess. I wondered if you might be free for a coffee or something.'

'A coffee?' Her urge to check her smartwatch is so strong it's almost visible, but she manages to refrain, wrist just twitching. She takes in the unhinged eyes I'm trying to hide and the slight tremor in my voice. 'Coffee . . . That, um . . . That sounds good. Come in.'

The door yawns wider as she lets me in, and I see she's in her pyjamas already. Guilt needles at me. Her slippers make a soothing shushing sound as she shuffles into the corridor, ushering me in. Her living room sits on the left, lights dark and booming sounds coming from within.

'We were just watching a movie,' she explains.

I poke my head in, and a handsome brown face looks back at me, confused. Her boyfriend. Must be. I withdraw and look back at Emily.

'Oh god, I'm so sorry. I shouldn't have just turned up like this. I'll just –'

'Don't be silly.' She pops her head into the living room doorway. 'Ash, you remember I told you about my friend Natalie? The one from school?'

Confusion morphs into alarm. I shudder to think what

328

she's said about me. Still, he does his best to sweep the concern away. Gets up, approaches with a warm smile. He has kind eyes. 'Hi. Ash. Nice to meet you.'

We shake hands and I almost laugh at the formality of it.

'We're just going to grab a hot drink,' Emily says. 'Fancy a tea?'

'Nah, I'm all right,' Ash says. He casts a look at Emily before he sits. 'Just let me know if you need anything from me, yeah?'

I follow Emily to the back of the house and down some stairs, landing in a bright and airy kitchen, a pretty kitchen island in the middle of it. The space is a little busy, but it's nice, homier than when I was last there and she was renting out the rooms to old uni friends. Certainly miles nicer than the place I was in before I lived with James.

A pang of guilt arrives with that thought. I have to wonder if I've turned a blind eye to what now seems so obvious about him for that reason. For the comfort he provides.

'Why don't you grab a stool?' Emily suggests, palm outstretched to a tall chair pushed against the island.

Of course. It's not normal to just stand stock-still in the middle of a kitchen, eyes glazed. I do as I'm told.

We're a little quiet as she busies herself with the kettle and mugs, taking a few moments with her phone while she waits for the kettle to boil.

'I'm thinking maybe tea would be better at this time,' she says. 'Or decaf?'

'You choose, I'm not fussed.'

Before long, Emily is plonking herself onto a stool beside me, big mugs of something faintly fruity and herbal steaming in front of both of us. I take a sip. I imagine it's meant to be calming.

'Not that I'm not happy to see you, but I'm surprised

you're here,' Emily says. 'Do you want to start by telling me about this day you've had, then?'

I go to open my mouth and choke on the words. Despair begins to take hold of me as I realize how futile this is. I've come all the way here, but I can't tell her about anything. Tears spring from my eyes. I don't know what to do. I don't know why I'm here.

Emily's shoulders hitch up and her eyes scan the room. There's kitchen roll within arm's reach and she grabs it, tearing off a sheet and shoving it into my hands.

'Nat, what's going on?'

'It's just . . .' What can I say? 'Things aren't great, I guess.'

Her brow wrinkles. 'What do you mean?'

'I mean . . .'

As I rummage through the clutter of my mind for safe words, Emily begins to assemble an image in her own.

'I saw your wedding on Instagram. Has your husband . . . Has he done something to you?' she asks, eyes flicking to the phone on the counter.

The tears begin to transform into tremors that gently ripple through my body. I'm unspooling in her kitchen and I don't know how to stop it.

'Has he . . . Has he hurt you?'

I shake my head hard.

'Sorry I've just shown up here. And it's so late. And I'm not even saying anything . . .' I pause, try to stem the flow of tears. 'I just . . . I realized I don't really have anyone else who knows me to go to.'

She stares down at her mug, runs her fingernails around the cerulean ceramic, artificial light glinting off the gloss in splotches of warm white. 'Wasn't that sort of the point?' she says quietly. I say nothing. 'I mean, at first . . . At first I thought you'd gone quiet on me because you were grieving.

That made sense. And I thought you might blame me for flaking that night. Not showing up. That you thought things might have been different if I was there –'

It's so shocking that it's sobering. The tears stop. 'Oh my god, Em. I never blamed you. Not even for one second.'

She shrugs, voice thickening. 'I wasn't mad. I mean, I blamed myself.' She pauses, finds tears escaping. 'Fuck's sake, now you've got me at it.'

We both laugh, and I'm reminded of why I felt so compelled to come here. Being with her feels like coming home.

'Anyway, it wasn't until you finally took my call that I realized why you were avoiding me. Why you'd been avoiding everyone we knew.' She pauses, looks at me with a question in her eyes. 'I guess we can talk about it now, then?'

I nod. 'Yeah, I . . . I guess that's partly why I'm here. I had to confront that today. Admit that she's . . .' I choke on the word '. . . dead.' And it's no one's fault but mine.

'Oh.' She sighs, then chuckles. There's sympathy, but also a little disappointment. I'm sure it doesn't feel like an event worth showing up like this for. 'I'm worried about you. You don't seem yourself – if I'm allowed to say that after so long apart – but I'm glad you came to see me.' A hand reaches out, squeezes my arm. And it's like that small bit of contact reminds her of the artificiality of the boundaries the years have built between us. She leaps out of her stool and pulls me up into a hug. Her hair still smells of the same apple shampoo. I come undone. The tears are free-flowing, but in her arms, for the first time in a while, I feel like I might be okay, a lightness rising in me.

And then Emily says, 'Who's James?'

I feel heavy again. We disentangle and I follow her line of sight. His name flashes up from the screen of the phone I've left lying on the glossy island.

'My husband,' I say.

'He's called a couple of times.'

The screen goes dark but flares back to life as he rings again.

When the doorbell goes, my body goes rigid. Emily knows me too well, brow scrunching.

'Babe!' she yells into the corridor. 'Don't get th—' But it's too late.

The sound of muffled male voices becomes clearer as we approach.

'. . . I think she might need a minute with Emily. But if you wait in the living room —'

'She's been having a hard time lately. I think it's best if we just go home.'

We arrive in time to watch James step around Ash. His eyes lock onto mine.

'Natalie,' he says. 'It's time to go.'

Chapter 49

Now

James's arm around my shoulders looks protective, but his fingers are digging into flesh, muscles engaged to push me out the door. I don't want this. But James is strong. Has always been strong. I try not to look at Emily's face, distraught. I try not to look at Ash's face, appalled. I know I look insane right now. I'm the madwoman in the attic, and James is my weary keeper. But I want to yell at them, to scream that he isn't some hard-done-by hero. I want them to understand that he's my captor, that he's made me this way.

'Em, we weren't done talking,' I say, throwing my voice over my shoulder as James pushes me down the short path to the pavement. 'Maybe I could stay?'

She takes a decisive step forward. 'Of course.' She taps James on the back, harder than polite. 'She should stay. When we finish catching up, she can sleep in our spare room.'

He doesn't stop. 'I'm so sorry, but she needs to come home,' he says. 'She has a lot going on right now.'

Emily falters. 'I just think maybe she should stay if she doesn't want to go —'

'Look, you seem like really nice people, but I've not met you once, so I imagine you have no clue what you're dealing with here.'

He's making me sound crazy. 'You're making me sound crazy!' I hate how shrill and unanchored my voice sounds. I watch Emily back away again, consider how many years we've been apart. How much I might have changed in that time.

'She's getting help. She'll get better. I know this is . . . Sorry, I just . . . I'm doing my best. Sorry.'

And James keeps apologizing. Even as Emily follows us out to the car, my jacket in her hands. Even as he pushes me into the passenger seat and fishes the keys out of my jacket pocket, gingerly handed over to him from Emily's hands. Even as I berate myself for letting this friendship go stale. If she could be confident she still knew me, there's no way she'd let him cart me away like this.

My breath is back in my mouth, and I know I've totally fucked this. I've fucked this. Because until now, I've been a good little actress in front of James, but now I've blown my cover. I look nervous, and I wouldn't look nervous if I wasn't suspicious of him. He's going to have questions. He's going to know something is up. And I don't have any answers. And I need to be anywhere that isn't right beside him right now. In the heat of an argument, Chioma accidentally gets pushed to her death. God knows what happens before Jade kills herself. His partners have a habit of turning up dead.

His car door clicks shut. The ignition switches on. I try my door. It's locked. How is it locked?

The child lock.

The engine revs.

Emily's face is suddenly outside my window. 'My number's the same. Please text me tomorrow once you've slept. Let me know how you are,' she says.

'She'll be fine.' James.

Emily is forced to take rapid steps back as the car begins to move out of its parking space. We're on the move, racing through the streets of South London. James's fury is felt in the speed of the car, throttling around turns. I find myself wondering how he's tracked me down and kick myself. He has my location on Maps. Idiot.

'What the hell is going on with you?' he manages to say. His voice is smooth and almost sweet, which would calm me if it didn't feel like the sweetness of cyanide.

I don't trust what my mouth will say, and so I say nothing.

'The silent treatment? Really, Natalie? What have I done to deserve this?'

He deserves a lot more than the silent treatment, but broken as I am, I've no idea how I'm going to get him what he deserves. I've made the mistake of thinking I'm someone I'm not again. This doesn't work. None of it works.

'What?' James throws distrusting looks my way as the car hurtles down another road.

Did I say those last words aloud? I'm losing it. I'm really losing it.

'Natalie, for Christ's sake!'

It's so loud I nearly jump out of my skin. He doesn't apologize, simply keeps the car going, snaking up through West London, eventually joining the M4. I think about texting Will, letting him know what's happening. Although how do I even describe what's going on? *Hey, my husband's driving me home . . .* Then I catch the gleam from James's jacket pocket. My phone, not his. Is it worth snatching it out? Worth the further suspicion this will raise? Not likely.

I stay very still. Perhaps if I'm perfectly still, I can disappear entirely. Perhaps all my problems will disappear entirely. But James's rough driving won't allow for this, each painful collision of my knee with the car door reminding me that I'm very much alive and here.

I've already built a picture of Chioma's face in my mind. Not that I have any details, really, but I can imagine her as clear as anything. She has expressive dark eyes. A cheeky quirk to the way she moves her mouth when she speaks. She's someone who smiles a lot. Or smiled, I should say. She has fine, dark braids. They're 1B with a tiny bit of 24 mixed in, creating thin blonde streaks.

Jade's face also floats in and out of my mind's eye as we continue to hurtle towards home, thick black liner and defiant stare. I want to tell James to slow down, but I'm suddenly scared that even the lightest allusion to what I know will give me away. And so I let myself be bounced around the passenger seat like a rag doll, waiting for us to arrive home.

And when we finally do, James wants to talk.

'Nat, what the hell is going on?'

He's marching up the stairs behind me, our shoes discarded. I need to do better. He can't know what I know.

'It was just a bad therapy session,' I say.

I make my way into the bathroom, quickly turn the lock in the door. We never usually lock the door when it's just the two of us at home. James knocks.

'I need the toilet,' I say, which is true. An insistent stream sounds loudly through the bathroom to confirm this.

When I emerge, he's waiting for me outside, arms folded.

'Talk to me, Natalie.'

'Not right now, James. I . . . I need to sleep. It's late.'

'Yes, it's late.' Vindication is so loud in his voice, it almost hurts to listen to it. 'So why are you turning up on people's doorsteps? I was worried about you. And from the state of you, I had every right to be.'

I've mirrored James's stance, my own arms crossed. I suppose I want to look as grown-up and sure of myself as he does, but I suddenly notice my right hand is shaking. I cup my rib cage with it to hide the tremor.

'I need to sleep,' I say.

'Baby . . .'

He reaches for me and I want to recoil, but I can't. He pulls me into his arms and I want to push him away, but I can't. He pulls my chin up, kisses my mouth, and I want to bite him like he bit me when we first kissed outside that bar, want to taste his blood, and I can't. I shouldn't. But I could. Actually, I can, can't I? So I do. I can't help myself. It's instinctive. A little revenge that pales against everything he's done to me, but it feels good. Incredible, even.

He lets go, steps back.

'Ow, Nat. What the fuck?'

And I slip away from him while his mind is distracted, finger dabbing at his lip. His eyes are transfixed by the blood and I'm doubly glad for these necessary moments. With the gift of a few seconds' time, I'm into the guest room, door pushed shut.

'Nat?'

But I'm already shoving the chest of drawers in front of the door. The door opens a fraction before colliding with the solid wood. Still, I know that if my weak arms could move the chest into place, James will be able to push the door open with a meaningful shove. And it's with this in mind that I'm already shunting the bed frame across the floor. It groans as it scrapes against the wood.

'Jesus, Nat. What are you doing in there?'

He tries the door again, but he's been too slow. The bed is already firmly against the chest of drawers, which is now more snugly against the door frame.

'I need some space tonight, James.'

'Nat, this isn't normal.'

'I need some space,' I say, already heaving the bedside table on top of the bed. It takes some effort, but I'm eventually able to get it on top of the chest of drawers. I bounce off the mattress and back to the floor.

'Nat, please . . .'

'Just . . . just give me the night, okay?'

One night to safety pin myself together. And then . . . And then . . .

I'm loath to lure myself back into the trap of thinking without foresight, but it's all I can manage right now. If five minutes is too dangerously narrow a field of vision, then perhaps I can take things hour by hour for the time being.

A confused James acquiesces. 'Okay, Natalie.' I can still hear him breathing on the other side of the door. 'Are you going to sleep in there tonight?'

I nod and then realize he can't see my nodding. 'Yeah. I am.'

'Oh, Nat . . .'

And he sounds so sad that I can almost believe that he loves me, that this part of our relationship hasn't been a lie. And maybe it hasn't. But I can't trust that feeling, and I can't trust him, not when he's made sport of misleading me.

'I'll see you in the morning,' I manage to whisper.

The sound of footsteps against wood strike up and fade away. I hear our bedroom door click shut. Our bedroom. Soft sobs stretch from there to here, and it makes me want to cry, too. And I do, the wood smooth and cold beneath my feet.

I'm tired. So tired.

And I think of drawing the furniture away, of running to our marital bed and burying my face in his chest. I think of us holding each other, sobbing together, and it feels good. Better than crying alone. Better than letting fear and distrust divide us. Because, after all, what do I really know for sure? How far might I be letting Will manipulate me? James has been so consistently kind, loving and patient. Can't I just trust that? Can't I just let him hold me, make everything okay?

Then I think of the lies he's told about his dating history, the finsta, the convincing shock on Will's face when he learned of my innocence, and it feels better to stay where I am. I'm sure James is crying due more to his house of cards collapsing than our relationship being on the fritz. Better than letting him get close to me again. Better than risking my safety in his suspicion.

I go to close the curtains. If I want even a semblance of sleep, I'll need to shut out the light. Beneath the street lamp across the road, a figure seems to stare up into my window. The form is female, soft curves reading through the cinched waist of the big hooded coat. Tight-coiled curls spring out to frame her face. A face I can't see. Claire. I know it's just what I want to see, but it feels like she's still looking out for me. Keen to finish the big conversation that we never started. I turn back to the room.

The bed's mattress looks inviting. I want to collapse onto it, but I eye the bedside table on top of the chest of drawers and fear that a shove of the door in the middle of the night could make it fall and crush me. And, so instead, I pull the duvet and the pillows from the bed. Arrange them on the floor. I curl up there, alone and cold.

Sleep doesn't come easy to me. My mind is too alive, too full of racing thoughts. I think of distracting myself with some mindless scrolling and then remember that James still has my phone. When drowsiness does come, it falls on me with a heaviness so deep and complete that, when I wake, it's with a gasp, as if I've been drowning and my face is just breaking water.

'Nat?'

I realize it's James's knuckles on the door that have woken me. His knuckles, and his pleading voice.

'Nat, I'm scared, and I don't know what to do. I called your therapist, asked for an emergency appointment if she could see you. She's booked you in for five p.m. I've told the office you're sick again. That I don't know when you'll be back in. Molly started to crack Mad Mary jokes and I didn't want that to become a thing that spread, so I've just told people it's a bad chest infection. Sorry if that was the wrong thing to do.'

He's certainly convincing. I can't quite believe that he'll just leave, mind trying to calculate if the blockade will really manage to keep him out. There's a heavy lamp on the floor, dethroned from its previous perch on the bedside table. I scrabble over to it, weigh it up in my hands.

'Nat?'

My voice is small, still unpractised after sleep. 'I'm here. I heard you.'

'Will you go?'

I nod and then realize he can't see my nodding. 'I will, I promise.'

And I mean it. Am grateful, even. But I don't leave the room until long after I hear the front door close. He must know I know *something*, and if I don't act soon, I fear I will become another dead mark on James's romantic scoreboard.

Chapter 50

Now

If anything has become completely clear to me, it's that I need to get out of this house. I'm in no fit state to get any kind of answers or revenge. And if my worst fears about James are right, I will die trying.

It's still early, a half-drunk coffee going cold on the dining table downstairs as I empty out one of the suitcases we've been using for storage in the guest room upstairs. A hot mouthful was scalding my throat on the way down when I decided I couldn't wait another moment. It was time to get out.

I've just finished shaking Christmas-tree decoration glitter out of the suitcase when the front doorbell goes. Annoyed, I pelt downstairs. You can imagine my shock when I see –

'Dimple,' I say, jaw dropping open.

'Hi,' she says. 'May I come in?'

I give a garbled acquiescence, watch the sleek bob of her hair slide past me. I wonder if this total wrong-footing is how it felt for Emily when she found me on her doorstep last night.

'How . . .' I begin, failing at my attempt to form a sentence. I try again. 'What are you doing here?'

Her eyes are scanning the hallway, peering into the kitchen, the living room. She does a graceful swivel to face me. Her head does her signature tilt, one side, then the other, as she takes me in. 'I was worried about you. You were clearly distressed at the end of yesterday's session, and James called to report some concerning behaviour. I know it's a little . . .' Her hands are hanging by her sides. I notice her index finger start scratching at her thumb. She's as nervous as I am. 'I know this is unorthodox, that we're scheduled to see each other this afternoon, but I was concerned for your safety.'

I shut the front door, turn back to face her. 'Well, I'm okay. Or not, I guess. But now's not a good time to talk. I . . .' I cast my eyes upstairs. 'I'm taking myself off to a hotel for a few days while I figure out a more permanent situation. I think . . . I think I have to admit James and I are done. I don't feel safe here any more.'

She nods like she understands, but her face is as impassive as ever. I'm about to suggest that she leave, that we catch up at our scheduled time, when she says, 'I understand. You don't mind if I wait while you pack, do you? I've already cleared my schedule this morning, and I notice your car isn't in the drive. I can give you a lift wherever you need to go, and maybe we can talk on the way there.' She's making her way into the living room before I can even respond.

It's unnerving having Dimple in my home. There's something distinctly feline in the way she prowls the space – slow, gentle and considered – while I flit around her to grab things. I assumed she'd simply sit patiently on the sofa, but she's inspecting the room with a soft touch, picking things up to peer at them before placing them down again. Occasionally, we catch each other's eye, and she gives me a quiet smile. I suppose for her it must be quite the trip seeing me in my home environment, like the frisson of strangeness one feels when bumping into your GP or teacher in the supermarket.

I leave her to it, heading up to the bedroom to pack some clothes. Working methodically, I make my way through drawers and cabinets, filling up one suitcase and then the next. I log in to the joint account and clear out the funds – I don't trust James with money. At first, I only intend on taking half, scared of opening myself up to accusations of theft. But then I remember my lost inheritance. It's hard not to take on a Claire-like rage at that thought, but in order to keep moving, to get out, I shake it off.

'Need any help?'

I jump half out of my skin. 'Jesus! Sorry, you startled me.'

'I've been told I have an unhelpfully soft tread.' Dimple is standing in the doorway, the picture of casual elegance in her cropped blazer and wide-leg trousers. She's looking at me curiously through her black-rimmed frames.

'I think I'm –'

And she's already strolling into the room, recommencing her inspection as she pulls drawers and doors open.

'You have some lovely things. Need any of these shirts?' She indicates a row of brightly coloured satin blouses.

'Actually, a couple of those would be great, thanks. Not too fussed which ones.' And I nod towards the open suitcase on the floor.

This house, although not ancient, has squeaky bones, the floorboards groaning in protest as we patter around.

'I'm unsurprised James found your hiding place given how loudly it announces itself,' Dimple says, three blouses in her hands.

I stop, brows scrunched. She catches the confusion. Elaborates.

'The hiding spot under the floorboards. Where he found your letters.'

The evening of the house-warming, the confession about the letters . . . It all feels like a lifetime ago. It's been mere weeks, but I feel like an entirely different person from who I was back then.

A small shake of my head. 'Those weren't hidden in this room. They were in the spare bedroom, next door.'

We both look to our feet.

'Do you think there could be . . .' Dimple leaves the question unfinished, but it's clear we're both thinking the same thing. We get to our knees. Dimple throws the blouses aside, presses her fingertips across the wood until she feels the weak spot. 'Here,' she says.

With the back end of a pair of sturdy tweezers, we manage to lever the floorboard up. For a moment, I'm ready to tell Dimple she is wrong, that there's nothing to see here. But then I see the white corner of a small box. It takes a bit more levering and a big stretch with my arm, but my fingers find waxy coated cardboard pushed out of immediate sight and pull out the prize.

We're both nervous as we stare at it.

'What is it?' Dimple asks.

'Fucked if I know.' But I'm desperate to find out, gingerly removing the lid.

And at first, the contents are almost a disappointment, sheafs of paper nestled together. It quickly becomes clear what they are as I pull some out and flick through them.

You never really liked me for me
I'm trying to starve it out
I was too stupid to realize that just because you said you liked me,
it didn't mean you respected me
I regret being too slow to notice what you were doing
But the worst thing you took from me was my sister

Copies. Copies of each of my letters. And then I see something that punches me in the gut so hard that it winds me.

Dear James,

I sometimes wonder, if we'd met at a different time, in a different place, whether things might have ended differently, too. I don't think there was ever really the possibility of a happy ending. So much stood between us – so much history, so much blood – that the way things have worked out is sort of fitting.

Despite that, I really do think it's a shame that things have turned out this way. I did love you. I think. Perhaps.

I would have certainly given you almost anything you'd have asked of me. I guess, though, when the chips were down, what you wanted was something I just couldn't give.

I'm sorry for everything I've done.

I'm sorry for what I've put you through.

But now, after everything, I think we both have to agree that what we have between us needs to come to an end. As much as we've been at odds, I don't believe you'd fight me on that. As much as we've been at odds, I think you'd agree that only one of us can come out of this marriage alive.

At first, I'm confused. The writing is so much like mine, and it sounds so much like me, that, for a moment, I wonder if I've finally cracked. If I've well and truly lost my mind. But then I reread it, read the sentiments that don't quite ring true.

I feel Dimple over my shoulder, hear a sharp intake of breath as she reads.

'This is him, isn't it?'

A nod. It must be.

But why? Why write this letter? *I think you'd agree that only one of us can come out of this marriage alive.* It makes me sound dangerous, like I'm going to hurt him, or myself. But what's the point in that? Whatever his plans, I'd obviously

345

just vehemently deny I wrote this. That would be a massive problem for him, no?

The final knife in the back lands.

Because I realize it would only be a problem if I *could* deny it. And I can't do that if I'm dead.

Oh god.

'Hold on –' And I'm racing to the chest of drawers on which my phone sits. I grab it and fling myself down on the edge of the bed. Dimple comes to sit beside me.

'What is it?'

'Those girls from his other Instagrams. I messaged to ask them about James. It's unlikely I'll get a reply, but maybe . . .' One. There's one new message in my finsta's inbox. 'Shit.' I read it aloud.

> *Hi this is Jade's mom and if this is serious you need to get away from him immediately. Jade died seven years ago and they ruled it suicide but I know that monster killed her. If you don't believe me you can call me on the number below but don't wait just get away from him now*

Dimple's hand fastens around my wrist. 'You've got to make sure you're out of here before James comes home.'

I'm still reeling from the message; James is exactly the monster I feared he was. Maybe worse. I know what Claire would say.

Natty, have you learned nothing from our parents? You take your shit and you get out!

My voice is shaky, breath a thin hiss, but I manage to say, 'You're right. I . . . I should finish packing and get out. Thank god you found the letters.' Something in my brain slides into place, and the weight of it triggers a wailing alarm. I shift away from Dimple a few inches. 'The floorboards,' I say.

Her eyes flick dispassionately to the doorway. 'How did you know I hid my letters under the floorboards?'

Her cool grey irises level me with a look void of emotion. 'You told me, in our sessions.'

'No. No, I didn't. I never mentioned exactly where they were hidden.'

I spring to my feet, step in front of her to block her exit. She stands, too, but where my limbs shake and I can't stay still, she's a resolute statue.

Warm in the places I've been cradling it, my phone sits in my palm. I bring the screen back to life. Flick through the call history.

'What are you doing?' Dimple asks.

I don't answer. Simply find the number, the number I found in James's call log. The number he's been making so many calls to for weeks now. I press dial, wait a moment.

And then Dimple's pocket starts buzzing.

Chapter 51

Now

We stare each other down, unmoving. I'm surprised by the strength of my fury. Because Marc, Luca, George, James . . . Their betrayal is one thing. But Dimple betraying me is another entirely. That anger helps me spit the next words out clearly.

'There's a number that James has been calling and calling for weeks. Long conversations. A supplier, he said.'

Understanding darkens her features.

'But that's your number.'

As I stare into her blank face, I have to wonder how much of her stoicism in our sessions has been a professional resoluteness, and how much an indication of something absent in her. Something very wrong.

'I've been trying to figure out how to tell you. What to tell you,' she says.

I find myself slowly backing away, Dimple's former sense of safeness swept away by the sense of something sinister.

'Are . . . are you sleeping with James?'

She cocks her head, a gesture so classically Dimple but eerily uncanny in this moment as the person before me morphs into a stranger. It's clear she's still assessing me. She takes a sudden step forward, and my tightly wound panic springs free.

'Natalie –'

I don't wait to hear more. Simply turn, spring out of the bedroom, race down the stairs, Dimple's footsteps behind me. I snatch my coat from the banister, knowing my keys are inside, and bolt out of the door.

'Natalie!' Although it's still morning, rain clouds have made the sky evening dark. I didn't realize I was running into a downpour, but it seems I've a habit of running into things unprepared. Rain beats into my face, icy, as my feet slap against wet concrete.

'Natalie! If you just stop, I'll tell you everything,' Dimple yells. 'Don't you want to know the truth?'

I want to get away from her, but I do want to know. Am desperate, even. I risk a glance over my shoulder and see she's stopped running. See there's a safe distance between us. I slow. Stop.

She removes her rain-fogged glasses and slips them into a pocket. A moment of relief washes over her, eyes closing for a micro rest before fluttering open.

'I'm just getting a little closer, so I don't have to yell,' she says, taking very slow, deliberate steps in my direction, palms raised to face me.

Some wet hair has fallen over her furrowed brow. The locks are coiling in on themselves, revealing a curl pattern I've never seen before. The only time I've seen curls in her hair is when they've clearly come from a wand. Glasses discarded and hair curling up, she's transformed. That feeling of familiarity returns, only this time it feels more like recognition. I'm transfixed.

'What?' she asks. 'Have I got something on my face?' The tight smile she tries to float the sentence on fails to add the levity I think she intends.

'Your hair' is all I say.

Surprise flickers across her face. 'Oh. Oh yeah. It does that when it's wet.'

'Dimple, I swear to god, if you don't just get to the

point . . .' That sense of familiarity intensifies the closer she gets. A visceral dread builds with every moment, but I want to push on, know more. I'm the girl in the horror movie, hand reaching for the handle of the closed basement door, eyes welling with tears, a scream building in my throat, but still, I push the door open. 'What the hell is going on? How do you and James know each other?'

She takes a deep breath.

'It's not James I'm connected to. It's never been about James. It's always been about you.'

Chapter 52

Now

Dimple

There's something deeply bonding about surviving mothers who can barely survive themselves. I think that's why Natalie, Claire and I clicked so well. Our mothers' mental health made for a roller coaster we were strapped into whether we liked it or not. There were moments everything was great, but predominantly we were just flung around in terror.

Looking back, I think our mothers were a little scared, too. Latched on to each other as two of the only nurses on their team who didn't sound exactly like everyone else. For whom the culture was so new, their mother having grown up in a strong West African community, and my mother raised in a strong South Asian one. And fear is a powerful emotion. Bonding. Which is why the bond lasted beyond that one hospital, even if it would eventually be broken by other things.

I remember the play-filled evenings and weekends, no border between their home and mine. It was all just Home. To all of us. I'd sometimes stay with Aunty Melissa for a few days, or weeks if my mum went back home to visit family. And vice versa. Nat and Claire were always welcome at Aunty Dev's. Wherever we were, Nat and Claire would curl up in one bed and I'd take the other. At theirs, it meant me being in Claire's bed, and at mine, it meant being on a mattress on the floor. Either way, we'd all get to play sleepover. We'd find torches, shine them in front of our hands and make funny shapes of shadow on the walls. When it thundered outside, we'd all cram together under one duvet and hold each other until it stopped.

The loneliness I might otherwise have felt with it being just me and Mum was curbed by the sense that we had a bigger chosen family. Until it all abruptly ended when I was still very small.

All I knew was that one day they were all there, and then one day they weren't. I ran away from home to Aunty Mel's more than once, but she'd simply take me straight back.

Mum was cagey about what had happened, although it was obvious her and Mel had had some kind of fallout. And then I felt it. The isolation. Mum was working shifts in the hospital all week and helped out at her friend's florist on weekends for extra cash. My days were lonely. And Mom felt the isolation, too. I shouldn't know what the inside of my mother's throat feels like. Shouldn't know my fingers pressed in there are the best way to get her stomach empty of pills she shouldn't have taken. But here we are.

I suppose it's what got me interested in psychology, really. I wanted to know how to help her.

She finally succeeded in killing herself before I finished my postgrad.

There was a lot of guilt in the wake of her death. I blamed myself for going off to uni, not being there. Wondered if I'd studied harder, learned faster I'd have been able to intervene. It was only in trying to downsize the storage unit of her stuff to save cash that I decided to fire up her old phone. Saw all the texts from Aunty Mel's husband to Mum. They started friendly. Too friendly. Lewd, even. And my mum was just as bad back. Then the tone turned.

She's already outgrown her shoes. I'm not asking for money. Please just buy her a new pair

She's your responsibility. You deal with it

And then they worsened.

You've got to keep Joy away I'm not asking again. It's upsetting Mel I can't have it

It's not fair on her. She's heartbroken separated from the girls. Not her fault she's starting to look like her dad

I'm done asking nicely Dev. Don't push me

Things got progressively sour as the messages wore on. I read through paragraphs and paragraphs of Mum begging for support, acknowledgement, anything.

My girls don't want another fucking sister. No two ways about it. So you'd best keep your kid at home where it's safe

It's irrational to connect the idea of Nat and Claire denying a relationship with me to my father's abandonment of me, my mother's worsened isolation and her eventual suicide. But it was a line that pulled me away from my crippling guilt, from the idea that Mum's death was my fault, and so I took it, a simmering anger helping me survive my grief. And the anger was only further fuelled by the idea that my sisters were my only surviving family – that they were the only things between my being totally alone and not.

As is the hallmark of unhealthy fixation, my life became about little else other than finding them again. Nat was easy enough to find; she was listed on the East London Chill website, and their office address was a simple Google search away. I waited for her outside her office one evening.

Watched her step out onto the busy pavement. There was a curated attractiveness about her. A little like a show home. Nice-looking, ostensibly, but devoid of a quality that makes it feel inviting. Feel real.

I'd every intention of introducing myself, finding the words somehow. But instead, I found myself just watching her disappear into the London crowd, cursing myself.

Claire was harder. There was a decent amount I could find about her online, her face beaming out of a series of Instagrams in which she's draped around a variety of young, artistic-looking people. But nothing recent.

I knew it was a risk, that if she could reject me as a little runaway, she'd just as likely reject me again as a young woman, but I still remembered where she lived. Aunty Melissa.

Her eyes went wide when she saw me on her doorstep. I suppose in me she immediately saw the ghosts of her former best friend and husband.

'Hi, Aunty,' I said. 'Can I come in?'

The tears flowed thick and fast, regret pouring out of her. She welcomed me in, offered me food, which I declined. We sat with cups of orange juice and talked. It was mostly her asking me questions about my degree, which I dutifully answered. When we got to the end of these, I summoned the courage to move us on to the more difficult questions. I asked her how much she knew about the affair my parents had been having. She was honest, at least. Told me she put two and two together when I started getting older. Told my father she'd take the girls away if he didn't keep me out of their lives. How much would have been different if she'd accepted me?

'Do you mind me asking how he died? My father, I mean. Mum told me when it happened, but I never knew how.'

'He fell. At home. It was an accident.'

Naturally, she didn't confess that she killed him. I didn't know that until Natalie revealed it in our sessions. I confronted Melissa about it after I found out the truth. *I had to protect myself, my family,* she'd then confessed, lined dark hands wringing against each other, eyes looking everywhere but into mine. *I should have known that it was too late to save Natalie. That she was headed the same way as her father. She's never been right, that one.*

Her inability to see how she'd created the daughter she reviled triggered something in me. I could see why Natalie didn't take her mother's calls. Was lucky she didn't; otherwise, my ruse would have been up.

'You know she died, too?' I found myself saying. 'My mum.'

Mel's chin pinched, knee jostled. 'I heard,' she said. 'One of our old nursing friends told me. I'm sorry she left you like that.'

Right. I mean, I wasn't so blinded by anger that I couldn't see how my mother's death was her choice. But I also didn't know how Mel could sit there and feel no blame. No shame.

As we traded a few happy memories of my mother between us, sunny picnics and home movie nights, I couldn't help but think how small Mel was. Much smaller than I remembered her. In her living room, faded carpet and thin curtains, she looked like a match in a shoebox.

Everyone else was the problem. Always. And her commitment to living this lie had pushed people beyond her reach. Stuffed her home with a loneliness I worried was catching.

It was a blow when she told me about Claire's death. The finality of never getting to know her was a lot. Although when talking about Claire, Mel's eyes sparkled. Her daughter, the future movie star. It was clear that memories of her were Mel's favourite company. Her only company, perhaps.

When I told her I wanted to seek out Natalie, her whole demeanour changed, frame going rigid, diction going from smooth to staccato. Words laced with acid dripped from her mouth as she told me how Natalie had killed her sister. Another shock.

In the end, I thanked Aunty Mel for her time and promised to leave Natalie alone. Which I did, in a fashion. Unsure of what I wanted from her, of whether she might be as callous and selfish as her mother described, I simply watched her from a distance. Eventually, I followed her to the clinic she attends for therapy. I couldn't help but spot an opportunity to really look behind the mask. Get to know her. And so I started following Dr Foster. Found out about her affair with her patient. It was easy enough from there to leverage her into retiring from the clinic and facilitating me stepping in as a replacement and the transfer of Nat onto my books.

Dr Foster's notes on Nat were both fascinating and terrifying. It became clear to me that she was a violent, dangerous woman. I'm not sure Foster bothered to look any of Nat's exes up, but there were grief-stricken messages for Marc and Luca plastered all over social media. I couldn't find anything about what happened to George, although the lack of updates on his LinkedIn profile suggested something dark had befallen him, too.

I'd wanted a sister and instead found a monster. A monster who deserved to be put away for everyone's safety. And I knew that getting close to her in this way could cost me everything. But after her family had already cost me so much, what did I really have to lose?

Chapter 53

Now

She's close enough now that I can start to study her face, rainwater running down the slope of her nose, the arch of her brow. It's easier to take the details in without the obstruction of her thick frames. The slate grey of her eyes is Dad's. And there's something in the curve of her lips, the rare tight coils, that reminds me of . . . Claire.

'Have you been stalking me?' The gravel of my anger cuts her, her face flinching in a rare show of emotion.

'I . . . I might have followed you once or tw—'

'Jesus!' I take another two steps back. To infiltrate my life, pose as my therapist . . . She's sick. Is she even really qualified? Who have I been talking to?

'Please, let's just go back inside. If we get out of this rain, sit down, I can explain the rest of it.' She's searching my face for an answer, and for the first time I can see her mask slipping, see the desperation naked on her face. 'Please,' she says again.

A storm of emotions rages inside me, but I want these answers. Am dying for them.

'Turn around,' I bark. 'You walk ahead and do exactly what I say. No sudden movements.'

And I march her back into the house, maintaining a distance between us, brain whirring. I send her up the stairs first, and after she's taken a few, I dash into the kitchen, grab the big knife out of the knife block. I find her paused at the top of the stairs when I emerge, eyes tracking down to the gleaming steel in my hand.

'I didn't tell you to stop. Back in the bedroom. Sit on the end of the bed.'

She does as she's told. We eventually find ourselves facing off again, Dimple looking up at me as I brandish the knife in my hand. I'm by the doorway, ready to run if I have to. Ready to gut her if I have to. Gut her. My sister? A flash of Claire, her bleeding temple, blinds me for a moment. And then Claire's face is suddenly Dimple's face. Bleeding, lifeless. I feel dizzy, try to shake it off.

'Explain. Did you have something to do with the letters? You know, I always wondered how James found them. He's smart enough, but he's not a particularly curious man.'

She looks at the knife, flicks her gaze back up to my face. 'Could you please put that down?'

My grip tightens. 'Answers. Now.'

Her jaw clenches. I don't know how she has the nerve to be angry.

'Yes. I . . . When I read Dr Foster's notes, looked up your exes, it felt clear to me that you'd probably killed them. And your mother had already told me you'd killed Claire. She refused to give me any details and I suspected –'

'Of course she didn't give you details – she wasn't the one reaching out to you, was she?' The barrage of calls a few weeks back makes sense now. I'd just told Dimple my mother killed her dad. Dimple must have confronted her about it. 'And you thought what? I'd *murdered* my sister?' Emotion swells in my throat, threatens to swell in my eyes. I won't cry in front of her. I won't.

Her brows rise, and for a moment I feel like I'm back in her therapy room. 'Well, you were living a fantasy in which Claire was alive. You clearly already had a violent past. I don't know about *murder*, but having some responsibility for Claire's death didn't seem so far-fetched. A compelling reason to create a world in which she's still alive, no?'

Rage, regret and confusion compete for attention as I stare down at her. She looks so different from us, and yet, the defiance gives her features a distinctly Claire-like flavour. I realize the knife is trembling in my hand, fight to steady it.

'You still haven't explained the letters.'

'You have to understand —'

My anger propels me forward, the blade suddenly at her neck. 'Fuck. You. What exactly was the endgame here anyway?'

She looks me dead in the eyes, fingers woven tightly into the sheets but expression unruffled. She's brave, I'll give her that.

In the silence of our heated stares, I hear the creak of the floorboards behind me. Dimple looks past my shoulder and for the first time she looks truly afraid. I risk looking away from her and cast my eyes over my shoulder. He stands in the doorway, giving new meaning to 'dangerously handsome'.

James.

Chapter 54

Now

James stares at the frozen figures of Dimple and me. His letters lie scattered across the wooden floor, secret hiding place still gaping open. He looks at them and then back at us with betrayal written clear across his face. As if we've somehow wronged him by finding him out.

'So you found them.' And then he looks at Dimple. 'And what the hell are you doing here?' Then he spots the knife, sucks in a sharp breath. I expect him to back away, but he takes a decisive step forward, closing the gap between us.

'Thank god,' he says. My confusion grows louder. 'Thank god, you found her out. I couldn't . . . I couldn't take any more.'

I hold my free hand up, stretch my arm out between us. It's not smart to let him come any closer. Then I realize my predicament, one arm pointing the knife at Dimple and one palm warning my husband away. I'm stuck between two vipers and don't know who will strike first.

'What are you talking about, James?' I ask. 'How do you know her?'

'You can't trust a word he says.' Dimple.

'That's rich, coming from you,' he spits. And the heat in his words feels too alive to be fake. He turns back to me. 'She came to me, told me about your letters. Told me you were dangerous, a killer. Unfit to be a mother. And I didn't want to believe her, but when I found them . . .' He has to choke the words out, but whether it's genuine emotion or simply tough to spit out these lies, I'm not sure. 'She put all this pressure on me. Told me I had to trigger you. Get you to hurt someone so she could have you arrested. Put you away.'

'That's a lie!' Dimple shouts, lurching forward a hair's breadth.

'Nat, she's *insane*,' James says.

'Yes, James was meant to try to trigger you,' Dimple says. 'But just enough for you to say something serious enough, incriminating enough, in our sessions. I didn't know he was threatening Will. Didn't know he had his own secrets to hide.'

'Can't you see she's lying?' James. 'She's trying to confuse you.'

'When you first started telling me things about James — the secrets, the suspicions — I thought you were just fucking with me. That maybe you were onto us, wanted to play us off each other. Or that Will was fucking with you. I still wasn't sure until I came here today. James told me where he'd stashed the copies of the letters he was sending you. Guessed if he had anything else incriminating, he'd stash it there, too.'

I move the knife a few centimetres away from her neck. Her words remind me of the forged letter — it could only be James who'd written that — and the message from Jade's mum. James is a good actor, but he's not a good man. And I don't know what Dimple is, but I do believe that she's my father's daughter. A flash of George's large frame, heavy hands. And there's Claire again, eyes unseeing, so much blood. My past feels like it's racing towards me.

She looks again to James. 'She knows you've been manipulating her. Will told her everything.'

He takes another decisive step forward. I spin, point the knife at his chest. He's close. Too close. 'What exactly did my alcoholic, pill-popping brother say?' he says.

A reel of scenarios is running through my mind. I can't stop replacing James with George in my mind. I have a shot to do it right this time. To fight him, and win. But he has a chance to hurt my sister again. A sister I feel nothing but rage for, but a sister nonetheless.

'James, I think we can drop all pretence,' I say. 'You know I'm capable of using this, or you wouldn't have sent me after Will.'

He tries to interject. 'Nat—'

'I'm talking,' I say. 'You're going to stay right where you are, and Dimple, you're going to leave this house.' I don't risk looking at her. If I look away from James, I'm sure he'll make a move. 'James, I'm being very, very serious. You're not to move a muscle. Dimple, get out.'

She doesn't have to be told again. She makes a break for the door.

'Be smart, James,' I bark.

His jaw clenches tight, but he doesn't even turn his head to watch her leave.

A naked fury is building on his face. 'What exactly is it that you think you know?'

I hear the front door slam shut. Feel a wave of relief and then another of terror. We're alone. I hope Dimple is calling the police but can't trust that she is. Can't trust anything about her.

'Do you remember how when you found my letters I just came clean?'

He surprises me with a laugh. 'Did you, now?'

'Listen, I know you clearly read those letters and thought I had a violent streak. Had hurt my exes. And Will . . . Will was falling apart about Chioma. Your confession.' James's jaw tightens further, the muscles straining. 'You saw two opportunities. The first, try to shut Will up with the threat of violence and my money. The second, push me to the point I might snap and kill Will to get rid of your problem for you. And for when you needed to be rid of me? A contingency plan.' He's shifting from foot to foot now, eyes flickering around the room. 'I want to believe that at the worst, you just wanted to paint me as unstable. But I can't help but wonder if . . .' I can't even say it.

James's eyes widen. 'You think I'm planning to kill you?' His portrayal of hurt surprise is so good I want to applaud. 'You really think I could be capable of that?'

'You tell me. What happened to Jade?'

His eyes lose their doe-eyed innocence. 'Who?'

'James.'

'How do you know about Jade?'

'I'm not even going to touch how weird it is, you lying about your dating history. Just answer the question.'

'She was a sick girl. Mentally, I mean. She'd been struggling for a long time and one day slit her wrists in the bath while I was sleeping. That's it.'

'Jesus.' I wonder if that was his plan for me, feel the breakfast I didn't have churn in my stomach, empty and acidic.

'It was a horrible tragedy.'

'Just like Chioma, right?'

He visibly flinches. I've got him.

'I know about the fake Instagram, James. Why is your relationship with Jade all over that but nowhere to be seen on your main account?'

His jaw clenches. 'She was putting pressure on us to be official on socials. It was too early for me.'

'I might buy that if you didn't have a few months of holiday and restaurant posts before she even appears. Why set it up unless you always planned to hide from people you knew? And why hide her? I can only assume you knew she might disappear in a way that was hard for you to explain.'

His voice has been stoppered up while mine has been uncorked.

'I get it now,' I go on. 'Why you were so scared about Will telling the police – or even just Chioma's mum – about what happened to her. You didn't want everything else coming up. But, James, it has to end.'

He cocks his head at me, frowns.

'How exactly does this end, Natalie?'

Chapter 55

Then

James

Chioma, Will and I ambled to the secluded beach, me trying not to hold Chioma's openness with Will against her. Beach bags deposited and towels weighted down, we stripped to our swimwear and headed for the waves. The water was calm and shallow. We splashed about, trying handstands like the very first day we'd met. And when we got bored, we looked to the sizeable rock a short swim away, jutting out from the water where the shelf of sand dropped into the deep. It was a good diving rock, and a few days prior we'd seen some locals using it for just that. Today, it was just the three of us.

Our first few turns were fun, effortless, but Will grew bored and swam back to shore. Shortly after, Chioma began to grow tired and in equal parts churlish.

'Can we head back now? I'm getting cold.'

The rock was cool and smooth beneath our feet. She was pouting, one hip jutting out.

'Can't we stay a little longer? It's nice it's just the two of us now.'

'You said that a while ago, James.'

I tensed. 'Eager to get back to Will, are you?'

'Are you joking, James? For crying out loud.'

'What? Even my mum's started cracking jokes about how inseparable the two of you are. "Thick as thieves," she said.'

Chioma was properly angry now. I don't know why I kept going.

'I can't do this with you, James. This insecurity is so –'

'So what?'

'You can't start spiralling every time I'm friendly with a guy. What are you going to do when we're miles apart at uni?'

'Exactly! Why d'you think I'm so worried about it?'

She paced away from me. 'And why d'you think I couldn't have us be together?'

Disbelief froze me solid before pure rage shook me loose. 'What did you just say?'

And I suppose she had no real reason to fear me, so she kept going, didn't read my sudden step towards her as aggression.

'I just . . .' She went quiet. 'I just couldn't give up UCL for Exeter. Not when it's one of the best medicine programmes in the world. And not when I can see what it'd be like, us at uni together. We'd close ourselves off, and –'

'You got in?'

At least she had the decency to look ashamed.

'You got into Exeter?' I try again.

'Yeah, but like I said, it –'

'You told me they rejected y—'

'I just didn't know how t—'

'You lied to me.'

'I'm sorry, James.' Her eyes were welling up, but she was just sorry she'd been caught.

'Why am I not good enough for you?'

She came towards me, tried to hold me, but I stepped back. 'I promise it's not like that.'

'So it's what? You just wanted to mooch off my family as long as you could and then disappear?'

Her face rearranged itself from sorrow back to anger.

'That's a fucked-up thing to say, James. This fucking holiday was your idea. Your family's idea! I didn't ask to come.'

'But you were perfectly happy taking the handout.'

At this point, I could hear myself. I wanted to stop, wanted to apologize, but I couldn't. All I could hear was *You're not good enough. You're not good enough. You're not good enough.* On a loop.

'Fuck you, James. I'm going back to the villa.'

'You can't go back on your own. You need someone to help you up over the verge and walk you back.'

'I'm sure Will can help. Either way, better than staying here and bearing the brunt of your fucked-up mummy issues.'

I physically recoiled from the blow. 'Sure, leave. Just like everyone else does.'

Tears and rage filling her eyes, she stalked to the edge of the rock, prepared to jump down.

'How can you blame people for leaving, James, when you make it so hard to stay?'

It was the most painful thing she could have said. In that moment, all I knew was hurt and rage. It was reckless of me, but as she began to spring away from the rock, I gave her a solid shove in the back, with a 'Fuck you.' But I'd mistimed it, shoved too soon. My aim was also a little too high, sending her chest keeling over, her whole body then twisting on her toes, as if to ensure she could give me that last look of shock and betrayal. I grappled with thin air as she fell, saw the back of her head crack against the rock, and the side of her body dash against it, too, a moment after. She crashed into the waves, doubtless into more hard rock below.

For a moment, I was ready to spring, dive in, scoop her up, and swim back to shore. But I thought of her panicked, flailing limbs, thought of how likely they were to drag us both down, thought of what she might say if I saved her, how it could ruin my life. And so instead, I stood paralysed, tears falling from my eyes. I just watched. Watched to see if her head of blonde-threaded braids would re-emerge. And I thought I caught a glimpse of a hand, heard a spluttered cry, but it was hard to be sure with the wind whipping around my ears.

In the end, I turned my back and sat down cross-legged. I watched the waves lapping gently against the shore. And when a minute or two had passed, I dove into the water. It was as I began to swim back that I saw her not far from the rock, the back of her head and stripy swimsuit bobbing in the water. I recalled absent-mindedly a fact she'd once told me about things floating in salt water and sinking in fresh. We were in the pool where we'd first met, taking turns to see how long we could sit at the bottom. It was the day we'd shared our first kiss.

When I arrived back on the shore, tears still falling, not quite believing it had happened, I choked out the best story I could. Chioma swam out too far and got in trouble. I couldn't save her. Will insisted on swimming back out but failed to find her. The local authorities never managed to retrieve her body and ruled the death a tragic accident, which everyone seemed to accept and quickly move on from. Except her parents, who kept pointing to her second-place swimming medal from when she was fifteen.

For a couple of years, I kept feeling like I'd get found out. But despite her parents' appeals, despite the truth of what happened, I eventually accepted that I'd got away with it. And even though there were days I still missed Chioma, I knew there were other girls out there who could think me special, worthy of love and attention. Girls like Chioma.

What I'd done to Chioma had frightened me, I must admit that. Because what if I did it again?

But her death also taught me that I had an untapped power. That if I chose the right person, I was perfectly capable of getting away with murder.

Chapter 56

Now

'How exactly does this end, Natalie?' James asks.

We're frozen, two cowboys in a Western, waiting for the other to draw first. But I'm the only one with a loaded gun this time; I have the advantage.

Perhaps James knows this, because suddenly there are tears in his eyes. 'I can't let people think . . . I've not . . . I'm just trying to do my best, Nat. Everything just keeps getting fucked.'

Outside, I can hear the slow grumble of cars ebbing and flowing. Life is just going on. I want to rejoin it, escape this dead zone.

'James, you've made your bed. I'm afraid you've got to lie in it.'

And I've got to lie in mine, too. The memories of my exes, what I thought I'd done, have haunted me for years. I can grow. I can change. I've only just got the ghosts of Marc, of Luca, of George, off my conscience. Do I want James's haunting me for the rest of my life?

And then he lunges, grabbing the wrist of the hand that holds the knife.

I'm thrown backward, back cracking against the foot of the bed. James now has one hand on my throat while the other thumps my wrist against the bed, trying to get me to relinquish my weapon.

Furious, I bring my knee up into his groin as hard as I can. He roars, collapses to the floor.

'Fucking bitch.'

I'm up, racing to the bedroom door.

And then I'm falling. A hand is around my ankle and I'm diving face first to the floor.

I manage to turn my body to protect my face from the blow, but my shoulder hits the wood, hard. My hand hits the floor at full impact, too, and the knife clatters free.

A huge weight is suddenly upon me, pushing breath out of my lungs. I realize James is scrabbling over me, trying to get to the knife.

The handle is just within reach. I punch it, hard, and it skids farther along the wood, falls over the lip of the stairs. We hear it clatter down.

But his weight is still pinning me down. I try to crawl out from under him. I'm not getting far. Then I think maybe if I can scratch at his eyes, he'll back off. And I manage to turn onto my back, reach up for his face. A nail, a few nails, find purchase, scrape.

He curses even though I don't manage to draw blood, lurches forward so that his wide shoulders push between my arms. And then his hands are on my throat, eyes wide, frightened. I can't breathe, find myself slapping at his arms. He doesn't budge, eyes filling with tears. Like it's him who's having the life choked out of him.

'I'm sorry,' he says. 'I thought you were different. I really did want a family with you.'

My hands flail, nails trying to find purchase in his skin again, clawing anywhere I can reach. But the silly little manicures I can now afford have taken the sharp edge off, tips softened by pretty pink gel. It's not enough to deter him.

'I'm sorry,' he says again. A tear splashes into the silent scream of my mouth. My vision is blurring; I know I'm in trouble. I don't want this to be the last thing I see. His face, self-pitying. Him winning. Because then, what was it all for? What has it all been for? One sister in the grave, another I'll never get to know. A future I'll never get to have. Just another Black woman whose murder won't even make the news. Another name forgotten.

A crack splits the air. I feel his fingers come loose and air rush in. His body collapses, the deadweight suffocating me for a moment more before I manage to roll him off.

I look up. Dimple. A lamp in her hand, arm still raised.

'Now, let's get the fuck out of here,' she says.

Chapter 57

Now

There's an old cuckoo clock staring at me from the dark green wall of the kitchen. I feel as broken as it looks. Dimple sits across from me at the small wooden kitchen table. The drive over here was as silent, as dead, as this kitchen is now.

Neither of us is smiling, but there's an expectant look on her face, the same one she wears when she's waiting for me to speak in a session. This is all so fucked.

'I'm usually good at crises, but I'm not sure what to say or do,' she says.

For a moment, I say nothing. I'm grateful that she saved me, but she almost helped James destroy me. How can I trust her?

'So what am I meant to call you?' I eventually ask. It hurts to talk, hurts to swallow. Each breath is a memory of James's thumbs in my larynx. 'Dimple or Joy?'

'Family calls me Joy,' she says.

It's a clever trap.

I look away from her, back at the cuckoo clock. Gaudy maple leaves carved of wood frame the clock face. I wonder why she has such an ugly thing in her home. 'Why "Joy"?'

Confusion tugs at her for a moment before she understands. 'It's my middle name. Came out of the womb smiling, apparently. Mum chose both my names to fit. "Dimple" first because it was Hindi and English. Then "Joy" because of how I made her feel. She always thought "Joy" felt more me.'

'Fuck. This is so fucked-up, d'you know that?'

There's a defiant look in her eyes, chin jutting forwards. 'I did what I thought was right.'

'God. You sounded just like Care then.'

'I wish I'd known her,' Dimple says. When I bring myself to look at her, I can see genuine pain on her face. I try not to let it, but it pisses me off. She doesn't get to show up in my life, fuck with it and then miss my sister.

I get up, phone in hand. She stands to meet me, arm outstretched.

'What are you doing?'

'I'm calling an ambulance to go check on James,' I say, my voice coming out in a husky wheeze.

'Are you s—'

I hold a palm out. 'Nope. Sorry, I'm not blindly following your instructions any more. Not now I know you're just as insane as I am.'

The call connects and I murmur the highlights of the evening. None of the salacious details. Just that my husband tried to strangle me. My sister – and I do find myself saying 'sister' – hit him over the head and we fled. I know 'sister' will provoke fewer immediate follow-up questions than 'therapist' and can't be challenged as a lie, unlike 'friend'.

'They want your address,' I say to Dimple. I can't think of her as 'Joy' yet. She shakes her head. I place a hand over the receiver. 'What other choice do we have?'

She relents, recites the details. When the call is ended, we find ourselves just looking at each other again. I don't have the best childhood memory, but think I can start to see a little of Aunty Dev in her. Especially now that she's discarded her towel, letting that same head of tight curls fall loose. There's a small chink of hope buried beneath my anger. Had I found out about Dimple five years ago, when Claire was still alive, before Dimple lied and manipulated her way into my life, I'd have been thrilled. I can imagine it. The three of us. It wouldn't have taken long for me to have loved and defended her as fiercely as I did Claire. Claire, who'd shown up at my lowest moment at Marc's party; swooped in to make Luca pay for humiliating me; sacrificed her life to save me from George. Now that the sting of betrayal is less fresh, I can see that these were acts of love. Loving me when I didn't know how to love myself.

I stare at the stranger who's conspired against me, tried to hurt me. She's still my sister. That sacred, irreplaceable role.

'You really wanted to put me away?' I ask.

'At first, I just wanted to find family. I was lonely, I guess. But then when I met Mel, the things she was saying about you . . . I got the measure of her pretty quickly and wanted to get close enough to you to find out who you were for myself. But then I read your files, found the trail of dead exes. I thought you were going to hurt people.'

'Don't you think what you've done to me hurts? You've destroyed my life. Although I suppose with James's history, you might have saved it in the long run.' I run my tongue over a small ulcer on the inside of my cheek. 'You know, Claire was always like that. Led by a strong sense of justice.'

She leans forwards in her seat. 'I'd like to hear more about what she was like.'

There's a familiar openness that's returned to her face with a little hope beneath it. More like the Dimple I knew. A frisson of irritation runs through me at the sight of that. 'Dimple, I can't . . .' How to find the words? 'I'm not going to immediately start playing sisters with you.'

She nods. 'I understand that. But I hope you know I did try to help in my own way. I tried to explain your innocence to your mother. I'm talking about your exes. Claire's death. I hoped it might help heal things between you. And . . . and

I know I pushed you too hard, but I thought facing Claire's death would be good for you, too.'

My mother's gasping sobs on the phone spring to mind. When I'd taken that call in the car, she'd been trying to apologize. 'So that's why she called.' I'm trying to see a way through the past into a relationship for me and her, but it's murky. My mouth is twitching around all the things I want to say and don't know how to. I'm overwhelmed and underprepared to deal with all the shit this whirlwind week has blown my way. And I no longer have a therapist. 'Anyway, we don't have time for this. The police will be here soon. And James might be . . . We should decide what we're going to say.'

It's strange feeling like I'm at the steering wheel. But then again, I suppose I'm the big sister. Weird.

By the time the knock lands on our door, we're ready to face whatever comes next.

Chapter 58

Later

Funerals are never easy. The priest's words bounce off the stone walls and zip through the yawning gaps between the bodies dotted among the pews. The turnout is paltry, although I suppose that's unsurprising given how far the rumours spread about James. Nobody wants their mourning to be misunderstood as support. Certainly not for trying to murder his wife. Nor for murdering his exes.

The police could only really try to pin him for trying to murder me in the first instance, but it didn't stop the claims from coming. Chioma's and Jade's parents took to the news. Ama surprised me by filing a report about Mad Mary. When I'd asked her about it, she was sheepish.

'I left my house keys in the office one day,' Ama had explained. 'I went back for them after a drink with a mate in the evening. And I saw them. Mary and James together in his office. *Together*, together. So I always thought it was weird how he shit-talked her to everyone else. Nicely, mind. Dressed up like concern. You know what I mean. And then he asked me out . . . I don't know. The whole thing felt off. So I started looking for other jobs. I'm sorry I didn't say anything sooner. I didn't think he was dangerous until everything else came out.'

I think of Mad Mary. The titters about her in the office. I think of James inside her. Of his faux concern as he says, *Bless her. She just wasn't quite right. I hope she's found the help she needs.* I didn't want to think of what he said about me when I wasn't around, but Molly sent me a guilt-laden voice note not long after the claims started coming out. A choice clip from the five-minute ramble: *You have to know we never believed it when he said you were losing it. The idea that not being able to have kids was messing with your head is so misogynistic. I should have spoken up.*

I didn't know what was worse — that James had weaponized such painfully private things, or that Molly had the gall to message me when it turned out she'd been sleeping with him all along.

In the end, it was all too much for James, who'd made enough rope to hang himself with. Quite literally. It was Hettie who found him hanging in the living room a few weeks after he'd attacked me. I guess she got her wish of having only one child in the end.

For obvious reasons, I don't speak at the funeral, although James's dad, Peter, invited me to. I'm sure the invitation would have come from Hettie had James's death not unravelled something in her. She seems to look through everyone and everything in the sparse church hall.

My guess is James's parents thought my speaking would rehabilitate his image. But I don't know how to speak authentically without bringing the mood down even further, and making a funeral more depressing is not something I desire to tick off as a life achievement.

Instead, I sit at the back of the church and let the ceremony wash over me. I feared it would shake something loose inside my fragile heart or mind, but I realize as the ceremony wears on that I've already grieved for the man I thought I married. Emily's beside me, hand clasped in mine. When it's over, we're the first out and into the car.

'You did well in there, babe,' she says as she fires up the engine.

It's nice having her back in my life. Not just nice. A relief.

Like a cool drink of water after hours thirsting on a long, hot day.

I hadn't realized that the wedge between us after uni wasn't just George-shaped, but Claire-shaped, too. That she'd figured out what Claire had done to Luca. Didn't know how to hold that information and be my friend at the same time. And then George and Claire were gone, but I didn't want to live in a world where my sister was dead. I wanted to remain in denial, and that's a place in which Emily could never reside.

It's not a place in which I can reside any longer, either. The app in which Claire's voice lived is now gone, deleted one night after a bottle of wine and an hour of talking myself into it. My account had already been suspended for breaching the terms of service – shocking that you can't use corporate technology to force a murder confession from your dead sister. It was a decision that was ultimately the right call, but it left me with an abrupt silence from my sister at a time I wasn't prepared to admit to her absence yet. A lot of the apps have been cracking down after a spate of bad news stories. It's easy to get too attached to something that feels so much like someone. Easy for that to send you off the deep end. No one in Big Tech wants to be sued by suicide victims' families.

But this deletion feels more intentional. More permanent. I cried myself to sleep that night, even though I know it was the right thing to do.

'Thanks for being there today,' I say to Emily as the car pulls out of the car park and onto the main road. I see the tall shape of Will emerge from the church door, Hettie tucked under one arm, doing a zombie-like shuffle. Peter trails him. Will's eyes gloss over our car as it rolls away and I think he sees me but he gives no reaction. His words echo in my ears, *He has to pay.*

I wonder how Will feels. While there's no hostility,

whatever camaraderie there was between us seemed to die when James did. While we endured a few stilted check-in calls after James's arrest and then suicide, the trickle of communication between us has since run dry.

By the time we reach my flat, it's still light outside, missing rush hour on this rare sunshiny day. I didn't stop to consider keeping the house. With everything that had happened there, including James's final moments, I wanted a fresh start. Wanted to not feel so isolated so far out of town. And I considered returning somewhere else in London with the past in mind, but I had loved East London before James and was determined to love it until his ghost faded from the street corners and coffee shops.

Emily shuffles into the small lift with me, the floor a patchwork of ominous stains. We ride up to the third floor and push open the door of my brightly lit flat.

'Hello?'

'Hi,' a voice says back.

We kick off our shoes and round the corner of the corridor. Dimple – I can't quite think of her as Joy yet – stands in the living room, expectant. It's minuscule, but her jaw jostles from side to side as it does when she's uncomfortable. Her signature glasses are pushed up her nose, although her hair is in its natural state, close curls fanning out from her face. Sometimes, I think she looks like Claire. But I think it's just that I want her to. My new therapist says it's normal to want to transfer feelings from one sister to another with the loss and the discovery, but we're working hard on my not doing that. They're very different people, and I need to respect that about them both.

Emily and I enter the living room. I give Dimple a hug I wish was warmer as I make my way to the sofa by the French windows. Emily gives her a narrow-eyed look and doesn't embrace her at all. Dimple notices it and glares at the back of Emily's head. I smile. Think of Claire. Try not to think of Claire.

'So, how was it?' Dimple asks, pulling out a dining chair to face us. It's a small, open-plan living area in a new build. Bright and airy with slightly high ceilings but limited space. The sofa isn't big enough for the three of us.

I tell her about the funeral. Not that there's much to tell.

'Sounds like you're taking it all in your stride,' she says in a very even voice. 'You've done an incredible job processing all of this.'

My mouth twitches in irritation.

'Jesus,' Emily blurts out. 'You know you can stop fake therapizing her now, right?'

Dimple frowns and sits on her hands. It's a childlike gesture. She does a lot of those around me. But she doesn't like me to point out her regression any more than I like her to use her therapy voice on me. Besides, she has her own therapist with whom she can work through these things.

'Emily, be nice,' I say.

'Hmm' is all she replies.

'Thanks for putting the lamb in,' I throw back to Dimple, who's chewing the inside of a cheek. 'I know it's stupid, but I felt like I had to cook something showy, and –'

'You don't have to explain yourself.' A small smile.

I get us all something to drink. With each of us on our best behaviour for various reasons, it's a very small glass of white wine apiece. Not long after she finishes hers, Emily checks the time.

'I'm so sorry, Nat, but it's time for me to head.'

'No, it's okay. I don't want you to miss your scan.'

Emily smiles and cradles her stomach with her hand. I feel like I've been kicked in mine, although it's not like when

I first got the news. When she first told me, I was winded. I'm not ashamed to admit that I went home and screamed into my pillow. But not because of what she has. Because of what I'm reminded I've lost. Beyond the selfish pain, the thoughts of 'what if' and regret, I'm thrilled for her. I've no doubt she'll make a great mum. And though I missed the years of her courtship and romance with Ash, on the few occasions I've met him, he strikes me as kind. That's the most important thing, after all.

Dimple and I say our goodbyes, although Dimple's is more mumbled than spoken. I usher Emily towards the door, hold her tight.

'I'm so proud of you for surviving everything you've been through,' she says, and I can feel that her cheeks are wet. And then mine are, too. We hold each other for a moment more, and then she adds, 'And this isn't anything at all like what she said.'

I laugh, dry my eyes. 'You have to be nicer to her, Em. She's trying.'

She makes a face. 'I'm not making any promises.'

'Em.' A word of warning.

'Okay, fine. Although I thought you'd be above harassing a pregnant lady. Jeez.'

With an eye roll and a wink, she's out the door.

When I return to the living room, Dimple stays where she is, even though there's room beside me on the sofa now.

'How are things at the school?' I ask.

I suppose it was an inevitability that Dimple's career would not survive what happened. Even without James's claims about her provocation of my poor mental health, that she'd orchestrated her way to becoming her sister's therapist was a significant issue. One the UK Council for Psychotherapy saw fit to strike her off their register for. It didn't actually stop her from practising, but it certainly didn't help, and she took it as an invitation to reconsider her career. Now she was working as a teaching assistant while she weighed up pivoting into social work.

'It's tough, and shit pay. God, the kids are having a rough ride of it.' Her frown transforms into something akin to a smile. 'But it's rewarding. I don't know.'

'I'm sorry you've had to leave therapy behind.'

She waves away the apology she's heard before. 'I got into it because I wanted to help people, and I still am. Besides, I knew it was a risk when I chose to get close to you, irresponsible as I was in doing so. I made my choice.' A proper smile now. 'We'll see how things go. What about your work?'

'I'm still figuring out what to do with James's shares. It's . . . I don't know. And Will's gleefully swinging his weight around. I mean, he's got his strengths on the business end, but I can't let a man like that run around the business unchecked. I think I need to sell. Find someone smart and decent. Or just hire someone like that. I don't know . . . At the very least, we've hired a replacement for me in the office. For the best, really. And James's parents have paid me the equivalent of what James stole. They needn't have bothered. Turns out that, yes, he was putting a lot of his money back into the business, but he was hiding a lot of money from me, too. I'm not exactly sure what for. Maybe to fund one of his many illicit affairs. Turns out he *was* shagging Molly, by the way.'

The doorbell buzzes and my body goes rigid. Somehow, it's already time.

Dimple points an elegant finger into the hallway. 'Do you want me to?'

I nod.

She gets up and walks into the corridor, saying a few words into the intercom. I hear the click of the door button. Some time passes and then there's a short knock at the front door. Before long, Dimple is re-entering the room, my mother trailing behind her.

Years. It's been years since we've been in the same room. Before she can say anything, tears are already springing into her eyes.

'My baby,' she says.

The skin around her eyes is a little more lined. Relaxed hair streaked a little more silver. But otherwise she looks the same. And I tell her to come in, make herself comfortable. It's quickly noticeable in the way she picks apart the meal I serve her – her favourite meal – that she hasn't changed much on the inside, either. She spends a great deal of time talking about herself. I watch Dimple panic as she swings between a desire to intervene and a promise not to. A shake of my head tells her it's all right. She's here as facilitator and witness, but it's not her fight.

It's hard not to be flung back into my teenage body, rising to every jab with an angry retort. But I manage it. Just.

I'm too distracted by her deep sadness, her deep loneliness, for my anger to take root. Despite all the ways in which she's failed, I know she has done her best for me. Her best as far as she was capable. And I can see the ways in which she has been left broken, too.

It's not my job to fix that. It's hers. But I can't hate her for being damaged by the hard life she's lived.

As we're clearing the last of the roast from our plates – hers suspiciously clean despite her complaints – she announces a gift.

'I have something for you,' she says.

And I'm inherently suspicious of this until she produces

a small journal. I recognize the cover immediately. Claire's old journal.

'I've already read it,' she clarifies. Because of course she has. 'I found it when I was finally clearing out her room a couple of years ago. There's some stuff in there I didn't understand before, but now it makes more sense.'

The red pleather stares at me. A promise and a betrayal. Claire's real voice. I'm dying to crack it open, even though it feels like a posthumous invasion of privacy. I tell my mother as much.

'You've always been so sensitive about things. So much like your father.'

I can't help but bite. 'I need you to stop saying that.'

She jerks backwards, nose scrunching, like I've waved a turd under her chin. 'Why not? It's true.' She shrugs. I take a sip of water to stop myself from firing back. 'You've both always been sensitive. Sensitive and too afraid for your own good,' she continues.

I set the glass of water down harder than I mean to. Ignore the narrowing of her eyes. 'Too afraid? Was Dad "afraid" each time he laid hands on you?'

A dry laugh. 'Of course. Why do you think he chose me? He was a coward, afraid of everything, and he wanted someone he could punch down to. Why do you think James chose you?' She rises from her seat. 'Where's the bathroom?'

I'm still winded, trying to catch my breath.

'It's just on the left as you come in the front door,' I manage to say, voice quiet. 'Do you need me to show you?'

She tuts, shakes her head. 'And your antibacterial wipes?'

I don't need to rise to this. 'I cleaned the bathroom this morning.'

'Today has been hard enough for me, Natalie. Please, the wipes.'

I fetch the packet from under the kitchen sink. She takes them and leaves. I reclaim my seat at the table.

'I'm sorry,' Dimple says. 'I can try broaching the topic of family therapy again, but –'

'It's okay,' I answer with a small shrug of my own. 'Trying to get an aunty into therapy is . . . Anyway, I wasn't expecting she'd have changed. And she's not wrong about Dad and James.'

My hands pick up the journal. Flick through the pages. Claire's teen rage is written in clear lines, only growing as she turns twenty. But amid the anger and the hypervigilance is her humour.

'Can I see?' Dimple asks.

I cast my eyes over to her. See her nerves pinning her arms to her sides. 'Sure,' I say.

She takes a moment to look through the pages. Laughs. 'I can see why you say we're similar.'

'Mmm' is all I can say.

She flips to the last pages of the journal. Reads. Smiles. Stops smiling. 'She was a very hurt girl.'

'She was.'

'She loved you very much.'

'I believe she did.'

'I think you should see this.'

The book is pushed down a canal of space between the dirty plates. I pick it up. Read.

I know one day, I'll have to tell Natty what I've done. And I hope she'll forgive me for it. At the very least, I think she's happier now than she would have been. And if there's one thing I want, it's for her to be happy. For her to come out of all the shit we've been through and stop pretending her feelings. Pretending to be happy or to like whatever or to care about whatever. And just fucking live, you know? One of us has to figure out how to do it, and I don't think it can be me.

I fight the swell in my throat and then allow the tears to fall.

'Do you think you could do that?' Dimple asks.

'What?'

'Let go of your anger. Try being happy,' she says.

I sigh, try to prise a few ossified fingers off the guilt I've been holding on to so tightly. A little falls away. 'I think so.' I consider the small relief that smooths out Dimple's forehead lines. 'But you have to try, too.'

Dimple frowns, nods. 'I guess that's fair.' And then smiles. And it's one of those unburdened smiles. Honest smiles. When she smiles like this, her whole face lights up, eyes beaming a pure warmth. And in these moments, I can't help but think, *Joy.*

She looks back at the journal. 'Mind if I borrow that after you? I understand if it's too much to share it, but . . . Well, I'd like to get to know her.'

I consider the journal and consider Dimple. 'I'd rather tell you about her, I think. If that's okay. From what I've seen, she's writing at her worst. I want you to know her at her best.'

Dimple considers this. Nods an acquiescence. 'I know there's trust to rebuild –'

'On both sides –' I concede.

'– but I want to know you, too.'

The bathroom door clicks open. My mother's footsteps echo down the corridor. Her eyes spot her empty glass.

'I suppose you're waiting for me to die of thirst, then,' she says.

391

A little of the camaraderie leaches back into Dimple and me as we catch each other smothering smiles.

'Joy was just about to refill your glass.' And at the sound of her name out of my mouth, she gives me one of those radiant smiles again.

I don't know if we'll ever completely heal what this thing is between us, but I'm ready for us to start.

Dear Care,

I'm sorry that the choices I made mean you're not here to see me do the work. Learn how and why I've chosen to walk the path I have. Learn how to forge a new one.

I'll admit I've been angry with you. Very angry. But when I forced myself to reflect on why I was choosing to feel that way, I had to admit that it was to push out the guilt. Easier to be mad than feel that pain. It's taken more work, but I can feel the guilt falling away slowly. I know what happened to you was ultimately his doing, not mine. I can't pretend there will never be a small feeling of culpability, but I'm no longer worried it will break me.

You'll be relieved to know that I have a new therapist. Not a secret blood relation as far as I know. She's good. I like her. I think you would, too. Speaking of, I'm trying my best with Joy. She'll never replace you, I hope you know that. But I think you'd like her — she almost killed James, after all.

Thank you for how ferociously you loved me. Thank you for looking after me when I didn't know how. I know some people might say what you did was monstrous, but if there's anything these past few weeks have taught me, it's that we all have a little monster in us. Some people are just better at hiding it than others. To be human is to be complicated, to live in the dark and the light. And if I'm being honest, I understand what you did on a cellular level. I'd kill for you, sister.

Love you, always,
Natty

If you loved *The Exes* and want to be first to know about new books or exciting offers from Leodora, then sign up to her mailing list at leodoradarlington.com/mailing-list

Author Letter

Dear Reader,

First and foremost, thank you so much for taking the time to read my novel. It's beyond my wildest dreams to have a real-life book out in the world, and I'm so thankful to every reader who comes across it. If you'd like to be first to know about exciting giveaways or my latest release, please sign up to my mailing list below.

leodoradarlington.com/mailing-list

I think almost everyone knows what it's like to want to murder an ex – figuratively, at least. In writing this story, I wanted to explore what happens to a woman to drive her to violence.

I've long been interested in how trauma and memory intersect. I'm no scientist, but I've certainly had my own experiences with blank patches I can't seem to access. At its most extreme, I would lose slices of my day while the day was still happening. During this time, I was primary carer for my terminally ill mother, a mother who had complex mental health made more complex by her medication. There's a lot from this time that I still don't remember.

There's so much more to say on how trauma shapes our personalities and relationships, but there is a particular experience women have when it comes to looking back at romantic relationships. Too many of us can reflect and see we've accepted behaviour that we wouldn't stand for now. For women of colour, romantic relationships can carry another layer of danger. The deaths of women like Asia Maynard, Lauren Smith-Fields and Brenda Rawls says it all. I thought of them while writing this story.

Ultimately, I wanted to write a story of hope, of self-discovery, and of self-forgiveness. With the state of the world, I think it's okay for women to be a little bit angry. I also think it's okay to escape, and I hope *The Exes* took you on a compulsive, twisty journey. At the end of it all, I also hope people come away from the book feeling that one can overcome even the darkest of times.

Thank you for taking the time to read this letter, and for reading the book. I hope Natalie's story remains with you long after the final page. If you enjoyed your read, it would mean the world if you could please share a review on your preferred websites. It can make a world of difference to an author.

Warmest,

Leodora

𝕏 @Leodora_
⬡ @leodora_
♪ @_leodora

Acknowledgements

I'd like to take a moment to thank my agents at WME for securing me such life-changing deals. First and foremost, a thank you to Hellie Ogden, who took on this chaotically half-finished manuscript – a real risk, but one that I'm glad paid off. Thank you for the considered edits and equally chaotic but speedy wrangling of this into an actual full manuscript. Thank you to Suzanne Gluck, who found me an array of brilliant editors and breathtaking offers in the US. Thank you to Laura Bonner for finding so many brilliant and passionate editors to work with in non-English speaking countries – amazing that this book gets to be translated! Thank you also to Ma'suma Amiri, who expertly works to hold everything together while building her own impressive list of clients.

A thank you to the other agents I was lucky to meet with; your kind words about my work were hugely appreciated, especially having been so nervous to go out on submission in the first place. You are incredibly impressive and accomplished individuals, and I appreciate the investment of time in reading my work and speaking with me about it. I know I would have been in safe hands with any of you.

Of course, a huge thank you to my editors, Joel Richardson at Penguin Michael Joseph in the UK and Maya Ziv at Dutton in the US. Your creativity and support throughout the editorial process has been hugely valued; I'm lucky to have been working with such a great editorial team. A big thank you also to Grace Long for stepping in as my editor while Joel was on leave, and for your enthusiasm and professionalism.

It can be nerve-wracking for authors when their acquiring editor leaves, but it was reassuring to be in such safe hands.

Further thanks to my international publishers across France, Germany, Italy, Romania, Poland and the Netherlands. And a massive thanks to my brilliant publicists and marketers internationally. Particular thanks to Sriya Varadharajan and Ellie Morley for all of the exceptional work on the UK campaign. It takes a lot of hard work to launch a debut, and I'm so grateful for all the brilliant campaign ideas and truly amazing things you've secured to promote the book.

Thank you to my mother for helping me fall in love with reading and writing. I'm so glad that books were such a fundamental part of my childhood, and that even when we couldn't afford to buy at the rate that I read, trips to the library were a mainstay of our weekends. I'm sorry that you're not here to see this publish, but I know you'd have been very proud and shouting about this from the rooftops.

Finally, a thank you to my partner. Thank you for your patience as my day job began to bleed into my evenings and weekends and I still had to find time for this book outside of that. Your support has kept me sane – relatively speaking – and I'm grateful to you for making the tougher months a little easier.